THE Tongues of Men or Angels

A NOVEL

Also by Jonathan Trigell

Boy A
Cham
Genus

THE TONGUES OF MEN OR ANGELS

A NOVEL

JONATHAN TRIGELL

corsair

CORSAIR

First published in Great Britain in 2015 by Corsair
Copyright © Jonathan Trigell, 2015

The moral right of the author has been asserted.

*While this story has necessarily been dramatized and historical holes will
at times have been filled from imagination, substantially the narrative
proceeds as the author's research has led him to believe events most
probably occurred. Quotations from the authentic letters of Paul and other
texts the author believes to be relatively reliable are generally embedded –
rather than italicized or placed inside quotation marks – in order not to
impede the flow of what is, in the end, just a novel.*

Quote from *Rabbit, Run* by John Updike (Ballantine Books 1971, Andre
Deutsch 1961, Penguin Books 1964, Penguin Classics 2006) copyright ©
John Updike 1960, reproduced by permission of Penguin Books Ltd.

A CIP catalogue record for this book
is available from the British Library.

ISBN: 978-1-84901-795-4 (hardback)
ISBN: 978-1-47210-223-2 (export/airside trade paperback)
ISBN: 978-1-47210-612-4 (ebook)

Typeset in Garamond by Saxon Graphics Ltd, Derby
Printed and bound in Great Britain by CPI Group (UK) Ltd, Croydon, CR0
4YY

Corsair
is an imprint of
Constable & Robinson Ltd
100 Victoria Embankment
London EC4Y 0DY
An Hachette UK Company
www.hachette.co.uk

www.constablerobinson.com

For the monkey who dances on the temple steps

If I speak with the tongues of men or angels, but have not love, I am only a resounding gong or a clanging cymbal.

Epistle of Paul 1 Corinthians 13:1

Are they servants of Christ? I speak as a fool. But I am more. I have worked much harder, been in prison more frequently, been flogged more severely, and been exposed to death again and again. Five times I received from the Jews the forty lashes minus one. Three times I was beaten with rods, once I was stoned, three times I was shipwrecked, I spent a night and a day in the open sea. I have been constantly on the move. I have been in danger from rivers, in danger from bandits, in danger from my fellow Jews, in danger from Gentiles; in danger in the city, in danger in the country, in danger at sea; and in danger from false brothers. I have laboured and toiled and have often gone without sleep; I have known hunger and thirst and have often gone without food; I have been cold and naked … I am not lying.

Epistle of Paul 2 Corinthians 11: 23-30

Of course, all vagrants think they're on a quest. At least at first.

John Updike, *Rabbit Run*

Four Days before
the Crucifixion

If I were you, I wouldn't start from here.

That's what Cephas's father said one time, when a foreign-faced Roman legionary demanded directions. A wile as hoary as the hyena's stripes: for the powerless to feign stupidity; to lull that they might deceive. Nonetheless, from *here* is where we must begin.

Cephas gazes down the Mount at Jerusalem, enthralled by its size. He's a country boy, a country man, a hard man, grown in a hard land. Cephas isn't his real name, it's a nickname. It means 'the rock' or 'rocky', 'stony' maybe; a tough man's name for a tough man. Cephas has a dense beard, matted and wired like the belly of a wild goat. His hair is knife-cropped against the heat, revealing folds of muscled neck. Skin baked dirt-brown from sun-blasted net-hauling. He was a fisherman once, an illiterate labourer, the sort of man irrelevant to the powers of this world. It is hard even to conceive of the ease and casual brutality with which people such as him can be disposed of, or the indifference with which they can disintegrate into dispossession and starve to death. Even so, only the very brave or the very dumb would fuck with Cephas one on one.

His unwashed feet are sandal-less and stiff with dust. His mutton-haunch right hand rests upon the cloth-taped handle of a cheap but sturdy sword, tucked unscabbarded into his belt. It is a belt much worn and much pierced; extra holes along its length betray times of relative plenty and times of near demise. He's a big man – it takes a lot of food to keep a frame like that – but Cephas has known days of eating bitter unground corn, picked from the fields in which they hid. Picked even on the Sabbath, once, so desperate was their state and need. Cephas has known flights into the desert, and weeks holed up in the brush of maquis scrubland, periods when they envied the holes of foxes and the nests of birds. Cephas's belly is fuller now: times have been better of late. Long may it last, though that lasting is in doubt.

Yeshua stares down at Jerusalem too. At the snaking walls of yellow limestone, mottled with grey like the camouflage of a horned viper, but too big to hide, cutting across the landscape like a leviathan. Visible even above those walls are the bulk of the Roman Antonia Fortress and the glory of the Second Temple – the Great Temple – not yet even fully finished, but already claiming the space between earth and heavens; making plain that only in Jerusalem can penances and sacrifices be made to God. Only in Jerusalem and only through blood.

Next to Cephas and Yeshua is James the Lesser, lean like a winter wolf. He is Yeshua's brother. Second in line to the throne if – as they claim – the blood of royal David flowed through their father's veins. But it is first-born Yeshua who will be king. And those who've met him would say that to be lesser than him is no sin, but only natural, inescapable, when Yeshua is a prophet and a prince.

'What should we do now?' Cephas asks James.

'As planned,' James the Lesser says, 'as we must for Yeshua's arrival to have impact. Word will spread about what has happened, if it's done right. Send Judas the Twin and Thaddeus back to Bethpage. If Yeshua's requests have been heeded, by now they'll find a donkey colt tethered to a stone watering trough. The donkey will be young, but strong enough to ride. Tell them to lead it here. If anyone questions their taking it, they must say it is for their master, as agreed, and that it will be returned shortly. There shouldn't be any problems.'

No, there shouldn't be any problems, Cephas thinks, but there will be: there always are. And he can't help noticing anew a marabou stork, which has trailed them at a distance all day. The stork hunches its bald pink head into the grey shawl of its feathers, like an eerie old man. From its throat dangles a purse flap of skin, like the goitres of the inbreds in the mountains. Does it use this skin to store food like the pelican or to roar like the bullfrog? It matters not: what bothers Cephas is that marabou storks feed on the dead and this one seems to think that carrion will come soon enough.

* * *

Few of Yeshua's followers have farmland to tend. His strongest support comes from day labourers, beggars, boatless shore-fishermen, corn gleaners, ditch sleepers, tax absconders. Those who could leave their families have come with him now. The freedom of poverty. The bravery of desperation. The front runners have done their work well in gathering spectators. Only James the Lesser and the other eleven walk beside Yeshua, to represent the tribes of Israel; they will be his ministers, they will sit on twelve thrones. The rest throw their cloaks on the ground before the colt he rides. They run in front scattering brush they've cut. They skip and shout *hosanna* – 'Save us, we beg you.' They clap calloused hands and cry that revolution is coming. The streets are thronged with people anyway: pilgrims coming to Jerusalem for the Passover. The city will soon be swollen and bursting out, like an overfilled wine skin. A good number of the pilgrims join in with the cheering. The others stand and watch. Some smile, some laugh, some marvel. But all watch.

The crowds aren't vast, not like some they have known in the past. Not like those the Baptizer used to pull in. Not like those who came to Yeshua at Bethsaida, after the Baptizer's execution. But Cephas knows they're not on home ground now. Galilee is many days' walk behind them. That time is gone. But there are enough people here to start it. Enough to disperse the whispers. Something is happening: one who claims the line of David, a man who would be king, is come to Jerusalem.

Word has been spread among the poor and dispossessed of Jerusalem that something is to be expected. And there are many poor and dispossessed in Jerusalem. Giving alms in the Holy City is a doubly righteous act, so people who would have starved to death in the countryside can scrape an existence from the kindly guilt of pilgrims in Zion. Which is not to say that people don't starve to death here too. There are too many dispossessed now for all to survive: property has been robbed from the peasant toiler. Laws created to protect them have been usurped. The Law of Moses says that land cannot be bought and sold, precisely to protect the lowly subsistence farmer.

But Rome has no need of peasantry in its provinces: the Italian wolf gorges on extortion, tribute and taxes. Yeshua says he can change this. Yeshua says he will free Judaea from the Romans and the quisling collaborators of the Judaean aristocracy; that he can bring about a new kingdom. And who dares say he can't, when Yeshua is a prince?

The young donkey is tiny beneath Yeshua's length. His feet reach almost to the palm-strewn ground. It might have been comical, but Yeshua has a way of making humble things look holy. He makes a virtue of the poverty that was enforced upon him anyway. He says the rich will come last once he is king. Had he entered on a charger, a man with his claims and his charisma could appear too proud.

* * *

Even now, on the other side of Jerusalem, just such a pompous procession is occurring. The Roman prefect and his cavalcade flood into the city. Pontius Pilate, bearing his flab like a badge of conspicuous consumption, face clammy with sweat. Riding a dappled giant of a horse, at the head of a phalanx of troops, marching to drum beat and horn blast. The blessed ground seems to tremble as they pass and their passing takes for ever, so long is the tail of this great snake. Three thousand scarlet shields like a tide of blood. The standard bearer beside Pilate is cloaked in a tawny lion skin, like Herakles, and holds the Imago, a beaten-metal portrait of the god-emperor. Their very presence and every act in the Holy City is blasphemy. But who can stand against them? They are a fighting monster. A war machine, before people who know not what a machine is.

The Romans, too, are coming for the festival. Pilate doesn't live in Jerusalem. He lives in the sumptuous marble surrounds of Caesarea on the coast. There is a permanent Roman garrison in the fortress next to the Temple, always a spot potentially requiring suppression. But this aside, the Romans try to maintain at least the semblance that the high priest and Sadducee aristocracy run Jerusalem, enforced by the mercenary thugs of the Temple Guards.

But Passover celebrates Jewish victory over Egyptian oppression. It is a time when feelings against current oppressors can easily explode. And the festival means the already dense population of Jerusalem is multiplied many times. Every bed and floor space is taken. People sleep in tents pitched in the streets and outside the walls; they sprawl over rooftops and in alleys, in nightly bivouacs, or unprotected save by cloak and God. Jerusalem, always a flashpoint, at festival times becomes a clay oil lamp, teetering above a straw floor. One strong wind, one clumsy move, and the whole place erupts.

Zion in these days is a city of zest and tumult. Traders shout and sing from their stall sides. Yearling lambs are driven down the streets by country-rough shepherds, leaving trails of damp, rich dung to be kicked up by the children who chase in their wake. Pharisees – the pastors of the people – teach in huddles with eager acolytes, or debate and discuss with their fellows. Even the beggars are a little lifted, with so many people around in such a spirit of giving.

But there is a dread never forgotten. An anxiety that lingers at the end of every street and every sentence. The high priest fears the Romans; the people fear the high priest's guards; the Romans fear riot from the people.

And this tremulous tinderbox is the city into which Yeshua rides on the foal of a donkey. Deliberately fulfilling the prophecy of Zechariah. Declaring himself to be kin of David. Declaring himself to be king.

> *Shout, Daughter Jerusalem!*
> *See, your king comes to you,*
> *righteous and victorious,*
> *lowly and riding on a donkey,*
> *on a colt, the foal of a donkey.*

* * *

Cephas, named 'the Rock', stares at the rocks of Jerusalem's vast walls as they pass through the East Gate. Boulder stones of ivory and ochre; pepper and salamander; dirty snow and threshed corn; soiled swaddling and first-fruit offerings. Wrinkled like camel knees, motley like a Roman pony, misted like a winter morning in the marshes. All of life is here in Jerusalem and all of Jerusalem is echoed in its walls. So shout, Jerusalem, shout. Your king has come.

Thirty-four Years after
the Crucifixion

Useful is his name. One of them, at least. Everyone has multiple names in this mixed-up modern world – Roman names, Greek names, state names, slave names, religious names. It can't always have been like that. It wasn't. But Useful is a good name for a slave. Even if he isn't.

If it wasn't for that name, Useful would be dead. Or, rather, the act that saved him also gave him his name. A foundling on the steps of the shambles, exposure the preferred form of family planning among the Phrygians. A child so young he was still draped in birth offal, left amid the blood and mess of the meat market.

'We could take the babe home, bring him up as a slave,' the master had said. 'He'll be useful one day.'

He wasn't.

Useful's master is an atheist now. He no longer worships our Divine Lord and Saviour, the Prince of Peace, God and Son of God, Bringer of Grace, Redeemer of Mankind, the Deliverer of Justice: Augustus Caesar.

Neither does the master now believe in the Great Mother Cybele, or Artemis, or Apollo. Not even Sabazios, the city's patron god. Patron of pit latrines and emptied bed pots, to judge by the summer stink.

The master worships only one god now, or two, perhaps, at most; there is some confusion as to whether one is a god or not. It seems to be complicated, this Jesus stuff, jealous and complicated …

Under his new faith, the master won't even eat meat if it was previously offered as a sacrifice to other gods. Which is near enough to say any meat. Sometimes he sends Useful to buy mutton or goat from the Jewish quarter. About the only place you can find flesh that wasn't first dedicated as an offering, unless you slaughter the beast yourself. You can see why the Jews are so strong, even though spread so wide: they separate themselves from the world, but in every city they are at home already. Their strange ways and laws are deeply familiar to them. Mostly the Jews seem to be a very moral people; many of the Greeks admire them for that. Though Useful has seen a stoning, which didn't look so moral. A choke-screaming girl dragged barefoot outside the city walls, crying that she hadn't done whatever it was they said she'd done, whatever it was that merited stoning to death.

It's hard to kill someone by stoning, it seems: requires a lot of stones. The mob struggled to find sufficient. People are surprisingly sturdy, when it comes down to it, even though death is all about: sickness strides through the slums, splashing in the street sewers; children drop from unknown ailments – perhaps two-thirds of those who survive birth are dead before sixteen – and even the kin of emperors and ethnarchs are not immune. Mortality in the cities is so high that their wall-confined claustrophobia would be emptied entirely, were it not for the hordes always pouring in from elsewhere. Death is not some distant future end to life. Death is life's constant companion. Death is the unloved neighbour of all who live crammed in unsanitary single workshop rooms. But if you actually try to kill someone, it takes a lot of effort. The girl being stoned, she survived long beyond the anger of the crowd. It took persistence to finish her off, her smashed-crab fingers still clawing at the dented earth as though some doorway might be found. Finally one of the kinder ones brought down a big corner-stone rock to crush her skull. Imagine such kindness as that: the kindness of crowds.

* * *

Useful is an over-sized urn-faced youth, with hips wider almost than his shoulders, but not in a womanly way, just as a bear's are. Possibly it is this that gives him his ambling gait, which makes him look as if he's taking longer than he ought. Which is not a good look for a slave.

Slavery is the way of things: you can't complain about it. It has always been there and always will be. Useful would likely be dead if it weren't for slavery: who but a wealthy man in need of slaves would save a foundling? Many slaves are freed on the death of their master, or can save up to buy their freedom. A favourite slave in a rich household often lives better than a poor freeman. In many ways, there are worse things to be than a slave.

But a slave is still property. A slave can be thrashed. A slave can be scourged. A slave can be raped. Or, rather, a slave can't be raped, not by their master. It is the master's right and therefore it is not rape. A slave is their master's to do with as he wishes. Even to kill, if he wills. A waste of a valuable asset, but it happens. More slaves achieve manu-mission than are murdered, but it happens …

And, of course, a slave who runs away is a challenge to the Roman state. Thereby receives the penalty reserved for those crimes and those crimes only: the lingering, gasping agony of crucifixion. The body left on the tree, so dogs can chew the blood-scabbed toes and crows can peck away the face flesh and claim the soft marrow eyes. Useful heard of a man who took nine days and nights to die on the cross. Nine days spent hanged from a tree, shoulders and wrists dislocated from the strain of hauling up on the holding ropes, bereft of hope of reprieve or release, without even the means to end it himself: his final right removed.

The master's new god was crucified, apparently. It's a strange sort of god that lets himself be crucified by the Romans. But, then, Philemon is a strange sort of master.

He's in the cloth and robe business, Philemon. Travelled frequently the length of the coasts, from Mysia to Cilicia, in his day, making the connections that still serve him well.

When Useful was growing up, Philemon had a shrine of figurines and idols he'd collected from all the great cities he'd visited. Carved from wood, moulded from clay, cast from bronze and then silver, the homely family gods echoed not just his travels but his rise in wealth. He smashed them all with a splay-ended tent mallet in the end, though. His new god doesn't like other gods, except maybe this Jesus.

Even later, in relative dotage, Philemon still journeyed, when business required it. Sometimes he'd take Useful with him, hoping he might prove himself worthy of his name. He didn't. They'd camp on the damp-dilated planks of the deck by night. By day watch the shores; rarely allowed out of sight; sometimes close enough to count the cliff-top flocks. Hair clogged with salt from the spray. Legs shaking from the roll of the waves. And, though he knew he was just a slave, Useful always felt a bit more than that, on those voyages. There will be no more of such trips. Not him and Philemon together. Not after what Useful has done.

* * *

Useful is on a solo journey now, compounding his first crime with two more: the theft of the gold coins required to make his escape and the escape itself. But this is his only hope. A slave has just one legal chance for life, when he has committed an act his master deems worthy of death: he can flee to the sanctuary of a higher-status friend or patron of his master, plead his case to them and hope they see fit to intercede. There is only one man Useful knows of whom his master respects to that degree and who might, just might, believe that Useful deserves his life. So Useful is on his way to Rome. The ambling foundling from the shambles on his way to the greatest city on earth: the centre of the empire. He could weep for the fear of what he's done and what he faces, but tries to stay cold and calm as a carved idol. For *fugitivarii* – slave-hunting bounty-killers – wait at every port, on the lookout for strangers who might be runaways. And any fellow passenger or traveller on the road would likely be ready to turn him in, for reward and through duty. The outlaw slave lives a knife-edge life of desperation and trust-less torment.

Useful keeps a blade under his cloak, but doesn't know if he would have the strength or skill to kill, if it came to it.

The coins Useful stole, they tell you a lot about this world: minted with images of different deities. Rome rules over all, but embraces all; there is no such thing as heresy. Every god is accepted and welcome to mingle in the imperial pantheon. But the master's god won't have that: the master's god says you can praise no god but him. Indeed, he says there is no god but him. It seems a bit selfish somehow, to Useful, a bit childish. Did no one ever teach this god to share?

Ten Days before
the Crucifixion

Mariamme's eyes drop demurely when she sees Saul. But he catches the flush on her cheek. It casts a sharp, scarlet shadow beneath her cheekbone, accentuates her fine-bred features. A tiny scar on her upper lip, vestige of some baby tumble, no doubt, for post-blossoming she does nothing so ungraceful that could create such an injury. Her wrists are as slight as cyclamen stalks, drooping gently in the sun. But her eyes – it is those eyes that draw Saul in. Like the twin gates of the Temple, they beckon, but they bar those who are not purified; those without permission. A girl such as Mariamme cannot even be approached without the consent of her father. So Saul must find the perfect moment, when he is certain he has demonstrated his worth. Saul is in no doubt that Mariamme loves him. But, then, Saul is not really a man of doubt at all.

She nods in a slight bow and Saul returns it. Then she hurries off, small feet pattering, little ghost rabbits on the mosaic. She finds it uncomfortable to be near me, Saul thinks, so great is her love. But soon they will be united. Soon he will ask her father. They are separated by station now, but her father must be aware that great things are destined for Saul.

Many men would feel nervous and cowed, on their way to see the high priest; not Saul. He strides the corridor on feet of confidence. His legs are a little bowed, but only, he thinks, in the way Roman cavalry *equites'* often are. Now in his thirtieth year, Saul's hair is beginning to thin and recede, but surely this serves to show the world his fine brow. His forehead is broad and strong-boned. And fronts above expressive features, his face can transmit charm or anger into the watcher, a useful skill for a guard. Or not a guard, but a chief of guards, a captain of the Temple Guards. The police of the high priest. The bulwark against blasphemy and disorder. The guardians of the Holy City. If they do not carry out their duties flawlessly, then the Romans will take over entirely and Jerusalem will be lost. The Pharisees can debate fine points of faith in street-corner assemblies; the Zealots can die pointlessly, flailing against the unconquerable might of Rome; the people can flock to every fool who calls himself a messiah; but it is Saul who is at the sword-point of preserving Judaism. If revolt occurs, then Roman boots will again soil the Holy of Holies and the crucified will spike the hills like porcupine quills. Two thousand men were nailed at once, when Jerusalem last rebelled against Rome. What joy did the learning of the Pharisees bring then? To be a Temple Guard is surely a grander path.

'I don't want any fuck-ups this year,' the high priest says. 'It damages my position when the streets stink of disorder.'

Actually, technically Annas no longer has a 'position': he is not really the high priest at all. He was deposed by the previous Roman prefect for having too many people executed, an over-indulgence the Romans reserve for themselves. But in Jewish law the high priesthood is for life, so Annas is still called high priest and still feels able to command the guard. Legally his son-in-law Kayafa is in charge, but he looks to Annas for instruction so often that Annas almost rules in his stead. Saul has every hope that he, too, will soon count Annas as father-in-law and wield some power in his name.

Annas has a noble head. If he were Roman he would doubtless have busts of himself scattered about his mansion. But such things do not do with the Jews, who disdain as blasphemy all depictions of man and beast. Saul can make out in the high priest's face the shadows of his youngest daughter. Dark eyes, a little downturn at the edge of the mouth, perhaps even the same gentle curve to the chin, though that is hard to tell beneath Annas's grey-splashed beard. His robes are made of fine linen, with perhaps just a little less purple than Saul would choose if they were his own. And one day such robes will be his own, of that there is no doubt. Saul has always felt a powerful sense of his own destiny.

Not that he could ever become high priest, of course. The priests can only come from the tribe of Levi and the high priest is chosen by the Roman prefect – generally on the basis of a considerable bribe – from among those few aristocratic Sadducee families who claim to trace their lineage to Aaron. Though Saul has confident hopes for a link by marriage to Annas's daughter, he still would not be eligible for the priestly class. But there are many alternative roles in the upper echelons of Jerusalem's rule for which Saul considers himself eminently well qualified.

The other guard captains summoned do not hold themselves with Saul's bearing, he notes not for the first time. One of them sucks at a locust-green plant stalk, as Annas gives his orders. None of them have shown much attention to their appearance. Temple Guards are obliged to supply their own uniform: short grey tunics, which do not show the dirt and the blood. Most have secured something passable as cheaply as possible. Saul has spent all he could afford to make his own stand out: it is made from a well-woven cloth and has a simple black pattern sewn around the hems of its short sleeves. He even bought a leather breastplate, though he could not afford one with a back section; the absence leaves him feeling curiously far more vulnerable from behind than he ever felt before he acquired the armour. Now he is ill at ease when anyone stands to his rear, as if all of Jerusalem hopes to slide in a blade like a Sicarii – the nationalist assassins, named for the cacheable curved daggers they favour. All the guard captains are Jews, but most, like Saul, are from the diaspora. They speak Aramaic with varying degrees of accomplishment, but often break into street Greek when they are together. None has acquired Hebrew learning, as Saul has, though coming to Hebrew late in life made its study arduous even for him.

So many of the guards are from Greek-founded cities because most Judaeans prefer not to enforce the will of the governing class, seen as repressing their own people, as being in cahoots with the Romans. The simpletons cannot see that they are in fact being protected from the Romans, that

Jerusalem can only retain some right to rule herself if she is seen to do as Rome wants.

Saul has been called a collaborator and a traitor, a stooge and worse, out in the city. Now he carries a short, dark-wood club – of the type fullers use to pound the wool – to deal with those insults, and alongside it, a sword, reserved for more serious challenges. It's a good sword: Roman. Found, so the seller said, after the razing of Tzippori. Perhaps it has cut the throats of Israelite rebels in its time, but now it serves in the hand of Saul. Serves in the high and holy name of Annas, Kayafa and the priesthood. This is a noble calling. Saul should feel no shame for abandoning his Pharisee scholarship.

Eight Years before
the Crucifixion

The gladiators move towards the centre of the arena, with stilted, unnatural steps. Each holds a *gladius* – the short sword favoured by the Romans – but has no shield. Their feet are bare. The hot sand of the arena is perhaps the last sensation of touch they will ever know, except the blade of the other. They are clothed only in loincloths and simple armour: each of their sword arms is protected by lizard scales of beaten iron – otherwise injury might end the contest too speedily – and each man wears a large helm with a sweeping brim and a face covering. The helms are scarred from former blows. These gladiators are not among the first to wear them. Many men have already died in them. The gladiators most certainly know this. Perhaps they weep. Only they know if tears fall, because the helms they wear have no eye-holes. But probably they don't. Probably they wept last night. Probably they barely slept last night. But now there is just this. Now they can only do what they can do, even if that is only to die. They are *damnati*: criminals condemned to death in the arena. And they are *andabatae*, who fight blind, for the viewing pleasure of the Roman crowd, who love such hilarities.

The band strikes up; the enormous hydraulic organ booms its buoyant notes, joined by the caw of long brass stork-leg trumpets and a drum that beats the rhythm as if on a galley ship. Blah-ta-da-da-blah, and two men edge towards each other. They swing blades in front of them as they come, like inept reapers. Sightless in the sunlight.

Those spectators in the good seats have canopies above them to create shade. Slaves sprinkle water on the plebeian mob, to ease the heat a little. All paid for as part of the sponsored spectacle. A man called Pilate of the Pontii Equestrian Order is the *editor*; he has organized all this, paid for all this. It is said he seeks office. Of course he seeks office. You don't near bankrupt yourself in such ostentation for love of the common man.

Pilate isn't in his conspicuous, elevated seat at the moment. He's probably gone to urinate or something – it will be a long day. These *andabatae* are just programme-fillers anyway. No one comes to the circus to see this crap, but they make the crowd laugh. Who wouldn't laugh to see two blindfolded men slashing their way nervously towards each other? Tilting their helmed heads when they think they hear their opponent. Walking flatfooted, so as not to risk slipping, like old folk on ice.

They made the *damnati* piss before they entered the arena. It's cleaner that way. More dignified. Men either take the punishment bravely, or they don't. But all men take it. Previously they may have had choices in life. But now there is just this.

To some it may seem strange that they don't pull off their blinding helms and run, or try to fight their way free. But it is not only resignation that prevents them. There is some pride to be salvaged in dying correctly; there is a right way and a wrong way to do this. One of them may even walk out alive from the sands after the fight today. Not to freedom, but to a temporary respite. A chance to die in another arena another day. There are no prisons in the Roman world, there are only gaols. Imprisonment is not a punishment: it is the waiting period before the trial or before the sentence is carried out.

One of the *damnati* it disoriented now. In his flailings with his sword he has finished facing the wrong way entirely and is setting off towards the place he started, still slashing in front of him. Many in the crowd are in tears of laughter at this. But, then, who could fail to be amused by such a sight: a man condemned to die, bewildered like that.

One of the arena guards prods the *andabatae* until he is facing something approximating the correct direction once again. The guard is dressed as Charon, the ferryman of the underworld, visored with a mask of iron set in an implacable expression, covered with a black cloak, which must be exhausting in this heat – but his is still an enviable role among those who must set foot on the sands. He carries a staff, one end finished with a steel spike. It is this he uses to goad the *andabatae* when they stray too far apart. Sometimes they fling wild slashes at him, but they cannot reach the end of the goad. It is futile to fight the goad. Though arguably it is equally futile not to. The result will likely be the same. The other end of Charon's staff is tipped with a hammer. This he uses to crush the skulls of the fallen, if so directed by the crowd and the *editor* of the games, who today is a man called Pontius Pilate.

Life in this world is so cheap that often it has no price at all. But here it does. Here in Rome in the arena everything has a precise cost. All has been calculated by he who pays, in a weighted gamble that such entertainments will bring him to the fore of public life and secure him a post in some province from which he can wring far greater wealth, from extortion and bribery.

And it's perhaps not the best system for running an empire, but these are relatively early days for Rome. Over time the Romans will improve, bringing sanitation and trade, education and engineering to the places they conquer. Bringing a paid-for peace, the *pax Romana*. For the moment, though, there is no *pax*, just taxes and crosses.

All this is, of course, irrelevant to the *andabatae*; they may not even know who has sponsored their deaths today. They are almost upon each other now. They can feel the change of pressure when the other cuts the air. They can hear from the crowd that they must be close. They crouch and duck as best as blind men can. They stab and slash and try not to puke. They know that one of them at least is about to die and can only do their amateurish handicapped best to try not to be him. But none of that much matters, except to them. And to the Roman mob, who, of course, find this hilarious; who wouldn't? The sand will be raked back ready for the next combat and the world will hold one less person, that's all. The death of a single man will never change much.

Four Months before
the Crucifixion

As was tradition for the kings of Israel, first came the salutation and then the coronation. Cephas made the proclamation, since he was to be chamberlain, the holder of the keys of the kingdom and protector of the King's person. Cephas was hard as carved Judaean rock; Yeshua's red right hand.

The inner circle knew, of course, that something was to come. But Cephas's words still fluttered in the hearts of the other followers and devotees, like a bird trapped in the Temple: full of tremble and wonder. Can it be? Yeshua – already healer, exorcist and prophet – now declares himself king as well.

The news caused nervous rejoicing. It even elated the Zealots in the camp, of whom there were many, including Simon the Zealot and Judas Sicarii. For although such rebels were inclined to be republican, they were in favour of urgent and violent action against Rome and its collaborators, and a coronation meant no going back. A king could be a rallying cry. A rival ruler is as good as a declaration of war.

Some whispered the words of the Sibylline Oracles: *A holy king will come and reign over all the world – and then his wrath will fall on the people of Latium, and Rome will be destroyed to the ground. O God, send a stream of fire from Heaven, and let the Romans perish, each in his own house!*

And others thought of the star prophecy: *A star will stream forth from Jacob; a sceptre shall emerge from Israel. He will crush the skulls of Moab, and destroy all the sons of tumult.*

* * *

Six days after Cephas's salutation of Yeshua as king, as tradition dictated, the ceremony was held. The service was witnessed by a great throng of followers, who journeyed up to Mount Sion, the highest mountain in the region. And it might have been the highest in the world, for all those men knew of elsewhere.

James the Lesser, Cephas and Jochanan climbed to the very pinnacle with Yeshua. The others remained a little way below, from where they could see the coronation, framed against the blue of God's sky.

The servants of one of Yeshua's admirers – a wealthy Pharisee from the Golan highlands – had delivered a gifted gown of dazzling white Egyptian linen. It was without seams, woven in a single piece, like the tunic of the high priest. Kept wrapped in coarser cloths throughout its travels, when Yeshua pulled it on it was the whitest thing the assembly had ever witnessed. It seemed near other-worldly to those men of the dust and the scrub, to see something so unblemished: like a babe's milk teeth; like a fish's wet wide eye, in the moment it is landed; a thing that comes from elsewhere and will not last long in an untarnished state in this dry, invaded land.

Cephas produced an alabaster vial of precious oil, of the purest Indian spikenard, and Jochanan anointed Yeshua's brow – with the cross of the sacred letter *Tau* – and wiped the sweet-scented unguent through his hair; and the air was filled with the fragrant perfume. When it was emptied, Cephas smashed the jar on the ground. Yeshua was now an 'anointed one' – a *Messiah* in Hebrew, a *Christ* in Greek – just as the kings Saul, Solomon and David had been called.

James then recited the coronation psalm: *'I have enthroned my King, on Sion, my holy mountain.'* And he repeated the words from that psalm, of God's adoption of all His kings: *'You are my son,' the LORD God said; 'this day I become your father. Ask of me what you will: I will give you nations as your inheritance, the ends of the earth as your possession.'*

From then on, like all the kings before him, Yeshua could be known by the royal title of *Son of the LORD God*. He would lead his people against the false rulers who oppress, and would shatter those foes like a jar of nard on a stone floor. Shards would fly to the corners of the earth, but the soothing balm would bring a new age of peace.

Then the followers built a tabernacle – a *succah* – a holy hut where the newly enthroned king could commune with Yahweh. It grew cold, up on the heights. And some wanted to head back down. Yeshua told them they should, but that he would remain to pray in the tabernacle.

Cephas said, 'Master, it is good for us to be here, with you.'

But Yeshua told him to go down with the others and Cephas did as he was bade, partly glad to be out of the encompassing chill and the cloud that had descended.

When he, too, finally came down, Yeshua commenced the politics of rule. He named James the Lesser, Jochanan and Cephas as the triumvirate beneath him. Then he chose nine others of his closest disciples, who would sit with them on the dozen thrones of the Twelve Tribes. And he picked seven wise and just elders to be his judges. Finally he selected seventy from among the rest of the gathering, who would become his Sanhedrin council, once the kingdom was established. And he instructed them to go in pairs to the towns and cities of Judaea and Galilee and spread news of what had occurred: to tell the people that they had a king once more.

Twenty Years before the Crucifixion

The rock badger goes where it will. It fears neither man nor beast. It is said that a rock badger will take on a leopard and make it back away. The leopard would be near certain to win, but it senses that the price of victory might be too high. If blinded, it would lose in any case: a sightless predator is the walking dead. And God armed the rock badger with whetted claws, armoured it with unyielding skin and gave it bravery beyond human comprehension.

Saul followed the rock badger across the scrub. It trotted, stiff-legged, nose to the air not to the trail. No objective in mind. The badger travels on a whim, and if someplace it finds something to sustain it, then that place becomes where it was going all along.

Saul would have liked to be like the rock badger, equipped with that self-fulfilling wanderlust; fearless and strong. Not yet knowing that one day he would be. This Saul, the boy, was still slight, not puny, but not one to scare a single soul. Certainly not a rock badger. The badger looked back at Saul – neck bending round almost to its stumpy hindquarters – un-nervous, barely curious. Blank black eyes stared, the beast perhaps coming to a decision as to whether the energy expenditure required to lose Saul, or chase him away, would be worth the stealth benefits accruing to a solo hunter. Seemingly the badger decided that Saul could stay for now and set off once again, on its low-slung lope, towards it knew not where.

The rock badger led Saul to and through a copse of dark pine where it might have been night, except for the scattered sunbeams that broke through the canopy onto a floor sponged with epic ages of dropped needles. Emerging onto a field at the other side, the badger cocked its head, then bolted into some goat's-thorn scrub, perhaps smelling snake or rat within, leaving Saul alone to face a brace of boys of about his own age: ten or so years old.

'Jew,' one of the boys said, a single-word sentence, which managed to be both definition and accusation.

The Jews of Tarsus did not dress markedly differently from the region's other inhabitants. Nonetheless, the other inhabitants could generally spot a Jew. Though to an outsider both would look more alike than apart, they remained separated in internal eyes, through subtle differences of cloth and cut. Even leaving aside the concealed cut the Jews regarded as of such high importance.

Of course the Jews were hated. Wasn't Joseph hated for being the favourite son? How much worse, then, to be the favourite race. And to refuse to worship other gods, any of the other gods who represent the city-state and the people. To be a Jew in any of the Greek-founded cities, which speckled most of the known world, was as much as to be uncivic. Holding a separating religion above and apart from the common faith of the populous. Many good Greek families and individuals had a patron god or a favourite god, but they didn't despise all the other gods, as the Jews did. Only the atheist Jews showed this disdain. And the Jews sent taxes back to a temple in a far-off land, enriching a distant exchequer in preference to the place that hosted them. And many Jews wouldn't dine outside their race, through fear of breaking their obscure and arbitrary dietary laws. Rules that came, it was rumoured, through Israelite origins as a tribe of travelling lepers, cast out and forbidden to eat at the tables of others. And the Jews were lazy, resting every seventh day. And the Jews were too industrious, thriving while others struggled. It was widely suspected that the Jews prospered only because they practised insidious nepotism, each Jew promoting the interests of his fellow Jews. And the Jews were too fecund, outbreeding through their lascivious nature or because to them abortion counted as infanticide and to them infanticide was a sin; they refused even to expose unwanted offspring. And the Jews did not cremate their dead, instead sticking them in the ground, like Egyptians or mole rats. And the Jews practised circumcision, an outward show of difference; a sever from the penis and from the polis. And despite this wilful separation, Judaism was a missionary religion: the Jews sought continually to swell their ranks with converts, drawing decent people into their excluding fiefdom, which already comprised a tenth of the population of most cities. It would have been well to be rid of the Jews entirely. But since the time of that Jew-lover Augustus, the Jews had been protected by Roman law. And the Jews were numerous.

Normally they were numerous. At the edge of a copse, where the black pine met an oxen-tilled field, for example, there was only one Jew. A small Jew, held to the floor by two boys, with his head pushed painfully down. A hand against his chin, forcing open his mouth.

'Lick it,' one boy said. 'Lick it, then tell me that the dirt here tastes good, better than in Judaea. Tell me that you worship a donkey and Judaean soil tastes of donkey shit.'

To Saul, the Tarsean ground did not taste good at all. It tasted of humiliation and blasphemy. And because even slight things can be strong, if pushed in the right direction – take a feather or a fibula – Saul managed to force himself up sufficiently to land a clumsy blow. A wild thrash that, from sacred destiny or beginner's luck, caught his assailant in the eye. This first boy stumbled back from Saul, leaving his companion, still sitting upon Saul's legs, temporarily bewildered by events. Confounded long enough for Saul to clutch up a handful of pine-needled dust and fling it at his face. Both attackers were then as good as blinded: one from the blow, the other from the dirt. Neither saw Saul stand and grab a fallen bough that Divine Providence or gravity had presented, but both boys felt the swing of it.

Saul was advanced in the Israelite religion well beyond many of his own age, zealous for the traditions of his ancestors. And he had the Zealot's look, as he wielded the branch. The fanatic's maniac glint. The look of a beast that might well go down, but would not go down alone. His two foes scrambled in a tangle of arms and legs to be the faster departed.

'I will be great,' Saul shouted at their heels.

'You'll grow up to be porters and labourers. Then you'll see what soil tastes like! You'll be fucking farm hands and I will be a famous Pharisee in Jerusalem.'

The rock badger plodded out of the goat's-thorn bush, a still twitching snake between its teeth. The rock badger knows that you do not have to kill the leopard: you need only make it fear for its eyes.

Thirty-four Years after the Crucifixion

People say that all roads lead to Rome. They don't: they lead *from* Jerusalem. But Rome is, nonetheless, where Paul's road has finished. At least for now, since Rome is where he has spent the past few years. Proclaiming the coming Kingdom of God and teaching the facts about Lord Jesus Christ quite openly and without hindrance.

Paul's back aches in the early mornings. A low lumber cramp, born from public thrashings or just from the terrible bed pallets of public inns. He pulls off the light gown he sleeps in through Rome's sweaty summer nights, groaning to himself at the effort. Beneath the wrinkled pig-leather of an old man's belly hangs his undeniably Jewish cock. What strange tricks God plays, to have set such an importance on thus a thing. To let men believe – to point of death sometimes – that the presence or absence of a flap of foreskin is of any matter. Paul moves over to his chamber pot to let out the near bladder-bursting accumulation that has built up inside him in the night. Though the fullness of liquid is almost painful, he still has to force it free, pushing out with some arcane muscle the piss that in in his youth would have sluiced from him as if from an aqueduct. Growing old is not for the weak. Age berates Paul daily now, like an angry unbeliever. But surely the return of the Lord Jesus is looming; that day could come at any moment, and when it does, Paul will be well again and so will all things.

The tile beneath Paul's bare feet is pleasant, a constant cool reminder of wealth. Or if not wealth, then of comfort at least, if those are different. He girds himself with a freshly washed loin covering – clean clothes being another gratifying benefit of prosperity – winding it about himself almost without thought. So many times has he performed this same action that his hands hold the memory of how inside themselves. Then he pulls on a robe, a gift from Lydia this one, or another admirer, Paul forgets, but it is cut from a fine fabric. Only when dressed does he call for someone to take his night soil away. As is only right for such a figure in the movement, Paul has a few servants to assist him – as nothing when compared to the wealthy of Rome, whose slave retinues sometimes trail behind them a full street length. But an apostle cannot both baptize and fetch the water.

Paul has trained himself to be able to use the word *apostle* without feeling that grating inside him. There are those, and they are many, who claim that Paul is not a true apostle. Who say that the apostles are those companions who were chosen by the Christ in His lifetime. But Paul knows that the people who say such things are wrong: Paul was chosen by the Christ after His death and is therefore an apostle of greater importance.

The movement is growing rapidly in Rome, overtaking even the sects of Mithras and Magna Mater, in pace of conversions, if not yet in size.

Paul didn't found the Roman groups: they were established before he arrived. But his presence in the city is largely, if not universally, welcomed by the followers already there. And he talks with such eloquence and passion that many of the leisured potential converts who visit him are swayed in just an afternoon to stand among the company of the sanctified. Even some of Caesar's household call on Paul and are counted among his supporters.

People will probably come to Paul's apartments today to listen to him, as they do most days, to hear Paul preach of his resurrected saviour-God; a figure like, but quite unlike, Dionysius, Trophonius or Orpheus, for they are misty deities of an uncertain past. The redeemer Paul talks about is a real man, was a real man, a real God, who walked the earth as a peer of this generation and who will return within it too. Who will descend to judge the quick and the dead inside these warped and crooked days. What listener could fail to be amazed by such apocalyptic urgency, especially when spoken of by a preacher so visibly certain of the truth in his every word? An apostle who can even reveal concealed proofs that all this was foretold in the ancient scriptures of the Israelites – a people renowned as mystical and God-devoted – yet Paul speaks of no age-old creed, already well-travelled with caravan traders and sailors, like the mystery cults of Isis, Cybele, Atargattis and Serapis were when they first arrived. His is a dewy neoteric sect of now, something too compelling to ignore: to think that this present moment exists in the imminence of the coming Kingdom of God, the arrival of which – expectantly pressing upon every fresh dawn - was signified by the risen Christ Jesus, the Messiah for whose sake Paul is currently imprisoned.

Were it not for the soldier who sleeps by the door, it would be hard to tell this is a prison. The building is a prison that some Roman nobles would be glad of. Not a senator, but a country landowner might not mind it for a town house and most merchants certainly wouldn't scorn to live there. Paul is obliged to pay the wages and upkeep of the soldier – a one-eyed Praetorian guard named Manius – as well as for the apartments, but he has sufficient funds for these expenses.

The whole household breakfasts together, eating fruit and bread spread with fish sauce and honey – Epaphras, Timothy, Silas, Aristarchus, Demas and Luke, as well as Manius and the three servant women. Paul believes strongly that there should be no division between Jew and Greek, slave and free, male and female. Except, of course, where such divisions are necessary. Whether or not there *should* be separation between Roman citizens and the rest of the world, this is unarguably the situation that exists, and it is entirely thanks to his citizenship that Paul now 'suffers' in this imprisonment rather than being dead, so it is a separation for which he is in some sense grateful.

But though Rome is the greatest city on earth it is still a city. A lamp of burning camphor gum struggles to keep the stink of the streets at bay while they eat; and still that stench of overpopulation almost visibly oozes from beneath the outer door.

There is a knock at that door before they have finished, still too early for Paul's usual acolytes and admirers. The soldier Manius gets up to see who is there, it being his duty to vet visitors as much as to prevent escape, though he has thus far never barred anyone from entering and Paul has absolutely no intention of escaping.

Without even asking their business, Manius waves the caller in, then lies back down on the cushioned floor to take another quince.

The entrant is well past his twentieth year, but still has the look of a giant boy rather than a man; a big moon-headed lad, somewhat uncomely. He wears a travelling cloak wrapped right up to his chin. His bland face poking out from it is like unadorned pottery, blank and functional. He walks in an oafish way as he crosses the room, almost insolent it looks, his swaying swagger, but Paul is sufficiently astute to realize that it is not. And in any case the caller almost immediately throws himself at Paul's feet. Prostrates himself like a stretching hound, face to the floor. Trying to kiss Paul's bare, road- and age-gnarled toes.

'My lord Paul, master of my master,' he begs, 'I plead with you to intercede. I will be killed unless you can help me.'

He must have seen Paul before to go straight to him or at least have had a good description because there are six other men in the room, not including Manius, and no reason to suppose that Paul is their leader, other than his greater age and perhaps his finer robe. But, then, Paul does rather exude being chosen of God; perhaps it is merely that.

'Look at me, boy,' Paul says. 'Do I know you?'

The supplicant raises his head. Tears, droplets that would evaporate in moments in the afternoon's heat, remain upon the morning-cool tile floor beneath him. 'I have seen you, sir, at my master Philemon's villa at Colossae.'

The boy's cloak has slipped down from his chin with his writhing on the floor and Paul notices for the first time the metal collar riveted about his neck. 'You're a slave. And from Colossae!

That's a month's travel away. What are you doing here?'

'Seeking you, sir. Begging for intercession. I have committed a wicked crime against my master, and further wronged him by fleeing his judgement and stealing the coins needed to make my way to you. Philemon is a great patron, he owes no one debts. You are the only man I knew who he might listen to. Please help me, Lord Paul.'

The slave glances at the soldier Manius as he speaks, as if fearful of being arrested on the spot. Manius has a scar, deep as the Kidron valley, which runs across his empty left eye socket. But his one good eye shows no interest in the importuning boy: it follows instead the ample rump of the serving girl, who removes the empty bowls, as if nothing unusual is happening.

'What's your name?' Paul asks.

The boy says, 'Useful,' choking out the word with hesitance, as though this final divulgence is what will see him condemned.

His fear is understandable, though, whatever his first crime, for running away alone he should face grave punishment. At the least, fugitive slaves are usually whipped near to death and hot-iron branded on the forehead, lest they try to flee again; but they might just as likely be crucified, or burned alive in cloths soaked in pitch, or whatever other exemplary death sentence their master dreams up – being eaten by lampreys was one, sucked and rasped to death by jawless eel-fish. The Roman world does not value the life of a slave. But Paul believes that even a slave can be a brother in the Christ.

'Come.' He places his hands on Useful's chubby shoulders and raises him up, so they stand level, though Paul's head is more properly level with the metal collar around Useful's neck. The shackle is inscribed and, almost without thought, Paul murmurs aloud what it says: *'If I have run away, then catch me. If you take me back to my master Philemon, you'll be rewarded.'*

'Would that I didn't wear this collar of shame. Then I too might read it.' Useful says.

'But you can read?'

'Yes, my lord, the master had me taught from a boy, by the same tutor who taught his own children. He thought it might prove me of help in keeping his records and accounts.'

'So you can write as well? Interesting. You look tired and hungry, Useful.'

Useful nods affirmation.

'Which ails you more?'

'Fatigue, sir. I have barely slept since I arrived in Rome a week ago. Terrified by night, searching for you by day.'

'Then sleep.' Paul turns to his companions. 'Aristarchus, find Useful a pallet and a blanket upstairs.'

Useful throws himself to the floor again and kisses Paul's toes, which are yellowed and scrunched, like the claws of some ancient fowl.

When he wakes, Useful finds Paul beside him in the chamber. He gives Useful bread, spread with thick *garum*, and a clay beaker of sharp, delicious wine.

'You were not so useful to your owner, Useful,' Paul says, 'but I think you will become so to me.'

'How, Master? Anything.'

'I want you to help me unravel a story, a tangle of circumstance and circumcision. I think it would be well to try to get the tale straight and have an idea of how it should be told, not least because a trial at Caesar's court awaits me. Its arrival is in a future contingent, it is true – in fact I have every expectation that the appointed time of God's judgment of all mankind will come first and my trial, therefore, not at all. But it would nonetheless be sensible to make some preparation.'

'Thank you for your confidence, Master. But I am unworthy to pay you this service. Surely, one of your companions ...'

'A couple of them write well enough. But they are also ... how can I put it? ... encumbered by their experiences. A fresh ear, I think, may be just what is needed. Some of the others were present at certain occasions and might bring too much of themselves to the history, or else they have already heard second-hand accounts, invariably inaccurate. With you I could have, as it were, a *tabula rasa*. You, Useful, will write my stories. You will tell the world how I am a real apostle because the crucified Christ appeared to me. The risen Jesus spoke to me!'

Seven Months before
the Crucifixion

What is vision, what is demon, what is insanity?

* * *

It was near noon when he first heard the voices, the sun at its highest, not yet it's hottest. The voices held out promises. They told him what he could become. They said the whole world would honour him, that he had been set apart from his mother's womb. The voices have rarely ceased since.

Legion. The voices are called Legion. Maybe they are emissaries of God, but there is one God and the voices are many, overpowering him as the Romans have overrun Judaea. A man in torment; a land in chains; both infested with legions.

The man, too, used to have a name. And back when he did it was Shuni.

There are pigs now. They did not exist round here when he was a child. The pigs forage through the sacred soil. Filthy, impermissible animals kept only for the Romans. Swine have skin like people, but are bristled like beasts. He slept with a whore once, in Capernaum, before the voices came. She wasn't bristled, but she was cleft in the middle like a swine's foot; she was pink and forbidden like the swine. Now Legion tells him he should take a pig like he took the whore. He tries, but the small ones are too quick and the big tuskers too fierce.

Sometimes he watches the pigs coupling with one another, shrieking swiny glee-pain. The noise hurts his ears, the sight offends his eyes: that such creatures should be here in the God-covenanted land. That such snouty demon-beasts, prohibited even as food to those who fear Yahweh, should be foraging among the tombs of the ancestors. Filthy animals, bred only for the occupiers, sows to feed the Roman blasphemers. Despoiling the soil. Cloven like whores.

The man who used to be called Shuni runs unclothed among the pigs, whipping them and himself with briars and sticks, raising welts and gashes on their backs and his own, the bristled and the bare. The swineherds sometimes try to chase him away, but they are afraid of him, because he is strong and he is wild and he is filled with Legion.

Once, his family had had him shackled. His cousins and his mother – *the sow who bore you*, Legion said – dragged him foaming and moaning to the wooden trammel they'd had a carpenter fashion. But it couldn't hold him for ever. Eventually he smashed the stocks with a rock, dug with bleeding fingers from the ground. It was like the big round eye of a behemoth, the rock, staring into him. Black like the bottom of the nearby sea whose waters had soothed his feet as a child. The blows he rained to break the wooden shackles gouged and bruised his ankles, but he found he didn't mind. Pain was at least sensation, something to bring him back to the world, away from the voices. After he had fled he continued to pound himself with rocks. But only round ones. Only ever round ones, like behemoth eyes.

* * *

Now he lives among the tomb caves. It's dry there, dusty as the grave, since graves they are. Legion makes him curl up in there at night, naked with the dead. When the pigs try to come in, he chases them away. Or, at least, he chases them and then they run away. Is that the same thing? Is it the result or the intent that matters? How are we to judge and be judged?

The Pharisees say that there will come another age, a time in the future when the righteous will be raised; the Sadducees say that this life is all, that we have just one go. He is alone in the tomb caves. No one is resurrected, lending credence to the Sadducees.

Bats dangle from the hewn ceiling though, like strange cave fruits. Still as statues of jackal-man Anubis: dog-faced, furred like cats, winged like beasts of myth. The cloth of their wings, wrapped tight around their fronts like Egyptian funeral windings, is woven finer and tighter than Alexandrian linen; the spiny finger-bones that run through them look too spindle-thin to stand the force of a single flap. It is through their frailty that bats create fear: he is scared that they will tangle and break themselves upon him, that he will somehow become infected with batness. But the cave-dwellers never collide: the bats make their eerie aerial way in the night without ever touching him.

The days are his alone. Alone but for the voices. Alone but for this land – the red desert rocks and the gorse scrub. The Sodom apples and flat-topped parasol thorn trees, which lean like the broken old, tired from resisting the wind, strangling each other in the fight for a place near water-carved cuttings. Seams of softer rock have been eroded into false pathways, narrow but not straight. Wind terraces, as wrinkles on an old baba, ring the hillocks. Boulders lie marooned in the scrub, tumbled from above. Shale piles up against the cliffs, like Roman ramps built to storm a city. Waterless wadis, some still cloaked in hopeful plants. Piles of post-brown brush, dead, waiting to be reborn when the rains come. If the rains come. Just because something has always been is not to say that it always will be.

In season, he eats brittle-skin locusts, because these are allowed by Yahweh, so long as the wings cover their body and they walk on four legs, using two to jump. He uses two legs to jump as well and two hands to catch his prey. Sometimes he cooks his locusts on the embers left behind by the swineherds when they move their tent settlements. More often he cracks the mottled grey locust shells apart and licks out the beckoning inner, as a Gentile might with a shellfish. The one-God of the Israelites does not approve of shellfish, but He likes locusts. The mottled grey at least, and the yellow and the red and some of the white. But never green. Eaters of green locusts will not be revived to walk the earth again with the Pharisees. Though the Sadducees say that now is all there is. Just one turn each, like beggars at the wedding leftovers. Be your time short or long, it is all you have.

Sometimes he sees ibex. They could be eaten. But the males grow horns as long and curved as Babylonian scimitars. And their spry feet carry them onto steep cliffs away from him. Their hoofs sound like masons' mallets as they scramble upon rock. White stockinged, dun as sackcloth. Brown patched, like robes repaired. Their eyes are amber, slit-pupilled and wise. Perhaps they see things on the mountaintops in the drear mists. Perhaps they know things that are hidden from man.

And oryx, they are allowed; they must be the pygarg then, for what else is?

These are the beasts which ye may eat. The ox, the sheep and the goat. The hart and the gazelle and the roebuck and the pygarg and the antelope and the mountain sheep.

Veins are visible on an oryx's massy flank legs. Horns twisted, like the speech of a liar. Ears as long and mobile as a rabbit's, flicking at the flies that buzz around its pale muzzle. Baby fringed with hair. Black marks descend from its eyes like tear-stains. Maybe the oryx mourns the Roman invasion of these lands. White-robed like a priest, maybe it prays in the desert sun that the legions will leave.

Night. Day. Night. Day. Night. Day. Night. Day. Night. Day. Rhythm as familiar and instinctive as the humping hips of the swine boars. Just as loveless. Cold in the tomb caves at night. Daily burned in the sun and self-bruised with round, behemoth-eye rocks.

* * *

Across the lake is Galilee.

The lake is too large really to be called a lake, so people call it a sea. But it is also too small and too land-locked to be a sea; still, it is the species of sea found here. Sometimes the sea seems to float above itself in the heat, a double body, a mirage of reality, so perhaps it can be sea and lake at once.

Somewhen, a boat puts to shore beneath the tomb caves. It comes from across the sea that isn't. Maybe an unseen boundary is breached, as the boat beaches, or perhaps it simply serves to remind, but he who watches it land remembers that he is called Shuni. Thirteen men descend from the boat. Or else one man does, with twelve companions. Shuni recognizes the man, from his youth maybe, or from his dreams. Shuni charges down to the intruders from the tomb caves; his feet are grown hard as ibex hoofs, but still they hurt from the pace of his descent, shale stones sliding as he goes, oblivious to path and pain. He howls and flaps his arms about, to scare them or to call them, he knows not.

The man from the boat calms Shuni. The man holds him and rocks him, like a wave-lapped craft. The man talks to him. Lays hands upon him and brings him back into himself. The man is a peasant – Pharisee-learned and vagabond-ragged, barefoot – but the disciples with him say he is a prince.

After the ragged prince has calmed him, Shuni understands for the first time in a long time what nakedness is. So the ragged prince blankets Shuni with his own outer cloak.

The ragged prince gathers his followers and together they herd up the swine – perhaps two thousand of them – and drive them off the edge of a cliff into the lake. The swine defile the sacred soil. The pigs are there to feed the invaders. The man's disciples say that the prince is appointed by God and that, as surely as he drives their pigs into the water, he will drive the invaders from the land. His followers swing their bill-hooks and iron-blades, to scare the swine and the swineherds. The pigs shriek like people as they fall to their deaths. Their screams are legion.

The swineherds flee to tell the townspeople of Gadara what has been done: what has happened to the demoniac and to the swine. A delegation comes and sees Shuni sitting there, clothed and in his right mind. The delegation is afraid. They are afraid of the ragged prince and his men and they are afraid of the sane demoniac, but most of all they are afraid of the Roman warriors whose pigs still bob on the lake, floated by bloating gases. The swineherds charged with the pigs' care will have to go into hiding and the rest of the townsfolk are dread-full of Roman reprisal. The delegation begs the prince to leave the area. The prince does not bow to anyone save the one-God, but he loves his people, so he acquiesces.

As the prince is getting back into the boat, Shuni pleads that he might come with him. The prince refuses, and says to him, 'Go home to your friends. Tell them what marvels have been done, and what mercy has been shown.' And Shuni promises that he will return to the town of Gadara and will proclaim and that everyone will be amazed.

As if it had been summoned, a gentle wind draws the boat of the prince and his companions back onto the lake. Sparkling fish, every colour in the world, play about them. Things of the water that have both fins and scales can be eaten whatever their hue. God hates shrimps but He loves fish, be they bottom-feeder brown or as bright blue as the flowers of the dwarf chicory. The ragged prince crumbles a piece of bread over the boat's side into the sea-lake's water. And the fishes all eat, but not as gluttons, each has a piece.

* * *

The man who had been possessed by unclean spirits waves from the bouldered coast. And the disciples, who will never return, believe that the man's attacks will surely never return either. The wind pulls the prince and his disciples back towards the dark uneven hills of Galilee, where they eventually put to shore, amid the thickets of poisonous dogbane oleander and the grunting of night frogs.

Twenty Years before the Crucifixion

Saul grew up in Tarsus, no mean city, named for its ancient patron god: Baal-Taraz, the dying and resurrected saviour. Tarsus was the metropolis of the province of Cilicia, blessed to be sited in the region of *Smooth* Cilicia: a place of bounteous fields and abundant grazing plains, the fertility of which was guaranteed by the tree-hanged god Attis, whose flayed, eternal frame dripped blood upon the land. A plenty to be contrasted with that of *Rough* Cilicia, where mountains descended right to the sea, an inhabitance of rock and scrub and scavengers.

Tarsus was a great port and a great portal to the world: to the east lay Syria, Egypt and Judaea; to the north and west, Asia Minor and Macedonia. Traders and seafarers from all these regions shouted in strange-accented but comprehensible Greek across Tarsus's river docks. It had fallen to Roman rule as a result of Pompey's ruthless, scorched-shore campaigns against piracy. But, though staggeringly successful, Pompey's victory cannot have been complete, because some of the scarred ruffian seamen, who spent clipped foreign coins in the Tarsean brothels and tent-taverns, were surely nothing were they not pirates. But the majority of native Tarseans were good people, law-abiders, given to philosophy and piety.

Only thirty miles behind the city, the cold, snow-cowled peaks of the Taurus Mountains towered like white bull horns. Tarsus was a territory of bulls. Bulls and blood. Like most significant cities of the day, Tarsus's foundation myths claimed links to the Greeks and their gods. Who knows if it was mystics or the linen workers who first spun the incredible tale that came to be credited? But Herakles, adventurer demi-god, it was whole-heartedly accepted, had founded Tarsus.

Herakles was said to have been fathered by God. Zeus, god of gods, had sired him with a mortal woman. And so Herakles – part man, who could suffer and die like us, part god, who could not – roamed the earth for a time, performing mighty works and giving hope to those who came across him.

The Tarseans worshipped Herakles – slayer of the Cretan bull – by sacrificing bulls in his honour. But the Herakles of Tarsus was also entangled with crops and harvests, the death and rising of Baal-Taraz, the vaguer, earthier god, who predated the unifying conquests of Alexander the Great and his Greeks. So every autumn Herakles died and a giant pyre, flower-garlanded and sacrifice-stocked, was burned while Herakles descended to Hades. Every spring, he rose again, like the sun, and the virgin girls who had come to marriageable age through the winter danced. Lithe, slight, girl legs sprited – in what finery their families could afford – to honour Herakles and to celebrate renewal and to be watched, while they did so, by the men who hoped to be suitors and the men who just enjoyed watching virgin girls dance. Then bulls, cloth-draped and painted, were pulled through cheering streets. And the people ate grapes and drank them and roared their devotion in the warming sun, a festival offering to Herakles and to the fecund vegetation spirits they no longer remembered.

The Jews did not give offerings, not to spirits or to Herakles and especially not to bulls. They had been punished in their past for honouring golden calves, and they would not be fooled again. Only in the distant Jerusalem Temple could the Jews make sacrifice to their God. Saul's father, as citizen Jew, occupied a curious position. He could not thoroughly take part in the life of the metropolis, as his Tarsean citizenship entitled him and almost obliged him. Yet he had paid the required 250 drachmas – more than a year's wage for most men – so citizen he was, among the elite, and citizen his son was by inheritance. Citizenships to great cities, and the privileges and protections they bestowed, were bought and sold across the civilized world. Though that rank most sought after, which few could afford, was, of course, to be Roman. A Roman could not be flogged or fined or executed, except by order of Rome.

There were few Romans in Tarsus. But those there were, soldiers and traders, brought their own cult of the bull with them: Mithraism. Its doings were secret, but the Jewish boys whispered to one another about what was known. Gleanings of what went on in the Mithraeum temple were more scant and secret than those about sex, since the latter acts – in cramped, city-walled dwellings – were frequently performed by their parents and others within earshot, when not in plain sight. Mithraism, on the other hand, was alien: a mystery religion;

an initiation religion; a thing of brother-bonded devotees and shared sacred meals, with foreign concepts of everlasting abundance in heavenly eternity. On holy dates, or upon induction of a wealthy neophyte, it was said that a blindfolded bull – cloth wrapped about its eyes to make it compliant – was led aloft a scaffold and its jugular was cut to drench the new devotee below in a tide of blood. They would wash with it, rubbing the hot life force into themselves, lapping it from cupped hands, caressing it frantically into every crack and crevice of their naked flesh. All the followers of Mithras drank the blood of the bull when they could; an idea anathema to the Jews, for whom the consumption of blood had been prohibited by God. But bulls are costly and blood is messy; it was said that outside festive events, the gatherers in the Mithraeum chamber would symbolically pass a chalice of wine, a surrogate that became blood, and just as effectively blessed them with immortality.

'They say that devotees of Mithras will live for ever,' Saul told his father once, as they passed the Mithraeum's descending stepped entrance.

'Well, it's nonsense. And we don't believe in such upstart muck,' his father said, looking for a moment as if he might cuff Saul, but just as suddenly softening again. 'We believe in an ancient God. Not all that is new is good. And ours is a jealous God. Remember that, Saul, and remain faithful to Him.'

Saul did so, though he still saw the passion in the eyes of the worshippers of Mithras, as they left their vaulted cellar temple; he saw that they believed and with what fervour. And he heard the revelling, on the twenty-fifth day of the twelfth month, when they celebrated the birth of their god, born in a manger. But righteous Jews didn't believe in frivolous rituals, heavenly hereafters, or wine that turned into blood, so he hardened his heart against it all. And he thought no more either of the civic ecstasies of Herakles-Taraz, who arose from the dead each spring. Or of the hanged god Attis, virgin born, who died for the sins of others and was resurrected three days later, whose followers ate his body in the form of bread. Such fripperies were put right to the back of Saul's mind.

One Year after
the Crucifixion

Saul has never seen Annas, the high priest, laugh before. But now his face is creased with it. He puts a palm upon his chest as if to stop a mirth so fulsome that it hurts him. His eyes are wide and watery, like a camel's. He wheezes, as if the sudden humour has left him short of breath. He has a horrible laugh: screechy and repetitive; it echoes around the chamber. Saul hates that laugh. Saul hates being laughed at. And now every laugh directed against Saul for the rest of his life will take him back to this one.

Annas lifts himself upright, from where he was apparently bent over with the hilarity of the situation. He wipes his beard with the back of his hand, as though it must be drenched with saliva from such drollery. He makes a great and deliberate show of straightening his mouth, as if it was a trial of strength, and then he releases a final deep pant, heavy as a high noon dog's.

'Oh, Saul,' Annas says, 'when you made an appointment to see me, I was afraid you wanted your wages raised. But now you have quite made my day. Marry my daughter, you say.' He looses another little chuckle. 'No, I'm sorry to say that I can't accommodate you there. Mariamme is a charming girl and I don't doubt that she's caught your eye, but I'm afraid I was rather hoping for a more equal match. You are a sturdy enough man, Saul. Not entirely without prospects. I'm sure that some father will be pleased to call you son, but not me.'

Annas pours himself a worked-stone beaker of water from a glass jug, with great ostentation. He does not offer Saul one.

'Do you know who made this pitcher, Saul? Ennion of Sidon made it, one of the finest craftsmen in the world. Do you know how much it cost? No, neither do I, it was a gift, but it is probably worth more than you will ever see in your life. Do you understand? My daughter can't marry you – in fact, I'm slightly taken aback that you thought she could. She will marry someone of her own station. She will live in a house a little like this one. Perhaps not quite so grand, but similar, and I don't intend to pay for it. My line is of the Kohanim, greatest of the Levites, the only tribe of Israel still able to call itself such. I am a high priest. My son-in-law Kayafa is the current high priest. My son may well be high priest one day, if the Roman prefects continue to be as greedy and fickle. My family has been of priestly class since the days of Moses. And you? You are a guard, a guard from Tarsus. You would have been much better off, in fact, asking for a raise ...'

And at this Annas doubles over again, roaring with laughter. Veritably bursting with merriment. Saul would like to take his sword and strike the high priest's white-turbaned head from the shoulders draped in luxurious linen, but instead he retreats from the room. Walking demeaningly backwards as he does so, as convention dictates.

* * *

Saul's chest feels tight about him, as he returns to the malodorous streets outside the mansion. It is as if some great force is crushing him. As if boulders were piled upon his ribcage. He loosens the straps that hold his leather breastplate in place. But it does nothing to ease the constriction.

He feels the loss of Mariamme as surely as if he had really known and possessed her; his mind is quite capable of fictive leaps. Her breasts like twin young roes; honey and milk under her tongue. Her garments scented like camphire and Lebanon, her hair of calamus and cinnamon. Her body a garden of delights, swollen with moist aloes and pink pomegranates. But Saul will never now go into that garden and enjoy those pleasant fruits. It is henceforth a garden enclosed, a fountain sealed. Or sealed to him at least. She will belong to another man, and this knowledge scorches Saul even deeper than the failure. Jealousy as cruel as the grave scourges him.

He used to wake hard and aching from Mariamme's dream visits, so real he swore he still heard her breathing in the night and was unable to reclaim sleep for the sound. He would find himself smiling whenever he whispered her name. A name so strong and sacred, it carried a sense that it should not be spoken out loud at all: a half Yahweh; a djinn who mustn't be summoned.

Mariamme was an oasis girl: the promise of safety and plenty. A store pile of harvest fruits, still ripening. Saul longed not just for her, but for what a match with her would have given him: position; station; connection. And so to lose her is a double loss.

He gulps back the bile that rises on burning acid wings within his throat.

* * *

Saul's men, all nine of them, are waiting for him, lounging on the itchy, mange-bare, camel-hair cushions outside Ephron's pothouse. They shouldn't be drinking on duty, but the wine there is so weak and watered it hardly matters. They're a dungy bevy, slope-backed and semi-subordinate. Most of them probably only joined the Temple Guard because the barracks offered somewhere for new recruits to sleep. Jerusalem is an expensive place to live and full of young men from the diaspora, whose journey to the Holy City cost them more than they had counted on; they arrive penniless and part-starved. Not that all of Saul's men are young. Midian barely has a beard to speak of, but old Korach already has aches in his joints, which grow worse in the winter. Though he's a bruiser, Korach: his knuckles may only hurt him so much through the number of men he's punched in the skull.

Saul is their captain; he was never one of them. He always felt destined for bigger things, as though set apart as special from birth; but now his greatest advance has just been wrenched from him, trampled underfoot by that lofty bastard Annas.

* * *

There's a man preaching on the Temple steps. His Aramaic has the guttural sound of a Galilean. Saul spoke Greek as a boy, but his Aramaic is good enough to be able to pick out strong accents, though in speech it is a little stilted and halting, and sometimes he's forced to take a slightly circuitous route to what he would like to say. The preacher on the other hand is evidently eloquent: he's gathered a small crowd about him. He's one of the sect of the Nazarenes. Followers of a dead messiah. Often they travel shoeless, like this man. Wearing ostentatiously shabby and worn-out robes. Making a show of the poverty they should find shameful. They hold all their meagre goods in common and preach that all men should be equal. They speak out against wealth and privilege, and they also preach against the occupation. To talk of messiahs is to spread sedition, which leads to riot and decimation as surely as clouds come before a storm.

Saul struggles to understand why the Nazarenes take so hard against Roman rule. Judaea has not had it the worst: when Caesar captured Gaul, more than half of its people – two million souls – were massacred or sold into slavery. And through their long unbroken history the Jews themselves have experienced uncountable generations of enslavement. There is more freedom under Rome than they have sometimes known. But, anyway, the Nazarenes' king died without freeing his people, was put to death by the Romans. Thus was self-evidently unsuccessful. The Romans are still here and he is not. It's not blasphemy to believe that this Yeshua was the Messiah, it's just bloody stupid.

Believing a man to be an anointed one, even a dead man, is no crime, but speaking out against the Romans, near enough calling for their overthrow on the very steps of the Temple, with the Roman Antonia Fortress in view just behind it, that is something else: that kind of dissent threatens peace and order. That is something which needs attending to. Something that needs paying for. Saul feels a very distinct sense just now that someone should pay.

Under Saul's motion, the guards belt themselves around the preacher's cluster, loose but encircling, like wolves about a lost sheep. Several of those who were listening notice and edge off. New spectators emerge, from stall sides and shaded spots, but stay at a distance, people more interested in what might happen now than in anything the Nazarene might have had to say.

'What's your name?' Saul asks.

'Stephen,' says the Nazarene. He has uncut hair long as willow fronds, uncommon among Jewish men. And his beard is parted at the front, like the hoofs of a goat. His face flesh is thin, bones visible, perhaps because of the laughable deliberate poverty these people practise.

'A Greek name, but you're from Galilee, aren't you?'

'Yes, I am, from Tiberius – there are many Greek names there. But Jerusalem is my home now.'

'Then if this is your home, treat it with respect. Cease and desist,' Saul says. 'Stop preaching against the peace. Your leader is dead. He failed. And if you bring more havoc to the Temple, the same will most likely happen to you.' Saul pronounces this with monotone menace.

'You say he's dead, we say he will come again and lead us to victory and a new age, a real peace, beyond this present servitude.'

'He was crucified, fool. Your king was executed by the Romans. He's not coming back.'

'Killed by the Romans, yes, but as much by you, the toadies and collaborators. The fearful and the lusters after wealth and advancement. The cowardly and the covetous. Will there ever come a prophet whom men like you wouldn't kill?'

It is hard to know if this Stephen is brave

through his beliefs, or plain sun-stroke stupid. But what is clear: he's really picked the wrong fucking day to have a go at Saul.

* * *

Stephen's dragged bare feet leave trails in the dirt of the street. After the first attempt, he does not struggle to get away, but neither does he assist them, even by standing upright. His toes, though toughened from sandal-less road-walking are bleeding by the time they get to the Dung Gate. The guards stationed there do not salute. Saul mentally notes who they are.

The spectacle of a captured miscreant gathered a small following as the guard party progressed through Jerusalem's streets. Most of the followers are idlers and part-time porters by the look of them. But they'll serve the purpose as well as the next man, if fired up sufficiently. Everyone's fired up in Jerusalem; Jerusalem can always be relied upon to erupt.

They drop Stephen to the ground outside the walls. Robe a little more torn. Hair a little more dishevelled. Nose a little more broken. Blood runs from it, down the divide of his beard, congealing into blackened tufts. They tie his hands to his feet, behind his back, so he is forced to sit in an awkward semi-kneel. His shoulders slump, head bowed. When he looks up it is directly at Saul. His eyes bore into Saul's. Like they can see inside. Saul doesn't hold the gaze; he turns and spits onto the bare dirt. It is little better than desert out here: generations of tethered camels, donkeys and goats have consumed or trampled every sapling, shrub and blade of grass that dared try to grow. Nothing is left now but dust and rocks.

It is hot work collecting stones. The guards leave their cloaks at Saul's feet while they gather, worried that the street trash who have accompanied them through the Dung Gate might try to take off with one otherwise. They pile the stones in a line of slack cairns, facing the now muttering Stephen. Perhaps he is praying. He is drawn white with fear, but does not sob or beg.

Judaea is a vendetta land under vendetta law. An eye might be gouged out for an eye lost. Relatives can seek retributive vengeance. But stoning means no one man is responsible for the death. It is the community enforcing the law. And here, outside the walls, the guards and the dreg riff-raff they've gathered on the way are the community and the law.

Stones can't be too big, or death will come too fast, nor too small, or the killing could take hours. The perfect stone, like the perfect orange, is the size of a woman's fist.

* * *

Saul counts them down and they throw the first stones together: nine from the guards and another ten or twelve from the rabble. Most of the volley misses. A few stones hit the man on the body, making him grunt with pain and knocking him more completely to the ground onto his flank. Though his hands are still tied to his feet, he seems to be trying to move away, in strange erratic twists like a broken-spine snake. The throwers pick another stone each. Their speeds are different now. Some stones thud onto the baked ground around the man's head. A stone hits him on the thigh. Another on the shoulder. He wails. He pleads, in Aramaic then in Greek. A stone hits him on the forehead: it opens and blood runs sideways down it straight to the ground. More stones hit him on the body. More stones hit him on the legs, the arms, the ribs. It is impossible to imagine the pain he is in, but he deserves it. Surely he deserves it. Someone has to keep the peace. Still the stones come. Even when the soil around him is covered with blood and his head is gashed open, a mangled mess, the man still writhes. Panting. Backwards hands clawing at the soil he supposedly wanted to free from Rome. The throwers run out of stones. They have to go further in, to collect the stones they've already thrown. Some are coated with blood. It gets on their hands. They wipe them on their tunics. Grey tunics of the guards. Rough cloth of the porters and idlers. In the pause the man raises his head. He stares into Saul again. 'God forgive you,' the man says. 'God forgive you.' It sounds more like a curse than a blessing. His teeth are broken and his mouth bubbles blood. For the second time today Saul feels queasy. But this man deserved it; he deserved what he got. Like his so-called Messiah leader did. Saul and his guards are the real holy ones. Preserving what is good for Judaea. Saul, who has not cast a stone, but stands with the cloaks of his men at his feet, ordering and approving it all. And guards like Korach, who now throws a big rock, which hits the man directly in the centre of his face. Smashing what remained of it flat. Blowing blood out from it, as if from a child's toss into a puddle. He no longer looks like a man, the man who deserved this. But sometimes brutality is necessary to preserve the peace. A little bloodshed can prevent a tide of blood. Someone has to take responsibility. Someone has to act. Someone has to face up to what is needed. We can't all escape into fantasies to flee the horrors of this world. It would be nice if we could. But we can't. We have to deal with life as it is. Stones bounce from the man's body. It does not even twitch now, as each fresh blow lands. Occasionally a low moan comes. The throwers' arms are tired by the time the moaning stops. Some of the makeshift mob have left. One of them vomited as he did so. Already dun sparrows peck at the vomit he deposited. The birds are too nervous to make their way to the blood-food that oozes from the man lying in the middle, but they would like to, you can tell they would like to. 'Stephen' he was called, the man. A Nazarene. A dead man who believes in dead men. And he deserved what he got, for that. He must have deserved it. Because that was what he got. And people get what they deserve in this life, so the Sadducees say at least. But Saul didn't. Saul hasn't. Saul deserved Mariamme, but he didn't get her. So what does that mean? And Stephen's bubbling lips won't shift from his mind. Is that face going to replace Mariamme's now, in his dreams? 'God forgive you,' Stephen said. 'God forgive you.' Why would Saul need to be forgiven? Stoning means no one man is responsible for the death. And, anyway, the man deserved it. And, anyway, all Saul did was hold the cloaks.

One Day before
the Crucifixion

The master told them to follow the man they would find collecting water, which seemed strange, because collecting water is women's work. But there he was, an ambiguous sister-brother, gathering and chattering with the women. They say that all things exist in Jerusalem, that if a thing is, it is there. And so, here was this thing. Here was this. Here was the man who collects water like a woman and the master says they must lodge with him. Perhaps other pilgrims did not like to lodge with this man-woman. Perhaps that was why he would have space when no one else did. Perhaps the master knew this. Or perhaps this was just one of the things that in Jerusalem are.

So they followed the cow-sway steps of the water-carrying woman-man. He had a head too big for his slight shoulders, like an ant, but must have been strong, like the ant is, too, because the clay urn of water he carried was large, larger than a full woman could carry. Its pottery painted with simple bands, a design timeless as the Torah.

Maybe he sensed that they followed him because he started to jerk quickly down alleys, only in the moment of passing, as if he tried to lose them.

Perhaps he had been beaten before, by drunks or Temple Guard thugs, who didn't care for one who wore a headscarf like a woman, but had a boy child's wisps of beard, visible but faint, like smoke in the daylight.

The man moved erratically, as a polecat will, unsure if it is pursued, but anxious in any case to be less exposed. But he also carried an urn and even though they didn't know the wool-tangle of streets, Cephas and Jochanan easily stayed with him.

The woman-man had eyes like a gazelle, wide and painted with kohl at the edges. Cephas stared into them and saw the fear as the sister-brother tried to close his gap-slatted door on them.

'We won't hurt you,' Cephas said. 'It's just that our master says you have a room here. A big room we can rent.'

And it was so.

* * *

Yeshua pronounced the Kiddush – the blessing – over the cup of wine. As was done at every significant meal by all the Jews of the world. It might seem magical, that blessing, to one who didn't know the rituals of the Israelites. Though perhaps it is no less magical in the knowing. Magic either exists or it does not. Then – also according to Pharisaic custom – to signal the beginning of the meal, Yeshua removed the cloth that covered the bread and he broke the bread and handed a piece to each of those present. It was a large room, but even large as it was, it could not nearly have contained all of the people who would one day say they had been in it that night.

All who really were there would attest that the blessing of the bread and the wine were no different from those they had all seen Yeshua perform before, and their fathers perform and their uncles perform and themselves perform in their turn. But it is true that Yeshua then spoke words uncommon, though not unknown, a Nazirite Vow: 'After this wine, I will not now drink again of the fruit of the vine until I drink it anew in the Kingdom of God.'

Because Yeshua knew what was to happen that night, if all came good. And he had to believe that it would. Because either everything would be won or all would be lost. He was in expectation and excitation of the imminence of the Kingdom. Which was why his hand shook when he held the cup of wine, so much so that tiny tremulous waves flowed across the red of its top. And why his long fingers clutched too tightly into the lumps of soft, blessed bread he passed, leaving imprints in the dough, like footprints in a desert.

* * *

They ate on mats on the floor, as always, and Yeshua held the disciple he loved close to him. Both men seemed to take strength from the other's presence. The disciple Yeshua loved reclined against him. At times lay back in Yeshua's lap, or alongside him, cupped in one another's curves. Two men accustomed to the consolation brought by the other in times of difficulty.

The room was full of unease and tension. For all of them knew some of what might come to pass that night and even the best would be a terrifying ordeal and the worst would be unthinkable.

Yeshua and his beloved shared not only this fearful future but also their past. And they whispered together a lot during the meal. Of revelation, perhaps, or of love. No one but them knew. And why should they? Even a king must have secrets. Especially a king. And the one he loves should be the one to share them.

Among the Greeks, it was considered quite commonplace and natural for a man to love another man. For them to lounge together and feed each other. For them to take solace and comfort from the other's touch. It was not so normal in Judaea. But, then, Yeshua was hardly a normal man and, anyway, he was from Galilee. But even enquiries into inclination are perhaps irrelevant for those who are celibate. And both Yeshua and the disciple he loved were. The other apostles all knew that Yeshua, who loved many, still loved one particularly. And that this man, quite naturally, loved Yeshua back. Quite naturally not only because everyone loved Yeshua – Yeshua was a prince – but because they were brothers: raised and grown together; born and bonded. Yeshua and James the Lesser loved each other as demonstrably and affectionately as any chaste men could. Just as King David loved Jonathan, so King Yeshua loved James. They loved each other only beneath their love for their land and their God.

* * *

When the meal was over. When all that needed to be said had been said. When Yeshua had washed his disciples' feet, the king as their servant. When all had embraced and looked their friends in the eyes for the last time in the world as it was. Then Yeshua told the Twelve to arm themselves. And they picked up their swords and followed him out into the night.

Thirty-four Years after the Crucifixion

Useful examines himself in the burnished bronze disc; he has never really seen his own image before. Only in still pools and polished platters. His master didn't have a mirror disc and, of course, no one else in the household could afford one. This is a world with little by way of reflection. People see themselves predominantly in the eyes of others. Perhaps that is why so much of a man's life is tied up with notions of honour that depend not on what he thinks of himself but on what others think of him. Is this why Paul is so enthused about dictating the events of his life to Useful? Does he mean to have the world reflect back to him the view that he wishes to see?

The view Useful sees in the metal mirror is not of great comfort: a face bland as goose fat and not nearly as appetizing. It is easy to understand how little interest Useful has ever been able to summon from other people. Even so, the reflection he sees is not unadulterated: it is stretched and indistinct, tinged with bronze. Useful is not really seeing himself as others would see him.

And this distorted view, Paul says, is how we look at the whole world for now: basic and vague.

He tells Useful that they will only see clearly when the Epiphany comes, but that day is expected to arrive at any moment: Paul is quite certain that this is the end time, that some of those who are now alive will meet with the Christ, soon to be returned to earth. Until that Day of the Lord, everything will remain blurred and incomplete, like staring into this metal mirror.

'We should continue,' Paul says. 'Who knows how long we have?'

Useful carefully puts down the looking disc and returns to his scroll of parchment. He practised a little on pottery shards first, to be sure he had his hand, parchment being of such cost. The summer stink – the Tiber, night-filth and fish – seems to disappear when Paul talks. He has such vigour and such infectious conviction – born of an unbreakable sense of his own inner divinity – that you would need to doubt your own senses to doubt the truth of his beliefs. What it is to be with Paul in these last days. And to think that Useful, a slave, has been chosen to record this story.

'Where had I got to?'

'You had just told me about the stoning of Stephen, over which you approved,' Useful says.

'Ah, yes, Stephen. Poor Stephen. But fear not for him, boy, he will be among the beloved, resurrected when Christ returns to rule on earth. Stephen was given decent burial by certain devout men, they made great lamentation for him, and he will be among the first brought back to life.'

Paul eases himself down into the chair. The Romans have 'chairs'. They are quite the thing: cross-strutted, canvas seat hanging between wood like a hammock. It is a marvel to be in this house at all, Useful thinks. But to be with Paul ...

'Back then,' Paul continues, 'the supporters of Jesus who were left were called followers of The Way, but they hadn't really realized His significance, strange as that may seem to you now. It was only to me that it was revealed that the Christ was a part of God, an eternal being. But, anyway, that all comes later. Back then I was ravaging The Way wherever I could – entering meeting houses with the Temple Guards, dragging off both men and women to be beaten or whipped. The high priest Annas sanctioned all this. He was well pleased with the stoning of Stephen. He was scared of The Way, because its followers continued to grow in numbers and knew of his part in the death of Jesus. Annas probably feared a Sicarii dagger would one day find its way into his kidney. But he would have been against them anyway, because they held all their goods in common, they were the enemies of wealth and preached against the sort of privilege that Annas and his family enjoyed. And they still railed against Rome as well. Those who actually knew Jesus in his lifetime never understood Him as I do.

'There was a big man in my troop who did my bidding: Korach. He was perhaps a little in awe of me – I was quite a sight, back then, in my prime. Though, of course, misdirected, until I was chosen by God. When we were interrogating those of The Way, I would always have Korach start with blows to the face. Once the face is all swollen and bruised the rest becomes easier. You make a beast of them first. Mess the captive up so that they no longer resemble a son of man. Then you can do what you want to the creature you've made. We gave many of them the forty lashes minus one. It's no small thing, that punishment. Maybe you've seen it.'

Useful shakes his head.

'I've received it on five occasions myself. Thirty-nine lashes, even with supple thongs and a fair hand, is agonizing and debilitating. You sleep on your chest for a month, when you can sleep at all. But upon the weak, with a whip stiff and weighted and a man the size of Korach swinging with full force from the shoulder and the knee, the forty-lashes-but-one can be a death sentence. One of the Nazarenes died before us, there at the holding post, hints of spine visible through his skin. It is not impossible that others succumbed from their wounds or infection after release.

'But in my delusion, I believed that what we were doing was commendable, that's what you must understand. Judaea held on to the last of self-rule and its religious rights by a babe's grasp. The Romans had confiscated the high priest's vestments and released them only by permission for the festivals. And worse: they chose and deposed the high priests. Pompey's slatted boots had marched into the forbidden Holy of Holies, desecrating the place of God. Judaea's ruling class lived in fear of orders to place statues of the emperor in Jerusalem, or even in the Temple, which would certainly have seen a rising of the people in rebellion and consequent war. Yet followers of The Way preached against Rome, threatening dissent and destruction. Those fools in the Jerusalem gathering, those so-called "Superlative Apostles" still threaten it, in fact: James and Jochanan and Cephas. They still can't see that the Christ's resurrection changed everything, that this is bigger than one land or one people. I learned a lot about The Way from those we interrogated, but it was from God that I received my true instruction.

'Anyway, many of the followers of The Way became scattered through our persecutions – some disciples even fled Jerusalem. Brother James and Old Stony seemed to believe they were untouchable – he was tough, Cephas, you have at least to accord him that – but many of the others fled, into the country districts of Judaea and Galilee and beyond, spreading their message wherever they went.

'I became more fired up by the day. The hate grew in me and over me, like a carapace. It enveloped me until the part inside was almost hollow. I had loved learning and it was gone. I had loved a girl and she was gone. All that was left in the space was hate. Hate for The Way and its leaders, so-called Holy Men and lore-taught Pharisees, lauded by the people as if they were some great things. Saying that the Sadducees and high priests, whom I served, were nothing. Saying, by their implication, that I was less than nothing.'

Even now, so many decades on, Paul's face drains as he speaks, as if his anger has been brought back to life by this memory. Resurrected, like all things will be soon.

'Word reached me that The Way was growing in strength among Jews in the diaspora, especially in Damascus. So, breathing threats and murder against the disciples, I went to the high priest and asked him for authority over the synagogues at Damascus, that if I found any leaders of the Nazarenes, I might bring them in bondage back to Jerusalem. And Annas gave me his permission for their rendition and a letter, which ordered the elders and priests of the synagogues to aid me by any means they could. The letter was sealed with red wax, round, like a wound.

'So we departed, my Temple Guards troop and me, with letter and provisions, cloaks and swords. We took the road to Damascus. And that was where it happened: where the fate of the whole world was changed for ever; where I was chosen for glory and for hardship. On the road to Damascus.'

TWO CHILDHOODS

Saul was set apart right from his mother's womb, as one untimely born. He was near enough two months premature. And back then, that was as good as a death sentence. That was as good as to say a swift kick goodbye to the world you've never known. His mother kept him in a little woven reed box, padded and blanketed with scraps of cloth. Resigned to his departure, she did what she could anyway, almost as a child might for a swallow chick, nest-tumbled from a rooftop: just to comfort and give it love, even if it would near certainly be in vain. She coated Saul with pig lard, to keep him warm; she knew Yahweh would forgive her that. She never washed him for fear that even heated water would spell the death knell. She fed him with breast milk, dripped from a whittled stick down his tiny, silent throat. He didn't cry. Perhaps he was too weak to cry. He was too weak to suckle. Too weak to do anything, except to lie in a little woven reed box, covered with a thick wax of fat, padded and blanketed with scraps of cloth. One stray spark from the fire she kept him by and Saul would have gone up, like a dropped oil lamp. But he didn't die, from fire or from anything else:

pneumonia; or heart failure; or sickness; or just from being an insufficiently finished creature to live. He didn't die and eventually he was too big for a little woven reed box and too hungry to be fed with drips from whittled sticks and his mother began to be more scared than she ever was at the beginning, because that was sad certainty, but afterwards she had to deal with the mustard seed of hope. But still Saul didn't die. And the elders said it was a miracle and the healer said it was a marvel of medicine. But Saul's mother said it was just lard and love.

* * *

So, from the very beginning Saul was blessed, but any boy who grew up in Tarsus was in some sense blessed: he could bathe in the salmon-scale silver river in the summer and watch the sun turn the snow on the sharp crenulations of the Taurus Mountains salmon-flesh pink in winter. A boy born to a family of reasonable means could be educated. Indeed, Tarsus was famed for its education: some said that the schools of Tarsus were comparable even to those of Athens and Alexandria.

Saul was tutored in the philosophies of the Greeks, and he was taught the Israelite religion and law from *The Septuagint*, the Greek translation of the Hebrew scriptures. But more than this: he was lectured in love because loved he was. A boy who is the unquestioned object of his mother's adoration will go through his whole life feeling like a champion. Saul had just such a mother: a gentle, doting mother, with brown eyes that shone in lamplight and daylight both.

Saul had a younger sister, and there had been other siblings, others who had died, a dark seam of parental anguish running through the years ahead of his. But Saul had survived, the boy his parents had sought and cherished. Not that his sister was not loved. She was loved, in a way. Just a different way. Though it is hard to measure the loves of other people, never mind other times. For many Greek families back then, love meant leaving a child out for exposure: sacrificing the latest comer entirely in order to feed those who had come before. Or selling them as a slave to a good master in good times, lest fear of starvation force them later to be *given* to a cruel master. Some families considered it dangerous to love at all: even on average five or six children born alive would see just two reach adulthood; occasionally, ten would mean none. Some Tarseans feared to name their children until they were grown enough to gather kindling. Before that they were called only 'the baby'.

Even past thirteen, when he could follow the Torah as a man, Saul remained his parents' baby and he was loved in the straightforward sense of being adored, indulged, maybe even spoiled. He was never beaten, as his sister was sometimes beaten. This was not by regulation. It was simply something that did not occur. Because Saul was the son that his parents had prayed for and Saul gradually became a son any Jewish family would be proud of: learned in his scriptures and devoted to his God.

And yet Saul was not greatly happy. Or at least he did not know himself to be. Perhaps we need some element of sadness to make a judgement on our happiness, just as a cold face measures the warmth of the body beneath a blanket.

Sometimes the boy Saul wondered if other people really existed at all: could they think as he could think? Were they truly separate beings, or was this whole world constructed as a thing to test him? Was he at the centre of a giant dream, which revolved around Saul as the sun revolved around the sky?

* * *

There were other people, of course, most of them in other lands. In Galilee, for example, there was a boy of approximately the same age as Saul. Yahushua he was named, though his friends called him Yeshua and many who didn't know him would come to call him Jesus.

Yeshua lived in a squat, single-storey home, part hollowed into a limestone hill. Its packed dirt floor was smeared with clay, so that manure could be more easily swept away because animals – a couple of goats, a milk sheep, possibly a donkey – were brought in at night. The walls were of stacked rock, with mud joints. The flat roof was also made of mud, layered with sticks and straw. When the nights were warm, the family would sleep up there; at colder times they would share the sole room below with the beasts. They cooked on a clay oven, fuelled with animal dung. They lived mostly on millet, emmer wheat and barley, in the form of gruel, bread or flat cakes. But also pine nuts, coarse horse beans, almonds, olives, sycamore figs, lentils and dandelion leaves. Occasionally they ate salted fish. The zenith of every year was lamb – an unblemished year-old male lamb – for the Passover festival.

Yeshua, like Saul, was devoted to his study of the Torah and the love of the one-God. In Judaea and Galilee, the Pharisees ensured that even the poor could have some education. Yeshua had four brothers and at least two sisters, of whom he was probably the eldest, although there is no definitive reason to suppose this. Someone would later write – a century later – that Yeshua was born in distant Bethlehem to a virgin; but this doesn't seem very likely. That's the sort of thing a mother would remember and Yeshua's mother quite clearly did not. Or else why would she later think he had gone insane and needed restraining when he started preaching? And why would she be amazed at a level of boyhood precociousness that would seem very underwhelming in one who began life announced by angels and implanted by God? The narrator of this nativity tale would say that the parental travellers must have come to Bethlehem – where it was commonly believed a messiah should be born – because of the census. This wasn't the case, but such mistakes are easily forgiven, because the storywriter spoke a different language from Yeshua and had never been anywhere near Judaea and wrote only after fables and tall tales had taken root, in an age when miraculous nativities were competitive and ubiquitous.

What little is known to be true is that in the year of Yeshua's birth there were riots in Jerusalem at the Passover and more than three thousand people were massacred, cut down by horsemen. The troops rode through the tent villages outside the Temple, slashing people to the ground and trampling them beneath hoofs. And following this barbarity, tens of thousands of Judaeans rose up, the garrison of the Antonia Fortress was attacked and long battles were fought for control of the city. Fire blackened the streets; Romans tumbled the cloisters of the Temple and looted its treasure; sieges were thrown up and destroyed again. And at the finish another two thousand of the defeated Israelites were crucified at a single time. It is impossible even to speculate as to how many men must have lost their lives in combat or fled into the deserts and the diaspora, if two thousand were taken alive, knowing they would face the agonizing state-terror of crucifixion.

Two thousand men were hanged and nailed from beams and trees, many surviving the suffering for days, cursed to cling to life without hope of release, in delirium and pain beyond measure. But large numbers conceal rather than express true horror. It was not two thousand men who were tortured to death, it was one man: a man who liked to stroke the palm of his wife's hand, to touch a little thimble of flesh, which remained soft, though all the rest was calloused by work; a man who knew just how to make his imp children squeal like goslings when he tickled them; a man who spat pips for accuracy with his father when they ate fruit, and pissed for distance when he drank too much wine with his friends; a man who didn't sing out of tune, only because he never knew what the tune was; a man who sobbed with joy on his wedding night, because he had not fully understood how great the gift he was to receive would be; a man with a laugh funnier than any joke and eyes warm as simmering soup. It was one man, only one man, to each family who lost one man; but this murder was repeated two thousand times.

And in the year of Yeshua's birth, at least three Israelites declared themselves to be a messiah; declared themselves to be an anointed king, that is.

There was Simon of Peraea, who temporarily took the royal palace at Jericho and was crowned with a diadem. His men were eventually slaughtered by Roman soldiers and Simon himself beheaded in battle. Though some of his followers believed that, at the command of the angel Gabriel, Simon rose from the dead three days later.

And there was Athronges the Shepherd, who had four brothers, like Yeshua had, and was a tall man, like Yeshua would become, and was put to death by the Romans, as Yeshua would eventually be.

And there was Judas bar Hezekiah who seized Sepphoris, which lay just a sunset's walk from Nazareth, where Yeshua and his family lived, their closest town. Judas spread the arms captured there among the multitudes that followed him. And in revenge the Romans burned Sepphoris to the ground and sold into slavery every surviving man, woman and child who dwelled there, perhaps twelve thousand souls. Doubtless the families in Nazareth all had friends and relations in Sepphoris – barely three miles away – who were massacred, or incinerated alive, or sold into slavery. The hills all about and humble Nazareth itself must have harboured that fraction who managed to escape alive.

In the year of Yeshua's birth, two whole Roman legions with auxiliaries – twenty thousand war-brutalized soldiers – marched unstoppably through Galilee, destroying towns and villages and killing in such swathes that the soil itself wept blood. The night sky of Yeshua's nativity was lit not by guiding stars but by burning flesh. Yet all this is curiously absent from the book called the Bible, with its strange tales of virgins and journeys and censuses.

There was a census; that much is true. But it was held when Yeshua was about ten years old. So it did not, of course, affect the place or the manner of his birth. The memory of it as an important event must have lingered, though, because the census was resented bitterly by the trampled people. It was conducted to assess the level of tribute the Judaeans would have to pay and it represented subjugation and humiliation, as well as fear of the crippling taxes that would inevitably fall heaviest on the poor: head tax; land tax; income tax; salt tax; meat tax; house tax; road tax; boundary tax; bridge tax; water tax; market tax; town tax. Roman levies were legion and the tax-farmers cruel, and the monies taken were shipped to the distant blasphemy of a demi-god emperor in a foreign state; there was no pretence that the funds were for the benefit of those people who were bled white. Rome was not big on pretence: its origin myths were of fratricide and rape; its first citizens, criminals and outcasts; its sacred animals, the wolf and the vulture; its murderous founder, a son of the god of war.

Another Judas: Judas the Galilean – a countryman of Yeshua – began the rebellion against the census. This Judas was a rabbi, learned in scripture and resolved to call no one master but Yahweh, even should that mean death. With a Pharisee, he founded the Zealots and once again the Israelites rose in vast numbers, against the census and against the Roman domination it represented.

They did not fail utterly, because they started a movement that survived. And they knew from the beginning that the odds were incalculably against them. Judaea was not a land Imperial Rome could ever allow to be free, sited as it was between the breadbasket of Egypt and the vital cedar forests of Syria. To push the Romans from Judaea, you needed almost to push them from the world. But the Zealot rebels were pious and righteous men and they fought in expectation that God was with them. They took their name from the Prophet Phinehas in the Book of Numbers who was 'zealous' for his God and defeated the entire Midianite army and five Midianite kings without losing a single comrade, because the God of Israel was on Phinehas's side.

So the Zealots fought with every hope that their God would help those who helped themselves, as they were convinced that He had in the past. They believed that their bravery and piety would prevail, if God willed it.

They were, of course, annihilated.

Decimation is a term inadequate: it means just one in ten stolen, when probably some villages of Galilee were left all but devoid of men of fighting age after the Zealot rising. Perhaps in Yeshua's little Nazareth there was a generation virtually missing as Yeshua was turning into a man. Many, maybe all, of the adolescents Yeshua had looked up to as a small boy were killed in battle or nailed alive.

Yeshua's father might well have been an old man by the time of his birth – too old to fight – but many of Yeshua's friends must have grown up fatherless from the rebellions that arose in that year. And all of them would have had kin and friends butchered in Sepphoris. And then another constellation of men was wiped out when Yeshua was ten, crucified in such numbers that, for years afterwards, carpenters built doorframes and well-hoists from trees that had once upborne convulsed and broken patriots.

The helpless wrath against the Romans and their unbeatable legions must have growled black in the dead eyes of every survivor, when Yeshua was a boy. Must have echoed from the hollow begging bowls of every widow and orphan. Prayers that God would save His people from this horror must have been shared and shouted in Nazareth's small synagogue. We cannot blame Yeshua, because he did not grow up to be entirely a man of peace.

* * *

Yeshua and Saul both would come to be men who changed the world for ever, for better or other. And each would find himself in Jerusalem at the same time, although they never met.

Saul arrived first: he came to the holy city with dreams of becoming a great Pharisee. But possibly he found Pharisee learning too much, struggling as he was to study in another tongue. Though he had excelled in his memory and scrutiny of the holy books in Greek, the Pharisees taught and debated in Hebrew. Saul began first to dislike and then despise the faction of the Pharisees, with their liberalizing and constant scrutinizing of the law. He came to conclude that he would better serve his God in the Temple Guard, on the side of the aristocratic Sadducees. And so he abandoned his education, but he did not return to Tarsus. Saul was equipped with stories about not looking back, from his Greek heritage and his Jewish: from Herakles' and Orpheus's descents into the underworld and from Lot's flight from Sodom and Gomorrah. And so Saul did not look back, after that first journey to Jerusalem. He never looked back again. The past to him became nothing; a thing to be spoken of only when needed; a thing whose memory is malleable.

When Yeshua came to Jerusalem, he arrived as a rebel king, a rival ruler to the Roman emperor, a rival leader to the high priest. He came with his brothers and his disciples. With the Zealot Simon and the Sicarii dagger-man Judas. With Cephas or Rocky. With the brothers Jacob and Jochanan, so fierce they were named the Sons of Thunder. Just as the charge laid against him would later be recorded: Yeshua arrived in Jerusalem to oppose the paying of taxes to Caesar and to declare himself the anointed king, the Messiah. He came to incite a rising, as Judas the Galilean had done in his youth; as Phinehas had done in the scripture. He came to free his people as Moses and David had done. He believed that he and his followers would suffice to defeat the might of Rome. Because the scriptures prove that God helps those who are His chosen ones, if they are faithful and prayerful and prepared to fight like fuck.

Three Years after
the Crucifixion

Saul and the guards leave by the Damascus Gate, the opposite end of Jerusalem's walls to where they murdered Stephen. No, not murdered: executed, righteously and lawfully executed.

The four ziggurat towers of the Antonia Fortress – named for Roman warlord Mark Anthony – obscure the sky as they pass by. Beneath its guileless fortifications – each stone-carved block as heavy as a hundred hungry urchins – are lines of spread blankets, baskets and handcarts of the traders who sell to the legionaries. There are also scarlet-canopied whore tents, sweaty delights hidden beneath cloth that sieves the daylight. Even now soldiery laughter erupts from one. Some trooper probably cups a pomegranate breast and strokes the wet pelt of a Judaean girl. The Romans snatch the best of everything from this life. But what is this life? Is it just a prelude or a waking dream? Is a new age soon to dawn, as the Nazarenes say? Saul no longer feels he knows these things; he feels his certainties slipping away from him, along with a once hopeful future. There is a hole in the fabric of things, a gap that can be filled only with blood.

The law requires that nearly everything be cleansed with blood, the Torah says, *and without the shedding of blood there is no forgiveness.* Blood sacrifices, blood circuses, blood feuds, blood libels, blooded warriors, bloody hands. Blood marks us and keeps us. With blood we end and start. And only in blood is there absolution: *For the life of a creature is in its blood, and I have given it to you on the altar to make atonement for your souls …*

Saul will have his atonement from the Nazarenes; Saul will have his blood.

A knot of Romans sit, proudly polishing their armour. Dark-eyed boys stare at them from a distance, loathing them, yet longing to be like them. A feeling Saul knows something of.

Saul has learned much about the Nazarenes through his persecutions of them. People of The Way. Mystical, ignorant, nonsensical followers of a self-evidently failed messiah; believers that the end time will shortly arrive. They must be eradicated. That much is clear. Surely that at least is clear. The rest of their beliefs are indistinct, like looking through a veil.

These streets around the Antonia Fortress are little Italy. The Romans are visibly in control here. But they only ever traverse the dense and narrow alleys of lower Jerusalem mob-handed. Too many quarter-turn stairwells and alley doorways where Sicarii daggers can lurk. Too many flat roofs for collecting rainwater that can become ambush platforms. Dead ends that can be barricaded in an instant, leaving seven-foot spears and armour impotent. Where the mightiest soldier can be killed by dropped building blocks. Go in too light and Roman soldiers might die. Go in too heavy and they might provoke a riot. So day-to-day patrolling of

Jerusalem is still best left to the Temple Guard and the vestiges of self-rule, the pretence of self-rule. A pretence that fools no one, but is nonetheless a mutually beneficial fraud. A lie that almost everyone can take part in trying to believe. Isn't it better at least to try to believe in what you cannot change in any case? You have to attempt to hear some harmony in the clangs and crashes of the world.

Not everyone subscribes to this view. As Saul and his men leave Jerusalem's walls behind, some of the non-subscribers are visible: those who think that this land must be changed. They hang, part-rotted, from a row of crosses. Flesh turned shades of rancid green. Heads lolled forwards, as if at rest. But eyes long since pecked free by the hooded crows. The hooded crows are black-cowled and dark-winged, but tabarded in grey, like Temple Guards. They prize the eyes, moist and globular; the eyes and the genitals are always the first to go. The hooded crows caw and hop their springing half-flight lope between the wooden scaffolds that uphold the dead. The crows stay off the ground; the ground belongs to the dogs. The dogs yelp as they dance and stagger, unstable on hind legs, trying to reach ever higher up. The flesh and bone that dogs and jackals could readily stretch to have gone already; the ankles of the dead are jagged. The bodies are cut-offs now: footless, faceless and emasculated, like damaged statues from some abandoned Alexandrian town. This is the fate of those fools who oppose Rome. And Deuteronomy says that anyone who is hanged on a tree is cursed. How can the idiot Nazarenes believe that a man who ended like this could be the Messiah? Those of The Way are wrong, like Stephen was. They deserve to die, like Stephen did.

Saul has a scroll from the high priest to give him legitimacy for the extraordinary rendition on which he is embarked. Annas has no legal jurisdiction outside Jerusalem, but he is still a high priest, so the letter should impress the Jewish population of Damascus, where some of the leaders of The Way have fled. The Jewish population may be swayed, perhaps, but the authorities won't. So Saul and his men are dressed like traders, daggers at their belts, their swords secreted in packs on the mule that carries their provisions. Mules are mixed creatures, prohibited by Torah, but the high priest seems happy to overlook this instance. Saul has the high priest's scroll tucked safely inside his tunic, the stiff parchment pressing into his side, like a comforting wound. How can there be such a thing? How can a wound be comforting? How can the freaks and fools of The Way think that a dead man can be a messiah? It makes no sense. And yet so many of them refuse to recant the belief. So many of them take the whippings and beatings with smiles on their faces. Smiles like those of the idiot child who sits in the midday sun on the Temple steps: unconflicted; contented.

* * *

The journey to Damascus is eight or nine days' travel on foot, a hard trek even for the fit and strong, like Saul and the men of his guard troop. All of them have made long journeys before, though. None of them was born in this land. They are all Greek speakers, Jews from the diaspora. Rolling stones that have gathered little by way of moss from their time in the hated Temple Guard. But, then, there is no moss in this land. Even the northern faces are too hot for moss. There is no place in Judaea to hide from the sun.

On the deceptive downhill of the first day they are often overtaken on the road, usually by ox-pulled wagons with solid wood wheels; occasionally by chariots with spokes. But the guards' pace is fast for pedestrians; they are travelling light, nothing to trade but their swords, nothing to give but the orders contained in a scroll.

They pass a gang of prisoners: Judaeans, probably enslaved for unpaid taxes, on their way to the province of Syria, where people fetch a better price: Leviticus states that Hebrews must be freed after seven years' service, so Jews do not often buy their fellows. The prisoners are roped together through iron neck collars, hands bound, trudging in a line, guarded by Roman freebooters. They are new slaves, but already carry themselves with the cowering of the broken. They wear identical short tunics of camel hair, the coarsest, cheapest cloth, impossible to rid of parasites. Their own clothes must have been sold. Their heads are recently shaved and pale, their hair gone to become wigs for the wealthy. The ropes that join them swing as they make their slow progress, rocking in a pendulum rhythm. Saul tries not to catch any of their eyes, he is not sure why: some indistinct fear that abjection is contagious. He need not worry: they stare only at the section of time-formed road upon which they must take the next step. They have no future but that. No thoughts but the eternal question of the Israelite: why do Your Prophets say You love us, my God, yet You let Your children be taken in chains?

* * *

The next four legs are through desert, sands strewn with black rocks, as dense as seed on bread, and the domes of scrubby, struggling rimth plants. Saul and the nine guards rest through the hottest sunders of each day, wherever they can find shade to do so. Making strongest pace from dawn through the morning. Throwing up their night-time camp, which is just fire and blankets, as the light begins to fade.

On the fifth day, as they prepare to eat midday food beneath the canopy of a spiral acacia, Korach seems to think that Saul serves himself too large a share. Perhaps he does.

'You need to watch your manners out here, Saul,' Korach says. 'We're not in Jerusalem now. If someone were to have an accident on the road, no one would know.'

Saul's breath is filched from him. He fissures his eyes and puts a hand to his dagger's pommel, looks around to the others of his men to be sure that they will be with him as he deals with this insubordination. And realizes, with spinning disbelief, that they will not.

Midian is chuckling openly; the others meet Saul's eyes without glancing away, follow his gaze as he turns to the next face and then the next. Korach nods and takes a shovel-fingered scoop of bulgur gruel from Saul's bowl and adds it to his own.

'You don't command any more, Saul. You politely request, at best. Remember that. You are in charge by our consent. You were only promoted because you're a lickspittle with a little learning. You think because you can read and write you're a scribe. You think because you can quote some Torah and have a smattering of Hebrew you're a Pharisee.

You think because you bought a fancy uniform and a breastplate you're an aristocrat? We all know you were laughed out of marriage into the aristocracy. Word gets around. We all know how that one ended. You think because you're in charge that you can look down on the rest of us. But you are no different from us, except that we know our station and you think you're some great thing. They used too much leaven in making you. You are puffed up, Saul. Too puffed up.'

There are a few cairns of rock behind Korach. Probably only the idle tossed way stations of generations of travellers, but they could equally be bandit burials of the murdered. Saul does not reply. He looks down to his cracked bulgur gruel and tries to eat it; he chokes it down, though his mouth is dry as a potsherd and his tongue sticks to his jaw.

Korach makes a great show of licking every last grain of the sticky beige goo from his fingers after each mouthful, making loud sucking noises, at which the others laugh, mirthlessly.

Saul drops his bowl to the floor when he has finished, saying nothing. Feigning something. Fooling no one. Thoughts imploding. The sky is falling.

Cattle pass by, back on the road, hump-backed and horned. The herdsman forces the stragglers on with his goad: a man-length stave, sharpened to a spike. Sometimes recalcitrant creatures kick back at him with dirt-caked hoofs, but they cannot reach him at the end of his goad and only earn further punishing stabs for the attempt. The man has no dog with which to steer the herd, only pain.

* * *

It is Korach who decides when the guards have rested long enough and Midian hands the rope reins of the pack-mule to Saul.

'About time you took a turn leading the beast,' Midian says.

The mule is aged and mange-wretched. Muzzle pocked with infected flea bites, fur missing clumps where some leprous equine skin disease has forced an untimely uneven moult. Flies flock about it, as though it is already dead. They swarm like a mist, like black dots upon the eye that you cannot get rid of. Like smears from staring at the sun.

The mule is a gelded male, doubly cursed to unfruitfulness. Sterile child of horse and donkey. Not one thing or the other. Saul feels like a mule himself: neither Greek nor Jew; neither Pharisee nor Sadducee; not Roman but still living in a Roman world, obeying Roman rules; not a slave or truly free; the servant of Annas, a man he despises, obeying orders to destroy people he can't help admiring; commanding men that he no longer commands, a band of rough vagrants, slouching towards Damascus.

And with each passed hour on the road, with each further mocking rejection from his men under the melting sun, with each time the mule halts to snatch a mouthful of rimth, or kicks back at the stick Saul is forced to use to goad it, there is a further dizzying descent. It feels as if the world is in motion. Everything is getting blurred, like the flies that swaddle the mule; like peering through a veil of cloth.

Saul barely sleeps that fifth night, his mind struggling with the unravelling of what has occurred. Not just what has happened that day but with this life: a destiny for greatness that is being robbed from him, rubbed from him. Saul, who was struggling to settle himself to the possibility of mediocrity, finds himself staring at dejection and failure. He doesn't even have the respect of his own men, his only friends. Not only do they not honour him, they don't even like him. They despise him. He came to Jerusalem to be a leader of esteem, an eminent Pharisee; to astonish and be admired for his erudition and wisdom. He finds himself runt-captain of a pack of perfidious rats, hated by them and by the populace as a whole. And as each of the bitter-gall humiliations of his life burns through his sleepless addled mind, it is replaced in turn with a newer, fiercer, humiliation that came after.

Things are out of kilter; his mind is weighted all to one side. And he searches for but cannot locate something to even it out again. To make the centre hold. He pictures the scales that a spice merchant would use to weigh out his precious commodities. Saul needs something like that, something to correct the tilt of mind and life.

When sleep finally arrives, it comes with the smashed face of Stephen. An image scorched into the very fabric of Saul's skin, as if branded by white-hot iron. A burned flesh scarification of the forehead. Like the marking of a slave who has tried to flee.

* * *

The plains last for days, flat as the Galilee Sea, empty but for parched bushes in dry runs of the streambeds of the Jordan rift and balls of old dung, gone white like desert eggs. Wilderness should be yellow and green and blue and copper and russet. These plains are cinereous as the scorching of Sodom.

You see faces in the sands if you stare too long. A form of small blasphemy, perhaps, since it is against God's law to depict animals or people and you have surely painted them in your mind's eye. But Saul is sick of such small blasphemies, worrying about the motes of Pharisee rules, while nations and mountains fall apart.

The flies alone could send men insane, them and the southern wind. The flies sing in their hissed flight of the death and decay that you must keep pushing onward to evade. They land on you and on your meagre portions of food and they do not fear you as they ought.

When Saul washes his face in a pool, he doesn't recognize the man who stares back at him. The man who looks back is sleepless and delirious. The man who looks back is a murderer. The man who looks back is close to madness. The man who looks back is a distorted fool who peers into a pool to see, as if in a glass, darkly.

* * *

This state of dissonance cannot go on for long. Collapse must come. And maybe what falls can be made better a second time. But before it can be built anew, it must be broken utterly.

* * *

They are finally within sight of the worry-lined walls of Damascus when Saul drops, non-resonant, to the dirt. He falls like a nest-tumbled swallow chick. Near motionless and staring at the sky. He wails about the brightness of the light.

If you stare at the sun you may go blind, but at least you don't see the flies.

* * *

And one might say it was hunger, sunstroke and the wind. One might say it was malarial delirium. One might say it was the product of a mind somehow split from itself, a mind fraught with disorder, a mind damaged from external pressures, which it could no longer square with an aggrandized view of itself. One might even say that some grain or fungus, entangled in foraged food, contained hallucinogenic fervour. One might very well indeed say that it was temporal-lobe epilepsy, well proven to cause deeply experienced mystical visions and lingering but temporary blindness. One might say any or all of these things, and others have. But Saul believed he heard Jesus.

And Jesus told him to stop kicking against the goad. Jesus told him to come towards the light. Jesus said: what is sown in dishonour, can be raised in glory; what is sown in weakness, can be raised in power. Jesus said the least can be great.

Three Days before
the Crucifixion

A saw-scaled viper lies motionless, shrugged over a boulder, trying to warm its night-cooled frame in the first of the sun. It slowly lifts its head and flicks a hay-fork tongue to taste the breeze, as if sleepily becoming aware of a presence. As it does so Cephas hacks at it with his stubby iron sword. The serpent's head is not cut cleanly: it is still attached by the leathery skin of one side, though its inner flesh is exposed and its cold blood spurts. The snake tries to strike, but its head flops away, past right angle from its body, like a snapped flower stalk. Cephas brings down his blade again and severs the neck fully this time. The viper's tail thrashes erratically, then falls off the rock and lies still.

'Can the snake help being a snake?' James the Lesser asks.

'No more than a Roman can help being a Roman, but he is still responsible for his actions,' Cephas says.

'And what were the snake's actions so worthy of death?'

'Being a snake.'

* * *

They withdrew to the safety of Bethany last night. Now, once again, they look down to Jerusalem from the Mount of Olives. The city walls zigzag across the horizon, in crisp lines like broken *matzah* bread – the unrisen loaf of affliction.

Below them – descending past Gethsemane to the Kidron valley – are excavated burial caves. Those of the aristocratic Sadducee families have carved entrance ways and inscriptions. Not for the poor such finery in mortality. This valley is the boundary line between the living and the dead. The scriptures say the resurrection will start here at the end of days. Yeshua says this is the end of days.

The valley is on fire. Even the Temple – high above the city ramparts – is part obscured by the smoke that rises from the steep side of the Kidron below it. The plume looks dirty-pink in the morning sun. It lifts to the same height as the holy white smoke that already flows from the pyre of the Temple platform, then both veer off in the strength of an elevated western wind.

Fumes would fill the tomb caves were it not for the round stones rolled across their fronts. Even so, some smoke must be seeping through the cracks and the fissures to mingle with the flesh-desiccated bones within.

The fire is probably a deliberate burning, started to encourage regrowth and to prevent bigger fires later. If the grass of the Kidron valley grows too long and dry it can burn in a conflagration fierce enough to make even those in the city fear. Grass fire could never pierce the great limestone walls, but sparks can fly on the wind and ignite from within. Jerusalem is a city under permanent threat of combustion.

'Moses was spoken to by a burning bush and below there is a multitude. Perhaps it's a sign,' Jochanan says.

'Yes, it's a sign. It's a sign that the goatherds are sick of the gorse scrub and the dumped rubbish,' says Cephas.

* * *

Though not the palm-fronded entrance of yesterday, Yeshua and the disciples have still accumulated a large following by the time they climb the great stone stairway of the Temple. Many know who Yeshua is – some have travelled far to be part of this; others are simply Passover pilgrims, who join the mass of people heading in the small-step crush of the crowd to the Temple gates.

The giant stairs – broad as a field that could feed a Galilee family – are carved from the very rock of the Jerusalem Mount; they are an integral part of this sacred country and the Temple is the holiest place on earth, the one and only seat in all the world where the Israelites can make sacrifice. It is bigger even than the Acropolis or the Temple of Jupiter at Rome; the Jerusalem Temple is perhaps the largest site of worship known to man. Even Gentiles journey here, just to wonder at the magnificence.

Cephas and the rest of the Galileans come from a place where few buildings even have a second floor and a village can mean a hundred houses, or half that. Throughout the year they have followed Yeshua, they have stayed away from the metro-polises and even large towns, sticking to rural backwaters when they entered habitations at all. And now they are facing a structure that soars as if it might scrape the heavens. Each hewn-rock

JONATHAN TRIGELL

block is as high as a man's chest, held together with no bonding material save their own unimaginable weight. Every new row looms just a finger's width back from the one below in an imperceptible pyramid, forty rows high. And that monstrous construct is just the platform for the Temple itself – white marble, plated with gold – to stand upon.

Cephas is a man built for battle, nicknamed not only Rocky but also 'Baryona' – Outlaw. He could be a gladiator if he did not belong to God. He might be one yet, if the Romans take him alive some day. Cephas has wrists as thick as many men's ankles. A head as broad, as jowled and as menacing as the giant mastiffs the Romans use as dogs of war. But Cephas is not a fool. And Cephas knows what they are about to do. And Cephas feels his stomach coil like a boat rope as he mounts the steps.

* * *

The first courtyard of the Temple is open to all, even non-Jews. Though covering most of the thirty-six-acre precinct, large as a great lake, it is almost a bazaar. Awash with traders shouting, the yawp and squeal of livestock and the Babel babble of foreign tongues. Someone watching from the Roman-garrisoned Antonia Fortress looking down on the scene – and such there are – would not be sure if the great crowd that entered the Temple at one time is spreading throughout the court deliberately, or only through necessity of the narrow spaces between stalls. But spread they do, dispersing in every direction, seeping into the corners, strolling in groups of two or three to admire the frescos, or to take the shade of a

98

colonnade, or to haggle half-heartedly with a stallholder.

The Twelve stay close to Yeshua, with his brother, James the Lesser, to one side and Cephas to the other, Jochanan behind, the Three Pillars who support and protect Yeshua always.

But for the opulence of the court and the magnificence of the Temple, draped with ornate tapestries of scarlet and purple, this could be any market square in the civilized world. Though peculiarly specialist: most of the table traders are money-changers and many of the stallholders selling animals for sacrifice. Doves for the poorest, oxen for the richest and, this being the time of festival, lambs for everyone with a family large enough to eat one. The trade is necessary: the sacrifices are laid down in the sacred law and travellers can hardly come – often from far-off lands – carrying a live sacrifice and keeping it pure. Likewise, the Temple tax must be paid – Moses himself commanded that every Jew over twenty years must donate a silver half shekel by the Passover of each year. The tax is a sacred duty and it is the one levy in this country that does not fill Roman coffers. The exchange of coins for a single Tyrian shekel, to ensure that all men pay the same, is a necessity; money-changing is no abomination. Yeshua is not against these things.

But if Judaea were free, she could mint her own coins and would not need to suffer using those with graven images and words like 'Divine Augustus' upon them. And in this occupied land, the Temple tax and this Temple trade silts the purses of collaborators and conspirators: the high priests, who bribe and fawn their way to their appointment; the Sadducees, with their lavish houses in the upper city, their servants and imported slaves; the Herodians and their aristocrat cronies, who profit from the status quo, with their Roman finery and Latin education and affected accents. It is they who decide who can trade in the courts of God's Temple. And they who determine how much must be paid for the privilege. On God's Mount, by the Holy of Holies wherein God Himself dwells.

Yeshua leads the Twelve to the slots in the wall where pilgrims post their donations. A widow precedes them there. Too old to marry again. Too young yet to die. There are many widows in Judaea these days. Her face is raisined from fieldwork. Her clothes would scarcely be worth a rag merchant's trouble of taking to market. Her bare feet are pocked from the bite of fleas or mosquitoes. She places one tiny copper lepton at the slot, the smallest coin there is, and turns behind, to see who watches her in her shame. But her eyes meet those of Yeshua and he smiles at her. Yeshua's smile is a half-smile, just one side of his face changes and this asymmetry somehow reinforces how symmetrical he is. How handsome. His eyes and skin dark, like a Bedouin's. His black hair a lamb's-wool tangle. Yeshua's bearing is humble, but even this widow – who knows nothing of him, whose eyes are clouded with cataracts – can tell that he's a prince.

Yeshua shouts, so all nearby can hear him, even through the chatter of commerce. A voice much practised in addressing crowds. An ability to carry born from crying in the wilderness. 'This poor widow has contributed more to the Temple than all the wealthy men of Jerusalem combined. For all of them have given a little from their great abundance, but she out of her poverty has put in everything she had, all she had to live on.'

The widow shrinks, to be suddenly the object of so much attention, then seems to feel a strength pouring from Yeshua's presence and straightens again. Straighter than she has stood in years.

Like a dropped anchor, the whole Temple is suddenly tethered to this point; ripples of awareness flow outward from it.

Yeshua motions to Jochanan, who hands the widow some coins. Perhaps a hundredfold what she has just donated.

The Sadducee priest who monitors this section of the courtyard – at his back a squad of Temple Guards – comes to confront Yeshua. The Sadducees don't like pretenders to the throne and they don't like talk of rich and poor, divisive talk, and they especially don't like those who speak openly against Rome. This priest must know the views of Yeshua, perhaps thinks to entrap him in arrestable offence. The priest moves forward, but he does not come quite face to face with Yeshua: he stops behind a money-changer – a corpulent man, seated at a small table – a human barrier between them.

'So you approve of paying the Temple tax at least, Rabban,' the priest says. 'Now tell me, should we also pay taxes to Rome?'

Yeshua picks up a denarius from the money-changer's table. The man looks affronted, begins to protest, but sees Yeshua's grim brow and glances to Cephas's bulk and sits the fuck back down. 'Whose image is this on the coin?' Yeshua asks.

'It is Tiberius Caesar's,' says the priest.

'But doesn't God's law forbid graven images?'

'You know that it does.'

'Ah, yes, I remember it now,' Yeshua says: '*You shall not make for yourself a graven image, or any likeness of anything that is in Heaven above, or that is on the earth beneath, or that is in the water; you shall not bow down to them or serve them.* And who do you say Caesar is?' Yeshua asks. 'Is he a man or a god?'

'There is only one God.'

'But this coin of Caesar's says he is a god, the son of a god. And now you say he is just a man. So, do you think Caesar is a liar or a fool?'

The priest stammers a non-response. The crowd laughs. Not just the disciples, but all who stand and watch. The priest should leave it now. The priest probably even knows himself that he should leave it now, but pride is a powerful wind.

'You still haven't answered me, Rabban,' he spits, and he motions the guards to draw closer to him. 'Should we pay the taxes of Rome?'

'If I pay tribute to a man who says he is a god, whose image is graven on the very means of payment, is graven on the standards of his armies, is graven on the statues of his towns, am I not bowing down and serving a graven image? Am I not breaking God's commandment?'

The priest doesn't answer. He looks conflicted because he has achieved his aim: he has Yeshua in publicly witnessed sedition, but it has not run how he would have liked.

'You look confused, friend,' Yeshua says. 'Do I need to make myself plainer? Render unto Caesar what is Caesar's! Italy belongs to Caesar. Let it pay him tribute. Let him tax Egypt, if he must. Syria, too, for what we care. But this is God's land. Covenanted to God's people. It is forbidden to give God's things to a heathen. The fruits of this land are tithed to God. Render unto God what is God's!'

And Yeshua grasps the edge of the money-changer's table before him and flips it full circle into the air. The Sadducee and the guards scatter to avoid its landing point. Coins spin and roll about the ground, graven heads of Caesar clattering upon paving.

'This place should be a house of prayer, but you robbers run it as your private den,' Yeshua roars now. And he pulls the bull-whip of cords from an oxen stockman's hand and slashes it across the face of the Sadducee priest, who crouches and cowers.

One of the Temple Guards comes at Yeshua to grab the whip. But Cephas drops him to the floor. A punch from Cephas is as compelling as the hand of Fate. The guard is not a small man, but he is knocked down as if a child by a horse kick.

And havoc has been unleashed now. The followers of The Way, who had dispersed throughout the courtyard, all begin to smash tables, to shake free the doves from their split-wood cages and to drive the bigger beasts onwards into the chaos; they need little encouragement to try to flee, for dumb beasts are not so dumb that they cannot smell death. And the followers beat those who try to resist them and some of the richer merchants they beat even if they don't resist. Because a new time is coming and the last shall at last come first.

The guard troop around the priest backs hastily away and the Sadducee himself scrambles up and flees with them. And the rest of the Temple Guards stationed there that day draw their swords, but only that they might safely escape: they make no attempt to intervene in the carnage. The numbers are unrealistically against them. They take flight through the western gate along the arched bridge that leads directly to the upper city, a route normally forbidden to anyone save the priests and the Herodians. But by the time the guards have forced their way to it, all the priests and Herodians have already fled.

The Romans who watch from the high towers of the Antonia Fortress do not intervene either. Not yet. Perhaps they think this is a Jewish problem, best left to Jews. Perhaps they rightly realize that such high blood will only be inflamed by Roman boots in the Temple. They cannot afford a full-scale eruption of Jerusalem at festival time. Or perhaps they just don't care. Perhaps the only reason Yeshua is still alive at all is that the Romans have such disdain for the Jews and their doings.

But Yeshua and his followers drive out those who sold and those who controlled the Temple, and they overturn the tables of the money-changers and take the money for the poor. And since so many of them are themselves poor, some find that transaction to be swift. And they smash the stalls of those who sell pigeons. And lambs and goats and unblemished oxen roam about the broken wood and the golden frescos. And the gates are blocked by men of The Way and no Sadducee-sanctioned trade is allowed in the Temple for the remainder of the day. And when dusk falls, in one unstoppable mass the followers of Yeshua – many laden with new acquisitions – flood through the twin porticoes of the Huldah Gates, still whooping and hollering of victory and Yahweh, out into the scattered safety of the hill country and the desert behind the Mount of Olives.

And the smoke continues to rise from the Kidron valley, long after they have shaken its dust from their feet.

Thirty-four Years after
the Crucifixion

Useful checks the time by the sun in the sky. It is later than he had thought. It's always later than you think. But it's hard not to get distracted by the atmosphere when you're out on the streets of Rome, strolling amid the grandeur and the vagabonds, the graffiti and the statues of emperors.

Though Useful couldn't claim to be among the comeliest of men, he would perhaps not fare so badly among the company of recent emperors: Tiberius's tired overbite is probably the best of them; Caligula, who came after, looks as fat-faced as a baker's son in the busts; and amphora-eared Claudius's chin recedes into a neck that threatens to engulf it. He looks as though, had he continued in his corpulence, he might have become entirely composed of neck. Perhaps it was rather in kindness that Claudius's buttered mushrooms were poisoned, if those rumours are true.

But now the emperor is Nero, and even in the statues – which are surely idealized portraits – his face is cruel. Above a chin-strap beard, a thin, grim mouth smirks, as though contemptuous of those not his equal, which is to say: everyone else.

This visible malice of Nero's visage is a blemish on the surface of Useful's world. A fear that spoils what otherwise would be perfection. Because Paul has appealed to Caesar for his case to be heard and sooner or later it must be. On the other hand, Useful trusts in Paul: he can make the very birds believe his words. So powerful and palpable is Paul's own faith that anyone who hears him cannot help but be carried along. As Useful has been: gladly and gratefully surrendering to the initiation ritual of baptism and emerging into a new spiritual world, losing fear and strife, gaining a surging sense of belonging, a binding commitment to worship, and the unfathomable solace that is the promise of eternal life. Perhaps that's how it will be with Nero too. Paul himself has every hope that he may convert the emperor when the time for his hearing comes – if, that is, the risen Christ does not return to earth first.

Beyond the row of emperors are some statues of satyrs. They are hairy and leering and their cocks are carved all curled up, like those of swine boars. A crooked man stands among them, cleaning spittle from a kitten, which isn't his but is a stray. He wipes the bag of bone and fluff with the edge of his robe, grinning at this moment of difference in his day. And passers-by stop too, though they have all seen cats before. Still, it is not every day you see one so small and alone as this one on the street. And the passers-by make suggestions as to how best to reunite the kitten with its mother:

'Put him on the wall and she'll find him.'

'Don't keep wiping him – you'll make him smell of you.'

'Hide him in the crook of that tree. He'll be safe there and she'll surely sniff him out.'

They make such fuss now, yet the kitten will shortly be forgotten by all of them and perhaps even the creature itself will eventually forget that it was once a kitten, should it survive to be full-grown, to fight and filch and fuck with the rest of the Roman cats. Cats were scarcely known of in Colossae, but in Rome – transported on grain-ships from Egypt – they approach commonplace. Though still not so rife that a kitten can't draw a little gathering.

Useful has a mission, though: he shouldn't linger any longer. He has been sent to buy more parchment, for the glorious work he does with Paul. His chest uprushes with the very thought of that work. Useful is filled with love, not only for his new God but also for his new life and the splendid task of recording this story. Because suddenly Useful is a person of significance and now he can leave an impression on the world. The world as we know it is soon to transform, of course, but Useful will still have made his mark upon it.

He falls into step behind a group of slaves formed about their master. The group clears a path through the throng of the streets, like the prow of a ship, which makes progress easier. Though Useful tries to keep a distance between himself and the slave who carries the sponge on a stick, jauntily slung over his shoulder like a soldier's spear and waving as he walks. Such sponges are used by the rich – or, rather, used on the rich by their slaves – for the cleaning of the fundament after defecation and Useful would sooner not catch it across the cheek.

Split in two by the Tiber, but divided all over, Rome is a polar place, a city of opposites, perhaps more so than anywhere else that Useful has been.

And he visited not a few cities in his travels with Philemon, his old master. The wealthy of Rome are among the richest of the entire world. People pass in sedan chairs, accompanied by retinues that might have made Cleopatra question the expense, and they are probably only going to visit a friend a few roads away. The toga, the civic dress, is just an elaborate show of how much cloth you can afford. And yet, because of the monthly corn-dole, Rome simultaneously supports a magnitude of poverty seen nowhere else to quite the same degree. Citizens of Rome can survive with nothing else to their name save that citizenship. If they could sell it, it would fetch them a sufficient sum to live in comfort a good few years. But they can't do that – though the state itself can; their station as a Roman allows huge numbers to survive in levels of destitution well below the point where others would be forced to flee a city or go into voluntary servitude.

Even more pitiable is the position of non-citizens, denied the corn-dole in their crises: ill-begotten creatures, hugging stall-fallen fruits to their chests as if they were babes. Others with babes by their sides, as uncared-for as stall-fallen fruit. Girls grown too filthy and skin-shrunken even to work as whores, at least by daylight, though by night outside the over-spilling taverns of the Aventine they might just scrape a meal from scraped knees.

Yet it is hard not to get swept away when you are in Rome. It is hard not to let the lustre get into your heart. Even the gutter in the middle of the street shines like gold in the sun. Useful becomes briefly bewitched by the beauty of it, more like lava than scum, though a handful of children beside it, at some game with stones and bone shards, look as if they only pantomime play. Too beset by hunger to lose themselves fully in imagination, too old already to produce more than a passable impression of childhood. Parents love against will and sense, it seems to Useful. It would be better to behave like beetles: to lay as many eggs as possible in some nook and hope that a few survive. To love in poverty is a commitment to a certainty of future pain. But Paul says that all of this is soon to change, in the blink of an eye. The Day of the Lord is shortly to come and Useful will stand with Paul when it does.

* * *

The parchment sellers ply beyond the slave market. By rights Useful should feel nervous, passing through that square, out in the open like this. But now he has fresh clothes and is fed and walks with purpose, no one will stop him. He looks just like any other slave out on his master's business. A valuable fact of life: if you look like you know what you're doing, no one will question you.

Not unaccustomed to barter from his travels with Philemon, Useful beats a reasonable deal from a trader with a disappointed slump and half-packed stock. And having saved Paul a good sum of money – probably enough to feed a family for a week – Useful thinks it not inappropriate to buy an apple to eat on the return walk. More so even than the apple, the scrolls of parchment under his arms feel prickly and delicious. It is easy to forget that these skins have been flayed from some poor beast. But, then, what is a beast, but a creation of God and what is Paul but God's chosen apostle and Useful his scribe? Happy beast, then, to serve such a cause.

And happy Useful, upon the pavements of Rome. Among the spice stalls that burn and awaken the nostrils, free them from a self-induced sleep. Among the floury aromas of food booths, selling round Roman pie-loaf and hot pastries. Among the open-air barbers, shaving and tattle-sharing. Among the chained wine flagons, advertising taverns. Among the yellow songbirds trapped in cages of softwood. Singing of God's creation, or to be free, or for a mate, or just because yellow songbirds are made to sing. What does the reason matter, when sing they do?

Useful dismisses the feeling that he is followed as paranoia, born from his weeks on the run. He ignores the sense that he is stalked, because whenever he turns to see, there is no such pursuer in sight. It is only as he knocks at Paul's door, to be let in by Cyclops soldier Manius, that Useful catches the glance of a man who watches him. A man who visibly marks the portal at which Useful raps and doesn't seem to mind being noticed. The watcher is elderly, or has a fistful of years over Paul at least. But if he is shrunken, in the state that Useful sees now, then in his days of glory he must have been a monster to make daemons scared of the dark. Probably a Jew, Useful would say. A giant, broken-nosed, frightening old Israelite, with cheeks drooping like a scent hound's and eyes that know altogether too much. Eyes that continue to watch at least until Useful has gone in.

Useful wonders whether he should say something about the watcher, but it seems a bit silly somehow, once he is back inside, with the surly legionary guarding the door and Epaphras, Silas, Timothy, Aristarchus, Demas and Luke all on hand. Feels a bit daft to say, 'Some old bloke was watching me come in and there was something a bit funny about him.' The house is, after all, hardly unknown: several years already Paul has lived there, teaching about the Lord Jesus Christ quite openly to all who would hear him.

* * *

When Useful goes upstairs, Paul sniffs the parchment and rubs it between his thumb and forefinger; he has worked with skins himself in his time, though more in shop awnings and the like, but he knows a thing or two.

'Pigskin,' he says. 'You've only bought bloody pigskin and me circumcised on the eighth day, of the tribe of Benjamin, a Hebrew of Hebrews,' but he seems rather more amused than angry. 'Don't worry. Swine vellum may serve just as well for our story, my boy – perhaps it is even appropriate.'

'Thank you, Master,' Useful says.

Paul waves him to think no more of it, with an affectionate smile. Great love and great ire seem to coexist simultaneously in Paul. Or perhaps they don't coexist: perhaps they fight one another for dominance inside, as Paul says Jacob and Esau did in the womb.

'Now then, where were we?' Paul asks.

Three Years after
the Crucifixion

Saul could see nothing. What had been bright was black. He felt as if something lay across his vision, like the film that forms on the eyes of the dying, not a lens, darker than that, darker even than his lids, something more like scales, which blocked the world entirely.

Still lying on his back, on the packed dirt track where he had fallen, dropped like a tortoise by an eagle, Saul is vaporized, unable to locate the pieces of himself.

He hears his men, if they can be called that, if they were ever that, discussing him and what to do. Their voices are far away, echoes of a world unreal. Compared at least to the voice of Jesus, just gone, which Saul thinks was the realest thing he has ever heard.

Still, from some delirium distance, Saul hears his men in conclave. He tries to form words of his own but they will not come. The guards, having arrived at their decision, desert to a man, taking with them the goodly purse of money that was entrusted to Saul for lodgings, bribery and transport to carry the kidnapped back to Jerusalem. And they also take the mule and the swords, the letter from the high priest, for parchment is expensive, and even Saul's own dagger. Then they leave.

But only moments afterwards, as if thinking better of it, they return.

Saul manages to speak now: 'I knew you couldn't abandon me,' he says, the words croaking out of him, like slinking cave creatures unused to an exterior.

The guards do not reply. They just unfasten Saul's sandals and his belt and lift them off. And then they take his outer coat and tunic as well. They leave Saul in his loincloth, sprawled in the dust, arms outstretched, feet pressed together, staring at the sun with eyes that cannot see.

And it seems to Saul that more people pass him by, leave him lying like that. It seems to him that he calls out and they do not respond. It seems to Saul that there is no love left in this land. He sits up and edges his way as best he can – crawling splay-fingered – to what he thinks is the side of the road and stays there, hunched like a hedgehog, but without even its feeble defence, with not a single spine to keep the world from him.

The air has cooled to night before someone stops. The man asks what has taken place. And Saul responds only that he has been robbed. Robbed and left like this, unable to see. The man's accent is strange; he might come from Samaria; Saul doesn't ask. The man gives him water from a gourd, sweet and flinty. The man leads him by the hand along the remainder of the road into Damascus. The man asks where he should take him to in Damascus, if he has kin or friends with whom he was to stay. And Saul tells the man to take him to the only place he knows of, the only man in truth he knows to live in Damascus at all:

to the house of Ananias on Straight Street, to the leader of The Way.

* * *

'This traveller was robbed and somehow blinded. He seems disturbed in the head by it all. He says he is a friend of yours.'

'Then he must be,' says a voice that Saul takes to be Ananias's, a man he was dispatched to Damascus to capture.

There had been another Ananias, in Jerusalem. Some of those of The Way whom Saul interrogated told of a rumour that Cephas had killed the other Ananias and his wife – or, at the least, had had them killed – because they hid a portion of the proceeds from the sale of a field from the rest of the group. Among The Way there were no personal possessions: everything was pooled and used as was required by those in want. The penalties for hoarding resources were apparently pitiless.

This Ananias, Damascus Ananias, is filled with mercy. He finds Saul a robe, leads him to a pallet and lays him there. He wets Saul's brow with water, above his crazed, staring eyes. He tries to feed Saul bread and Saul tries to eat it. Saul is without speech, like an old man taken to bed at the end of life. The things he has to say are too big; he cannot find a path to them.

'He has spoken to me,' Saul says finally. 'Jesus, whom you follow, he has spoken to me. He appeared to me as a light, so powerful that it blinded me. And he told me to come to you here.'

'Were you also robbed then, as the Samaritan said? How did you come to be so near nakedness?'

'My men became beset by devils and the devils in them led them to turn upon me.'

'Your men? Are you a merchant then?'

'I am, or was, a captain of the Temple Guard. I did much evil to your brothers at Jerusalem and I came here with authority from the high priest to bind his enemies and take them back to him. But Jesus told me I have been selected as his vessel, to bear his name before kings and the children of Israel. Jesus told me that I, whom they thought was weak, like a nurtured runt, will become strong. What the powers of this world scorned, God has chosen.'

Ananias pats him on the head and smooths Saul's thin, damp hair. 'I think you need to sleep,' he says. 'Sleep now and we'll talk tomorrow.'

* * *

Maybe Ananias thought Saul delirious, but Saul's story does not change when he wakes. Nor does it the next day. And when, on the third day under Ananias's roof, Saul wakes to discover that his sight has returned, Ananias is forced to concede that this is a fully paid-up fucking miracle.

And all the followers of The Way in Damascus come to his house to witness the wonder and to talk with Saul. As do not a few other Jews, who have not yet been baptized into The Way, but nonetheless recognize and respect Ananias and the others of The Way as devout men and strict observers of the Law of Moses. And some even take the miracle of Saul as sufficient provocation to belong to The Way themselves.

So three others join Saul to be baptized: an old awning maker, with eyes that wander independent of each other like a skink's; a tinker, who sharpens knives and trades in the farrago of the Jewish quarter; and a young widower, near beardless and eviscerated, because his wife, soft as blossom, has lately died in childbirth, murdered by a curled, self-hanged creature that would have been a son.

The baptism is a practice taught by John, who founded The Way, whose disciple Jesus was at first: the submersion an induction and a sign that a new sinless life is begun; a mark of repentance and regeneration to speed the arrival of the Day of Yahweh.

Though the river Abana coils through Damascus, the followers of The Way do their initiatory rites out of town, upstream. Not just because Baptizer John and Jesus both preached in wilderness places but also because the Abana's waters are holier before every household and stall in Damascus has flung their waste and night-soil into its flow.

Saul is, of course, used to submersion, the ceremonial cleansing practised by all Jews who wish to enter the inner courts of the Temple. But there it was in man-made pools designed for the purpose, entered one at a time, a private purification between one man and the one-God. Here Saul strips, with his fellow acolytes, before a small crowd of other followers of The Way, naked and humbled in public. The parts of Saul's body long sun-hid beneath his soldier's tunic are pale, like the inner flesh of bitten fruit. The old awning maker is withered as a winter prune and the tinker is as slight as kindling once disrobed. Four circumcised penises are presented to the river and the hills and the watchers, as evidence of God's eternal covenant with Abraham and all his descendants. As evidence of God's love for His people, soon to be demonstrated in the new age, which His anointed King is going to return to inaugurate.

The shock of the water's cold cuts through time. The ceremony, the rebirth, severs a life into the portions before it and after. The acolytes buckle their knees into the water so that they are entirely sunken from sight and when they resurface they cry out, '*Abba!* Father!' as new mystical children. Saul clambers onto the bank dripping like a fish but dewy as a babe. And fresh white robes are put on him. And Ananias hugs him, and all the new adherents clutch each other, and there is love once more in the world. And Saul surely feels the thing that Ananias talked about: the Holy Spirit that descended upon him there in the water and is now with him. Saul feels it in each fingertip and in his lips and in the hair that prickles upon the breeze, and he wants to sing of it, overcome with a strange tongue, so he does, and though no one understands his words they all do understand. And some join him, singing of the mysteries of the heavens and praising God in rapid involuntary languages known only to Him.

* * *

Later Ananias tells Saul of how a great number, perhaps as many as five hundred at one moment, felt the Holy Spirit upon them like that, coming through them like a wind, and all began talking in tongues, as though drunk, though it was only morning. And how, after Jesus's death his followers were at first destroyed and distraught, and scattered, returning to Galilee and their homes. But when Cephas, James the Lesser and others had visions, encounters perhaps similar to Saul's own, they began to realize that this must surely all be part of God's plan. That Jesus's death was a necessary thing because he was to come back as a resurrected king, the first to be resurrected, but all the righteous would be resurrected in the age he was shortly to bring. And they began searching the scriptures for the proofs of this, and they found in Isaiah's writings of a Suffering Servant, the very things they were searching for.

Ananias shows Saul these passages. And Saul at first protests, because the passages do not mention a messiah and they had never been taught to him as having anything to do with a messiah and they seem clearly to indicate that the suffering servant described is Israel the nation. But Saul comes to realize that maybe they could also refer to Jesus, if looked at in just the right way, as if the true meaning is obscured by a veil. And once you accept this premise, then how many other great secrets might be hidden in the Torah and Prophets, just waiting to be discovered, perhaps ready to be revealed by Saul himself?

* * *

During weeks and then months under Ananias's tutelage, Saul begins to reconstruct himself, piece by piece. Like shards of a shattered sword reforged. And, as sometimes happens with a bone that heals, he is afterwards formed thicker than ever at the breaks. He is stronger than before. But the bone never forgets, even if stronger, that once it was broken. And Saul, even if rebuilt, even if he appears to be the same man, is not the same. The parts recovered from a thing so obliterated can never be placed together just as they were. We are not just altered by such events. We are other.

One Day before
the Crucifixion

Three days ago, as the disciples first approached Jerusalem, Yeshua told them a parable, about a rightful ruler coming to a city to inherit his kingdom. It ended with the words:

> *But those enemies of mine who did not want me to be king over them – bring them here and kill them in front of me.*

It was not one of Yeshua's more cryptic metaphors.

* * *

Yeshua and the Twelve leave the upper room and the house of the man who collects water like a woman. The man checks that the crescent side-street is clear before he waves them out, flicking a wrist that is somehow more flexible, less joined, than a wrist could be. His head is covered with a scarf, in the manner of a maiden; he readjusts it self-consciously, pulling it low to his eyes, as if it controls his own looking as much as the way others look upon him.

Yeshua thanks the woman-man, taking her hand. And Jochanan pays her twice what was agreed. Perhaps he thinks the disciples will have little need of money henceforth.

The moon is full; its light is blue on the faces of the Twelve, as they make their way to the southern gate. Their clothes, damp with day-sweat, are cold. Some of the Twelve had to sell their cloaks to buy swords; all have a blade with them now.

Outside Jerusalem's walls are the overflow camps of pilgrims and the bivouacs of the dispossessed. There are tethered camels, sleeping in their strange angular crouch, and canopied bowers of the tender, mercenary Eves, whose tent slits comfort men far from home.

The Kidron valley beneath is dark and the Twelve have no torches. But God is their light and salvation, as the psalmist says, so who shall they fear?

A hooded crow pecks at the maggot-riddled carcass of a thing that was once itself a hooded crow.

Even now, after several days, the burned ground of the Kidron still faintly smokes in places. With the scrub removed, stones are visible, baked brown and scalded like oven bread. All is grass ash, but for occasional long strands of scorched bushes; straggled like seaweed, grey as an old prophet's hair. Though *old* prophets are rare.

Everything is charred, like the Hades of the Greeks. And perhaps that is fitting enough for what must happen tonight. A year and more has led the Twelve to this point. Maybe everything has always led to this point. And, as Cephas's mettlesome father would say: if you could choose, you wouldn't start from here. But here is where they are.

Days of panic, days of doubt. Days when they couldn't go on. But they did go on: there was no going back. All those days have carried Yeshua and his disciples to this now. Only the Twelve must accompany him tonight. Only the most loyal and most noble and most pious. For Zechariah said, *God will come, if all with you are holy.*

The Romans are a pestilence of warriors. Numberless as the locust; ferocious as the lion. The Romans are an apparatus of destruction forged by four hundred years of continuous battle. They cannot be beaten by men. But only by God. And to believe that they will be beaten might seem madness, but not to believe it is to believe in nothing.

The valley is scorched black.

They pass through it and climb the Mount of Olives among the tombs – grave caves, hollowed caverns in the rock – into Gethsemane's groves. In the dark, the gnarled and twisted trunks of the olive trees loom out suddenly; malevolent, like a coven of withered-limb witches. Galileans are not ordinarily scared by shades and night-creeps. But this is no ordinary night. Success and failure both are to be dreaded in their ways, and so this fearful place is as fitting as any. More fitting, the fittest: for here on the Mount of Olives is where it must occur, as the Prophet Zechariah said it would:

> *On that day his feet shall stand on the Mount of Olives, which is in front of Jerusalem on the east; and the Mount of Olives will be split by a vast chasm, so that half of the mountain will move toward the north and the other half toward the south ... earthquake ... Then the Lord, my God will come, if all with you are holy. And this will be the plague with which the Lord will strike all the peoples who have gone to war against*

Jerusalem; their flesh will rot while they stand on their feet, and their eyes will rot in their sockets, and their tongue will rot in their mouth. A great panic from God will fall on them; and they will seize one another's hand, and the hand of one will be lifted against the hand of another ... So also this plague will be the plague on the horse, the mule, the camel, the donkey and all the cattle that will be in those camps.

Yeshua is the Messiah, of that there is no doubt, not in the hearts of any of the Twelve. He is the anointed one, the King, but filled with so much more in hope than that. Yeshua is the King who will tonight fulfil what Zechariah prophesied, who will inaugurate the new age. Who will restore the dynasty of David. And God will destroy the Romans just as Zechariah promised He would. God will smite them and the very animals they ride upon. The odds are so incalculable that they need not be counted at all. The Twelve have swords to fight, but God will do most of the mighty work. Perhaps the Twelve will each lead a legion of angels.

Because if you believe it to be true that God killed the firstborn of every single family in Egypt, why would He suffer the Romans? It is no insanity to think that God will provide victory, not if you trust scriptures that say Yahweh killed a hundred and eighty-five thousand Assyrians in their sleep for the sake of His people. Not if you believe that God sent giant hailstones down on the Amorites, and stopped the sun in the sky to give Joshua sufficient daylight to butcher the survivors. Not if you believe that God bewildered Sisera's army, so that they slew one another, without the Israelites having to draw a sword. If you believe that this is

God's country and these are God's children, then how could you believe that He could let them fall? If you believe that Gideon, with just three hundred men, slaughtered a hundred and twenty thousand Midianites, why would an entire nation fear a few cohorts? If you believe that Samson killed a thousand men, with just the jawbone of an ass. If you believe that God smote fifty thousand and seventy Bethshemites. If you believe that David massacred every male in Edom and all the people of Ammon and sixty-nine thousand Syrians. If you believe that Ahab killed a hundred thousand foes because they mocked the God of Israel. If you believe that the Lord slew twenty-seven thousand men in Aphek by crushing them under the walls, and uncountable by the same act in Jericho, why would you think He could let the Antonia Fortress stand? If you believe that God struck dead a million Ethiopians in a single day, for daring to attack Judah, it hardly seems possible that He would not assist at all in fighting Rome.

For the covenant says that God loves His people. That is the one known certain truth. That is the foundation of a nation and its faith. If that could be a lie, then what isn't?

The heavens are deep-water black and the stars are like spined urchins and the olive leaves slender and silver, like minnows in Galilee shallows. And if Yeshua was doing this again he wouldn't start from here. He might ask for this cup to pass from him entirely. But here is where he is, so what must follow is this.

Yeshua and the Twelve kneel among the serpent olive roots and go into the pain of prayer, into the supplication required to make this thing come to pass. And the first hour is an ecstasy as they pour their every strength and heart into their words. They bay fearful at the skies to bring the thing required. Needed not just by them, but by this very land.

The olive trees about them shift and dance in the wind, swaying like gladiators made drunk for the crowd's amusement. The olive trees are hollowed out in the centre, as if they should be dead. But they do not die. They thrive, as little else has thrived since the Romans came. There are twists and shards of iron nails embedded in some of the trees. When a multitude of men are executed at once, they are sometimes nailed to living olive boughs, to howl in the dark like mandrake fruit.

The second hour, in an agony, Yeshua prays more earnestly, and his sweat tumbles as if it were great drops of blood falling down to the ground. And the Twelve pray with him. This event must come to be and they have nothing left to make it but their own force and belief.

God will come, if all with you are holy.

The third hour, though anguished and distressed, the disciples pray on. They cry and beg. Through souls filled with sorrow even to death. Past exhaustion from their efforts, they prostrate and petition. And Yeshua sees that some start to tire but he says to them: 'Rise and pray. Don't enter into temptation. Don't give up yet.'

Steeled, re-girded, they discover new strength. But such energies are hard to maintain: even for men as pious as the Twelve, even for those as filled with faith and conviction as they, the spirit is willing, but the body is weak.

Yet they continue. What else is there but to go on, but to fall once more onto the ground and pray? They are in the Valley of Decision and this must be decided. God will come. There is no space for doubt. Hesitation cannot be allowed. In.

Slowly disquiet creeps. A black beast crouched in the shadows. One after another the Twelve begin to fail internally, unable to command their own belief. They continue their wailing praying, but they falter in their conviction. They catch each other's eyes and see the uncertainty there, and the doubt once released cannot be recaptured. The beseeching and the chanting continue. Yeshua is building once more into a crescendo of supplication and the Twelve are with him, but they are not with him. All of them have now confessed to themselves that this is not going to happen, not now, not tonight.

What is going to come to pass is the only thing more dreadful, more to be feared than earthquakes and plagues and angels: nothing. Void. Absence. The darkness is devoid of anything but olive trees and the wind. And their hopes are as hollow as the olive trees and the heavens are as empty as the wind. And if you could choose, you would never start from here. But since they cannot choose, the Twelve continue praying.

* * *

The Romans bring a terrible relief when they at last arrive, but at least it puts a stop to this. At least it is an ending. At least the Twelve can now admit – staring in disbelief through eyes drained and straining, tear-streaked and rubbed raw – that this isn't working. At least they can fight now, and maybe God will be with them. Maybe this is how He wants it to run.

So Cephas charges them, one man into the mass. A bull into a pack of dogs. He storms into the traitorous men of the high priest, who head this cohort of Romans. They scatter and he hacks an ear from one as they do. But Cephas is smashed to the ground by the shields of the Romans behind. The Romans don't scatter. The Romans train daily for moments like this. And their shields are impregnable as the walls of a fort. Some of the shields are new. Some are dented and battle-blooded. All of them are stained with dust and crossed with the blasphemous thunder bars of war-god Mars.

Charging such a shield line unarmoured is suicide. But the rest of the disciples draw their swords and make ready to run at it anyway, exhausted from effort, but mad with God and anger. They were to have had twelve legions of angels. But the angels haven't come and the Romans have. With them Temple Guards and slaves and men-at-arms of the high priest. One without an ear, but all with blades and clubs and torches that flame in the darkness, showing the warped and wretched shapes of the olive trees.

And only now does Yeshua rise, only now does he, shaking, stop his prayers. And even the Roman who is about to fling his spear into floored Cephas ceases when Yeshua cries: 'Enough!'

Yeshua is a prince.

Cephas shouts that they will prevail. Cephas shouts that even if the whole world falls away, he will not.

But Yeshua answers, 'Enough, Cephas, enough, brother, it's too late.'

And Yeshua asks the Romans who they want. And when they say *Yahushua son of Joseph*, he tells them it is he.

Then he says, 'And since I am the one you want, let these others go.'

Jochanan shouts: 'My King, let's fight? We brought the swords!'

But Yeshua shakes his head.

Flanked by a phalanx of Roman spearmen, the Temple Guards advance towards him. Encircling but skulking, like jackals about a lion, they bind Yeshua's hands.

Yeshua recognizes the guard who ties the thongs that bite into his wrists and says to him: 'I remember you. I saw you in the Temple courts. You didn't dare lay a hand on me then. But now it's your hour: when darkness reigns.'

The *centurio* of the Romans – cold-eyed and stiff as lance – gives his command to depart and his men pull back into formation.

The man of the high priest who has been cut, who clutches a bloodied lump of his own cloak to the gash where once was an ear, says, 'Wait!' He lisps from the blood that has oozed into his mouth, 'Aren't you going to arrest him too?' He points at Cephas.

The *centurio* laughs. He turns and laughs in the face of the bleeding man: 'Our orders are to arrest the Nazarene Yahushua, this "dangerous revolutionary" here. And since we have done so, without injury to any of my men, we are now leaving with our prisoner. Should you wish to seize any of the others, I suggest you fucking do so. I obey your master only under the specific command of the prefect. I'll obey a servant when the crows start shitting silver.'

And he spits then, at the bleeding servant of the high priest, who recoils from it, like a flinching child. And it's clear that this priest-servant isn't going to be seizing anything but his own wound. But Cephas stumbles up anyway and backs away, sword slowly waving like the head of a horned viper, and when none of the Temple Guards come at him he runs into the night. And all the other disciples turn their backs to Jerusalem and flee the other way, towards the hills and the safety of the scrub.

The Romans trudge, implacable, through the charred Kidron back to Jerusalem, Yeshua dragged by the Temple Guards at their tail.

Cephas stalks the flames of their torches at a distance.

* * *

The other disciples hide in the darkness, weeping at their failure, wondering who betrayed them. Not that a defector is necessary because previously they had gone out to the same place on the Mount of Olives, preparing for this night. And anyone could have followed them or informed on them. Even still, eventually a traitor must be chosen, a betrayer will be found. Literary completeness demands it.

Thirty-four Years after
the Crucifixion

'We really should write to Philemon soon, Useful: your former master must be told where you are and what has happened so that he may forgive you.' Paul shuffles on his chair, face cut in jagged squints, like a cracked tile, as he does so, his bad back clearly paining him.

'Maybe what I have done is beyond forgiveness,' Useful replies.

'Nothing is beyond forgiveness. Didn't I explain to you how Jesus has made himself a sacrifice for all the sins of the world? Any who believe in Him are now forgiven anything they have done. I add here that you must still try not to sin. That may sound obvious, but we had some problems with the community in Corinth on that score. I'm sure we'll come to it presently in the story, but the idiots seemed to think that because all was forgiven they could do what they wanted. Orgies were going on, flesh writhing upon flesh, like serpents in a pit; drunkenness and debauchery became normality. They devoted themselves to pleasure. Many stopped working for a living, because they assumed the end time would arrive any day. The form of this world is indeed passing away, but that doesn't mean you shouldn't work in the meantime! Or ignore basic decency: one chap in Corinth married his mother! There was talk of doings so bestial that it would shame my lips even to mention them. The whole thing was a disaster. So now I always have to couch it in these terms: all your sins are forgiven, but you still shouldn't sin.

'Anyway, what we really want to say in this letter is that Philemon must forgive you, but that you ought to remain here with me. You should continue to serve me, only with Philemon's blessing. I don't want to order him, he must decide of his own free will, but he must decide to do what I direct him towards. It's probably a bit like the sinning thing: God gives you the freedom to do what you want, but you must still do what He wants …

'What was your crime, anyway, to so upset Philemon that you fled in fear of your life? Actually, don't answer: we can discuss it another time. We really should return to our work: my story, God's mission on earth.

'So, after my baptism, filled with the Holy Spirit – are you getting this down? – I learned all I could from Ananias. Several weeks I stayed with him in Damascus. But soon I realized that I could draw little more from him. After all, I had spoken with Jesus himself. Ananias had never known Jesus, before his death or after. The greatest lesson Ananias taught me was the first one he showed me in the words of Isaiah's Suffering Servant: that everything which is to come is written in the phrases of the past; that the scriptures can be mined for prophecy and direction; that words may look as though they have one meaning, when encased in context, but with the Holy Spirit's inspiration we can lift them free to reveal their true meanings, and present them to the world.

'Ananias having said that my vision of the risen Christ was similar to those experienced by Cephas and James, it became obvious that I must have been chosen as an apostle of equal standing to them. Perhaps my destiny then was to carry The Way into new quarters. So to this end I left Damascus and went into Nabataean Arabia, alone, to preach the word of God and the message about Jesus.

'To be honest, Useful, we probably don't need to dwell too long on that year in Arabia. My gospel and my preaching were not yet wise and persuasive and the Arabs weren't ready for the word. To add to this, Galilee and the Nabataeans were in a period of conflict, which made the struggles of an itinerant preacher even harder. You could just write down something like: *And Saul had many great victories there among the Arabs and showed them how the Messiah had to suffer and rise from the dead and that verily Jesus is the Christ.* Put something like that.

'So afterwards I returned to Damascus. I was half starved and ragged as a beggar's step-child. It is hard enough to survive in a foreign land, dependent on the kindness of strangers, without the extra encumbrance of adhering to the Israelite dietary laws. Thinking back, maybe it was during this period that the Christ first began to whisper to me that He had redeemed us from those outworn Torah bonds. In any event, I certainly realized that if I was going to go on such missions in the future I would need some kind of trade to support myself while I preached.

'In Damascus, there was an aged awning and tent maker, who was baptized with me. And when

I returned to the city, I lodged with him awhile. He was a droll old soul, of whom I grew fond. Though boss-eyed as two sides of a coin, he could stitch as neat as any man on earth. And he patiently taught me his trade, which I thought a good one for a traveller. Because there are always people who need things patched on the road: clothes or tents or blankets; and ships need sails mending; and every town has awnings and shade cloths to be replaced. You need carry nothing but your awl and punch and other gubbins and you can find employment anywhere you are. And the old tent maker gave me his tools in the end too, when he became too weak to work, and because of the communality of The Way had no further need to.

'It was good that I learned his trade, because afterwards – almost three years since I had left Jerusalem as a Temple Guard – I was forced to flee Damascus, as an apostle of the Christ. Perhaps it was a Jew still loyal to the high priest and resentful of my change of allegiance who betrayed me, or maybe it was a Jew of The Way, whose bones were rotted by envy of my rise to prominence. However it was, someone reported me to the Damascus authorities, and told how I had originally been sent to kidnap residents and forcibly render them to Jerusalem as prisoners. And relations between the states being barely short of all-out war at the time, the governor ordered my arrest. God saved me by disposing me to take a walk through the bazaar the very night that soldiers came to my lodgings to arrest me. But the city of the Damascenes was always rigorously guarded. Day and night men kept close watch on the gates and might have arrested me, or killed me, if I had tried to leave.

'I had to stay with one member of The Way after another, each wanting urgently to move me onwards, for fear that I would be discovered. Finally, knowing I was so desperate to keep preaching the word in the synagogues that I might expose myself any day, and with almost no one left for me to stay with, Ananias came up with a plan.

'It was common in Damascus, as in most cities, for householders on the upper floors of tenements to raise and lower baskets down to the street sellers that they might buy bread and other produce without descending the stairs. And Ananias procured a stout example on a strong rope and scouted out an unlit spot where the city wall was low.

'One night, he and his followers took me there beneath a cartwheel moon and proposed to ease me down in the basket through an opening in the wall. Even in the dark the drop looked high, the rope thin, and the basket was barely large enough to contain both my feet at one time. But I knew that God would protect me.

'"When you get to Jerusalem, find Barnabas the Cypriot," Ananias said, as I readied myself. "He knows me well. He'll introduce you to the others and to James and Cephas."

'And so I was lowered, helpless as an anchor into the deep. I had the line twisted round my arm and it bit as it tightened. So I untwisted it, but then – still a death-drop from the ground – my robe got snagged for a moment on the wall and the basket fell away from me. I had to slide down to it again, gripping the rope in my hands alone. It burned a track down both my palms, but apostles count such pains as tallies to their good. And the rest of the distance, I dropped as softly as an angel descending from the heavens.

'Ananias then raised and lowered the basket again, this time with provisions for my journey, and I crept away into the dark to find the road on which it had all begun.

'Now, I want you to be sure to insert here, Useful, that although I went to Jerusalem to meet with the Pillars of the Church, it was entirely of my own volition and decision that I went. I wasn't summoned by them. I was appointed by God and do not think I am in the least inferior to those "Superlative-Apostles". James has no authority over me. If he and Cephas and Jochanan were held in high esteem – and whether they were or not makes no difference to me: God doesn't acknowledge such favouritism – I was called as an apostle of Christ to be their equal, at least their equal.'

Paul seems as though he may continue on this theme, but thin-lipped Timothy comes into the room and whispers something to him. Something that turns Paul's face a seething skull pale. He grips the arms of his chair so hard that the veins spring from the backs of his hands, like rivulets renewed in a desert.

'He's here,' Paul says. 'He's spoken already in some house churches. The man pursues me like the stench of a polecat. How many times have I begged the Lord to rid me of that thorn? And now he's back again: Cephas is in Rome.'

Five Years after
the Crucifixion

He is no longer James *the Lesser* now. Yeshua is dead, James is the oldest. But there are many other Jameses in the movement, so James still carries a cognomen: the people call him James ha-Zaddik: 'the Righteous' or 'the Just'.

Some of the disciples have scattered, but the Three Pillars remain in Jerusalem: James and Jochanan and Cephas. Every day they continue to meet together in the Temple courts. They remember their brother, murdered by Rome. Yeshua, who was the brother of them all, but was the brother of James through flesh and blood, mother and father.

The Pillars go to the Temple at the time of prayer and they do not flip the tables of the money-changers; they do not whip the lackeys of the aristocracy; those moments have passed, at least for now. They go to the Temple and gather at Solomon's Portico with others of The Way and they pray. They are continually in the Temple blessing God. Celebrating the sacrifice of unblemished lambs, whose portions are burned to ascend to the heavens. There is no smell sweeter than the unguent luxury of lamb fat; it is little wonder that it pleases Yahweh.

Though the Temple is the most beautiful edifice on earth, above it the sky is born daily of such new blue that the greatest arts of mankind can seem like the pebble and twig assemblies of a child. Even still, it is only through the prescribed sacrifices at the Temple that God's people can truly worship Him.

The roof of the Temple building is covered with sharp spikes to stop birds resting upon it and soiling, but at the western wall swallows swoop. Black daylight bats, with wings that cut the sky, like reason through myth. Plucking from the air the flies that might despoil this most sacred place. They build their nests in the fissures between the giant blocks. The renovations of the Temple – started by Herod the Great, whose bones are already shard and dust – even now are not completely finished. But the works have taken so long that many generations of swallows have come back here to nest each year and to die here, or to die en route or to die in distant lands not blessed with a temple like this one. There is no temple like this one. The swallows were the first pilgrims and they will be the last.

Sometimes the Three Pillars walk past the Antonia Fortress as they go to the Temple. Sometimes they pass Roman soldiers, men who stiffly raise one arm and bark, 'Hail, Caesar,' when they greet each other. Men who brandish spears with spikes as long and cruel as that Gethsemane night. Men who speak in a tongue that the Three Pillars do not know and do not wish to know, or even wish to hear. And when the Pillars pass such men, Cephas drops his head to avoid meeting their eyes, not because he is scared but because even a glance held too long from someone who looks like Cephas can seem confrontational. And the Pillars do not wish to challenge again the might of Rome. Not for now.

Cephas was Yeshua's right hand. But James was his very heart. James was his beloved brother and James rules the movement now.

Increasingly, as The Way has gained more adherents, there are many who never saw Yeshua, who will naturally ask what he was like. And when they ask Cephas this, he will usually say: 'He was a lot like James. Though even more like James than James is, if there can be such a thing as that.'

And those who then look at James to see his brother see a man who is tall, though not abnormally so, handsome, but not quite enough to make maidens blush, and celibate, so they would have no need to, dark of eye and skin and hair, as most of the desert dwellers are, a man who walks and speaks and delivers judgements with confidence, but not with pride, who bears some kind of secret fire in his chest, which pulls others to him, as iron is drawn to lodestone; but first, of course, they see a devout and pious Jew.

And of the other Pillars – the three leaders – there is Jochanan, a man who has a space where his beard doesn't grow. A place that must have been a scar – that is a scar, rather, that must have been a wound. That must have been an injury hard to survive, from blood and breathing alone, without the risk of infection, in this world of gangrene and running sores. And yet Jochanan remains alive, a man with a deep wide scar across his windpipe, not so strange perhaps, in Jerusalem, where all things are.

And then there is Cephas, who has not been cut open, but if he were to be, his innards might surprise. Cephas is like the sabra, the cactus fruit: an exterior calloused and thorny, hard as bark and sharp as swords, but sweet and tender inside.

* * *

The Three Pillars are in the house of John-Mark's mother, where they often meet, when Barnabas the Cypriot comes in and with him another man. A man of thirty-five or so, with thin wisps of hair that sprout from his scalp, like faint feathers on the head of a just-hatched chick. He has legs too bandy to block a bolting dog, but they are sturdy, calves bulged as if accustomed to walking great distances. A man with faraway eyes, which glint with things that others cannot see.

'So this is the one you told us about, Barnabas,' says James, in a grim whisper. 'Saul who persecuted and now claims to belong. The one who had a man flogged until his bones were bared of flesh and he died at the whipping post. This is the Saul who stoned Stephen and crushed his skull. Do you think we're pacifists here, Temple Guard? Do you think that when struck we turn our heads to be hit again? Should we believe that you haven't come to spy on us or provoke us? Tell me why Cephas shouldn't gut you like a goat while we have you here alone and unarmed.'

A quiver of fear shifts across the face of the man called Saul – quick as the ripple on a pond's surface as a fish snatches a fly – but then it is calm again. Whatever else he is, he is brave.

'God has forgiven me,' Saul says, 'so those who would follow His will must, I suppose, forgive me too. I have been called, and since you must know how this feels, you should know what it looks like.'

And it is undoubtedly true that Saul looks like a man who, with his entire mind, is convinced that he has spoken with God. It is present in his piercing eyes and in his almost eerie smile.

James smiles too. 'I'm testing you a little, or toying with you perhaps. Yeshua once had us eat with a tax enforcer – a son of Abraham who profited from the misery he inflicted on his brothers. Just as long as he repented and made the restitution written in the Torah, Yeshua said he was as worthy as any of us. We must draw all our fellow Jews into the coming Kingdom and those who come last are the most treasured. The man who is hired at the eleventh hour will have the same wage as he who has toiled all day. So you are welcome too, Saul. You are the most welcome of them all.'

And each of the Pillars in turn then embraces Saul and kisses him. James holds him last and longest. It is a strange and marvellous thing, perhaps, for Saul: to touch and smell the physical brother of a person previously encountered as sound and light. Stranger still when James sits him down and slowly, gently, washes the dust and dirt of the world from Saul's feet. The act is almost too intimate for Saul to bear: he feels as if it would be easier to flee than to take such forgiveness. But he remains, while James presses his feet dry with a cloth.

Then together, with earnest pleasure, they all recite the prayer that Yeshua taught: hallowing the name of *Abba*; calling for the remission of debts; for enough bread for all; for deliverance from this present evil; for God's Kingdom to come, here on earth.

* * *

Later, they eat, the oldest bond of men, and they talk and chew by turn. Jochanan tells Saul how attitudes have softened to those of The Way in the years of his absence. Perhaps because the high priest and his party now see the Nazarenes as no immediate threat, since they wait for the return of Yeshua before further action. The aristocrats are all Sadducee fools and don't believe that the dead will rise. And if you doubt that simple fact, it is hard to be afraid of one who is coming back. But The Way has grown in political strength too: it now counts many leading Pharisees and other well-respected Jerusalemites among its number. Even the great Gamaliel is a sympathizer, so perhaps the Pillars are harder to persecute openly.

For those of The Way, the communal meal is especially symbolic. Saul is familiar with the practice from his time in Damascus, but it is given more meaning in the house of James. For James, though he is the leader and the Messiah's brother, waits upon the others. It is he who serves the grilled fish – white-fleshed and unspiced, wrapped in leaves – just as Yeshua would have done, had he been there. Among the Nazarenes it is the mightiest man present who takes the role of the wife, the mother, the servant, the slave. The first shall be last and the last shall be first.

James pours the wine and blesses it: 'We give thanks to You, our Father, for Your holy vine of David, Your servant, our once and future King, soon to be returned.'

And he breaks the bread and passes it: 'As this broken bread was scattered over the hills and was brought together becoming one, so gather Your people from the ends of the earth into Your Kingdom.'

James doesn't taste the wine himself, because of his vow. Like Baptizer John, who founded The Way, James drinks no wine or liquor; neither does he eat flesh. And no blade or scissor touches his head. Of all the reverent Jews of Jerusalem, James is hailed among the most pious. But strangely, although James eats no meat, he seems to wish for a return to a time when all men stalked their supper. 'When men hunted,' he says, 'men were equal. The successful shared, because the carcass would quickly spoil in any case. And by doing so each knew that others would share with him in the future. That was how it first was after Eden. When men turned to agriculture they could produce a surplus. And so they could be taxed. And so they could sustain the parasites who don't toil but only threaten and burden.'

Like Yeshua did, James believes that wealth is an obstacle to piety. They come from a poor family, after all, despite their royal blood. Two doves were sacrificed at Yeshua's birth, the cheapest, lowliest offering, made only by the humblest of society. But even the penniless must make sacrifice for a first-born boy and they were a dutiful family; all their sons were circumcised on the eighth day after their birth, as God had decreed those of Israel must be. James and Yeshua's father was a *tekton*, not a carpenter as such but a builder, a day labourer, one who has insufficient land to farm to support a family. Most houses are made from baked clay, mud and stone in this arid country; there aren't too many carpenters. Wood is used sparingly. Except by the Romans.

Hours before
the Crucifixion

Cephas follows the train of torches across the blackened valley and back into the city. Once inside the walls, on paved surfaces, the boots and spear butts of the Romans resound about confined and quiet streets; sufficiently so that Cephas doesn't even need to keep the cortège in sight to pursue it. He stays permanently a half-road or an alley back and because of this he sees the faces appear at window slots and heads poke mongoose-like around doorways after the Romans and the high priest's men have passed by. Even in Jerusalem such a procession of soldiery in the dead of night is a thing unusual. Many of the faces mutter inaudible curses; and the paving in places sparkles with mucus spat at distant Roman backs.

The cohort escorts the prisoner, still encircled in a throng of Temple Guards, to a building in the upper city, which can be nowhere if it is not the house of the high priest. Though to call Annas's residence a house is to mistake a harrier for a songbird, or a warhorse for a donkey. It is a mansion, and even then a mansion like no other: the bastard offspring of a scared man's castle and a Latin villa. No doubt trapped with Roman fancies:

mosaic floors; marbles; floral frescos of crimson and gold; defrayments of a traitor's guilt.

Once the high priest's men-at-arms and the fettered Yeshua are ensconced inside, the cohort of Romans clatters off again, eastward, doubtless returning to the Antonia Fortress. But the gate to the courtyard of the high priest's house is left open; the whole household is awake, it seems, and various servants, slaves, guards and attendants are gathered there, awaiting instructions or intrigued by events.

Cephas pulls his sword from out of his girdle and submerges it in the shadow-blacked bottom of a stone horse-trough on the street. His wet fingers immediately start to numb, so cold is the night. He pulls up his cowl and slips through the gate into the colonnaded courtyard, trying to be as stealthy as he can, without looking like a man trying to be stealthy.

A group, mostly of female servants, is gathered round a charcoal brazier and Cephas makes his way there to warm his hands and watch and wait.

* * *

Yeshua is inside the building, wrists still bound, alone but for the former high priest, Annas, his son-in-law, Kayafa, the current incumbent, and a handful of Temple Guards. The guards look to Annas for their orders – it is clear where real power still lies – though it is Kayafa who questions Yeshua.

'You attacked the property and business of the Temple. And the authority of the priesthood. Do you deny it?' Kayafa says.

Kayafa is portly – most priests are: they dine well. You can tell the children of the priests on

Jerusalem streets: little fat princelings who eat meat every night when most boys taste it just a few times a year.

'What authority of the priesthood?' says Yeshua. 'You are like one of your own grand Sadducee tombs: fine and whitewashed on the outside, but inside filled with dead men's bones and all kinds of filth. So it is with you: the exterior of honest men, but brim-full of hypocrisy and crimes of collaboration.'

One of the guards strikes him then, a blow to the jaw. 'Is that how you answer the high priest?'

Yeshua raises his head again, from where it was knocked low by the blow and looks at the man, who twitches a little from that look alone. Yeshua moves his jaw, as if in test that it is unbroken; his dense beard ripples as he does so, saltbush in a desert wind.

'If I spoke amiss,' Yeshua says, 'state it in the evidence. Why strike me? I have spoken openly to the world. I have taught where all people congregate. Why question me? Ask my hearers what I told them. I have said nothing in secret.'

'We have witnesses who say that you have threatened to destroy the Temple,' Kayafa says.

'Not the Temple,' says Yeshua, 'but your rule of it, you truckler puppet, you toad-eater. You wax fat from supping with Rome and oppressing the poor ones. Your obeisance to the heathen is ungodly. You aren't worthy of your office.'

The guard strikes Yeshua again, and smirks at it this time, pleased to have overcome his fear.

* * *

Out in the courtyard, a servant girl recognizes Cephas.

'You're one of his disciples,' she says. 'I saw you walking with him on the day the crowds cheered him into Jerusalem. You're with the Galilean, aren't you?'

'You are mistaken,' Cephas says. 'I don't know who you mean.'

* * *

'Tell us,' Annas says, 'are you the King?'

'If I say so, you won't believe me. And if I deny it, you still won't release me. So I'll tell you the truth anyway. Yes, I am Israel's King and you will yet see the coming of God's Kingdom, just as Daniel prophesied.'

* * *

The servant girl stares at Cephas and insists, 'It was you I saw. You are a head taller than the rest, I would hardly forget. And you speak like one of them too. You're from Galilee. You are definitely with him.'

'I am not,' Cephas says. 'I told you, you are mistaken. Half the Jews of the world are here for the Passover. There must be another hundred Galileans who look like me. I do not know him, woman.'

* * *

They don't need witnesses. Annas and Kayafa have heard sufficient from Yeshua's own mouth. The two high priests retire to a smaller adjacent chamber to talk in private.

On their own they seem different: sager and grimly sorrowful. They know what must be done, but there is neither pleasure nor malice in it. It is just one of those things necessary for the survival of the chosen people – like cutting a lamb's throat in the Temple – an act best performed quickly and quietly. Judaea balances on the point of a Roman javelin. A pretender to the throne could tumble the whole country.

Strictly the Nazarene should be tried, but they can't call the council of the Sanhedrin: it never takes place outside the Chamber of Hewn Stone in the Temple and it never meets at festival times and it certainly never meets at night. And even Annas's palatial home doesn't have a room where seventy-one men could hold court. In any case, the council is half filled with Pharisees who consider sedition against Rome a righteous path and in most things hold the view that they should be left to their own course: 'If The Way be of men, it will come to naught, and if it be of God, you will not be able to overthrow it.' That would be the talk of the Pharisees, were they here.

But they aren't here: it is only Annas and Kayafa and this is no trial, just a decision-making process, the result of which is all but predetermined anyway. Not by prophecy, but by pragmatism.

'Should he be allowed to continue until more of the populace believes him, the Romans will destroy the Temple and the nation,' Annas says. 'They have crucified men before for dropping a coin with Tiberius's head on it to the privy floor. Just to wear a robe that faintly resembles the emperor's is a capital offence. If our people start to follow a rival king, the streets will soon enough be ankle deep in blood.'

'Agreed, of course,' Kayafa says. 'More expedient that one man die than that the whole nation be destroyed.'

* * *

A Temple Guard comes over to the group by the brazier now; perhaps Cephas raised his voice more than he intended; perhaps the guard just likes looking tough in front of servant girls.

'What is your business here, fellow?'

'I warm my bones, nothing more.'

'I know your face from somewhere.'

'He is with Yeshua bar Abba, I tell you he is,' the maid chips in.

'I swear to you that I am not. I do not even know the man you're talking about. I have to go now anyway. I have orders to attend to and not enough time to blather with gossips.'

Cephas storms away as if offended, but breaks into a run as soon as he is back through the gate. He abandons his sword where it lies in the trough. Bolts the other way and takes every narrow alley and sudden turn he can. Though he hears no one pursuing, he runs until his lungs overcome him and he cannot do other than stop. And there he crouches, panting, trembling, heart of melted wax, hunched in the shadow of a tanner's vat.

A cockerel crows then, a boastful warble, which marks the moment sufficiently for Cephas to know that every dawn henceforth is going to shrill with the agonizing shame of this dishonour and desertion. Every proud-combed rooster in the world is going to sing about Cephas's crime. He curls, impossibly small, on his side. The ground is cold – so very cold – and Cephas's bitter-salted tears will not warm it.

* * *

Annas has authority to order the death penalty for religious offences, but there is no blasphemy committed here. Declaring yourself to be a king is not blasphemy, it is sedition against Rome. And for that crime the prisoner should be sent to the prefect. Pilate is expecting him to be turned over anyway: lending the priests command of a cohort of soldiers is not a normal occurrence. Better to get on with the deed, then, and have it done, Annas thinks. Maybe the Galilean really is of the royal line of David; probably he's just another madman. But either way, the best thing now is for the Nazarene to be dead and gone before Jerusalem even hears what has happened.

* * *

Kayafa is not as sturdy as his father-in-law. Kayafa lacks the stomach for this role. Some days he can barely believe that once he wanted nothing more than to be the high priest. After he gives the guards their orders, he rends his robe with horror and sorrow and sickness and self-pity at the shit he has to go through. It is a hard path to be this figure of half-rule. Even harder being hated for it. About the only thing the Romans and the Judaeans can agree on is that they all despise the high priest and yet they all still need him, as their go-between and negotiator: the Romans with the people; the people with God.

Thirty-four Years after the Crucifixion

In the week since Cephas was first sighted in Rome, Paul's followers have gathered more information about his doings: Silas and Aristarchus have even been to one of the house churches to hear him speak. Evidently Cephas is steering away from the villas where the wealthier Christians worship, sticking to the shop-front and tenement-courtyard gatherings of the poor.

Appropriately, perhaps, because they say Cephas's speech is rough and unlearned. Worse: Aristarchus says that Cephas is still using images of Galilee fishermen, deserts and shepherds, which really don't work in this urban world. Paul reaches the people of Rome with metaphors drawn from the arena sports that are their entertainment, and with martial talk, to which they are accustomed from their politics and history.

'I think that elderly pestilence, Cephas, is going to find it harder to buffet you here,' Timothy says.

Useful has noticed before that Timothy has this way of involuntarily pursing his lips, when he thinks he has made a fine point, as though kissing his own brilliance.

'No, Cephas will not defeat me again. I am too

aware of his schemes now,' Paul replies. 'He is nothing but a false apostle, a deceitful worker, given to me by God as a thorn in the flesh in case I should become too proud through my abundance of revelations. Cephas is no better than the slave who always stands behind a Roman general in his Triumph, who whispers throughout the ceremonies, "Remember you are only a man," to prevent the general thinking too much of himself.'

'But how did you come to be opponents in the first place?' Useful asks. 'Surely your purpose was the same.'

'Well, there, Useful, lies a story. And since that's so, perhaps it would be as well to get some more of our tale down. Leave us now,' Paul says to the others. 'Useful and I have our work to attend to.'

Paul peels a russet apple, the blade of his ivory-handled knife towards his thumb, while Useful readies the writing materials. With an old man's perfected practice, Paul carves the peel, furled into a single unbroken snake.

'So,' Paul begins, 'after Barnabas the Cypriot introduced us, I stayed fifteen days with Cephas in Jerusalem and got acquainted with him. And he appeared to be a servant of righteousness. He told me about his time spent with the earthly Jesus and of his visions of Him after His death, which, if anything – I might add – were not as spectacular as my own experience. And word spread among those of The Way that I, who had once persecuted them, was now preaching the faith and there was much glorifying and rejoicing.

'By this time, Nazarenes had travelled as far as Phoenicia and Alexandria, but aside from my own brief travails in Arabia, the message had been passed solely to Jews. However, in Syrian Antioch,

Greek Gentiles, too, were beginning to listen and join, and when news of this reached the ears of the Church at Jerusalem, Barnabas and I were sent to Antioch to preach and encourage the faithful.

'We lived some years with the community there. The people of Antioch called our movement Christianoi. I suppose you'd translate it as "the faction promoting messianism", a dreadfully insulting and derogatory slur. But Antioch was nonetheless a place of marvels, perhaps the third greatest city in the world, and more beautiful than any save Rome herself, so it was well to be established firmly there. And we increased the numbers of brothers considerably, until perhaps two hundred believed, or maybe three ... No, write five hundred. Now I think about it, it was much closer to five hundred.

'But at the end of that time, the Holy Spirit came into Barnabas and me and told us that we must once more travel and spread the word. And the Holy Spirit thought it best that we start with Cyprus, because that was where Barnabas was originally from, plus it was just a short sail across the strait from Antioch. And so, sent on our way by the Holy Spirit, that was exactly what we did: myself and Barnabas and another brother, John-Mark. Or, at least, I thought him a brother back then.

'We landed at Salamis and straight away went into the synagogues to proclaim Jesus as the saviour soon to return. And our successes were such that very soon word reached the proconsul of Cyprus himself, a great man called Sergius Paulus, who then summoned us.

'Barnabas was afraid, for fear of what the governor might do. And John-Mark didn't want to go, because he still regarded Rome as some kind of enemy. But they were both quite wrong in the event.

'Because the proconsul was a magnificent man, statuesque and noble, and it was the Holy Spirit that had guided us to him. Our meeting was doubtless destined, for many great things were born of this encounter.

'Sergius Paulus was a prudent ruler. If he had a single character flaw, it was that he was too open to superstition, because from the moment we were led into his court, I could see that he was part in thrall to a worm-tongued hanger-on of a magician. A lizard-faced, bulge-eyed, curtain-creeper called Elymas. Though a Jew, Elymas was shaven smooth, but for a little thumb-stump of beard in the manner of the Egyptians, and he was covered with queer blue tattoos, quite against the proscriptions of Leviticus. And he wore so many bangles and amulets that as he moved it was as though cheap timbrels tinkled after him. He called himself a sorcerer and fancied himself as a magi of old and as an interpreter of dreams. But if he had any powers at all, they were as nothing next to mine, as you will presently hear.

'Sergius Paulus questioned us – Barnabas, John-Mark and me – and I expounded at length and with some eloquence of all that we had learned and seen. And of how the ancient texts, with which the proconsul had already some familiarity, contained within them the evidence that Jesus was the Messiah. And it was clear that Sergius Paulus was becoming persuaded by me, and no doubt by the Holy Spirit also.

'Fearful of losing his influence, this Elymas began to whisper into Sergius Paulus's ear after each and every thing that I said. And I could tell from Elymas's crooked-slit smile, like a spider's leg, that whatever he was whispering, it was done to undermine and denigrate my words and to clench his master to himself.

'So I accused him straight to his face of being a child of the devil and an enemy of everything that is right, and told the whole assembly that Elymas was full of all kinds of deceit and trickery and was determined to pervert the right ways of God.

'Shortly after I said this, Elymas was taken dizzy and had to sit down, while I continued to preach. And then Elymas said he felt unwell and asked to be excused. Of course, it was the hand of God that had struck against him. Because, before he could depart to his chambers, he became blinded, barely able to see the light of the sun. Mist and darkness came over him, and he wailed like a babe and groped about for someone to lead him away by the hand. And when the proconsul saw what had occurred through my power, he was amazed and believed with all his heart that Jesus is the Christ.

'This blinding of Elymas was the first and perhaps the greatest of all the miracles I would perform. What happened to him afterwards, I don't know. Maybe he was sucked off to whichever power of the underworld he served. But Sergius Paulus, his entire household and not a few of the others were reborn that very day, baptized in the sparkled fountain at his villa. And there was such joy and rejoicing in the name of the Lord. And not a little humility on the parts of Barnabas and John-Mark, who had counselled that we should not go to the proconsul and were then forced to concede that I had been right all along.

'But further momentous things were to happen

in that place because, in a manner of speaking, I was reborn as well. Sergius Paulus insisted that he become my patron and gave me a letter of recommendation. And, as is not uncommon in Roman patronage, he suggested that I henceforth use a part of his name, as a mark of his special favour. And I was eager to do just this, so others would know of and celebrate the great miracle that I had performed in blinding the sorcerer. From that day onwards, I shed the name Saul, just as a man who has come into a great inheritance would throw away the clothes he had worn in poverty. And the world would come to know me as Paul.'

Twenty-four Years after the Crucifixion

This arena is small, provincial. It's probably in Galatia or Asia or somewhere, judging by how hot it is. But it might be in Hispania or Gaul, or even Britain, if this is just a particularly sultry summer's day. It is hard to tell precisely where this is because all Roman arenas are as similar as their shields. The Romans have a certain manner of doing things and it involves making each new place where they arrive identical to everywhere they have been. Often the natives – who previously had different ways and might have got a little stuck in them – initially don't approve of this. But once a sufficient proportion of the men of fighting age have spilled their innards onto the fields; once enough families, split, raped and wretched, have been sold into slavery; once an adequate number of villages have been razed to the ground and their shrieking occupants put to the sword, the locals generally come around. Rome is a civilizing influence, after all. And arena sports are just one of the many marvels of civilization they bring.

This being a provincial arena, though, the band isn't up to much. There's a man on some kind of trumpet, curled like the shell of a snail, another beating a goatskin drum, and that's about it. But to judge by the blood seeping into the sands, the morning's games have been good.

It's just a couple of *andabatae* on the programme now, condemned criminals, flailing about at each other in helms with no eye-holes. It's not the best of the arena sports, but you would have to have a heart of stone not to laugh a bit. To add to the fun, this first one is rather fat: his flesh wobbles with his every thrust into the empty air. He's so corpulent, in fact, that you could bet his penis has all but disappeared into the flappy folds of his groin. Really they should make him battle unclothed to be even funnier, but he wears a loincloth, like all the *damnati*. Most men don't fight well when they're naked: they instinctively feel bested and defensive. For *andabatae*, who can't see anyway, you wouldn't think it would make much difference, but seemingly it still does. What is really hilarious currently, though, is that the fat man's adversary isn't even out on the sands yet, so the flabby fool is wasting his energy slashing away like this.

But here comes his opponent now, prodded out from one of the arena entrances. The iron-latticed portal that closes behind him is quite poorly made, ill-fitted for filling the doorway. Wherever this place is, it is apparently somewhere with a dearth of decent blacksmiths.

Logically, they should have chosen an absurdly skinny man as the second fighter, to make the contest even more entertaining, but perhaps they were out of luck in the ranks of those sentenced to the arena, because he is quite normal-sized. He is altogether unremarkable, in fact. We cannot see his face beneath the all-concealing helm, but his body is distinctly Everyman. He could be a neighbour or the fishmonger. The only thing we know for sure is that he is a donkey thief, because the programme announcer said so, and this land – wherever it is – would doubtless be a better place with a bit less animal larceny. The crowd was jeering too much to hear what the announcer said the fat guy had done, but you can be pretty confident that it, too, was something well deserving of this fate.

They do a lot of proclamations at the arena: it's a good way of getting information spread, particularly among people who are illiterate, as virtually everyone probably is in whatever Empire's-edge place this is. There's a messenger waiting to do a proclamation after this bout. Some important news has just arrived: there's been a change of emperor.

He's already been in power a few months, truth be told, but it takes a while for news to filter to the provinces. He's only seventeen, the new chap, a bit of a turn-up for the books. Claudius held power for thirteen years, a good spell, but now he's dead and his adopted son Nero is the ruler. Doubtless there will be some big shifts in Rome, but round here nothing much will happen, except the face on the few newly minted coins in circulation will be different. Imperial intrigues don't amount to a whole lot in Bithynia or Cappadocia or wherever the hell this place is.

At least one man will never even hear the news. It's probably going to be Fatty – he looks exhausted already from his strikes at emptiness. Though a layer of lard is a definite advantage in some ways: there's extra weight behind your blows and it keeps the vital organs better protected from sword cuts. And you never can tell with the *andabatae* anyway: one lucky slash can sometimes decide a fight. Other times they manage to get a grip on one another and stab and grapple in a brutal brawl that might see both injured before it's through. Prone on the sand to have their skulls smashed by Charon's hammer.

They are close to each other now and they know it. Inching their feet onwards, pushing little mounds of sand as they come. The one who strikes first will give away his position and be left open if he misses, but might just land a devastating wound if he connects. What are they thinking, under those helms? Have they reached a point of strange warrior-calm, a readiness to face this and do their utmost to win? Or, like the Empire itself, do they keep moving forwards only because if they stop they may collapse?

A Decade after
the Crucifixion

From Cyprus the three preachers catch a ship north to the Mediterranean mainland. Saline winds smell of victory: a Roman governor converted and a miracle publicly performed. Final proof, if any should need it, of the apostleship of Paul. A name still glistening, like a cocoon-damp butterfly, veined wafer wings drying in the sun, exhausted from the effort of emergence, but proud of this alien form.

For a second time, Paul is embarking on a mission to a strange land with a letter tucked into his tunic, but on this occasion he is confident of his election and in elation.

John-Mark's hair is a tangled wild globe, like the head of a thistle, though in his manner he is imperturbable and precise. His eyes have almost no discernible colour around the pupil and look still and black. He is a good person to have along on such a mission as this. Not only because of his faith. Or just because his mother was one of the first Jerusalem followers of The Way; the Three Pillars frequently still meet in her house. But because he is young and he is strong. Roads and boats both are haunts of robbers and worse.

John-Mark, however, is sullen as they trudge lateral to the coast towards the city of Perga, along roads curtained with undulating silver-green grasses.

'Personally, I would sooner have no dealings with Romans beyond absolute necessity, but if you must preach to them, don't you think you should have insisted that Sergius Paulus and his household become circumcised?' John-Mark says finally, revealing the tick that has been biting him. 'They cannot be committed to The Way yet not be Jews – that makes no sense. And they cannot be Jews and not be circumcised.'

Paul gives a cheery clasp to his back, as one might to a downcast child. 'Don't worry. All that is coming to pass is as it should be. That's all you need to know.'

John-Mark shrugs Paul's hand from him and strides onward at an increased pace, heels coughing up little mushrooms of dust. Paul and Barnabas share a wary glance.

* * *

They pass abundant fields, worked by iron-collared slaves, evidence of a region as rich as Paul had heard. Perga, when they approach it, is a fortified city, walls the off-white of a rock-rose, boosting from the flat coastal landscape. In the safety that Roman domination has bought, tiled villas, some quite imposing, have spilled out beyond the defences.

Barnabas himself had such an estate at one time – he was a wealthy man – but he sold all his possessions and gave the money to James the Just and the poor ones of Jerusalem. Now he travels as emissaries of the Nazarenes are supposed to, like those Yeshua first sent throughout Judaea, with just a staff and a single cloak, no bread, no bag and no money in his belt. Paul carries the purse.

On the Sabbath they go to Perga's synagogue and preach in turn. John-Mark tells the gathering about The Way, about its founding by John and the baptism practised by him to purify and regenerate. And of his follower Yeshua – or Jesus, as they call him when they speak in Greek – who proved to be greater still. About the necessity of redoubling piety to prepare for the new age shortly to arrive. Barnabas talks about the communal meal, about the fellowship instituted by Jesus, about the last coming first. And Paul? Paul talks about different things entirely.

Afterwards John-Mark comes to him. 'Where are you getting these ideas?' John-Mark asks. 'I have never heard from James or Cephas that praying to Yeshua will cleanse sins. That sounds more like a scoffable pagan tale about Osiris or someone. We shouldn't even need sins forgiven – we have the Day of Atonement for that – and do we hate ourselves like tormented harbour-side harlots that we think our every action is a sin? Those who worship God faithful to the Torah have no reason to doubt His mercy. As the psalmist says: *He does not treat us as our sins deserve, or repay us according to our iniquities.*'

'You needn't quote scripture at me,' Paul says. 'Don't forget that I have spoken to the Lord Jesus.'

'That's another thing. Why have you started adding "Lord" every time you say the name Jesus?'

'Shouldn't we respect the Messiah?'

'Yes, of course. But for those who read the Torah and Prophets in Greek you are using the same word as for God: "*Kurios*" should not be applied in a synagogue to describe a man, even a king, even the King who will return. Neither should you be telling people to pray to one. You are coming perilously close to declaring that Yeshua is a god. There is only one God, Saul.'

'*Paul*. I am called Paul now. I am not the man I once was.'

'No.' John-Mark looks at him through slits that accentuate the darkness of his eyes. 'No, you are not.'

* * *

John-Mark leaves them that night. He returns to the port to find a ship to take him home to Judaea. Paul shrugs when Barnabas tells him.

* * *

The three-become-two continue passing from town to town, speaking in the synagogues, trying to sway these diaspora Jews to The Way. And many do come across – persuaded by Paul's unfakeable passion – and are baptized in the rinsing waters of city rivers. Most are not convinced, but anyway enjoy the speeches and the debates that follow them, because it is enlivening to listen to diverse voices and original subjects in these Sabbath sessions, and there is no harm in hearing the views of Judaism's newest sect.

But others take against Paul's words, more vehemently than John-Mark did. Others eject Paul from their houses of teaching and make threatenings that chase him and Barnabas from their neighbourhoods. These others are fearful, maybe, that the precarious position of outnumbered Jews in Empire cities risks unbalance in talk of messiahs. Or perhaps Paul's words begin to sound less like a fresh sect of Judaism and more like the first bursting fungus of something otherwise and strange.

* * *

At the city of Lystra, Paul feels ready to perform another miracle. Upon a lame man, whose eyes gloss with belief as Paul speaks. Who clutches a crutch of carob wood, shaft almost as thick as the thighs of his brittle cripple's legs. And he walks some steps, when Paul bids him to, more than he has walked in years. Hands floating before him, as though grasping for support that isn't there, unsteady but advancing nonetheless, like a dark-alley drunk. And he swears, to those who gather round to lift him up again, that within days he will be strolling the town as blithely as any of them.

* * *

But those who have taken against Paul begin to cluster. Malevolent scarecrow men afraid of change and enfranchised speech. They follow him and counter him. They attack his words. They shout, 'Blasphemy!' And when still he will not cease, they take up rocks.

The weight that crushed Stephen can crush again. Not that these are the same stones: every land has stones of its own. Those of Judaea are lime and pale, while these are grey and dappled; but they would serve just as well, to silence a voice.

Caught unexpectedly and alone, Paul is pelted and bloodied, left for dead. They do not drop the final boulder on his skull. Who knows if this is mercy or thought unnecessary? He did not move or scream for minutes while the stones still came. Consciousness left him with the first blow to the crown, which opened a seam to spread his blood upon the ground. Head wounds bleed heavily. It must be hard for those unaccustomed to murder to be sure when it is accomplished. The attackers flee, leaving Paul dripping blood into the soil, like the flayed god Attis of a Tarsus childhood. That dying and resurrected saviour, hanged from a tree. For without the shedding of blood there is no forgiveness, as Hebrews says.

Thoughts reel and tumble on the frontier of concussion and oblivion. Paul, who is Saul, sees Stephen and Jesus and himself in a jumble of faces, all of them red-wet and resurrected, circling like spokes, joined at a hub of blood. And Jesus, who looks like Stephen – goat beard split, hair clotted with black – is in Saul, and God is in them all. And Saul is in his body and out of it. But the body is just a tent, a temporary shelter, or else how can he see it there, broken on the ground, and yet be alive and elsewhere and here and looking at it? And Saul's blood is smeared on the stones and leaching into the soil. And Jesus is in Saul, who isn't Saul but Paul. And a man who is them or isn't, but is in Christ, is taken up to the third Heaven. Whether this is in the body or out of the body he doesn't know – God knows. But he is taken up to Paradise and hears inexpressible things, things that no one is permitted to tell. The revelation of mysteries hidden for long ages now revealed and made known. Those who knew the Christ in the flesh know Him no longer. But Paul is in Christ and Christ is in him. Whether in the body or apart from the body he doesn't know, but God knows. And Stephen says, 'God forgive you,' with his broken teeth and his mouth bubbling blood. And the consumption of blood is prohibited, but a chalice of wine could serve as surrogate; could just as effectively bless with immortality. And Paul will have his atonement; Paul will have his blood.

Nine Hours before
the Crucifixion

He breaks his nightly fast – at an ungodly time, when by rights he should still be peacefully dreaming about chewing the nipples of some full-breasted boat-fresh slave – with a cutlet of pork, faintly gilled like the underside of a mushroom, served red-rare, still swampy in its own grume. There is pleasure to be taken in such small things. Don't eat blood. Don't eat pig. Don't do any fucking thing on the Sabbath. These tiresome, touchy Judaeans. After all the expenditure, planning and petitioning for a chance to govern, of all the lands in the Empire, to end up with this one.

Pontius had only just arrived – four years back, this was – when he almost had his first full-blown riot. Over nothing. Nothing that would cause a problem anywhere else in the known bloody world anyway. *You can't put up statues in Jerusalem.* He knew that, was advised of that – multiple times – before he left Rome. Not even in your own bloody apartments can you put a statue, never mind in the Temple, where there bloody well ought to be one of the emperor or Jupiter or some decent Roman god. But, no, the Israelites won't even have a statue of their own bloody 'Lord of Hosts'. But Pontius was grudgingly fine with it; it's ridiculous pandering, of course, but if that's how it's always been done, then so be it.

The centurion, Gaius, enters.

'The high priest is here with the prisoner, Prefect.'

'Well, what are you waiting for? Bring them up.'

'Prefect.' The centurion looks uncomfortable.

'What is it?'

'The high priest won't come up, Prefect.'

'No, no. Why by the arse-of-Medusa would he enter such an unclean habitation as this?' Pontius gestures about the mar-less palace, marble as white as Alpine snow, shining ivory that might have come from Hannibal's elephants. 'These people, Gaius, these fucking people.'

Pontius rises and spreads his arms so that a slave can place a thick wool cloak across his shoulders and fasten it by the two rings attached to the front of his breastplate; it hangs through them in twin puffs of scarlet cloth.

'I have to keep the place statue-less, for their sensibilities – not so much as one image of Venus the Modest, half hiding her little titties – and they won't come inside anyway. So tell me why I bother.' The instruction is left to drift, not aimed particularly either at Gaius, or the slave, or any of the other attendants.

And, of course, Pontius knows full well why he bothers: so he doesn't have another incident like there was when he arrived. Not that he even put up a statue back then. It was just some standards of the legions, placed around palace walls, that was all. But, of course, some of the standards have an image of the emperor's head on them and the emperor is a god. And that was sufficient to have volley after volley of priests and merchants and Pharisees and Sadducees and Herodians all pleading and imploring for the standards to be taken down. Pontius should have been congratulated for uniting factions ordinarily in discord. But when he declined all of their entreaties as insulting to the emperor, he had found his palace surrounded. Not by warriors, but by people protesting. For five bloody days, great crowds gathered round, bringing commerce to a standstill and creating a hubbub and a spectacle that could not be allowed to go on indefinitely.

So, on the sixth day, Pontius had the assembled multitude all summoned to the stadium, as if he was going to answer them. But then, upon his signal, they were encircled by soldiers, three ranks deep, with swords already drawn, and ordered to desist protesting.

Whereupon the fucking Israelites only all flung themselves on the ground, extended their necks, and cried that they would rather die than transgress the Torah. Bloody hundreds, if not thousands of them, baring their napes so their heads could be cut off. What can you do with a people like that? Pontius could hardly massacre them all in cold blood, having only just arrived. The Emperor Tiberius might even have rescinded his appointment. So Pontius had to let them have their way in the end and take the standards down. Bloody incorrigible people.

* * *

Pontius and his entourage descend to the walled courtyard adjoining the palace, where Kayafa and several squads of Temple Guards stand before the dawn. The prisoner himself is framed by the rising sun; it glows around him, making his white robe look orange.

Four slaves place the prefect's judgement seat on the paving. A skinny lizard – morning-slow – skips away from it into a crack.

Pontius sits and folds the two sides of his cloak across his bare legs. A large tan and white Mollossian mastiff ambles down the steps after the rest of the party and settles at his side. The toes of its paws are longer than a child's fingers. Pontius smooths the shaggy mane around the loose-hanging fighting flesh of its neck.

'You will forgive me for not entering your palace I hope, Prefect?' Kayafa says, to break the silence. 'We have the festival, as you know, and I have to be pure for it.'

'Of course, of course, I understand, Kayafa. I have been having your laws and prophets read to me each night by one of my slaves. Do you know, I think I must be as well versed as most Judaeans by now? If you were somehow to incur uncleanness you would have to be purified again. A ritual that consists of … Remind me.'

'The impure man must descend naked into the water of the *mikveh* and emerge again from the other side.'

'So, like a bath?'

'A bath, Prefect, correct.'

'A bath, that's right. And such baths are near impossible to find?'

'The prefect knows that there are many *mikveh* in the Temple surrounds, but these would be exceedingly busy at festival time. They must be entered one at a time and the queues would be lengthy.'

'Have you ever thought of having one installed

in your own villa?' Pontius asks. 'I would have thought that could offer considerable advantages.'

'I believe the prefect is aware that I do have one in my villa.'

'Well, now, that sounds more convenient. And yet you still prefer to drag me outside my palace rather than use it?'

The high priest begins to say something but Pontius waves him to be silent. 'Let's just get to the business, shall we? So, this is the prisoner. Behold the man for whom I have to rise before dawn. His name again?'

The prisoner is many-named, Pontius is informed, as many people are, common and great. His given name, Kayafa says, is Yahushua bar Joseph. But apparently most people call him Yeshua. Yeshua of Nazareth; Yeshua the Nazarene; Yeshua the Rabban; Yeshua bar Joseph; Yeshua the Messiah; the rabble know him best as Yeshua bar Abba, perhaps from his habit of asking followers to call God 'Abba' – Father – in the special prayer he teaches. The words of people who know God personally, who speak with Him directly; an over-familiarity, in the view of Kayafa. Though possibly the prisoner is called bar Abba because *Son of the LORD God* is a royal title and he claims to have been anointed and adopted as king.

'Presumably he's not a Roman citizen?' Pontius asks. It's ridiculously unlikely, but best to check these things since Romans have the right of appeal to Caesar's court.

'No. He's not even strictly a Judaean. A landless Galilean. He was at first a follower of the Baptizer John.'

Pontius was told about the Baptizer: executed for preaching dissent and for criticizing Herod

Antipater's incestuous marriage. Some stories blamed the bride's daughter, painted her as a stunning little cunny – Pontius wouldn't have minded meeting that one. It's probably all a lie, though: these people are always blaming women for their sins … They say Baptizer John's head was put on a plate when it was severed and a banquet held before it. They say it rolled around in the last of the blood, John's long curls coated, then congealed in it. They say they had to put a cloth over it to stop the flies swarming on it. But still it drew them and eventually they moved it away from the food to the opposite end of the banquet hall. Wonder what happened to it afterwards? Probably no one knows. The bodies of the executed are given no ceremony. They are dumped in ditches and ravines or buried in hasty holes. They are never returned to their family: that is part of the punishment.

Thoughts of banqueting make Pontius hungry. But he is running a little towards fat these days, it must be said. So he resists the urge to call for food. He calls for wine instead. Anyway, best to keep the liquids up for the heat, which will certainly arrive later in the day, and the local water tastes to Pontius like it was bucket-bailed out of Charon's leaking vessel of the dead. It is tainted, half cut with decaying flesh. And not surprising, when the hills all about Jerusalem are covered with tombs. The water flowing to the pool of Siloam must have percolated through every shrouded skeleton and rotted funeral winding and sack of part-decomposed flesh lumps of all the deceased of the land.

But you try to put up an aqueduct to get in fresh water direct to the city. You try to do that to help them and leave Jerusalem a better place than you found it and you have more riots on your hands. It is un-bloody-believable.

* * *

Quite recently, this was: Jerusalem needed more clean water and the Temple Treasury was sitting on huge piles of gold. Sacred money, yes, but Pontius had the high priest's permission – albeit under some duress – and Jewish law permitted the use of the fund for social welfare and public works. Now, what is an aqueduct if not public works? And welfare at the same time, for that matter: not dying, squirting out your own innards of bloody dysentery, is bloody welfare, isn't it?

You would have thought they would be grateful; but instead, at the next festival, Pontius had found a palace surrounded once more. By several thousands this time. They probably thought they'd repeat the offer-their-necks thing, which had worked over the standards, if he sent in the troops. But Pontius wasn't about to be tricked like that again.

This time he had auxiliary soldiers – Samaritans, who look pretty much identical to Jews – dress up in civilian clothing and mingle with the protesters. And when the rabble refused to withdraw, the troops broke it up by force.

Pontius had forbidden them to use swords, permitting only quarter staffs and clubs, perhaps a few daggers, just to rough the crowd up and scare them a bit. But, of course, the soldiers had got carried away once the blood mist set in, as Pontius had half known they would. It's about as optimistic as commanding a war dog to savage someone gently, to think that Samaritans would use restraint against Judaeans, the enmity between them being age-long and bitter. Any protesters who resisted were stabbed or beaten to death on the street and probably even more were trampled or crushed while trying to flee. Several hundred were dead by the finish, but it didn't much matter because the result was good: order was restored.

* * *

Pontius's wine arrives, a vintage from the hills of Alba. The gold beaker is richly blistered with amber and crusted with beryl; condensation glistens on cast stags. There's a crack in part of the amber, Pontius notices. He's never owned such a fine goblet before. And now he owns one with a fucking crack in it.

'I won't insult you by offering you a cup of my dirty idolater's wine, of course, Kayafa,' Pontius says, taking a sip so deep that his nose is wetted.

Kayafa manages to produce a look that a charitable man might possibly construe as a polite smile. Pontius is not such a man.

Pontius strokes the giant mastiff beside him. Judaeans don't seem to like dogs, but as far as he knows they have no specific proscriptions against them. Obviously they can't eat them, but who does? Except in times of siege, of course. It's not like Romans eat dogs, but they still use them as companions and guards and for herding and hunting. Judaeans seem to despise canines and be extremely uncomfortable around them. Which is partly why Pilate likes to go everywhere accompanied by his favourite *Canis pugnax*. In the heat it often has long dewy strands – like the threads a witch might use to drip poison into a sleeping man's mouth – swinging from its sagging maw. Pontius delights in seeing the Judaeans recoil from the sight. They visibly flinch if the beast should turn its crop-eared head too sharply, as if it were a madman flicking his own seed at passers-by not a little bit of dog dribble.

Pontius takes a sip of wine and sucks air in through his teeth to feel the tannin on his tongue. 'So that is the charge is it, Kayafa? The prisoner says he has been anointed as King of Judaea?'

'As you know, Prefect, he caused uproar and stopped all trade in the Temple, but he also opposes payment of taxes to Caesar and claims to be the Messiah King, descended from David.'

'Well, in that last regard at least he is probably correct.'

'Prefect?'

'Well, it struck me as I was having your books read to me. Solomon – King David's son – had a thousand wives and concubines and this was a thousand years or so ago. Think of all those children over that number of generations. My mathematician confirmed it: there is probably not a Judaean alive today who is not descended from David. You and the prisoner and the gangly eunuch who brings me my fucking bedtime broth are all descended from David. Probably why this land is so interminably cursed with would-be messiahs ...'

'You are wise, as always, Prefect. The prisoner Yeshua, though, claims to be the rightful king, through a line of first-born sons.'

'Yes, yes, of course. And who could doubt that such records were carefully and indisputably kept by illiterates, exiled, enslaved and decimated countless times over that thousand-year span? Not I. If a man states something so foolish as to say that he is king of a country that already has an emperor, then you would have to think that he truly believes it. And if he does, that's good enough for me.'

Pontius flicks two fingers to summon the centurion. The mastiff, now lying at the prefect's feet, looks up, hopeful that the movement beckons something of relevance to it. Disappointed, it settles down again.

'Gaius,' the prefect says.

'Prefect?'

'Crucify this man.'

'Prefect.'

The centurion motions and his troops approach the Temple Guards. With the surly uncooperative look of a gang of street-tykes being forced to make peace, the guards surrender their prisoner and the legionaries lead him away.

'What should we put on his *titulus*?' the centurion asks, for the sign displaying the condemned's wrongdoing.

'Well, legally speaking, his crime is *laesae maiestatis*,' Pontius says. Then he looks at the high priest and smiles. 'But write "*rex judaeorum*". That means "King of the Jews",' he translates, into Greek, for Kayafa, probably unnecessarily, with a further warm smile.

Kayafa protests: 'Surely it would be better described as "He claimed to be the King of the Jews"?'

'Write "King of the Jews",' Pontius repeats to the centurion. 'And write it in Aramaic and Greek as well.'

Kayafa nods shut-lipped approval, clearly aware that he is being mocked. But, then, that is rather the point of mocking.

'Have a good festival,' Pontius says to the high priest. 'Don't let me keep you.' He turns and begins to walk away, mastiff at his heel, its claws audible on the stone. But then Pontius pauses and looks back to Kayafa again.

'You know, Kayafa, some of us have a bath *every* day. Next time you wish to see me, you come into my fucking palace, Passover or not. Or I choose myself another high priest ...'

'Prefect.' Kayafa drops his head.

'These people,' Pontius mutters to himself, as he goes inside. 'These fucking people.'

'You don't think I'm dominating and cruel like these silly Jews seem to think, do you?' Pontius says, as he crouches and scratches the dog's white-blazed chest. It wags its butt stump of a docked tail. 'You know I'm trying to rule them as justly and wisely as I can, don't you? And, of course, earn a little to put aside for my dotage, as any man would.'

The dog licks his face, seemingly in agreement. Which is about as much confirmation as is coming. Pontius is pretty much resigned to the ingratitude of these bloody Judaeans. But such are the sorrows of leadership and he can't say he didn't court them. Some men are born to greatness. Some have greatness thrust upon them. And some are forced to claw it, howling to the empty heavens, from out of the bosom of mediocrity.

FORTY STRIPES, MINUS ONE

Time passes in strange ways, when you are waiting for the end of days. Paul marks its passage with lashes.

It is a few months after the split with John-Mark that Paul receives his first flogging. Elders of a Pisidian synagogue don't like his talk. Perhaps because Paul tells them that their revered and ancient Torah was given only by angels, through intermediaries, while he has spoken directly with God. Perhaps he just keeps coming back, long after they have warned him to take his new sect elsewhere. Perhaps they are baleful or savage or scared.

A physician – forehead walnut-wrinkled with thought – prods Paul's flesh and declares him sufficiently strong to take the punishment. Paul knows these procedures well enough – he has officiated over them – but even strictures laid down in Deuteronomy have their local flavours and here whippings are conducted with the condemned stretched along the ground.

Sun-baked paving warms a bare chest, heaving with apprehension. A fear that seems to create focus: with his hands bound before him, Paul notices how grubby his fingernails have grown, black sickles cut across their ends.

The elders ask him if he has anything to say – they do not know him well – and Paul quotes Lamentations:

> 'Who can carry out his will,
> unless it is the Lord's order?
> Are not weal and woe alike
> decreed by the Most High?
> Then why should mortal men complain,
> when they are punished for their sins?'

Paul continues grunting out these words, as and when breath allows him to speak, while the stripes are laid upon him. First they are just welts, but where a further lash falls across a fellow, blood begins to be drawn. It runs in lines down Paul's ribs and is splattered by the whip and flicked into the air, drops flying like augur birds. But God is in Paul's heart and chest and head, and Christ is in him and he is in Christ; and like this, the lash is of soft leather and the whip hand is not heavy.

Paul was sentenced to forty lashes, the maximum the Torah allows. But, as practice dictates, the punishment is stopped at thirty-nine. The missing blow is a sympathy, and a surety against accounting error.

Barnabas and some other brothers have procured a handcart and they lay Paul in this, face against the grain, and wheel him to the house of a supporter, where his wounds can be dressed and he can recover. At every jolt of the wheels into a rut or hole, Paul groans, louder than any noise he made during the punishment itself, as if he used up the last of his resources in that demonstration of resolution.

Three buckets of water are made red in the cleansing and still the bandages bleed through. Paul sits hunched, the pain squeezing everything but itself out of his mind. When finally the exhaustion draws him to sleep, or he passes out, Paul looks almost contented. And he whispers something as he drifts away, a word that might be 'atonement'.

* * *

The elders' warning is finally heeded, though, and once Paul is sufficiently recovered, he and Barnabas move on. A two-man odyssey of wandering Jews. But they leave behind them a nascent group of believers. Men and women newly convinced by the fearful yet thrilling message that this very generation exists on the brink of the Kingdom of God: that the day of reckoning is coming and now – thanks to their salvation – they will be transformed from vile bodies into imperishable, indescribable, everlasting splendour when it does.

* * *

Many Jews – not only the Sadducees – do not believe in resurrection or immortality. Though it is perhaps a creed of the wealthy and the blessed: to trust that God gives men their just deserts during life. A majority of Romans, too, think we come from nothing and return to it. The maxim *I Was Not, I Was, I Am Not, I Care Not* is carved on Roman tombs so frequently that it is reduced to acronym.

Romans make offerings to their gods, but for many this is akin to a transaction, performed through civic duty, rather than a truly spiritual exercise. Those Gentiles more mystically inclined may gravitate to the elective initiation sects of the mystery religions, which promise individual, intimate relationships with loving gods, as well as eternal life. Sects that are distinct, yet similar to each other, and perhaps also to another faith, currently still some way from achieving a finished form at its journey's end.

* * *

Road systems designed for the rapid deployment of Roman armies serve just as well an itinerant missionary like Paul. Built of dense-packed gravel, atop a bed of rock, crested in the middle to encourage water runoff, paved with hewn stone, bound with kerbs and drainage ditches, they are a marvel of efficiency.

Back in Judaea, paths are still flowing things, living things; if a tree falls, or boulder tumbles, or a stream moves its course, or a succession of people simply change the route to take in a vantage point, a path can shift. Here roads are laid and constrained by the Roman machine. And it is easy to feel appreciative of that machine, with a new Roman name and a scroll of recommendation and the realization that, were it not for Rome, there would not exist roads as fine as these.

* * *

The second time that Paul is sentenced to the forty lashes less one, he shows those who condemn him that letter from Sergius Paulus, in hope that fear of Rome may stay the punishment. But the enforcers only laugh and say that if they were in Cyprus then a letter from the governor of Cyprus might very well hold weight. But this is Galatia, friend, go back to Cyprus, if that is where you are loved. And one of them says he has a letter from his brother in Sardis and they are still laughing as the whip hand falls. And Paul knows they are right – not to laugh, not to reject his revelation, but they are right that a letter is not sufficient. If he were a Roman citizen, then they could not do this. If he were a Roman he would have the right to appeal to Caesar himself. A Jew caught whipping a Roman citizen would find himself beaten with Roman rods. But only at vast expense can such citizenship be bought and Paul has little enough left of the money the community at Antioch gave them to live on. New believers provide a bed for him to recover upon, face pressed into the pallet, and they buy balms for his wounds and donate money for his onward journey, but funds sufficient for Roman citizenship are as distant as the drifting griffon vultures.

* * *

Paul's back is time-healed and strong once more, when – outside another synagogue in another city – he receives his third set of the thirty-nine. The pain is not a thing to which anyone but a madman could become accustomed, but Paul is getting somewhat habituated. He knows by now that he can take such scourgings and survive them, so his fear is lessened. He finds anger rather in its place. Fury that these Jews who flog him reject the gospel he brings them. And something – the Holy Spirit or the delirium of laceration – sends the text of Jeremiah into his pain-addled mind: *Before I formed you in the womb I knew you, before you were born I set you apart; I appointed you as a prophet to the Gentiles.*

The realization comes as quickly as the lash descends. Of course: if the scriptures held well-hidden foretellings of the coming of Jesus, why would they not also predict the coming of Paul? And was not Paul set apart from birth, just as Jeremiah wrote? Then Paul must be that prophet to the Gentiles. The leather strikes and proves the truth of it. The scars of earlier rejections by Israelites interlace with the stripes of blood on Paul's back, which criss-cross in a fisherman's net. For Paul is a fisher of men: Paul is the Apostle to the Gentiles. The fact is scored into his body, as if in a script of blood. Paul is carried once more to a haven, to be nursed by friends and followers, too agonized and bewildered even to know which way his spit would fall, if his mouth wasn't too dry to spit. But he remembers those words; a man can hardly forget being chosen by God.

I appointed you as a prophet to the Gentiles.

* * *

Twice more Paul is flogged, before his first epic journey is done. Five times in seven years he is publicly whipped by diaspora Jews, who think he is a perverter of the Torah, or a troublemaker, or both. It is understandable, perhaps, that a man so brutalized should begin to see each torturer not as a person but as a people. And it would be a mighty man indeed who would not, at least subconsciously, start to withdraw the great good that he has, the secrets he thinks he has been shown, from such a people.

Thirty-four Years after the Crucifixion

Two old men – beards of bone-grey – circling one another, like stiff-legged gladiators. Though wrinkled, withered and diminished from who they once were, they both look of a type who might have wielded a weapon when in their fluorescence. They are unarmed now, though, nothing to battle with but their wits and perhaps arthritic fists, should it come to that. Their arena is just the main chamber of an apostle's apartments, but followers and servants and a Roman guard have nonetheless formed intuitively into a girdle of spectators around their master and the man he argues with. If he even is a man, this eternal pursuer, for their master has called him more than once a *Servant of Satan*.

Paul used to believe that the future was out there waiting for him, but time has taught him that the thing lurking around the next corner is invariably the past. Sometimes the past emerges as an ill-suppressed memory and sometimes it comes as a person, this person: Cephas, the old, stony nemesis.

'So here he is again,' Paul says, 'the man of threes: the third Pillar of Jerusalem, the third disciple, who leaped to deny our Lord three times, before the cock could even crow. And three times I've asked God to rid me of him too. Yet he's back.'

Cephas still has something toughened about him, but he is age-dried and seamed now, like well-seasoned wood. 'Yes, I've caught up with you again,' Cephas says, 'and I'll keep coming after you until the grave claims one of us, or you stop peddling your lies.'

'The gospel I preach is not of human origin. I didn't receive it from any man, nor was I taught it,' Paul says. 'I received it by revelation direct from Jesus Christ, so how can it be lies?'

'But can anyone really be educated for teaching by visions? And if the correct way was to be shown by vision, then why did Yeshua live with and preach to waking men for a whole year? How can we believe that he appeared to you, when your sentiments are so opposed to what he taught during his life?'

'Why can't you understand that He must have been changed by death? You who knew Him in the flesh know Him no longer ...'

'Changed, perhaps, all things can alter, but to become opposites? Impossible! They tell me you now preach that followers of The Way must be subject to Caesar and his governors, that all authority has been established by God. That whoever rebels against Rome is rebelling against what God has instituted.'

'Of course: rulers hold no terror for those who do right, but only for those who do wrong. Caesar is God's ruler and protects those who obey. But if you do wrong, be afraid, because rulers will bring the sword when there is reason to. They are God's servants, agents of wrath to bring punishment on the wrongdoer.'

'Spoken like the Temple Guard groveller you once were, but that isn't what Yeshua thought, that isn't what he said. The Romans bleed our lands. God didn't appoint them to rule us any more than the Egyptians, or Babylonians, or the Seleucid despots whom the Maccabees defeated. Your gospel is so opposed to what Yeshua believed that it simply cannot have come from him. He was executed by Rome, have you forgotten that?'

'He wasn't executed,' Paul says. 'He surrendered himself to be our redemption offering. He was the Passover Lamb, who atoned for the sins of the world. That's why He was sacrificed on the Passover.'

'Yeshua surrendered to save those of us who were with him that night, not the world. And he wasn't even crucified on the Passover – it was the day before.'

'Details, details, what difference does a day make?'

'Time means nothing to you, I know. You think you spoke with a vision for a single hour and became an apostle through that. If you truly are an apostle, then preach Yeshua's words, those he spoke in life, expound his meaning, love his disciples, don't fight with us who knew him. Instead of slandering me and reviling the preaching that I heard myself in person, become once again our fellow-workman.'

Paul turns to the circle of his followers now. 'You hear how the poison of vipers is on his lips. I let him under my roof only so that you could witness for yourselves the blasphemy of the false brothers. But if Cephas, or those others, or even an angel from Heaven, should preach a gospel other than the one I preached to you, let them be cursed by God! I repeat: if anybody preaches to you a gospel different from what I tell you, let them be cursed by God! This dog, this evildoer, this mutilator of foreskin flesh, would lead you away from the path of Jesus and back to the ways of the Jews.'

'But Yeshua was a Jew, a devout Jew, and to follow The Way to its fullest you should become Jews.'

'See? I am not lying, the messenger of Satan confesses it with his own tongue. If this agitator is so obsessed by circumcision, why doesn't he cut the rest off too? I wish he would go the whole way and castrate himself.'

At this Cephas lets out a curse of exasperation, as a child might at one who has bested, not his argument, but his self-control. He comes at Paul with poultry-skin hands extended in a shaky grip, as if to grasp his throat and throttle. Magnified by Cephas's great size and the tremors of age, the act looks exaggerated, almost comic, as an actor might perform it, so that those at the back of the amphitheatre could see. Perhaps Cephas would have restrained himself again, but Demas and Silas thrust themselves quickly in his path anyway. Then Manius draws his *gladius* and raises the tip up at Cephas's face, and like this Cephas is forced out of the still open door, though in his prime he might have thrown all three of them through it closed.

* * *

So even this vast city, it seems, is not large enough to contain both Paul and Cephas. The Way has long since passed a parting of the ways. But now one route or the other must be forbidden. One path must be blocked with felled trees and covered with cut brush until the wild reclaims it and humankind forgets that there ever was a track along there. The winning trail must be broadened and marked, laid straight and solid like the roads of Rome, paved with hewn stone, bound in with kerb and ditch. There can be only one right way. Intersection is heresy, if all roads lead to Rome. The alternative route must be hidden and returned to the forest; it must get overgrown until even the wolves forget it was once a path.

* * *

It is words that will win this struggle. The writer of the story chooses the ending. The teller decides the truth. And later Paul continues his tale to Useful.

'In Antioch, it was, upon return from the successes of my first missionary journey, that this still-weeping wound was carved open. Though it would be some time before the pus and fester took hold. Assisted by the Holy Spirit, I had founded daughter churches and communities of believers right across the provinces of Pamphylia, Pisidia, Phrygia and Galatia, from the viridescent Mediterranean Sea to the tusks of the Taurus Mountains. I preached in sombre synagogues, and market squares amid the sing-song cries of sellers and the hubbub of slaves and housewives. I was spat upon and stoned, flogged with rods and lashes, laughed at as a madman and revered as a god. But in each place I visited, I planted a seed, which through God's grace would continue to grow. In every city I located a patron who could become the foundation stone and host a gathering, where baptisms and the sacred meal rites could be performed, where believers would leave the sins of the flesh at the door and inside be one with the spirit and rejoice in prayer, united in fellowship and God's love. But, at the end of seven years – exhausted by my efforts and the innumerable hardships suffered – I returned to the mother church at Antioch, from where we had first set off. And I spent two years there, not at rest, but regaining strength and nursing the already large community, teaching and preaching, commemorating and telling of all the wonders we had achieved, and innovating ways to glory God and Lord Jesus.

'But then there came to Antioch false believers, secretly brought in, like snakes that slide through the holes gnawed by rats. They slipped in to spy on the freedom we enjoyed in Christ Jesus. False brothers crept into our church at Antioch. Men sent up from Jerusalem infiltrated our ranks, intent on disruption and provocation and informing upon us, to enslave us to old ways. Individuals of The Way came from Judaea and started teaching the Greek brothers, *Unless you are circumcised according to the custom of Moses, you cannot be saved.*

'And they caused such dissension and turmoil – because more than half the devotees at Antioch were non-Jews by then – that it was decided that Barnabas and I would go to Jerusalem to debate it with those apostles who were supposedly such great ones – those who measured themselves by themselves and compared themselves with themselves – those reputed to be the Pillars of the Church: James and Cephas and Jochanan.

'So, fourteen years after I had last met with them, I went again to Jerusalem.'

Nineteen Years after
the Crucifixion

Inside the Jerusalem Temple complex, the initial tiled precinct – twice as large as the Forum of Rome – is open to all people. Here, dilated-eyed animals for sacrifice are sold and money is changed and trinket-sellers peddle. But an elegant low balustrade separates this area from the holier courtyards of the Mount and from the Temple proper. And around this easily crossed but symbolic guardrail, there are numerous near-identical notices, each one stone-carved in a different tongue, and in every language the signs state: *No Gentile is to enter beyond the balustrade into the forecourt around the Sanctuary. Whoever is caught will have himself to blame for his subsequent death.* That is how it has always been in Judaism: Gentiles are welcome to admire from a distance but they are not allowed in through the Beautiful Gate, clad with golden vines, where the Levites sing, unless they first convert.

Which is why Jochanan can't really see how they got to this present problem with The Way. It's not even as if Yeshua left any doubt over his views. He was always saying that The Way was strictly for the lost sheep of Israel. And when the Messiah

188

sent out his Sanhedrin council to spread the word, he explicitly told them – though it hardly needed saying – *Do not go among the Gentiles or enter any town of the Samaritans*. When a Canaanite woman asked him to heal her daughter that time, Yeshua more or less called her a dog – about the strongest insult there is among the Jews – and told her that dogs couldn't eat the children's food. Yeshua was no lover of Gentiles. So why must there now be a debate about Gentiles joining?

* * *

When Jochanan and his brother Jacob joined The Way, they stumbled into it. They emerged from forty days hidden in the caper scrub – sharing caves with the sand cats and tuft-eared caracals – onto a bend of the Jordan river, to discover a multitude gathered there. An orderly line of a people who ordinarily know no queues. All waiting on the silt banks to be baptized, apparently unafraid of crocodiles, drifting timber with eyes as old and cold as flint. But, then, there were too many fearful things in that land for anyone to be afraid of them all. There were countless dangers in the wilderness nights, and Jochanan and Jacob were two.

Though Jochanan was still weakened from his wound at that time – he was led by his brother, riding on a stolen camel. A beast still clear in the realm of memory: draped in a colourful collage of blankets, the wooden pommel of a baggage-saddle barely visible from beneath them. Its eyes watery and weeping, lashed like a harem girl's. Petulant lower lip, and knees dry and cracked as parched earth. How it used to scratch its neck with a split-toed front foot, in a way impossible for a mule or a donkey. They named the camel Herod Agrippa because it was gangling and stupid, yet arrogant and wilful, like some entitled young royal.

But it wasn't the theft of the camel that led to the brothers' flight: Herod was merely the means of escape. Jochanan couldn't have made it a mile on foot at the time. He barely survived as it was.

The act itself was a quarrel with a tax-farmer, a *publicanus*. Jochanan and Jacob had been two-thirds of the way across a thin footbridge and in plain sight when the tax-farmer set off. Yet still he expected them to turn back, to make way for him and the two legionaries who accompanied him. He said that the camel carrying their chattel couldn't turn around. And, in that at least, he was probably correct. With the wisdom of reflection, perhaps the brothers should have retreated and sucked up their pride. But they didn't. They were both cursed with fierce tempers, though that wasn't why they were called the Sons of Thunder.

There was yelling and swearing in at least three languages, maybe more. But the brothers didn't turn back and they couldn't make way, and it eventually became apparent that, on a narrow and strangulated bridge, fishermen's knives were of more use in a fight than long Roman spears, which could be caught in hand and stepped inside. And Jochanan and Jacob, bred and raised in hauling nets, had arms and shoulders more powerful than any soldier's. So the tax-farmer had a smile slashed across his haughty, traitorous mouth and he was tumbled into the creek, with a screech like a goat-kid torn from its mother. And the first legionary had an iron blade, sharpened that morning with Galilee stone, thrust up under his leather breastplate into the clutch of amorphous organs that men need just as much as fish do. But the second Roman let go of his spear and drew his sword and put a wound across Jochanan's throat, before Jacob could force him to the ground. The cut was already made, before Jacob could put the Roman to the floor of the bridge and beat him to death with his own shield. Repeatedly slamming it into the man's head until first his helm came off and then the crown of his head came off, like the lid of an amphora, revealing grey furls like crab gills. But even though Jacob killed a Roman with his own shield – caved in his face and carved off the top of his skull – plastering with blood the shield's blasphemous Thunder Bars, that wasn't why the brothers were called the Sons of Thunder.

Jochanan was amateurishly patched, by a fisher-brother who knew a lot about knots and nets but little about bandages. And they fled then, Jochanan camel-carried like a sack of spice, into the hills. Jacob led them on foot, leaving a deliberate trail at first, outside inhabitation, so that their crime – if killing traitors and invaders is a crime – would not be blamed on others. Only when they had left civilization behind did he start to choose paths across rock and through streambeds. Only then did he start to leave false clues and dust their true tracks.

Jochanan was cut across the throat – he could hear his own breath whistling through the wound – and carried far into the wilderness. And yet somehow he survived. It was a miracle. But then, as Jochanan realized when it began to seem possible that he would not die, what isn't? The sun and the clouds and the ants and the words. They are all miracles. Every life and every day is a miracle. There is nothing so special about not dying, except that it allows you to witness every other miracle as if for the first time. It rapts you with awe at the overbearing wonder of everything and teaches you what it means to love, to truly love. To love your life and your family and your land and your brother Jacob and your God.

And weeks later, on a path they thought to lead them home again, among the silver of tamarisk and willow, the brothers stumbled upon The Way.

* * *

And now The Way has led Jochanan here, to this meeting of leaders. Jacob is not in attendance: The Way led Jacob to his death, seven years back. Beheaded, angry until the end, a true Son of Thunder. Though the trial court, if you could call it that, called him Son of Zebedee.

Zebedee their father is dead, too, of course. He was a big man, in a small way, Zebedee. *I'm world famous, in Galilee*; that was his joke. It's important to be someone's son. And Jochanan was always proud to be Zebedee's. Then suddenly Zebedee was gone and so was Jacob; and Jochanan was a singular *Son* of Thunder, but one of Three Pillars. The Three Pillars of The Way, who now apparently must rule on the admission of Gentiles.

The man Saul, who says that he should henceforth be called Paul, lays his case before them. Jochanan last saw him fourteen years ago. Back then Saul had the look of a wild, half-fledged creature; by now he must be the thing that he is. But what that thing is, Jochanan couldn't say.

Paul states his case: that Gentiles must be admitted, because divine visions told him that he is the Apostle to the Gentiles. And it's hard to refute him without calling him a liar. It's hard to deny him when he has achieved so much, founded so many communities. When he has been stoned, flogged and beaten.

All the disciples carry a rock of guilt within them, a stumbling-stone suspicion that their belief at Gethsemane was not sufficient, that it was they who failed Yeshua; that it was they who betrayed him. Paul, of course, was not with them, but you need only to look at him to see that he does not share this burden of doubt. Faith floods from him. But does that mean he's right?

He lays his message before them, the things he has been preaching. John-Mark once reported some worryingly odd beliefs in Paul, but John-Mark isn't in Jerusalem at the moment: he has left on a solo undertaking, and Paul doesn't mention any such things. He presents the gospel that he has preached among the Gentiles most respectfully to the Three Pillars. Wanting to be sure, he says, that he has not been in error, running his race in vain.

Jochanan and Cephas both tend to follow James's lead – it is hard not to, when he is so much his brother's brother – and James seems impressed by Paul's stories. But Jochanan notices that Paul's smile fades faster than it ought to as he turns away. It doesn't linger quite as long as a smile should, but is instantly snuffed, like a candle flame.

James the Just tells Paul that the Pillars must discuss the matter among themselves and that he will be summoned when they are done.

Paul's posture alters at the word 'summoned' and momentarily he looks as though he is about to say something, but then he doesn't.

* * *

Through the slit window of the room where the three talk, they can see smoke sailing skywards from the Temple's sacrificial pyre. It marks the spot where Yahweh gathered the dust to mould Adam. The same location as where Abraham, faithful to God's command, would have sacrificed Isaac and where King David then built the first Temple. It is a strange thing to debate the admission of Gentiles in such a place.

'But these are strange times,' Cephas says.

'More than strange: the times are treacherous,' the Just One says.

Jochanan nods. The meaning is clear: even peace of the occupied, hostile form endured in Judaea seems to be coming to a close. Mere months ago, a Roman soldier on the Antonia battlements bared his hairy arse and waved his uncircumcised cock and swore obscenities down at the Temple crowds, gathered for the Feast of Unleavened Bread. The fiery youths of Jerusalem of course took up in revolt and the Romans charged into the very Temple plaza and the young men were hacked down and hundreds of innocent people died; butchered, or trampled in the stampede to get away from the violence.

Judaea but barely survived the threat of the placing of a statue of mad Caligula in the Temple. The catastrophe – which would certainly have meant open battle – was only averted by the emperor's death. But the threat remains: a new emperor was heralded, as swiftly as a crow drops to a corpse, and if a blasphemous statue is installed, war will follow.

Perhaps the worst was in Alexandria, where Jews settled for three centuries were massacred by those they had lived alongside. Exterminated with a systematic horror for which a word does not yet exist. As if they were some vermin being rinsed from the city. Venerable men who had sat on the Alexandrian Senate, were flogged to death like criminals. Free men were sold into slavery. Whole families were burned alive in pyres of their own furniture, and scorched and tortured bodies were scattered promiscuously about the streets. The survivors were confined to one cramped and crammed quarter, with death the penalty for leaving it, even to buy bread. And the Roman governor not only approved it all, but crucified those who made complaint.

In Rome itself, this very year, many Jews have been expelled. Forced to leave the city they called home. In waves they have flooded to Jerusalem, in states of desperate hunger and poverty that the Nazarenes have done their inadequate best to alleviate.

Something is on the wind. Things have not got so bad that they cannot get worse. And the new age that is to come may well be birthed in blood, for what isn't?

Which is why James finally rules: 'Better that the Gentile followers remain separate than that men who will not die for Judaea are called brother. Hate against the nation is on the rise. We should be strengthening our blood, not diluting it. So, for those who don't wish to convert fully to Judaism, let us not oblige them, at least for the present. We cannot deny what Paul has achieved in the communities he has founded, and perhaps they can help to fund our work with the poor ones.'

* * *

So Paul is called to hear the Pillars' answer, standing before that window where the Temple smoke is visible, drifting up into the nostrils of the unknowable.

'We have reached the decision that those Gentiles who are turning to God shouldn't be impeded. You say that Greeks can't rest on the Sabbath, or else they will lose their jobs, and that they balk at circumcision. Our judgement then is that, to begin on the path of The Way and have a share in the new age that is to come, they need only worship the Lord of Hosts, to the exclusion of all other gods, and follow the simple instructions given to Noah, before the times of Abraham and Moses, such as were once obeyed by foreigners who stayed in the land of Israel. Namely, that they of course do not commit crimes and that they also cease idolatry, sexual immorality, blasphemy and the eating of meat with undrained blood still within it. They must not consume blood! If you agree to these rules, then, since you believe that God told you to preach to the Gentiles, you can continue to do so and we will go to the circumcised.'

Paul smiles, a bright smile, close to laughter in its joy.

'But one further thing,' James says. 'Just as all the Jews of the world send their silver shekel to the Jerusalem Temple, so your Gentile converts must make donation to The Way, to support the poor ones here in Jerusalem. And you, Paul, are charged with ensuring that this is faithfully carried out. Do you agree to all these terms?'

Paul agrees, cheerfully and readily, and crab-scampers out sideways, in bandy-legged haste to tell Barnabas and those others who came with him from Antioch.

Jochanan leaves too, to take a walk outside the walls. Noticing suddenly how confined the room is.

During his time following The Way, Jochanan has come to be good at reading faces, and it seems to him that Paul might have left believing something different from what James meant. Though maybe the fault was with James, because what does that really mean anyway? *You go to the Gentiles and we to the circumcised?* In Antioch there were both, they were all mingled, surely that was the problem: God has forbidden wearing clothes of two cloths; forbidden working with beasts of different species yoked together; forbidden sowing mixed seeds in the same field; forbidden growing grain or herbs in a vineyard. What, then, is a community such as Antioch, if it is not just such jumbling as that?

But James must know best. Jochanan just needs to walk it off.

The Kidron valley is so thick with growth that it is hard to picture it as charcoal and cinder, as it was that blackest night. The emerald grass has dried to amber in the sun's heat, bleached almost to hay while it still grows, but poppies survive amid it, even if a little bowed. A sparrow balances on the stalk of one, which cannot possibly hold its weight. And yet it does. A small miracle for Jerusalem.

Jochanan picks a blade of the grass and sniffs it, as if it might be new. Feels the texture of it in his fingers. It's all a miracle. God created all of it. Maybe that's all that matters. But Jochanan knows that isn't all: God told them what they must do and what they must not do and how they must worship Him and He was extremely precise about it. And Yeshua agreed: *Do not think that I have come to abolish the Torah or the Prophets; I have not come to abolish the Torah but to complete. I tell you the truth: until Heaven and earth pass away, not the smallest letter, nor the least stroke will pass from the Torah until everything is accomplished. Anyone who breaks the least of the six hundred and thirteen Torah commands and teaches others to do the same will be called least in the Kingdom. For I tell you that unless your righteousness surpasses even the Pharisees and the teachers of the Torah, you will certainly not enter the Kingdom.*

That was what Yeshua said, and Jochanan can't see how that left a single strand of doubt, not even sufficient to perch a sparrow.

The Penalty
Begins

Unlike Judaeans, the legionaries are beardless, shaven, their faces rough and blotched like stored fruit. Most have teeth missing; gaps like the battlements of the fifty-feet-high walls that surround this palace courtyard, where the foreplay of the death warrant will take place.

Every man sentenced to crucifixion is first scourged. So the prisoner is stripped of his fine white-linen robe, which by now is grubbied and torn from a night of manhandling. Then he is tied by his shackled hands to one of the stone pillars of the colonnade. Every second pillar around the courtyard has a metal ring set in it. They are too high for tying horses, but perfect for holding a man's hands above his head and preventing him collapsing to the ground. They must, therefore, have been fabricated and fixed in the pillars specifically to expedite the scourging process. The logistical difficulties of flogging and then crucifying, often tens, sometimes hundreds, occasionally thousands, of men at a single session, should not be underestimated.

The soldiers assigned to the duty are doubtless pleased to discover that there is so far only one man to be flogged today. A full shift spent at the whip will leave your shoulder muscles aching.

Unknown languages sound strangulated and devilish. The legionaries do not speak the tongue of the prisoner. Neither does he understand theirs. But, then, there is nothing they need to say to each other.

The Roman flagellum is not like the lash of the Jews. Though the prisoner has doubtless seen the torn and tortured bodies of crucified men, he has probably never before seen the device that inflicted such rending: three plaited leather ropes, the length of grown wheat, attached to a wooden handle and on each strand, shards of lamb pelvis, bored and knotted in place at intervals. The prisoner is a brave man, but Nature does not equip men to suffer such things as this: he trembles like a river willow and the cloth about his loins blooms warm.

The two legionaries designated as lictors alternate blows. The pieces of lamb-bone, chipped and cracked from much use, bite into the condemned's skin and splatter blood up the arms of the Romans. Occasionally they stop their work to wash themselves, or to have a drink of diluted sour-wine.

The prisoner is lacerated, head to foot, rended and torn. Slick with blood and sweat and urine. He hangs – all but totally suspended now – from his wrists, pressed onto the front of his feet, soles visible, as though he would collapse but for the pillar supporting him, which undoubtedly he would.

Some call the pre-crucifixion scourging the 'half-death'. There is no limit to the number of blows the lictors can deliver; it is left to their conscience and the necessity that the condemned must not be killed, not yet. Though accidents can and do arise. No one is perfect.

But during the everyday happening of the scourging, an unusual thing occurs: from over the high walls there comes shouting. Even at this early hour, word must have spread that this prisoner has been condemned and is held here. The crowd – for by their voices they must be many – begin to call for his release.

'Free Yahushua bar Josef.'

'Free Yeshua of Nazareth.'

'Free the Galilean.'

'Free the Rabban.'

'Free the Messiah.'

The crowd yells its demands. Pleadings near certain to be in vain, for, even by the standards of Roman prefects, Pontius Pilate is renowned as insolent and grievously inhumane. And it is not as if Rome is in the habit of releasing prisoners on the whim of a conquered people.

But what else can those who love the prisoner do, what else is there? If they could choose, they would never start from here. But since they cannot choose, the crowd continues shouting.

'Free Yahushua.'

'Free Yeshua.'

'Free the King.'

'Free the Nazarene.'

The clamour grows as more join the throng. The people who cheered Yeshua into Jerusalem as a saviour-hero mere days ago could not forget him so soon. And in the way that crowds will, the demonstrators soon begin to slide into rhythm, begin to slip into shouting the same thing, the name by which many know the prisoner best: as the son of the Father.

'Free Yeshua bar Abba,' they cry, many also crying tears, which streak dusty cheeks and tumble to the pale Jerusalem stone.

'Free Yeshua bar Abba.'

'Free Yeshua bar Abba.'

'Free Bar Abba.'

'Free Bar Abba.'

'Free BarAbba.'

'Free Barabba.'

'Free Barabbas.'

The memory of this cry will linger. It will echo down the ages, but distorted, just as wails of distress can sound in the desert night like the cruel howls of wolves. It will reverberate, this shout, words twisted by time and purpose. It will echo until the people who yelled for the release of their hope and king, Jesus bar Abba, will be painted as fiends who shrieked for his death and the freedom of another man: Jesus Barabbas. A confusion, at its kindest, or an obfuscation, or a deliberate libel, but which will curse their descendants for ever.

Not the cruellest critic could say that they deserve that curse, the people here today; even so, they do not keep up their protest for as long as they should. They do not continue once the legionaries of Pilate troop outside the palace. The crowds remember the protesting multitudes – many times more numerous than they – slaughtered on these same pavements by soldiers not many months back. They remember and they disperse. That world is lost, which might have been born, had Zion arisen at this moment. The Jerusalemites yearn to erupt. But they do not. Not yet.

* * *

Inside, the prisoner is cut down, to collapse like a sack of bloody skin. Gasping for breath like a shored fish; gashes in his flesh as open as gills.

A legionary comes back from an errand with something held cautiously in his hands: it is a ring, plaited from long thorns.

'I've got a diadem for the King of the Jews,' he says, and the others cheer.

The soldier was cursing as he pricked his fingers while cutting the fronds from a spiny jujube shrub, then weaving them into shape, but the laughter of his comrades makes it all worthwhile. What is life if we can't bring a bit of joy to our friends?

He cuts his hand again, while forcing the crown onto the prisoner's head, but the others are applauding, so he continues. From the scores the thorns cut in the Jew's head, it is as if he weeps tears of blood.

Twenty Years after
the Crucifixion

Yeshua might well have approved of this community in Antioch, Cephas thinks. It is a strange thing, all right, to have Gentiles and Jews sitting down together like brothers. But strange is not the same as wrong. The prophets of old said that, when the Kingdom of God comes, every people will look to Israel for rule and guidance. Just as Zechariah put it: *In those days, ten men of every language and nation will hold tightly to each Jew by the hem of his garments saying, 'Let us go with you, because we have heard how God is with you.'* In the time shortly to arrive, the Israelites will be the priests of all the world. So perhaps these people here at Antioch are just the first fruits of that.

This is Cephas's debut trip to a foreign land, if you don't count Samaria, and you can't count Samaria. Scar-throated Jochanan didn't think it was a good idea for Cephas to come. But Cephas is heartened now he's arrived to witness this curious symbiotic synagogue and to see it so thriving.

Because it's all very well for Jochanan to say that things should be this way, things ought to be thus and such. Things are as they are. It's been a year since the meeting with Paul at Jerusalem, and Cephas thought it was past time that one of the Pillars visited the following at Antioch, to see what it was all about.

The church meets in a riverside warehouse, which a wealthy merchant has given them on permanent loan. It was damaged in an earthquake and parts of its stone walls still bear the marks of that, cracks jagged and random as the tracks of startled hens.

Paul, Barnabas and some of the other brothers live there, in canopied quarters they have fashioned, a kind of tent-village within the building, like internal Bedouin. But any of The Way are welcome to pass by at any time, and daily they do. And all of them gather for the commensal meal and prayers, held on the first day of every week so that the Jewish brothers can continue to observe the Sabbath, but all can join in together on the following evening.

And it's on his first such evening that Cephas witnesses the collection being taken for the poor ones of Jerusalem, just as James had laid down to Paul. A Phrygian cap is passed around and each person places their donation deep within it, so that no one can note how much or how little a fellow can afford to give. But by the time it is returned to Paul, the cap is bulging and heavy, lumpen like a face stung by bees.

Perhaps they give especially generously because Cephas is here. It is hard for Cephas not to get a little swept away by his own celebrity. He is the first person these Antiochenes have met who knew Yeshua and they beam and gaze at him. Cephas is, of course, recognized and respected by many in Jerusalem too. But here believers even try to touch the blue-threaded tassels of his robe, as if they expect a little magic thereby to come upon them. Before the meal, some jostled and jockeyed one another for position, like boys at the beginning of a running race, to try to secure a place closer to Cephas's.

Paul tells Cephas that Antioch's dense-packed population is said to be more than four hundred thousand strong, with eighteen different ethnic districts confined within its walls. Not two years ago there were riots against the Jews and a great many died. Outside this warehouse of The Way is a city of mistrust and misunderstanding, gangs and rivalries, enmity and poverty. But in here all men are brothers and all men are fed.

And so Cephas breaks bread with them. Drivers, drovers, porters, bathhouse cleaners, tin-workers, merchants, shop attendants, carvers, coopers, labourers, blade-grinders, masons, sweepers, weavers, artisans, tanners, spinners, stallholders, tailors, sailors, silversmiths, and even some slaves. Pierced and painted and branded, with hair and hat and apparel of every folk and fashion of the Empire. It is a marvel to behold. And Jochanan probably wouldn't approve of it, but Cephas can't help feeling that Yeshua might have.

For while it's true that Yeshua never went to the Gentiles, didn't he also say, in that parable about the feast: *Go to the street corners and invite to the banquet anyone you find.* Yeshua only ever ate with Jews, it's true, but within that he dined with sinners and whores, he welcomed any who would accept his message of rededication and repentance to bring about the new age. And, when you think about it, seemingly Yeshua never expected to die – he said back then that the new age would come within his lifetime; but since he did and it didn't, everything subsequent has to be re-evaluated.

Paul calls the communal meal the Lord's Supper, Cephas notices, which is a little odd. And he reverses the normal Israelite order, first blessing the bread and then the wine. And even the blessing is unusual: 'We, who are many, are one body, for we all share the one loaf,' Paul says.

And he calls the wine the Cup of the Covenant. But aside from that, things are not so very different from community meals as the Nazarenes practise them in Jerusalem. And the table is spread with better food and Cephas has a belly for food. And the company is good. Though Paul, who sits next to Cephas, is also the most distant.

* * *

Paul has a livid blotch on his forehead. When Cephas first arrived, he thought it must be some minor injury. But over several weeks he notices that it has formed where Paul clutches his hand to his head when he seeks God's guidance or prophesies. He pushes his fingers there – as if to govern utterances threatening to overwhelmingly burst forth – so hard that the place is becoming permanently bruised. It is a visible mark of Paul's prodigious faith. But it must ache, Cephas thinks. It looks sore.

Cephas is unlettered – illiterate – and he admires Paul's learning while watching him teach the community and new converts over those first weeks at Antioch. But Paul can also seem slightly shifty somehow. Cephas can't quite batten down the sensation, much less define it, but it's as if Paul is trying to be all things to all men. Around the Jews he acts like a Jew and accentuates and exaggerates his Jewishness. Around the Greeks you would never know he was a Jew at all: he acts like one of them, like a former pagan – even his accent changes. Perhaps that's just the sign of a gifted orator, though, not disingenuous. There is no doubting that Paul has a compelling charisma. Whether he exhorts the followers to work, to pray, or to praise God in strange and startling tongues, he sweeps everyone along with his passion, like a mighty wave. Cephas half suspects that he is only really noticing little eddies of his own jealousy at Paul's great gifts.

If Cephas hadn't been chosen by Yeshua, he would still be a Galilee fisherman. His back would likely be strained and shredded as an old net by now. His face would be as dark and lined as the bruised skies before a storm. But he couldn't in all honesty say he'd be less contented. There was something to be said for the simplicity of his life before The Way. When Yeshua was still around, Cephas had felt so alive and filled with hope. But he hadn't needed to make any speeches or decisions back then; he had needed only to believe and protect. Now people look to Cephas to lead them. And Cephas doesn't know if he was formed to lead; he doesn't always know if his choices are the right ones.

* * *

James suffers from no such indecision. James is known as James the Just. And a few weeks into Cephas's stay at Antioch, certain men of James's come up from Jerusalem. At the head of them John-Mark. They wear black travelling cloaks and they bring black news.

'I've spent the last year and more passing through all the communities of Paul's I could find,'

John-Mark tells Cephas in private. 'I back-tracked along the route he took in founding his groups. And things are not as he told you they were.'

* * *

Burdened with the news, Cephas begins to draw back and separate himself from the Gentiles of Antioch. He no longer eats with them. The other Jews follow his lead. The hall divides into two. Split and separated, like the shell of a forbidden oyster.

* * *

Paul is energized and angered. He doesn't even take Cephas aside. He confronts him publicly.

'You are rending our community, Cephas. You're a hypocrite: you were eating with the Gentile brothers contentedly and suddenly you break with them just because certain men have come from James.' His face is puce with rage, the whole of it turned the same shade as the self-made bruise on his forehead.

'But I didn't know what I now do,' Cephas says. 'You haven't been telling us the truth. With lies you might get ahead, Paul, but you can never go back. Yes, I sat with the Gentiles, but I presumed we were not eating forbidden foods. But now I hear you have been telling your followers to *eat anything that is sold in the meat market without raising any question about it on the grounds of conscience.* So how can I trust in what you serve us? How can I know it is not pork? How can I know that the meat was not strangled, or sacrificed to idols, or boiled with the blood still in it?'

'You have lived like a Gentile in the weeks that you have been here, Cephas, not like a Jew. How is it that you suddenly remember to follow Jewish customs only when John-Mark comes? You told me yourself how with Yeshua you picked and ate corn on the Sabbath. Why was it all right to break the Torah then but not now?'

'Yes, we did one time. We were starving and we were on the run. The Sabbath does not apply to men on the march. But in any event, like the Pharisees say, the Sabbath was made for man, not man for the Sabbath. And there was precedent: King David's men ate the consecrated bread, so why shouldn't King Yeshua's men have picked corn? It wasn't that we wanted to break the Torah, we had to and it was allowable. It is not the same thing as in a period of plenty to eat meat sacrificed to idols, as I might have in your Lord's Supper. Can you tell me with any surety that I haven't?'

But John-Mark interrupts before Paul can reply. John-Mark's dark eyes are as cold as those of Paul are on fire. 'Why do you even call it the Lord's Supper?' John-Mark says. 'Those are the words they use in the rituals of mystery religions. They have no meaning in Judaism.'

'Who was speaking to you?' Paul says. 'You who deserted us at Perga and I hear have since been spying on our fellowships, following our path, like a jackal hoping to poach the prey of a lion. How can you of all people confront me, John-Mark, you who witnessed the miracle of my blinding the false preacher Elymas?'

'I saw a man taken from the room, struck sick. But I couldn't say that I saw you do it and I couldn't say it was a miracle. There seem to be a lot of false preachers around of late, there seems to be a lot of blindness ... James the Just told you that your converts must follow at the least the simple restrictions given to Noah, especially not to eat blood. You have not only broken this, but you are telling them the very wine they drink is transformed into blood. Turned into Yeshua's blood! What insanity is this? If it were true, it would be cannibalism, it would be akin to human sacrifice, but since it is not true, it is blasphemy and lies. Deceits have no place in this movement. Leave rites of wine turning to blood and food turning to flesh to the magical papyruses and the devotees of Dionysius and Mithras. These things are abhorrent to Israelites and would have been to Yeshua.'

'But that is the whole point. You do not know Him. Your Jesus was a fleshly man. Mine is the resurrected Jesus. He has spoken to me directly. You cannot presume to know Him better. You know only the things that He was, not what He is.'

'What he is,' John-Mark says. 'What he is! You have been telling your followers that your Jesus is a pre-existent being, a god-spirit-thing formed from before the creation of the world. The Son of God, not as all Israel's kings were known, but as quite literally the birth child of Jehovah. After the fashion that pagans believe Alexander the Great to be the son of Zeus and Caesar Augustus the son of Apollo. Do you deny it?'

'Give up this madness, Paul,' Cephas says. He is pleading, but from a person of his size even petition can seem like a thinly veiled threat. 'Yeshua was something more than other men, of course he was. He was a prophet and a king, the anointed one. But he was not a god. I knew him. I saw him spit. I saw him shit. I saw his feet scabbed from brush and stone; hard though they were, they were mortal feet. I saw his skin blistered with mosquito bites from sunsets spent hip deep in river baptisms.

I saw him eat, I saw him piss. He was no god. There is only one God.'

'Yet you can believe this very mortal Jesus is still alive and returning to earth to bring the new age?' Paul says.

'Yes, he is now with God and will be back,' John-Mark snaps. 'Like Methuselah, King Hiram, Bithiah, Serach, the sons of Korah, Eved-Melekh, Elijah, Enoch and Eliezer. They did not die, but they were not gods.'

'But you know your scriptures better than any of us, Paul,' Cephas says, trying to be conciliatory. 'Reread the Prophets and the Torah. Don't trust only in these voices that you think you hear.' Cephas opens his arms. There is still time; he would hug Paul and end this fray. But Paul shrinks from him.

'Come to me, Paul,' Cephas says. 'Embrace me once more as a friend and we will forgive and forget your errors. These have been confusing, uncertain years for us all, but we must follow James the Just and the path that Yeshua laid in his lifetime. Return to your brothers and to the Torah.'

'The Torah of Moses was never intended to be permanent. It came only through the tongues of angels, through imperfect mediation, and now it has been superseded by the new gospel given to me directly by God.'

John-Mark folds his arms in such a way as to push out the muscles, perhaps unintentionally but with inherent menace. 'You say our laws came *only* through the tongues of angels. Only! Well, I say your words are only the words of a man. You're a liar, Saul of Tarsus, and you should leave.'

Paul looks about the hall; the Antiochenes stare at the floor, at their dust-dragged toes, at the cracks in the walls and the holes in the surfaces of things. They are not with him.

'Leave I will,' Paul says. 'I'll be glad to, happy to have you gone from my sight. And the Lord long since decreed that mine is to be a missionary existence. Come, Barnabas, old friend, let's get our things. The pilgrim road is calling us once more.'

Barnabas the Cypriot has tears not just in his eyes but down his cheeks and dripping into his beard. He looks like a cloth torn in two. But he shuffles to stand with Cephas and John-Mark.

'I love you, Paul,' Barnabas croaks, struggling to speak at all. 'You know that I do. But Cephas was Yeshua's right hand, his hearth guard, his chamberlain. James was his most beloved disciple and his brother. How can I go against them and still say that I follow The Way?'

'Even you, Barnabas, even you?' Paul looks through him. 'So be it. I will follow my own way then. We'll all know soon enough who was right. Already the axe of God's judgment is poised, eager to sever the roots of the trees. And every tree that does not produce good fruit will be hacked down and thrown into the fire.'

Thirty-four Years after
the Crucifixion

'Fire!' Useful says. He stares out of the window at Rome's night sky, now lit with a scarlet glow to the south like a shipboard sunset.

Paul looks too. 'It's a long way off,' he says, and pats Useful's knee with an affable hand. 'Nothing for us to be concerned with. Let's finish the dictation.

'So, when Cephas came to Antioch, I opposed him to his face, because he stood condemned. For before certain men came from James, he used to eat with the Gentiles. But when they arrived, he drew back and separated himself from the Gentiles, because he was afraid of those who belonged to the circumcision group. The other Jews joined him in this hypocrisy, and by their hypocrisy even Barnabas was led astray.'

Useful shakes his head in bitter wonder. It is hard to believe the troubles Master Paul has been put through by those Judaizers.

Timothy enters; his face is smeared and spattered with ash, as if in some sackcloth ceremony of mourning. 'The Circus Maximus is completely aflame,' he says. 'It's already spreading to the streets nearby.'

The Circus Maximus is the largest wooden structure ever built. Yet beneath the imported Syrian-cedar rafters of its benches and floors are the cooking fires of bakeries, pastry shops and hot-food booths; lamp-lit taverns ply their trade the night through, so the inebriated can cavort and brawl next to naked flames, all among rows of plank-walled shops, stocked with combustibles, like cloth and oil.

'That it is now ablaze is perhaps less astonishing than the fact that it has never happened before,' Paul says.

* * *

Hand bells of the *Cohortes Vigiles* – the night watch – ring out across Rome, summoning their fellows to assist and warning residents to flee.

The *Vigiles* try to extinguish the fire. But they have only buckets against what is by now a whole district in inferno. It is as fruitless as pushing the wind. They try instead to make a break against the flames – a fortress of absence – removing flammable objects from the fire's path, ramming buildings to collapse them. There are seven thousand *Vigiles*, porting heavy loads like a baggage-train of termites. But they are not enough.

The flames laugh as they leap the ancient Servian walls, once the boundary of a city long since swollen and spread beyond them. The walls are of volcanic rock, impervious to fire; but this barrier, which might have stopped Hannibal, does not block the flames for an instant. *So perish all who cross my walls*, said Rome's founder, as he murdered his brother. But the fire doesn't perish as it breaches from within. Embers fly and land behind. And more floating windblown sparks start further blazes, apparently spontaneously right across the city, adding to the rumours of arson.

Arson isn't needed for this conflagration. Rome is dry as an Ethiope's tinder; these are the dog days. Mutt-star Sirius is in the ascendancy, rising as fast as the new movement of the Christianoi, whose speed in gathering converts is suddenly out-stripping the cults of both Isis and Atargattis. The poor of Rome gaggle after every new thing.

The wealthy have largely deserted the city for their country estates, as they do at the worst heat of every summer; only those obliged to by high office remain in Rome. Many among the landed rich should shoulder some blame for the fire's spread: owners of the four-, five- and six-storey tenement blocks that form most of Rome's housing have over many decades kept extending their rentable space. Now the faces of square-jawed apartments jut out well over the streets, smelling the breath, staring into the eyes of the blocks opposite. Almost touching, as if about to deliver a head-butt or a kiss, the streets beneath their chins too narrow for two carts to pass. Many of Rome's roads are sunless even at midday, so complete is the enclosure of buildings. But now they are lit up in the black of night. Now the near-kissing frontages are finally locked – sharing spark spittle – tongues of flame licking like over-eager youths.

Horses can scream. Those trapped by the fire make a noise that most of the fleeing people have never heard before. A screech of horror more than human and less than it. The shriek of a flight animal denied its basest urge even in death. Do horses know of their own mortality? The screams proclaim that they fear death at the finish, but do they know of it before that? Perhaps they think it isn't so. Perhaps they believe in an equine afterlife, delivered by a stallion saviour.

The fire is a tidal wave now. The flames roll unstoppably onwards like the foam of breaking surf, surging and bursting through every crack and fissure, breaching the portals and the fenestrations.

On the narrow streets the people push and crush. Some draped in blankets they have soaked, which cling about them tight as clothes carved on a statue. Many holding sacks and sheets filled with their precious belongings, or objects looted, if they had nothing of their own worth saving. The encumbrances add to the struggle of making progress and to the disarray. The strong try to force their way forwards, as the strong will, shoving swirls of the frailer into the walls, slowing the whole mass. Parents try to gather little ones in danger of submerging, but can only grasp an arm and hope. Here and there a person desperate to return for a loved one or a treasure tries to fight against the tide. Struggling contraflow towards the swarm. Shouting: *my wife; my sister; my son.* Words hard to hear amid the noise of a crowd in panic and the roar of fire and the crackle of shattering timbers and the tumble of buttresses and the screams of such infidel horses as don't believe in the Great Stallion in the sky.

The air is cut with smoke and so scorching that it feels like skin itself could ignite. And some citizens flee into the sewers, preferring to take their chances with darkness and effluent. History does not record if that decision was wise, but above ground walls fall and roofs fall and Rome falls. Unconquerable Rome flees on bloodied knees, bent from the baggage on her back. Rome who rules the world is violated by flame. Walls built against siege engines are felled by embers; men who have led legions are trampled beneath the cinder-stained sandals of slaves and immigrants. And toothless children wail and toothless crones sob and dogs as toothed as Cerberus bark and howl, because even their brave jaws cannot protect their homes now.

* * *

As the fire draws closer to the apostle's apartments, Manius the one-eyed Praetorian puts a shackle on Paul and attaches it to himself, more afraid that they will be separated in the chaos than that the prisoner would actually try to escape. But it is in any case a guard's duty to chain his own wrist to his captive's, if forced to leave the site of house arrest.

They exit the building, in a ring of the followers and servants, into a stench of smoke and cries of warning and panic and loss. They head up into the hills, from which distance the city below glows, like the coals of a dying cooking-fire. Though this inferno is far from over.

* * *

For six days and seven nights the fire burns, before it is finally brought under control. By the finish, ten of the fourteen districts of Rome are levelled utterly or left as but blackened shells, husks as desolate and charred as Carthage. The Temple of Jupiter; the Palatine and the Capitoline; the Temples to Apollo, Luna and Hercules; the Villa of the Vestal virgins and numberless brothels; the palaces of Augustus, Tiberius, Caligula and Nero; the mansions of the wealthy and the tenements of the poor; booths, boutiques, barrow-shacks, pothouses, emporia and workshops; the libraries and archives for the erudition of the elite and the corn-dole warehouses that placate the plebs. All are tumbled and burned, rubble and ash, collapsed and consumed.

Considering the scale of destruction, the loss of life is not great. The *Vigiles* succeeded in the alarm, even if they were impotent against the flames. Most of the dead were either too infirm to flee or were crushed by the crowd or falling masonry in the attempt.

But now hundreds of thousands of people, fearful, filthy and destitute, are crammed into refugee camps, overcrowded and under-nourished.

And in the camps, though the coughings of encumbered lungs drown even the cries and moans of the injured, whispers can still be heard. The whispers say that Nero did this. The whispers say he has architects' plans pre-drawn, models already made, of a new city: Neropolis. The whispers say the fires were lit deliberately on Nero's orders by the Praetorian Guard.

The Praetorians, in their cloaks of black, are obvious villains. They are the only legion allowed near Rome. The emperor's protectors and the kingmakers. They guarded even mad Caligula up to a point. But they can never indefinitely repress the mass of the Roman people. The mob will ultimately have its way. Not that the mob ever knows precisely what it wants. But it knows the kind of things it likes: bread and circuses; wine and blood. The mob doesn't yet know the particulars of how this story will proceed. But it knows how stories should go. And if you do not present it with a traitor, the mob will choose one of its own. There must be a betrayer: literary completeness demands it.

Because someone started the fire, of that you can be sure. There is always agency behind evil. And who if not Nero? Nero is perhaps half-god, but the gods of Rome are many and various, quite capable of malevolence. Romans and Greeks face no confusion over how a loving God could allow such horrors. For their gods are not loving; at least not to all men, all the time. Their gods can be capricious and selfish; they have favourites and enemies. Their gods can be sly and fickle. Their gods can be lusting and self-serving. But, for all such faults, they are at least not jealous gods. They do not demand that adherents worship no other gods. They certainly don't make the claim that other people's gods do not even exist.

And yet this new cult of the Christianoi does. This new cult says exactly that. An action clearly certain to have enraged and outraged those gods who always protected Rome in the past. And these Christianoi, so it is said, believe in prophecies that the end of the world is imminent and may come through fire. How natural, then, that they should seek to start one.

So Nero's people begin to disseminate this deflecting tale. The writer of the story chooses the ending. The teller decides the truth. Rome's official handwritten newssheets – the *Acta Diurna* – are posted up city wide. And in the squalid camps and on such street corners as remain, the criers read fresh proclamations. They give the people what they need to hear.

For the mob must have its vengeance; the mob must have its blood.

Twenty Years after the Crucifixion

Lydia knew little of love.

When she was thirteen, Lydia had still been a freckled child, with showers of auburn sunspots flocking over her shoulders and even down the gentle channel that was beginning to form on her chest. And when she was thirteen, Lydia was married off. And parts of her body that were barely budded, felt still new even to herself, became groped and opened and broken.

The man who bought her – or 'wedded' her, as her father referred to the transaction – was carelessly brutish. He treated Lydia as an object among his other objects, with her perceived value apparently lying not even at the upper end of those possessions. Sometimes he would have her in the way he would have a slave-boy and he didn't care if afterwards she cried. He was vain and mannerless; full of sly gibes and cruel passions. But he did have two great virtues: he was rich and he died.

And so, while scarcely twenty, Lydia had become that rarest of things – in this world, at this time – a woman in charge of her own destiny. Lydia took over her husband's slaves and his houses and even his business. Lydia became a dealer of purple, of dye and cloth. A seller of the secretions of predatory sea snails. Waxy juices discharged in such tiny amounts that ten thousand of the spiny-shelled snails barely suffice to dye the trim of a toga. But wealth flowed in the viscous form of this liquid. Freedom – the colour of blackish, brackish, clotted blood – pooled in Lydia's vast vats of decomposing molluscs.

The mythology of the purple murex merchants was that their precious dye was first discovered by demi-god Herakles or, rather, by his dog, the mouth of which turned plum upon crunching the snails. But Lydia declined staid Herakles as her patron deity: she was a seeker after a more exotic religion.

She followed at first the cult of Attis: son of a virgin; sacrificed on a tree; resurrected from the tomb; whose body was eaten by celebrants in the form of bread. And Attis's worship was entwined with that of his consort god: Cybele, the Great Mother – *Magna Mater* – Gaia, some called her. She was foreign and mysterious and alluring; bringer of dance, wine and misrule; rider of lions and ruler of emasculated men. Cybele was a fitting divinity for an independent woman like Lydia, pleased to be free of a virile tyrant of a husband.

The priests of Cybele and Attis were eunuchs, castrated that they might be chaste and celibate for a greater place in the heavenly banquet that was to come. But who nonetheless ran amok in celebration of the mysteries to which they were party, torchlight night-time ecstasies, which eventually became tiring and troublesome for Lydia, a woman with a business to run. And there was something more than a little untoward about the castrated priests with long bleached hair, cavorting in women's clothing, with dangling earrings and flouncing pendants, made up like cheap flesh-peddlers, some with breasts of carved wood.

In gradually recoiling from the excesses of Attis and the Great Mother, but still on quest for spiritual meaning, Lydia fell into the embrace of the comforting conservatism of Judaism, which had much to commend it, with its rich and long history and its carefully codified morality.

But it was, for all that, a little bland. For those who travelled to the fiery splendour of the immense Temple at Jerusalem, covered with weighty plates of silver and gold; who saw the majesty of the high priest – in his mitre, breast-ornament of treasure stones and fringes of bells – attended by seven hundred lesser priests to make the ritual sacrifices; for those who marvelled at the Beautiful Gate of Corinthian brass, adorned with embroidered veils from India, interwoven pillars, and clusters of golden grapes larger than a man; who saw the altar awash, its gutters flowing, as if in summer flood, with the blood of countless thousands of slaughtered beasts; for those who smelled the pyre-sized piles of burning cinnamon, saffron and frankincense; who descended the steps to feel the cool, cleansing waters of the purifying baths and heard the linen-robed Levites sing; for those people it might be a different thing entirely. But in the humble, dusty little synagogue of Philippi, they read the sacred texts in Greek, prayed and debated, and Judaism was a rather plain affair.

Not that Lydia actually converted to Judaism, but she was a regular Sabbath visitor to the synagogue, outside the gates, next to the river. She was a 'God-fearer', as the Jews called them: fellow travellers, who recognized the God of Israel as an ancient and powerful deity, but were reticent of full conversion and unwilling to take on all the arduous dietary laws and proscriptions of Judaism. However, as Lydia was to discover, to her great pleasure, such things were no longer necessary for salvation.

Because one Sabbath morning a man came to Philippi's synagogue. A man of perhaps fifty, his age was hard to tell, his face darkened like a field slave's from decades of days on the road, wrinkled before time by the sun he walked under, or the Son he talked about. A man of short but sturdy stature, with crooked legs, crisp, scanty hair, a single thick eyebrow perched on a broad forehead like moss upon a rock, a bent and bowed nose, and teeth that seemed rather more an assortment than a set. The unkind might even say he was an unattractive man. But it seemed to Lydia that only those who glanced for an instant could ever say that. Not those close enough to feel his forceful eyes. Certainly not those who heard him speak. To Lydia, the man could at times seem like an angel, which perhaps he was, since, like an angel, he was a messenger of God.

And to Lydia, who had known so little of love, he sang a hymn of love.

'If I speak with the tongues of men or angels, but have not love,' he said, 'what am I?'

And because no one in the synagogue answered this riddle, he answered himself: 'I am just a clashing gong or a clanging cymbal. Even if I have the gift of prophecy and can fathom all mysteries and all knowledge, and if I have a faith that can move mountains, but do not have love, I am nothing. If I give all I possess to the poor and render over my body to hardship, I may boast of my deeds, but if I don't do it through love, I gain nothing.

'Love is patient, love is kind. It does not envy, it does not brag, it is not proud. It does not dishonour others, it is not self-seeking, it is not easily angered, and love keeps no record of wrongs. Love does not delight in evil, but rejoices with the truth. Love always protects, always trusts, always hopes, always perseveres. Love never fails.'

And it seemed to Lydia that you could forgive a lot of a person who brought to the world such words as those. It seemed to Lydia that you could forgive him anything.

* * *

Lydia was baptized, there in the river, outside the walls. She took a deep gulp of air to prepare as the preacher held her by the crown and pushed her under. She released the air, as she burst free from the water and cried, 'Abba.' She released the air and so much more was released with it. She let go of envy and enmity and injury. She let go of a hate she had all this time harboured against a deceased husband. And a place inside her, the space cleared of all those toxins, was filled with love.

* * *

Man cannot live on bread alone. But without bread he cannot live at all. And Lydia begged the evangelist and his two companions to stay in her villa awhile. They did, and her whole household was baptized too, by the stranger-angel, whose name was Paul.

Paul's message was an elegantly simple perfection of form. The Jesus he told Lydia about, though new to her, was a figure comfortably familiar from cults she had known before. And Paul's faith was linked to the exquisite tapestry of the Israelite scriptures, but without their strictures. Being attached to those ancient texts added an authority lacking in other salvation-sects, but like them, Paul's followers were promised eternal life. And Lydia retained the powerful sense of belonging that she had experienced from committing to belief in just one God; but rather than being an appendage in the synagogue, she was a fully fledged member of the *mystes* of Christ. More than that: a sponsor and founder; among the first of equals; though all were equal in the eyes of Jesus.

'Should I give my slaves their freedom?' Lydia asked Paul one day, having come to an obvious conundrum of equality. 'If we are all united now, brothers and sisters in Christ and love, how can I keep them as slaves?'

'Let those called as slaves remain as slaves,' Paul said. 'Slaves should obey their masters with fear and trembling. The new age will dawn at any moment. This generation will not pass away before these things take place, so it is best that everyone just stand as they are. Time is short. From now on those who have wives should live as if they do not; those who mourn, as if they did not; those who are happy, as if they were not; those who buy something, as if it were not theirs to keep. Because the world in its present form is passing away.'

Which is why, to Lydia's great sorrow, Paul could not stay with her for long. He had to continue to spread the word, wherever the Holy Spirit would send him. And the Holy Spirit seemed to think the further away from Jerusalem the better. Travelling with only two disciples: strong-armed Silas, who had come with Paul from the community at Antioch – where Lydia sensed there had been some kind of discord – and Timothy, a half-Jew they had recruited en route.

Lydia pleaded that she be allowed to continue to send money for their work and Paul gracefully agreed that she could.

'Because the Lord has commanded that those who preach the gospel should receive their living from the gospel. He who shepherds the flock drinks the milk of the flock. Just as those who serve in the temple share in what is offered on the altar. So give what you have decided in your heart to give. God loves a cheerful giver. If you sow generously, Lydia, you will also reap generously.'

* * *

And surely it was so because, as if by divine intervention, Lydia's profits increased dramatically only shortly afterwards: one of her slaves discovered that there was another way to get dye from the sea-snails: they do not have to be crushed; they can be milked.

The Exaction of
Penalty

Cloth is costly and the robe is fine and seamless, indivisible without irreparable rending, so the legionaries play dice, to see which of them will claim it. Strictly speaking, gambling on games of chance is illegal for Romans, though betting on contests of skill – gladiators or chariot racing – is a national pastime. But there is no one here to judge the soldiers. No one but the prisoner anyway, and who is he to judge? A crumpled mess, less like a man now than the skin of a shape-changer, something left after the creature itself has departed. But that's just the way they get, following the half-death of the scourging. He has sufficient strength remaining to suffer awhile yet.

The soldiers were sent from a far-off country to be here. They are blood-sworn to serve Rome; many will not live to retire. They cannot marry while enlisted; they have no family now, save each other; no loyalty, save to their legion and its banners. They are hardened by regular war and constant fear: death is the penalty for nearly every and any infraction of military code. The soldiers probably think themselves no crueller than other men. It was not them who made the rules. They are just obeying orders. And those orders being as they are, what must follow is this.

The prisoner is raised to his feet. He is naked save for a loincloth. It is hot under this sun but he shivers. Whatever energy his body is using to keep him alive has not left enough to keep him warm. He shakes with pain and cold. Blood, some of it scabbing, some of it wet and weeping, coats him. He looks like a corpse pulled from a burned building, so riven is his skin from the scourging, so covered with black and red. Even his teeth are maroon glazed. His beard is matted like the wool of a Passover lamb, throat cut on the altar.

Two soldiers, in their breeches and their breastplates, with their beardless faces like clay golems, bring out the crosspiece beam. It is heavy even for two of them, but the condemned man must carry it on his own. They don't make the rules. Other legionaries hold him up and they tie the olivewood rafter across his back. They fasten his wrists tight around it. If he keeps dropping it the walk will take all afternoon. It is not so far from this palace courtyard to Golgotha, but it is far enough. Being tied to the beam stops prisoners escaping or being freed in a crush of crowd. And it reminds those who watch the party pass of the fate of all who stand against Rome. The beam itself is stained with blood by the time the soldiers have finished fastening it; the wood and the ragged old ends of rope that hold it in place have been dyed, as if with madder.

And so it begins. Legionaries open the heavy palace gates and the procession leaves Rome and enters Jerusalem. Past the pedlars and the bread-sellers; the beggars and the lepers; the stockers of pots and cloth. Past baskets of mint, with their

Elysium smell of soft meadows. Past the ragged, shadeless palms. Past marbled flanks of skinless sheep, swaying in the meagre breeze.

Most of the legionaries hold javelins and carry shields, as if going into battle. Two soldiers at the front use short whips to clear space through the crowds, steel-bladed *gladii* ready drawn in their free hands.

When the prisoner walks too slowly, he, too, is whipped; though he is struggling to walk at all. There are many faces in the Jerusalem crowd who love him. None of them jeer at him – why would they, who could? People wail and people weep. Not just because they know who the prisoner is, although some of them do, but because they would weep for any man being taken by the enemy to be tortured to death. Women cry and hold their hands up to the sky. Young men tense their young men's muscles and measure distances with their young men's eyes, as they try to calculate how many others might join them if they were to rush at these Roman guards. And the young men all arrive at the same total as always: insufficient.

The soldiers try to take the broadest streets – for their own sakes, because it is harder for their spears and swords and training to protect them in narrower passages – but even still there are points where the prisoner's burden must be turned sideways to fit through. Where an arch or a cart or a stall blocks the way. There are places where the beam jams and the prisoner must be manhandled to advance.

At one such place he falls, having been dragged too fast past an obstruction. As he stumbles, the weight of the wood on his back drops him face first to the flagstone. Unable to put down his hands, the force of his jaw hitting the floor makes a crack, louder even than the dropped-log bong of the beam. The soldiers pull him up again swiftly. Eager to be gone from these narrow streets and to the open ground of Golgotha outside the city walls, where they will once more feel in full control.

The beam has a slot in it, behind the prisoner's head. It has been auger-bored, chiselled and scraped by a carpenter, so that it will lock over the post at Golgotha. Perhaps they are each numbered and this beam forms part of a pair; or maybe they are all cut to identical size, so that any crossbeam will fit every post. Romans favour such standardizations.

Which is why these legionaries all look so similar, with the overlapping plates of their armour, which deflect blows; with pattern-formed javelins, designed to bend as they strike, so that they cannot be thrown back; with shields that lock into a barrier near impervious to arrows; and with pitiless eyes that know no other way, or other world.

Further times the prisoner falls. And each time he does, dust and dirt from the street stick to the blood, so that he rises again with skin like flour-baked fish, in agony from the grit in his wounds. And each time he does, the plaited diadem of thorn branches bites as his head hits the ground. And each time he does, Jerusalemites wail and mourn.

Once, as he stumbles, a man from the crowd catches the prisoner, holds him up, takes the weight of the wood. And for a moment each of them shares the strength that flows from the other. But a legionary pulls the man away and punches the side of his head for his effrontery in stepping into the soldiers' line.

It is strange, perhaps, that the prisoner continues at all. What could the Romans do to him here that could be worse than what awaits him at the destination? Yet he does continue, as they always do.

The group hears the howling dogs of Golgotha before they even get there. The dogs stay away from the procession, wary of spear butts and boots, but they know what such spectacles mean.

Golgotha – the place of the skull – is a stony basin, with limestone-cliff walls. Once it was a quarry. Formerly men from Jerusalem took rocks from Golgotha. Now Golgotha takes men from Jerusalem.

The land has almost overrun the carved limestone in the years of unwork. Pitted earth rolling forwards, motionless to the eye, yet relentless. Faces baked hard by the merciless sun, pocked with the nest holes of birds for which the heat is a blessing, allowing them to soar on the thermals that scorch from the ground below.

The stones all around are tawny and blunt, good Judaean stones. But everything is brown and grey and tan. There is so little colour in this place. Only the sun and the blood of the prisoner break the veil of numb beige.

The ground is littered with broken bone fragments, marrow licked free by the dogs, all covered with dust now, all the same colour as the rocks. Even the dogs are sandy-coloured; sandy and skinny, with tails like ragged flags, not so far from wolves. Scavengers; predators without prey.

The dogs snarl and snap at one another. And the air is thick with the flies that have no imperative to leave this place. Their whole circle of life, emergence, maggoty crawling, feeding, mating, spawning and death, takes place within Golgotha.

The vast rock bowl is scattered with crosses, like the abandoned crutches of cured cripples. Numerous posts standing permanently in place; many of them suspending rotting corpses.

Two at least of those who dangle from the crosses are still alive. They periodically try to heave themselves up on the iron pinions with which their ankles are pierced. They both look as though they near the end now. But such things are hard to judge: some men look like that for days.

And hooded crows circle and hop and try to stay out of reach of the dogs. And jackals, too fearful of men to come down by daylight, watch from the hillsides. And a marabou stork – hunching its bald pink head into the grey shawl of its feathers, like an old man – sits upon the cliff edge, waiting; waiting as if it has been always waiting for this.

And if you could choose, you would never end it here. Not in this place, please, God, not here. But the prisoner cannot choose, so he is pushed to the earth next to a ground-lain post, either numbered or standardized. Where he drops, the dust rises, a puff of smoke as if a pot is lifted from a clay oven.

Some women, who have spent hard lifetimes lifting such pots from such ovens, have followed to Golgotha and they watch from a distance.

The Romans allow the women that place and no closer. They do not threaten them off, but their stares and spears prevent further approach. A single man is with the group of women, apparently unafraid that his presence might be seen as collusion with the prisoner. Most men are fearful of coming to Golgotha, entry into which, without permission, can in itself be seen as cause for capture. The soldiers do not arrest this man, though. Perhaps because he looks so clearly like the prisoner, because they are so obviously brothers. Seeing the two men like that is a reminder of how we all can fall: one brother clean and straight and tall; the other drenched in blood and ragged with cuts, shortly to be naked and nailed.

All men are crucified naked. They leave the world as they entered it: covered with blood, a mother howling. And so the legionaries strip the prisoner of his loincloth; they don't make the rules. Though one of them laughs at the prisoner's circumcised penis, the only part of him unstained by blood, where the loincloth formerly blotted and soaked.

'Look at that,' the soldier says. 'Imagine doing that to a little baby. These people are fucking barbarians.'

And his friend nods agreement, as he fetches the hammer.

The beam is slotted into place on the post and soldiers hold the prisoner, while one of their comrades readies the nails. They are reused, these nails. This one has probably been through the arms or ankles of others already.

Can it even be called a nail, that crude, cruel spike? It is a nail, if siege engines and sling shots are both called catapults: it is a nine-inch dark-iron wedge of a nail. It is placed at the midpoint between the prisoner's wrist and elbow, where flesh and bone are still strong enough to take the force of holding a man up without tearing free. Even so the soldier places a rough lump of wood on top of the arm as a wad; to stop the nail head, the size of a double sestertius coin, eventually pulling through. The wood also prevents that first spurt of blood going into the hammerer's eyes.

Though the soldiers always try their best, occasionally one will inevitably spike an artery – nobody is perfect – and the condemned man will bleed out quickly. This prisoner is not that lucky. But, still, it is something of a kindness to be nailed at all. Prisoners who are only tied to the crucifix often survive for many days longer.

At the sound of the hammering the women in the near distance start to shriek and clutch one another and cling to the man in their midst. A man trying to be strong, but in danger of submerging, beneath his mother and the others and the horror.

The prisoner's legs are restrained, held either side of the prone post, and spiked in turn through the heels; further bits of wood are used to ensure that they won't tear free. The lumps of wood were found on the ground. Most probably, in this treeless quarry, they are bits of former crosses.

And, as regulation dictates, the plaque with the prisoner's crime inscribed is also hammered in place. *King of the Jews*, it reads; in triplicate.

The whole mass – cross and man – is rope-hoisted and pole-pushed up by the soldiers, straining and hauling. It drops with a jolt when the post, fully upright, finds the slot of its hole in the rock. And the prisoner cries out, as that force multiplies the pain of his own weight, for the first time fully suspended from the nails. His hands are held up skywards. Fingers curled in pain, in the shape they formed at the instant the nails were struck. Frozen like that.

Now he has been raised, the prisoner beholds the woman and her son, his mother and brother.

Though he has three other brothers, this one will be her eldest now; it is he who must take care of her. The prisoner mouths something to them, but he has not the strength left to hold up his head for long.

* * *

A few hours later, he loudly cries his last words, which are, *Eloi, eloi lama sabachthani* – 'My God, my God, why have You forsaken me?'

Maybe he is trying to recite the psalm that begins with this line, using the final shreds of energy that remain to him; perhaps he is only asking what any man of faith might, in circumstances such as these.

If those who watch from a distance were still holding hope for a miracle, it has not come; at least not yet. When they realize that the prisoner's spirit has left him, the women howl and shriek the shrill ring of Middle Eastern mourning.

The miracle didn't come and the Romans did. The man died, as men will, when nailed up high, beyond the length their lungs can take. Though he died mercifully quickly: he survived only hours on the cross, when many last multiple days and some pitiable few can suffer for over a week.

Surprised at the speed of the prisoner's death, wary of trickery, a soldier pierces his side with the long prong of his spear. The blood that flows is already sluggish and the prisoner makes no gasp or groan.

The half-death of the scourging must have carried too far, or perhaps the kindness of some poison was smuggled to the man in the mêlée of the crowds, an action not uncommon among Judaeans, trying to aid the condemned in the only way they can.

Normally the corpses are guarded and left where they hang. That is part of the penalty: for the condemned, while they still live, and their families to know that the birds and beasts will take what they can reach of the body and that the rest will rot. Fear of remaining without grave or pyre is a profound extra punishment in most of the societies that Rome has subdued, but especially so in Judaea. Crucifixion does not only consist of the public dishonour and the inhuman agony, but also this final assault: that even the corpse will not be given the proper rites.

But an admirer they call the Highlander, a wealthy and powerful Pharisee, has paid a large sum of money so that this last insult will not be so for the body of the prisoner. The Highlander couldn't stop the execution, but he has begged and bribed the prefect, Pontius Pilate, for the right to take the corpse at least. That it might be given the proper ceremonies and a decent burial.

The women watch and follow the Highlander's men, who take the body down and wrap it in a clean linen cloth and carry it to a newly excavated tomb. A tomb where no one has ever been laid, cut into a hillside not far from Golgotha. An honourable sepulchre, not the criminal cemetery, where those condemned by Jewish trial would be interred, and not the rotting shame of Rome. From a distance, the women carefully mark which grave-cave it is and watch the stone-carved tomb-cover being rolled into place over the entrance.

It is little comfort. But on such a day, it is startling to find any comfort at all. And at least the dead man can be given the proper rites. He can be gently washed of blood and tended with oils and spices. He can be shown the duties he deserves.

But not now: darkness is approaching. This is the day of preparation, tomorrow is Passover and the following day is the Sabbath: all other obligations must wait. Already the ram's horn blows from the corner of the Temple, to warn the goatherds and the fieldworkers and all others outside the walls, these women included, that the double Sabbath approaches. The horn blasts remind devout people that they must cease all work, down all tools, return to their dwellings. Until three stars are visible at nightfall the day after tomorrow, nothing must disturb sacred rest, not even the honour of the dead.

Twenty-one Years after
the Crucifixion

In a world composed largely of city states, there are many great cities. Paul has by now tasted not a few of them: Philippi, the home of his new sponsor Lydia, from which he has only recently departed; Tarsus, his birthplace, itself is no mean city; then there is Jerusalem, site of the Temple, which in turn houses the Holy of Holies. Though Paul now doubts those twin pillars are as important as the self-elevated Jerusalem fellowship would have you believe; Pharisees and hypocrites, chief among them those other Pillars. But Jerusalem remains undoubtedly a hallowed place: where the Saviour was sacrificed. And then there is Rome, where Paul suspects he must eventually head to win this battle of wills with the phoneys who plague and beset him, trapped in the world of their outdated Torah laws. How Paul would love to be a citizen of Rome, the centre of the Empire, the centre of the world. But for all that, for all these great cities, there is something more marvellous about Athens: the cultural pinnacle.

Every man of worth should stay in Athens for a spell, soaking in the learning and knowledge that swells from its every street and shaded grove. Paul's travel-calloused feet feel quite light as he trips the paving of Athens. At each corner there is a sculpture, and though the outdated gods depicted are imaginary, you can still admire the skill of the men who created the stone marvels. Statues are just empty shells and offer no temptation to the strong in spirit. Only the feeble need to fear graven images. How James would likely tremble in this place. And Cephas, Old Stony himself, scared of mere stones!

The Athenian buildings seem dusted with white light, as if God's favour is poured out upon them. Even the tenements and the store fronts have an otherworldly glow. And over it all, the Acropolis, built up on giant casement blocks merged into cliff rocks, as if it all surges as one from beneath the earth.

Paul has every confidence that, after a span preaching in the marketplace, these noble philosophers will realize the wisdom of his words and insist that he preach to them all in the court of the Areopagus. Or in one or all of Athens's great gymnasia, the schools of learning, where philosophers refresh and instruct the minds. Tarsus was a city of great schools, places wise men studied and taught, but Athens has schools far grander. Centres of learning to which the whole known world owes a debt.

Silas and Timothy, Paul has sent away to check on the community founded in Thessalonica, perhaps even now suffering interlopers from Jerusalem. Paul must stay here alone, fearful for the state of his children. But what is quite certain is that, upon his companions' return, they will find Paul has firmly established a new church – a new base of operations, to replace that of Antioch – in this great city.

Paul is misdirected initially, when he asks passers-by to show him the way to the marketplace. It seems the agora he seeks is more properly the *old* marketplace; most of the vulgar daily trade is now carried out at a new spot to the east; it is the old agora where philosophers pursue intellectual pleasures and where Paul is sure he will finally encounter minds as great as his own.

But even the new marketplace is not entirely to be scorned: it, too, has its merits. A man plays a kithara, the more learned brother to the lyres you would find in marketplaces in other cities. Even in its street markets, it seems, Athens exceeds. The seriousness of the player's face echoes the beautiful notes he produces. Paul has half a mind to chip a copper quadrans coin into the earthenware pot the player has set out for just such procurements. But ministry must come first. Nothing can be allowed to precede the mission, and who knows what future need Paul may have of that one small copper coin?

A sword-swallower eases a thin blade down through his mouth into a straightened and straining throat and Paul mentally logs the picture. It is perhaps an image he can use to win converts: 'Just as a sword-swallower engulfs the blade, so will this world be swallowed when the Christ returns.' No, not that. But something. He knows he cannot expect any acquaintance at all with Israelite texts among these pagans, so he needs to form some other point of connection.

At the edge of the market square, a boy child flips up a wicker ball with his feet, keeping it in the air lightsomely, motiveless. Oblivious to passers-by, no platter out for bread or coin. Dancing the more beautifully because he dances only for the dance.

Even the tongues of the errand runners and stallholders sing. They do not speak street Greek here, they speak with the elaborate high Greek style of Pericles and Aristotle. Paul is invigorated and enlivened by the chance to debate with the thinkers of this great city and to sway them to his beliefs. Oh, how will it be to have such great men at his side: the elite of the world? While James's Jerusalem church holds sway only over its own parochial confines. Those in that introverted fiefdom claim to be the chosen people, but who could be better chosen than these fine Athenian citizens? Here people even smell more pleasant. You can tell they bathe with an urbane regularity. There can be no place more cultured than Athens, more learned, more devoted to erudition, purely for enlightenment's own most sacred sense.

* * *

Eventually Paul finds the agora he seeks: the marketplace of ideas, where the Athenians, with their renowned thirst for knowledge, prefer nothing better than to hear of and discuss every new belief. Paul knows the conventions of Athenian debate from his own boyhood lessons: each man has a chance to present his own case and will be listened to attentively, without hassle or heckle. It is most certain that among the minds of these most noble, refined of men, Paul's risen Jesus will find a haven.

It is easy for Paul to gather a small crowd about him before he begins. The sophisticated philo-sophers can doubtless perceive him to be one of their own. And on the way to the agora Paul came across something that gave him an idea with which to link to these people, who, though highly cultivated, are nonetheless unknowing of the scriptures.

'Men of Athens,' Paul begins. 'You are too superstitious.' There is a slight murmur at this accusation from the gathering, but Paul shocks them only to save them.

'On the way here today, I found an altar inscribed *TO THE UNKNOWN GOD*. So anxious are you not to miss out on a god that you have made a place to worship one you don't even know about. You are unaware of the very thing you worship. But let me tell you, the God you are blind to does not live in altars built by human hands. The divine being does not abide in images. In the past God overlooked such ignorance, but now he commands all people everywhere to repent. Because I bring you good news: this world is soon coming to an end.' Paul pauses, to let the crowd take in the grandeur of his words.

'The world is soon going to end,' one man says. 'And how is that good news?'

A titter ripples through the crowd. The man who spoke has a pate as unadorned as Paul's own, as bald as Plato's. Paul wishes that God would similarly dash a tortoise into it. But no such wrath is evidenced. The man has a neck like a tortoise for that matter: stretched out and crinkled along an over-elongated length.

'Idolatry must cease, all other gods are nothing,' Paul continues, 'for the one true God has set a day when He will judge the world. Time runs short and shouldn't be wasted in worshipping statues.'

Another man from the crowd interrupts, against everything Paul had been taught about Athenian convention: 'But our philosophers have long said it is wrong to confuse a mere statue with the god represented by it. You'll not find people in Athens who believe that an idol is a magical creature. In fact there are many who believe that all the deities are merely manifestations of a divine urge, which might well be not so different from your one-God. Plato wrote as much more than four centuries ago. This is no new idea. But we are not so rude, or so certain, as to push our feelings on others as fact. What makes you so convinced that you are right, that all the tutelary deities who've served us well enough are nothing?'

'God has given evidence of this to everyone, by raising from the dead the man He has appointed to judge you all in the day soon to come.'

'So, a bit like Osiris, then?' someone says.

'This isn't philosophy,' another Athenian mutters, already turning to wander off. 'He's just a propagandist for foreign gods.'

'No, not like Osiris,' Paul shouts. 'Jesus was taken and tortured and killed to become a sacrifice for mankind's sins and reborn to be a proof and a judge over us.'

'Sounds precisely like Osiris, then! Who is this charlatan? He picks up scraps like a sparrow on the docks, but he mistakes plagiarism for learning. He has woven bits of other religions into a nest of his own and thinks himself a prophet.'

'But this is no Oriental myth. This is true.'

'How do you know?'

'It came to me in a vision.'

The crowd erupts into laughter now.

Paul's cheeks scald, like a bronze in the sun, with discomposure and anger.

'Well, there's no more certain evidence than a dream.' It is a gangly beak-nosed man who says this; curse his mother's encounter with a heron.

'Not a dream, a vision. A waking encounter with the risen Jesus.'

'There's a beggar to be found by the Odeon steps who daily encounters Zeus and by night is visited by Hecate. How are his gods imagined yet yours are real, or he a madman but you a mystic?'

'The true God does not come and go,' Paul says. 'God is all around. In times of trouble, famine, war, hardship, loneliness, God is always to be found.'

'Which begins to look suspicious ...'

People are openly laughing now. The old man with the tortoise neck who started it all is visibly weeping with mirth, wiping the tears with the back of his hand. But Paul is made of stronger stuff than they can know. Paul has been stoned and scourged; these wiseacres will not best him with words.

'Jesus died and rose again, and we who are now alive will witness the Lord himself, with a cry of command, with the archangel's call and with the sonor of God's trumpet. Jesus will descend from the skies, and the dead will rise.'

'But if he doesn't come, it won't be the end of the world ...' another man heckles.

'Through the death and resurrection of the Messiah Jesus, God has promised eternal life to all who are faithful to The Way.'

'But that's just what's offered to those reborn into the sects of not only Osiris and Isis, but Dionysus, Atargattis, Mithras, Orphism, the Eleusinian Mysteries and the Great Mother cult as well. We've seen many so-called "Mystery Religions" arrive. What is no mystery is that their fantasies of a blessed, plentiful, heavenly hereafter resonate with people who suffer with servitude, hunger and despair in their present. But just to wish for something doesn't make it true.' The man who says this wears a tunic off the shoulder and carries a bag and a staff, like a Cynic philosopher.

'Are you calling me a liar?' Paul yammers, at the edge of self-possession.

'To call you a liar would suggest that I see some deliberate volition on your part. There are many types of liar in this world. But the best liars, the truly great liars, are those who can fool even themselves and they are not really liars at all. So, no, I'm not calling you a liar,' and the man says this with a look almost of sympathy, which vexes Paul even more than the laughter.

'Doubters! You'll see the veracity. We'll all know the truth of this soon enough: the Day of the Lord is coming. Like a thief in the night. You will not know the hour, but it will be soon. The new age will dawn within our lifetimes. It could be any moment. Sudden destruction will arrive as certain and inevitable as labour pains on a pregnant woman. And when it does, your mocking will sound as hollow as your pride, O great Athenians, wallowing in the grandeur of times that will never return to you. The glory of Jesus will live for ever.'

Paul snatches his things from the ground. He would force his way through the ignorant idiots, but they peel apart for him anyway.

In his affronted hurry he leaves the agora the wrong way and has to double back a circuitous route to avoid bumping into any of the people he has just stormed from. The imbeciles, clinging to history: they are not ready in this city to absorb any new thing.

* * *

The city stinks, Paul notices, making his way back

to his lodgings through the new market. Filth cakes the buildings. Rats run in the gutters and barely larger worm-riddled dogs roam everywhere.

He spends a copper coin on a loaf of bread to supper on. The stall maid passes it with a flash of hairy dank armpit, but speaks as though she's spouting Socrates. Plum in her mouth, she has. You would think nothing of importance has happened to these poor sods since the death of Demosthenes three hundred years back. Can't they see the world has moved on?

The kid is still inanely flicking a stupid wicker ball about. The people watching him are probably pederasts. Athens is famed for them. And even worse: men fornicating with their own kind, with grown men.

The pompous kithara player is still there too. Making dumb expressions, like a cow drunk from eating fermented apples. As if there were something oh-so-important about the process of twanging strings on a box.

* * *

Paul is forced to spend nearly four weeks in Athens. An elderly and infirm city, sick from decrepitude. Mired in the memories of a great past. Unable to accept any new thing for fear it would signal Athenian irrelevance to the future. You should weep for that future, elderly Athens, Paul thinks, because you will have no part in it. He is anxious for news from Timothy and sick of this scum city, but cannot leave because Timothy would be unable to find him if he did.

Instead of preaching, Paul wanders through the Acropolis. The Parthenon is adorned with an elaborate frieze running all about it, depicting an

Athenian festival, illustrating yet again the overbearing overconfidence of these vain fools: who but such deluded snobs would place themselves so high? Ordinary Athenians carved from unblemished marble, painted and gilded with no thought of the cost to purse or soul. Such pretentious glories will yet be snatched away, Paul is sure of that. These proud and self-important Athenians will rue the day they scorned the Apostle of the Gentiles: Paul, who will judge the angels, will surely judge Athens.

They can keep their giant Parthenon temple with blasphemous statues of skirted Athena, holding up the ceiling with her head. Goddess of wisdom supposedly: all they give a shekel for is knowledge in this half-damned hell-hole; Paul would sooner be a fool, if this is what wisdom looks like.

Thirty-four Years after
the Crucifixion

'I won't lie to you, Useful, there was a setback at Athens.' Paul adjusts himself on the stuffed rugs that are currently functioning as a couch.

Manius, the Praetorian to whom Paul's wrist is chained, trying to doze, looks irritated by the movement. But then Manius has seemed to find annoyance in everything these past weeks. It appears that his good graces were only ever based on his stomach and they have vanished with the last of the pomegranates and dove preserves. Though Paul's disciples have managed to salve adequate alms to secure the group a large tent of their own in the refugee camp, the conditions are far below those that have become customary during their years in Rome. The days of shellfish, snails and dormice are gone; occasional eggs are now a delicacy. But Paul, who in his time has suffered greatly worse, is undaunted by the deterioration. Paul has been stoned, flogged and beaten with rods; a little discomfort is as nothing to him.

Paul continues: 'Athens was the first city I had visited where men didn't flock to my words. Because they were obsessed with "wisdom" in that place and my message about Jesus appears as nonsense to those who think themselves wise. But it is written: *I will destroy the wisdom of the wise, and the intelligence of the intelligent I will reject.*

'So where's the wise person? Where's the scholar? Where's the philosopher of this age? I'll tell you. God has turned their wisdom into foolishness. In His true wisdom, God saw that their supposed wisdom impeded them from knowing Him. And so God chose to save those who believe the "nonsense" of my preaching. Because the wisdom of this world is foolishness in God's sight.

'Sages think they can use logic, experiment, observation and reason to explain away the spiritual. But God doesn't follow those rules. God has chosen the foolish things to confound the wise. Jews ask for signs, and Athenians look for wisdom, but I preach of a crucified Saviour, an impediment to Jews and nonsense to Athenians, but God's nonsense is wiser than human wisdom. God chose what is foolish to make the wise feel ashamed.

'So my message *is* wisdom, but not the wisdom of this world, which is passing away. Instead, I speak about God's wisdom: a hidden secret, which God destined before the world began. And I don't speak about these things with human wisdom, but with words taught by the Spirit. I explain spiritual things to spiritual people. A person who isn't spiritual can't accept the things of God's Spirit, for they are nonsense to him. But to us, nonsense is wisdom. Do you see?'

Useful nods, though uncertainly. He couldn't pretend to understand all of it, if the truth be told. But the thing is, Paul says that you don't need to: to be saved you only have to declare with your mouth and believe with your heart that Jesus is the Lord, to eat and drink of His body and blood, and be baptized. There is a beautiful sufficiency in that.

'So when I left Athens and came to the city of Corinth, Useful, I was resolved to know nothing. My message and my preaching were not accompanied by clever words, but by a display of the Spirit's power. And there in that great place I found a multitude of followers eager to embrace the self-same things that those wise Athenians thought so ridiculous. And a great and numerous community was founded there at Corinth.'

'And then from Corinth you came to Rome?' Useful asks.

'Eventually, though not by a straight road. But I don't think we even have time for you to finish writing this story, Useful. I fear that, because of my love for you, I must send you away, while I still can.'

'What do you mean, Master?'

'I have been persecuted enough times by now, Useful, to recognize its stirrings.' Paul half cups his hand, almost as though he tries to mask his words from Manius, though that is hardly possible with the legionary lying right beside him. 'Since the fire, things have grown grim for the people of Rome. They need someone to blame. And from the tattle I hear on the wind, I suspect that the scapegoat has been chosen.'

'Then I must stay here to support you through whatever hardships may be coming,' Useful says.

Paul smiles at him. 'No, my fellow soldier. The greatest kindness you can do me now is to be safe. I will write a letter to commend you back to Philemon, your former owner, and bid him to forgive you. He won't refuse my wishes. I am an old man and a prisoner for Jesus, and you have become like my son while I have been in chains for the message. You are my very heart and I would not have you endangered. I will implore Philemon to take you back – no longer as a slave, but better than a slave, as a dear brother. And if Philemon believes that you have done him any wrong or owe him anything, then he must charge it to my account. I will write so with my own hand. Though he can hardly ask me to pay anything, since he owes me his very soul.'

A single droplet descends Useful's giant boy's head and he clutches Paul, tight as to a mast in a storm. Manius glances scornfully at the emotional display, then shuts his one eye again, in so doing renewing the intimation of violence in that abyss of scar, which runs across the void of his other eye-socket.

'Don't cry for me, Useful,' Paul says. 'I don't fear death and through my bravery the Messiah will be exalted always, whether I live or die. If I continue living, fruitful labour will be the result, but to die is also to gain. Life or death, I don't even know which I would prefer of the two: for my followers' sake it is better that I remain alive, but I have the desire to leave this world and be with the Messiah. Once I was scared that I would die before my work was done. But now I grow impatient of the Christ's return. I want to participate in His sufferings, become like him in His death and so attain resurrection.'

Twenty-two Years after
the Crucifixion

The tomb was empty. Of that there was no doubt. That was the unarguable fact. The women and James had seen the rich man's servants put the body there, in a freshly excavated cave, where no one had ever been laid. The women had watched from a distance. They had marked the spot well. And all of them agreed which burial-crypt it was. But when the women returned, on the morning after the Sabbath had ended – very early, just after sunrise – they found the body gone. The new moon of the tomb cover had been rolled away and they could see the place where Yeshua had been laid. But he was not there.

Miriam from Magdala fetched Cephas and James, yelling: *They have taken the Master out of the tomb, and we don't know where they have put him!*

So Cephas and James ran together, bare feet upon the hard ground. Fleet James, faster than Cephas, was crouched down staring into the glimless tomb interior by the time Cephas got there. But Cephas was first inside, squeezing through the narrow entrance hole. Cephas saw the linen cloths, sprawled as if shed on the stone niche, and the handkerchief, which must have been placed on Yeshua's head, not lying with the shrouds, but rolled up in a separate place.

Cephas and James and all the women witnessed that the corpse had vanished. But they did not yet understand what that meant. So afterwards they went back to their lodgings.

* * *

The tomb was empty. Of that there was no doubt. That was the unarguable fact. No one could dispute the empty tomb. But the rest of it hadn't been clear to begin with, not to Cephas.

And maybe things get even less clear with time. Memories are like bait-fish scattered in a lake, gradually drifting from sight, eventually to be consumed or just to disappear into the darkness.

At the end of the eight days of the Passover, the disciples wept and mourned and each one returned to his home, grieving for what had happened. Cephas had journeyed back to Galilee, slumped under a burden heavier than any pack-mule's. Sleepless with grief in the small-hour paranoia of the silent roadside nights.

Cephas came home to a dingy room, lit only by the light from the wood-barred window; walls whitewashed with grey; floor of baked clay. He returned to the sorrowful but knowing embrace of his stoical wife. To his sallow, edgy children, grown fearful of him in his long absence, standing well back, tattered shawls and the rear wall making each other dirtier.

When his wife brought a basin to wash the road from him, Cephas saw his own face, looking not just lined but channelled, as if the numberless tears had actually eroded it.

In the weeks that followed, persuaded by the hungry stares of his children, Cephas resumed fishing. He launched his ramshackle little craft back onto the Galilee Sea. And he became like that great lake too, like a body of water: so sorrowful was he that the tears became him and he became the tears. He was wet with them and filled with them and composed of them.

But Cephas discovered that he didn't love Yeshua any less, just because he was dead. If you can love a man enough to leave your work and family and wife and life, then that is a man for whom you have an ocean of love, wider by far than Galilee's presumptuous lake. And Cephas's love if anything grew even stronger, coloured by grief and guilt.

Neither did it feel like Yeshua loved Cephas any less, through being dead. It didn't seem like mere death had conquered that love.

And sometimes, when out on the sea that isn't, when letting his net drift or repairing a rent, Cephas would be quite certain that someone was sitting in the small vessel just behind him. And he knew that the someone was Yeshua. Cephas would speak to him; Cephas would say he was sorry, for his failure and betrayal, he would sob that his great love had not gone. And ask what he should do.

And sometimes Yeshua would answer.

If Cephas turned too suddenly, Yeshua would vanish. But if Cephas could be content to believe that Yeshua was there. If Cephas had faith sufficient not to look, but just to trust, then he could keep hold of Yeshua's presence and even see him on occasion, reflected on a knife blade, or from a sunlit wave. And Cephas was sure that afterwards the nets curled in the stern were a little flattened and warmer to the touch, just as if they had been sat upon.

And Yeshua told Cephas that The Way was not over yet, any more than it had been after Baptizer John's death. Yeshua told Cephas that he would come back. Yeshua said that soon the Lord God would wipe away the tears from all faces and swallow up death for ever. Just as the Prophet Isaiah said He would. Yeshua reminded his friend of a promise that this generation would not pass away before the dawn of the new age on earth. Before their lands would be free and peace would descend. Yeshua said that God's Kingdom would still come and God's will would still be done, just as he had pledged while alive.

And Yeshua said that Cephas was forgiven.

* * *

And among the followers of The Way, there were others who did not stop believing in Yeshua; many of those who had loved him at the first did not forsake him.

James and Cleopas were walking to a village called Emmaus, about sixty stadia from Jerusalem, when they met a stranger on the road and travelled with him awhile. The man was pious, wise and kind. And afterwards they came to realize that the stranger had been Yeshua. He had not looked like Yeshua: his face was quite different and he was older and his accent was of the south, but still, the two of them were close to certain that it had been him.

More and more of the disciples also came to believe that Yeshua lived on and would return to rule, though some had doubts. There were visions, through moisture-cloaked eyes, and there were those who searched the scriptures to see what these events meant. To see if somehow this might have been how it was all supposed to run. And there were those who pondered back on things that Yeshua had said and wondered if he hadn't always known that these happenings would come to pass. Perhaps they had not only failed him at Gethsemane, but had failed to understand him all along.

* * *

It has been a strange and tangled path, which has led from those baleful days to here. In the disciples' grief it was as though the very sky was darkened at the moment of Yeshua's death. It was as if the veil of the Temple was torn. But it was not torn: the veil remains. The Temple remains. Life goes on. Not as it was, but nonetheless.

Twenty-two years have passed in Jerusalem, and The Way continues to attract believers, who celebrate the Jewish festivals and the sacrifices along with Cephas, Jochanan and James the Just.

Often the Three Pillars still spend Sabbaths together in the house of John-Mark's mother, just as they did in those first years following their return to Jerusalem; after they were jointly persuaded that this thing had not ended.

John-Mark's mother has long since passed away, so the building would now be more properly called the house of John-Mark, but he is seldom there and old ways of speaking linger like winter in middle-aged men.

James the Just, who always was lean as a wolf, now is also grey like one. But through his piety, his popularity among the people continues to grow.

* * *

When John-Mark comes back from his latest journey, he does so wearing the most threadbare cloak the Three Pillars have ever seen; rather than cloth, it is more like a series of connected holes.

'You want to sell that cloak,' Cephas says, with a smile, 'before someone steals it.'

'A memento of Corinth,' John-Mark says. He is the youngest of them by some distance, but even so his black eyes have aged on this last trip alone and his shock of hair is beginning to winnow thin.

'Corinth is a hideous place,' John-Mark says. 'Fish heads and faeces all over the streets, you're happy when you step on a clamshell or a cornhusk. Even the icons stink of piss. And they practise sacred prostitution in a fashion worse even than the Canaanites: women giving themselves to strangers on the steps of the temple of Aphrodite, believing that they serve their goddess through that and their husbands' revelling in it – I dare to say aroused by it. And this is the place that enemy Paul has made his latest base.'

'I'm telling you, Paul does it all for money,' Jochanan says, 'so that he might trick wealth from those rich and impressionable women whom John-Mark tells us are led astray.'

But Cephas says that he doesn't think this can be true. Paul must believe what he preaches, or how could he have suffered so much for those beliefs? He is not deceitful, just deluded.

'Then wait until you hear this,' says John-Mark. 'Paul has made the final move into madness: he replaces the name of God in the words of the Prophet Isaiah and says that *every knee should bow and every tongue confess that Jesus is God*. He has at last made his Jesus fully equal to the Lord of Hosts and to be worshipped. And he now calls the Torah *so much dung*. He says that *all who rely on the Torah are under a curse*. He says we Jews *have a veil over our eyes*.'

'This is the consequence of leniency,' Jochanan says, not quite openly reproving James, but very nearly doing so. 'We should never have countenanced the idea of Gentiles joining without full conversion.'

* * *

Even now Cephas wavers. The community at Antioch became once again a fine and loving place, after those errors instituted by Paul were corrected. Must the Gentiles really convert fully and be circumcised if they want to follow The Way?

It's true that Yeshua said he was sent 'only to the lost sheep of Israel'. But even still, it is not quite so simple as sheep and goats: there was one time that Yeshua almost approached non-Jews – you can't really call Samaritans Gentiles, but they aren't quite Jews either. Yeshua and the gathering had gazed down at a Samaritan village and the Samaritans didn't look so different from Israelites, when you actually looked at them. They lived in the same houses: flat roofs of mud-packed reeds, walls built of bricks of sun-baked clay, with windows narrow and few, to keep out the glare and the dust. They wore the same clothes: half-sleeved *ketonet*; *simlah* with dancing fringes and tassels; leather girdles, to belt their skirts and hold their knives. And didn't they all worship the one-God?

But the Samaritans say that the sacrifices should be made at their temple on Mount Gerizim, when right-thinking people know that they must be made in the true Temple at Jerusalem. And because of this the Samaritans wouldn't accept Yeshua as the Messiah – though they, too, waited and prayed for one. Just because Yeshua's face was set towards Jerusalem and not to Gerizim. And the messengers Yeshua sent ahead, who entered the village of the Samaritans to make preparations, came back and said they had been told that Yeshua was not welcome. The Samaritans had rejected the King, just because his face was set towards Jerusalem.

Perhaps that was a message then, Cephas reflects. Maybe this was the signal that all must convert and look towards Jerusalem.

But back then it was taken as insolence, not prophecy; when Jacob and Jochanan heard how their master had been scorned, they had wanted to burn the bloody village down. They had wanted to torch the fields and spoil the wells. They had wanted to bring fire on the Samaritans as if it were lightning from the heavens.

Only Yeshua had stopped them, with a laugh like rolling waves and a smile wide as a rainbow. Yeshua had said their zeal was good, but their target was wrong. Yeshua clasped the brothers to him and named them his Sons of Thunder.

* * *

Jochanan's thunder has still not fled him in middle age. 'We need to counter these colonies of blasphemy that Paul is founding,' he says. 'We must pursue his path like John-Mark has, but as an army, no longer like scouts. In every place where Paul has founded a community, we need to send loyal messengers of The Way, relentless men who won't stop until the members of those churches embrace the Law of Moses and that polluter of waters is exposed.'

'Agreed,' James says.

They both look to Cephas: there must be consensus.

Cephas's brow furrows, deep as the wrinkles of the ram's horn that even now blows from the corner of the Temple. This decision cannot be left for ever.

'Agreed, then. Let us pursue him.'

THE
PURSUIT

Israel means 'He who struggles with God'. According to the Book of Genesis, the patriarch Jacob was renamed Israel because down by the ford of a river he wrestled an angel for the length of a dark night, until day broke upon them. Even when Jacob's hip was dislocated, he would not submit. And through his enduring strength, or his perverse stubbornness, he founded a nation.

God told him, '*Your name shall no longer be called Jacob, but Israel, for you have fought with God and with man, and have won.*'

So the stranger with whom Jacob wrestled was angel and man and also God. From the beginning, the scriptures left space for confusion and place for confrontation.

* * *

By the time the pursuit of his challengers begins in earnest – twenty-two years after the death of Jesus – Paul has come to believe that his congregations of the sanctified are the true Israel. They are Israel according to the spirit. The Jews are Israel only according to the flesh, now severed from God, withering, drying and dying, like pruned branches, because of their own outdated intransigence. Paul writes that *the Jews ... displease God and are enemies of all men ... they fill up their sins to the limit. The wrath of God is to come upon them to the uttermost.*

As ever, this will be a battle of words. The teller decides the truth. The men who pursue come armed with epistles and instructions. They say to those communities they try to sway away from Paul: *Observe the greatest caution, that you believe no teacher, unless he brings from Jerusalem the written endorsement of James the Messiah's brother.*

But Paul is also a man of letters and his followers carry his arguments to all the assemblies of believers he has founded, across the Mediterranean seaboard and into the heartlands of Asia, Galatia and Macedonia. Jesus and Baptizer John preached in wilderness places; Paul favours great cities and province capitals.

Some of Paul's antagonists make claim that he is a *scoundrel* and a *crook*. He is not, but he is a man of polar contradictions and he is at his worst when he feels that his mission is under threat.

Paul can be bullying: *If anyone thinks that he is a prophet, or spiritual, he must acknowledge that what I write to you is what the Lord commands. If anyone ignores this, he himself must be ignored.*

And he can be condemning: *Even though I am not with you in person, I am with you in the Spirit. And as though I were present, I have already passed judgment on this man.*

But Paul can equally be magnanimous: *Anyone you forgive, I also forgive.*

And touching: *Just as a nursing mother cares for her children, so we cared for you.*

He can be boastful: *Do you not know that we will judge angels?*

He can be crude: *As for those agitators, I wish they would go the whole way and castrate themselves!*

And yet he can eulogize about love with sufficient beauty to be read at every wedding of Christendom for ages yet unimaginable. Unimaginable, not least, because Paul believes this to be already the end time.

The Paul revealed in his epistles is simultaneously self-deprecating and self-aggrandizing; kindly, contemptuous and venomous. At times he sounds like a genius; at others like a fool trying to throw away the basket he is standing in. He can have an incisive clarity and yet be obtuse and confused. He can be intellectually cruel, piercing and mocking; he can be gentle, loving and tender. Sometimes he sounds like a wise old sage; sometimes like a baby, wailing with frustrated rage, because it cannot make people comprehend its needs.

Again and again Paul tells the hearers of his letters – for they were written to be read aloud and in public – that he is not lying, clearly against the claims of opponents who say that he is. Who must state, indeed, that Paul is not an apostle at all, for he replies to his followers: *Even though I may not be an apostle to others, surely I am to you?*

Those antagonists who come from James, Paul says, *are false apostles, deceitful workers, masquerading as apostles of Christ. And no wonder, for Satan himself masquerades as an angel of light. It is not surprising, then, if his servants also masquerade as servants of righteousness.*

Identifying his own needs and commands as identical and indivisible with those of Jesus – *Christ is speaking through me* – Paul harbours the funda-mentalist's urge simply to dictate that all views other than his are heresy, requiring no further reason than that he says it to be so. Yet he is sorely, gratingly, aware of the inherent weakness of his position, when contrasted against that of the brother and closest companions of the Saviour he preaches about.

Maybe the most damaging blows of Paul's opponents are the accusations of financial indiscretions. In an age where almost every holder of office sieves into his own purse, where rights to taxation are auctioned, where bribery is normality, such charges resonate and perhaps seem not improbable, even to people Paul has personally preached to. Though he tries to practise his trade of leather work when he can – separated from the support of Antioch, constantly moving and frequently in misfortune – Paul is greatly dependent on the patronage of donors; the allegations that he is profiting from them wound him worse than scourging.

Yet these indictments are hard for him to refute. Not least because, remaining true to his word, Paul has had his followers earnestly pooling their money for the poor ones of Jerusalem throughout these past years. They have carefully adhered to Paul's instructions: *On the first day of every week, each one of you should set aside a sum of money in keeping with your income, saving it up, so that when I come no collections will have to be made.* But those men sent by James the Just can report in all honesty that they have come from Jerusalem and so far the coffers of The Way have not seen so much as a single copper lepton arrive from Paul.

At one time, in great Ephesus, Paul might have been making so many converts that the silversmiths threatened to riot, fearing decline in selling images of the goddess Artemis. But the emissaries of the Three Pillars begin to force such inroads into his communities that eventually Paul is not welcome in the city.

Amid the fear that his other foundations could similarly come undone, Paul arrives upon a stratagem, perhaps not shrewd but admirably brazen and daring: he will gather the entire collection – by now a sum of money large enough to make the Pillars choke – and he will deliver it to Jerusalem in person. When they see the magnitude of his deeds, he hopes that his critics will be silenced, and by his generosity to his opponents, he will heap burning coals on their heads.

In his last letter of the period, Paul writes to the Christianoi of Rome, people he does not personally know but who are seemingly already aware of this great and growing division in their young movement: *Pray to God for me, asking that I may escape unhurt from those in Judaea who are disobedient, and pray that the donation I take to Jerusalem will be accepted.* To speak thus to strangers shows how great his anxiety for the endeavour must be.

* * *

For a dark night five years long, the two camps wrestled, like Jacob with the stranger beside the river, but which was the side of men and which of the angels, and where was God all the while?

Twenty-seven Years after
the Crucifixion

'They know who you are and mean to drown you like a three-legged whelp, once we set sail,' Timothy says. 'We must leave the ship tonight.'

And so, feet creaking across the salt-caked planks, beneath the stars and the howl of a Minerva owl, the party disembarks, returning to a *terra firma* that feels barely safer. Who knows what murderers lurk in the shadows of stacked amphora on the Corinthian dockside? Even still, better that than being cast overboard to flail against the waves. The close confinement of a boat is no place to face foes.

They had booked passage on a ship chartered by Jewish pilgrims heading to Jerusalem. But word about Paul and his views of the Torah had evidently oozed out among the other travellers and a plot was laid against him before the cargo was even fully loaded. All arrangements are aborted by the night-time absconsion, and a good deal of coin wasted too; but, for once, money is not among Paul's problems.

Over seven years, across seven provinces, Paul's congregations have been gathering their collection, each member faithfully giving what they could afford on the first day of each week. Copper coins in time being changed up to higher-denomination pieces: bronze; then brass; then silver; before transmuting a last time into easily transportable gold. Finally, the full crop is harvested.

Travelling with such funds would be a dangerous business, even for a man without burgeoning infamy. But Paul has used his skills in leather-working to fashion a variety of coin stashes: a multi-pocketed under-girdle; a bag suspended from his neck and twin thin bandoliers, concealed beneath his clothing; even his robes have gold coins sewn into them, in tight bundles so that they do not chink, or evidently alter the hang of the cloth. His companions, too, have money secreted about them, lesser amounts, but still considerable sums.

Demi-Jew Timothy purses his lips with pride at his discovery of the plotters, whenever the avoided adversity is mentioned. But Paul is visibly unnerved by the experience: if he cannot even sail there safely – encircled by followers – what threats might await him at Jerusalem?

He keeps Silas close by at all times. Silas has a tree-feller's arms and a chest broad as a boar. And Silas came with Paul from Antioch, the only one from that community who stood by him. If Silas cannot be trusted, there is no trust left on God's flat earth.

Not that the fidelity of the others is in question – Timothy; Sopater from Berea; Aristarchus and Secundus from Thessalonica; Gaius from Derbe; Tychicus and Trophimus from Asia – they have all proved themselves often enough. All of the group are Gentiles save for Timothy and Paul, if either can still consider themselves Jews by now.

* * *

The group heads inland again, then north towards Philippi, where Lydia lives, journeying by wagon, wheels churning in the scars eroded by other wheels; as foot travellers they once trudged in the spaces left between.

The parable is a Pharisee method of teaching, a story to illustrate a point. Paul does not normally use them, though the fleshly Jesus apparently did. But from Paul's troubled mind a parable surfaces and he tells it to the others as they go.

There was a great flood and the land was all submerged and a pious man, a believer in God, was trapped by the rising waters on the roof of his house. But God spoke to the man, saying that He would save him, so the man was not afraid.

On the first day, a neighbour of the man paddled to him in a small craft and said he would transport him to higher ground. But the man remembered that God had promised to protect him, so he declined the offer and, though the water was still rising, he was not afraid.

On the second day, a warship passed near to the roof, rowed by soldiers of the prefect. They shouted that they could take the man on board, but he told them that the Lord of Hosts had promised to watch over him, so he had no need of their help. The level of the flood reached almost to the roof now, but the man had no fear of it, because he had God's promise.

On the third day a group of villagers on a raft built of salvaged goods sailed close, but the man said that they should sail on, God would save him.

On the fourth day, as the cold waters swallowed him, as he choked upon the muddy waves, the man cried out against God. Even as he gagged and drowned, the man shouted that God had broken His word.

But God said: I sent a rowing boat, a trireme and a raft for you, and you spurned them all!

* * *

'What does the story mean, Master?' Trophimus asks later, having pondered the matter for a while along the trail.

'It means,' Paul says, 'that in order for God to help you, you must also help yourself.'

* * *

Paul and Silas stay with Lydia in her villa, but the others are sent onwards to the port of Troas, accompanying a slave of Lydia's, who is experienced in chartering ships.

'Should we really spend such money on our travel?' Secundus asks, as they are leaving, 'Surely it would be better just to take passage on a vessel rather than hire one.'

'We need to get to Jerusalem safely,' Paul explains patiently. 'Our protection is paramount. The money has been collected not only for the poor ones of Jerusalem, but also for the glory of Jesus Christ, and what could be more important to that work than the survival and safety of His apostle?'

In the event, Lydia's man finds them a ship on half-charter at a lesser expense. It has already been rented to sail for the city of Tyrian purple at the behest of an acquaintance of Lydia, another murex dye merchant. So for a share in the costs the apostle's party is able to direct the voyage to some degree with regard to stops, provided they charge cargo at Tyre and take no goods of their own.

The captain is a Thracian, habitually bare-chested; he has a tattoo of a skeletal hand on his shoulder, as if some daemon is pulling him gently aside.

* * *

And Lydia also helps to arrange something else for Paul: a business for which contacts with officialdom are required. Paul shows the bureaucrats his prized letter of recommendation from the proconsul of Cyprus. By now that papyrus scroll is as tired and travel-worn as Paul himself is, but it demonstrates his good standing and his character. And Paul pays five hundred drachma – a sum worth several years' wages for a labourer – in return for which he receives nothing but twin inscribed bronze tablets, folded together and wax-sealed. But Paul is more than happy with the transaction, which goes at least some little way towards easing his trepidation.

* * *

Paul and Silas join the others at the port of Troas, where they pass a week, waiting for the ship to be loaded and then for favourable winds.

As Paul is walking, in a loose formation of followers, along the beach past Troas's broad-basined harbour, he comes across a shell, large and spined and bright and lying there before him. He picks it up; it is rare to see such a fine example, not already scavenged away. It is shiny and pink on the inside of an alluring slitty opening. But it is also spiked and barbed. Glossy and inviting; but treacherous as well.

On that Damascus road, during his first debilitating ecstasy, Paul received many great gifts of God. And not least of them, in his esteem, his sexual desire was all but extinguished from that moment onwards. Paul is of the view that it would be better if all men were as he is, chaste and celibate, eunuchs for God, but sadly not all are so blessed.

* * *

There is a community of Christianoi in Troas, a few converted by Paul himself, when he passed through some years ago. And since he intends to bid the ship to leave the next day, Paul addresses them at their gathering on the first day of the week.

As Paul speaks, for longer even than normal, a young man sitting at the third-storey window drifts into sleep and slowly topples sideways, drops from sight. Paul, who watched it happen, charges down the stairs, still quick on his robust legs for his fifty-six years. And he lifts the lad up in his arms, at first fearing him dead, then exploding into relieved laughter as the youth comes round. A little dazed and bloodied but none the worse bar that. It is the first time Paul's followers have heard him laugh in weeks. And the whole group breaks bread and worships together, and they all talk with their master until dawn, renewing their bonds of faith. They think perhaps the spell of Paul's fear has been broken.

But then, the next day, instead of boarding the ship, Paul erratically decides to travel overland to Assos, to foil anyone who might be waiting in ambush at the Troas port, leaving his disciples further unnerved.

The ship, as ships do, though, hugs the shore and hops from port to port and Paul joins it at Assos, and from there they sail to harbours in

Mitylene, then Chios, Samos and Trogyllium. Paul refuses to let the Thracian captain make the obvious next stop, at great Ephesus, where Trophimus is from, instead ordering the ship on to Miletus. Paul is nervous of porting in Ephesus because those men who had come from Jerusalem have so turned the congregations against him. But he holds the ship at Miletus, further down the coast, and from there he summons certain members of the Ephesus community, who, Trophimus says he thinks, remain loyal.

They come, to Paul's relief, but still he cannot conceal his sadness when he sees them. 'Since I've been gone, I know that grievous wolves have come among you and harmed the flock. Some of your own men even arose and distorted the truth in order to lure others into following them. But, despite what they may say, I never desired anyone's silver, gold or fine clothes. You witnessed how I worked with my own hands to support myself. And now I am on my way to Jerusalem, not knowing what will happen to me there, or what suffering is waiting for me. Though I don't place any value on my life, I have a great fear that none of you will ever see my face again.'

And all of them cry as they put their arms around Paul and kiss him affectionately and pray with him. They urge Paul to abandon his visit to Jerusalem, but he won't and he rejoins the ship.

From Miletus they sail to Kos, then Rhodes and on to Patara. The greatest stretch of open water, the distance most to be feared, is where, from Patara, the ship crosses far to the west side of Cyprus to reach Tyre, risking wreck and storm. Most ships take the safer but greatly longer route along the coasts of Cilicia and Syria. But Paul hastens now, hoping to make Jerusalem in time for the Feast of Weeks.

And instead of crashing waves and dark skies, three dolphins accompany the travellers much of the way. As if to show that the Lord of Hosts, His Son and the Spirit that moves are with them. The dolphins leap across the bow and ride in the wake. They dive and circle alone and all as one. They roll and hang and flick their sideways flukes. They shine and smile. And there is such visible intelligence evidenced in the insentient fish that it is clear that Yahweh, whose hand moulded every creature, is at work in these ones this very day; so Paul cannot but take it as a sign that God will keep him safe.

Thirty-four Years after
the Crucifixion

When the Praetorian Guards finally strike, they come with the wrath of Mars. Wooden bolts are shattered as strapped boots kick in doors. Those who protest are hacked down where they stand. The delay in the round-up was not through mercy but efficiency. The black cloaks draw up plans, before drawing their long knives.

They take the congregations as they meet for their communal meal on the day of Solis. Those house churches not destroyed in the fire are encircled, dark sharks around a raft; the Christianoi who assemble together in the camps are even easier to take captive. Most of the arrests are made within a single evening.

Paul needs no tracking down. Manius hands over his prisoner to his comrades with an unapologetic shrug, then rubs his wrist and stretches his arm as though his predominant sensation is one of pleasure at finally being rid of an encumbrance.

Aristarchus tries to make escape, sliding on his belly beneath the back flap of the group's marquee. When half his body has passed, he gives a dog-yelp of pain and his legs go limp. They are wrenched out of sight from the other side and that is the last Paul will ever see of his friend.

Paul thanks God that Useful and Timothy at least will be safe enough at Colossae. The boy was sent away in plenty of time, back to his old master, Timothy with him to ensure Paul's letter would be publicly read and Useful forgiven.

Epaphras, Demas and Luke, if God wills it, will also evade capture: they left just days ago, armed with epistles to continue the ceaseless argument against those false apostles who would Judaize and circumcise the whole world if they were able.

But for Paul and Silas, it is gaol. And the imprisonment is truly that this time: no house arrest or manacled wrist, but a black and barred pit of filth. Floor slick with piss and faeces from stinking slop pots knocked over in the dark. A reeking dungeon into which new prisoners are lowered by rope. One of the ropes has a seat attached, for those who are too disfigured and broken from torture to hold on.

Roman citizens cannot be tortured, but many of the captives are immigrants, freedmen and slaves, and they are put to the rack as a matter of course. They return to the pit prison with their spines twisted and their arms dislocated, without fingernails, sometimes without fingers. They find it hard to speak when they come back, with their broken jaws and holes from pulled out teeth; but, by the rate at which the Praetorians find more Christianoi meeting places after each questioning, it seems they speak enough at the time. And to look at those misshapen, bloodied creatures, it is not possible to hold them responsible for anything they might have said.

Silas is taken away one morning. If morning exists in the murk of the prison cavern. He walks away as a broad, proud son of Adam; he comes back two days later as a shuffling beast, sightless and tongue-less. Paul weeps.

It is becoming clear that the Christianoi are not even to be scapegoats for the fire. Because the lot of the scapegoat is not so bad: on the Day of Atonement it is prodded and spat at and driven out of town and poked with reeds and heaped with scorn and maybe in the wilderness the wolves will one day catch it. But the other goat is taken straight to the altar to be held down and cut through the jugular. Perhaps it would be better to be the scapegoat.

Many of the Christianoi are resolute: they take first the fire and now this persecution as final evidence that the end of days is here, just as they have been told to expect. Paul encourages them in this belief and they are greatly lifted by his presence among them. He seems to emit a field, like the change of air around a fountain, a force invisible, yet tangible. To be with such a figure of the movement at this time of horror is a poultice of great comfort. Paul draws strength from the solace he gives to others and endeavours to be stoical and strong. If this is how the trumpet is to sound, he will not be found wanting. If this is the shape that battle must take, Paul will still wear faith as a breastplate and salvation as a helm. He will not thrice deny the Christ, like Cephas did.

Some prisoners do break, though, and can hardly be blamed for it. Some wail – whenever guards appear at the heaven of the ceiling hole – shouting that they are not of this sect, never were really of this sect, or in any case they recant. Lips spittle-flicking in their desperation, they cry that they still pray to the good gods of Rome. They say they know not who this Christ is.

The guards are immune to such pleas for clemency. Innocence is in any case irrelevant. The crime of the condemned is not that they are members of a newly arrived initiation-religion, but that they razed Rome; it is beyond improbable that any were genuinely involved, therefore all are equally guilty. Much of the city is in cinders, but the prison remains and must brim with criminals. The plebeian mass must be sated, with death and bread.

In the pit there is not even bread. For those whose gag reflexes have adjusted to the stink sufficiently to allow them to eat, there is only *puls*, a mashed-up corn gruel. As watery as fish-piss. But Paul performs his rites on it nonetheless. Paul tells those hallowed to share suffering in this persecution that even this gruel can become the body of the Christ and through it they will have immortality.

Some of the few Christianoi Jews prefer to eat their thin porridge without a magical blessing. But that aside, there is little separation between them and the Gentiles in this cavern-prison. All observe the Sabbath, if nobody works. Everyone keeps the dietary laws, when the only thing to eat is runny *puls*. And not the fiercest Judaizer would suggest a circumcision in this pit of cess and infection: it would be a death sentence. Although it has come to seem near certain that this is the fate they all now face.

Twenty-seven Years after
the Crucifixion

After a frustrating week of waiting, while charging cargo at Tyre, the ship finally ports at Caesarea in Judaea. Though Caesarea is hardly Judaea proper: it is a predominantly pagan city now, renamed for Caesar Augustus – and furnished with a temple to him too – filled with foreigners and foreign gods, the centre of Roman administration and commerce. The seat of the prefect, although, the Feast of Weeks being near, possibly the governor is currently in Jerusalem.

Pontius Pilate, of course, is long since gone, recalled for a readiness to resort to mass slaughter, cruelty and extortion, exceptional even by Roman standards. The prefect is Marcus Antonius Felix now, a freedman who has risen to control a province, though his buoyance doubtless owes much to his brother, embroiled in imperial intrigues, said to be the lover of the Emperor Nero's mother. Felix himself has lately married a Herodian princess.

If it were possible, Paul might have preferred to remain in this haven of Roman security but, for the sake of his mission, rapprochement with the Three Pillars must be accomplished. There are other supporters loyal to Paul in Caesarea, though; arrangements have been made, and Paul's group is swollen by seven Gentile men from Caesarea itself and a further ten who have travelled from Cyprus with Mnason, one of Paul's earliest disciples, converted at the court of Sergius Paulus.

They hire horses to take them to Jerusalem, pad nags, accustomed to being ridden by those unaccustomed to riding. Almost all of Paul's previous land journeys were made on foot, but each hour grows more essential now; this is not a moment for questioning every last expense.

The ostler they rent from trades camels, too. It has been years since Paul has seen such beasts. Knees worn black from their strange crouched wait. Fur like sheep's wool on the sides of their great chests. Faces of sad patience, deceptive faces, ready at a moment to hiss and spit. A slave boy cleans the camels' teeth, scraping bits from between them with a green twig. The pegs of the camels' rear spikes look carnivorous. If the Romans came across more camels, they would have myths about man-eating ones – camels that can thrive only on human flesh: that's the sort of story Romans like.

* * *

It is an extravagant comfort to be on horseback, the mounts' heads nodding in time to their gentle trot, flanks black and oily as cormorant feathers. And, despite some trepidation about meeting with the Pillars, it feels good to be back in Judaea.

Alongside the road are fortress cliffs of red rock, which have sheltered patriots and bandits, but there will be no fear of robbery on this trip. There is a certain sense of power, in fact, in travelling with such a large party: Silas, Timothy, Sopater,

Aristarchus, Secundus, Gaius, Tychicus, Trophimus and now Mnason and seventeen others.

Neither do they fear the Asiatic lions, the symbol of Judaea but snub-nosed like Roman dogs of war, asleep under the acacia trees to escape the sun. The lions have long learned to fear man and even at night would not attack a group like this one. But at the moment it is too hot for lions to hunt at all, and the gazelles know it. They eat mockingly close by, bodies twitching, though they stand still, as if an excess of energy is squashed into their small frames. Leaf-clipping muzzles pushing into bushes. Short satyr spikes of their horns like metal styluses.

The apostle's party passes villages. Some real, quiet and nervous. Others illusory: sand sculptures, layers hardened and built on top, like flat-roof dwellings; false streets wind-stripped between them.

Paul falls to the ground as he tries to remount after they eat by a dry-walled well. Unused to steeds, he slips and lands breathless on his back, staring at the sky. And in the moment before his companions lift him up again, he returns to a time more than twenty years ago, when he lay, like a shell-stranded tortoise, on a road outside Damascus. All he has achieved over those two decades, surely it would not have been possible were he not chosen and aided by God. Surely he can make James understand this. Beside Paul is a high thistle, spiny fronds reaching out like a beggar's plea for coin.

* * *

Mnason has secured the group lodgings in Jerusalem in advance of their arrival. Fortunately, because the city, as usual, is beyond bloated for the festival. As soon as they are settled, before even eating, Paul dispatches Timothy to arrange parley with the Three Pillars. Timothy returns to report it done, they will meet the following morning, and he grinning bears the tale that James seemed every bit as wrong-footed by the news of their presence as Paul had hoped.

* * *

And so the two sides assemble, in the broad, bright courtyard of the house of John-Mark's mother. Paul with Silas and Timothy, Trophimus of Ephesus and the others who came with them by sea and also Mnason of Cyprus. The Three Pillars with an entourage of elders of The Way and four younger men, long-haired and sinewy.

It has been seven years since Paul last saw Cephas, at the time of the Antioch incident, longer since he saw James and Jochanan. None of them looks so changed, but they must be: not only older, but altered.

There is none of the kissing common among reunited men of these regions. A cognized gap remains between the two groups. Paul hopes it is a space wherein the Holy Spirit might abide.

A cockerel – a fighting breed – struts about the courtyard, king of this small corner, golden-plumed, crested with a comb of flesh as red as the petals of the blood orchid. And on a paving beneath the arch of a roof a baby bird lies dead, its skin translucent, legs, not fully formed, curled uncomfortably into itself.

'You wished for an audience with us, Saul of Tarsus,' James begins.

He speaks in his native Aramaic, dictating the language in which this conclave will be held, putting Paul at a slight disadvantage, but cutting his companions from the conversation entirely.

'I wanted to see you, yes,' Paul replies, the rarely used tongue returning like familiar scripture, 'so that I could give you the very great sum of money I have collected for you and the poor ones of Jerusalem. I have been a man of my word, James. I have honoured our agreement. It was made, you will recall, at the time of the decision that I would go to the Gentiles and you to the circumcised. I have kept to my side of that bargain.'

'Bargain, was it? Like something struck by a stall hawker or a whore? The Pillars don't bargain, Saul, we decree. But it's fortunate that you bring up the matter of circumcision, because I have something to say, for your own safety. You see, Brother Saul, many thousands of Jews who follow The Way are here at Jerusalem and all of them are zealous for the Torah. But they have been informed that you teach men to turn away from Moses, saying not to circumcise or live according to the sacred laws. They will certainly hear that you have come, so we have been worrying over what we could do to protect you.'

Jochanan now speaks for the first time: 'What's the matter, Saul?' He laughs. 'You've the face of a man trying to suck honey from a hornet's nest.'

'There is nothing to be afraid of, Paul,' Cephas says, 'but you must know that we have been read copies of your letters. They circulate widely, widely enough for us to know that you have sometimes written ill of us.'

'And ill of the Torah,' James says. 'You compose epistles filled with thimblerigs, where you switch the peas before the eyes of fools to turn fraud into fact. We are not simpletons to be tricked by street swindlers, Saul. We know to watch the hand and not the cup.'

Paul's lips move, but no words come; it is easy to be disdainful of James the Just from a distance, but his presence is a force like the Boreas wind. James's face is drawn and dark.

'So we have decided that you must publicly demonstrate that you recognize the Law of Moses,' James says. 'You will show these Gentiles who have come with you and the Jerusalemites that you submit to us and to the Torah. When you have completed a Nazirite Vow to prove that you remain a faithful Jew, only then will we accept your gift for the poor ones and we will rule on what the future holds.'

'You know the process of the temporary Nazirite Vow, no doubt,' Jochanan says. The beard surrounding the scar of his throat has gone badger-striped with white. 'But perhaps I should refresh your memory, because it seems you have been prone to forgetting certain practices of late. You must make purifications to enter the Temple and also abstain from wine and other fermented drink for seven days. When the period of your dedication is over, you are to present sacrifices to God: an unblemished male lamb for a guilt offering, an unblemished ewe lamb for a sin offering, an unblemished ram for a fellowship offering, with grain, wine and bread offerings. You will present these at the Temple, before God and man. Then, in front of all, you must shave off your hair to symbolize your subservience to the Torah and put your hair into the fire of the sacrifice. Thereafter everyone will know there to be no truth in these reports about you, and that you are still submissive to the Law.'

'But we will protect you through this,' Cephas says, gesturing to the four gaunt younger men, who are with his group on the shaded side of the courtyard. 'These comrades will take the Nazirite Vow with you. They will look after you and ensure that the purification rites are carried through correctly. Though you will, of course, have to pay their expenses, because the sacrifices mean no small cost.'

'Do I have a choice in this?' Paul asks.

'God gives us free will. We always have choice,' James says. 'You could perhaps leave Jerusalem immediately and pray to outrun such deadly men as would most certainly pursue you.'

* * *

After they have retired from the meeting, Paul clarifies to his followers what has come to pass because they don't speak Aramaic. He explains how he has come up with a course of action to soothe the situation, as hot sun calms the lion.

'I have decided to perform a Nazirite Vow, as a balm on this fever of discord. To the Jews I become a Jew, to those subject to the Law of Moses as if I too am under that Law. God has made me all things to all men, the better to save some.'

'So you did not explain to them how the Torah was only a temporary measure until the arrival of God's Son, that all who rely on the Law are now under a curse, that salvation comes only through faith in Jesus Christ?' asks a puzzled Trophimus.

'Not precisely, no.'

* * *

Apart from its size and splendour and the fact it contains no statues, the Jerusalem Temple barely differs from any of the countless other temples that Paul has seen on his missionary journeys: people travel there to worship; the priests make sacrifices; the supplicant hopes their God has blessed them.

What separates Paul's new sect is that he has come to believe and teach that Jesus was the perfect and final sacrifice. That no more sacrifices are needed. Yahweh sent His own Son in the likeness of sinful flesh to be a sin offering. Jesus is the Lamb of God, the final atonement before the imminent reign of God on earth, when the righteous dead will rise from the grave and the saved among the living will have their lowly bodies moulded into a new and glorious form.

But that being so, Paul has no particular problem with the strictures of the Nazirite Vow that he has undertaken to complete. Aside from an uncomfortable lump of undigested pride in his stomach, the act is simply meaningless to him.

So he descends into the purifying *mikveh* bath, as do the four long-haired acolytes of James. Men who are cordial but cold. It is hard to say if they are to protect Paul or to curtail him. They remain so close by that their shadows blend with Paul's, but he is unwilling to trust his safety to them. He has Timothy take the rites of purification too, so that he can enter the inner sanctums of the Temple.

And as far as possible, during the seven days of the dedication, Paul keeps the rest of his disciples about him as well. A fish school of protection, in the centre of which Silas guards his master, like the pupil of his eye.

The Temple is the point of greatest danger. The Israelites are always fired up when so close to God. Which is why the Romans watch its courts from the towers of the Antonia Fortress and why, in recent years, fearing revolutionary activity on the part of the festival crowds, the prefect has even taken to stationing a company of soldiers at armed alert by the very entrance porticoes. To remind those Jews mounting the great stone steps that insurrection may be quelled with spears.

But Paul takes comfort from seeing the legionaries there, as he passes through the double gates with the four Nazirites and his retinue of followers. Paul himself wrote: *Let every person be subject to the governing authorities ... the authorities do not bear the sword in vain. They are servants of God to execute wrath on the wrongdoer.* So Paul has no fear of these troopers' blades; in fact, he steals the eye of Mnason and shares a nod, to emphasize the soldiers' presence. Because Mnason knows the ways of Rome well, having served the Cyprus governor. And Mnason has some specific instructions to follow in the case of calamity.

Past the porticoes, the party enters into the great bazaar of the first court, filled with bleating beasts and sweating traders, crying repeated words about their wares so fast and so frequently that they become almost an unintelligible stream, like speaking in tongues. Money-changers and pedlars ply and, occasionally, priests glide by amid the pilgrims and peasant farmers carrying reed-tied sheaves of wheat as offerings. And Paul sees also the short grey tunics of Temple Guards, a uniform he knows well.

Paul is beyond certain that the world has altered utterly – the Christ's sacrifice and Paul's revelations have transformed everything – and yet to be here, you could almost believe that it all remained the same.

There is still the waist-high wall, which separates this area from the holier courtyards of the Mount and the Temple itself. The decorative palisade has many unguarded entrances – it is purely symbolic, easily crossed – but the fate of transgressors is made clear by numerous notices in every language: *No Gentile is to enter beyond the balustrade into the forecourt around the Sanctuary. Whoever is caught will have himself to blame for his subsequent death.*

So Paul cannot take his formation of followers with him as he passes through with the four Nazirites; only Timothy accompanies him. The others wait outside, as instructed, as close to Paul as the wall allows, alert for his return. A large group, but not so incongruous in this vast open courtyard, filled with strangers and wayfarers drawn from every cranny country of the earth.

* * *

But as Paul passes back through the barrier to rejoin his companions, there is a man he identifies, hazily, as at the frayed edge of a dream; a man from Asia, from Ephesus. Is he a follower of The Way or just a Jew from Ephesus? Paul can't remember.

But the man clearly remembers Paul, because he shouts in anger, 'Men of Israel, help! This is the fellow who preaches everywhere against our people, the Law of Moses, and this edifice. More than that: see how he has just brought a Gentile into the inner Temple and desecrated this Holy Place.'

Does the man think Timothy is a Gentile, then? It is true that he is half-blooded and looks none too much Judaean. Or does the man recognize

Trophimus the Ephesian and assume that Paul had taken him, too, into the Temple? Or, worst of all, was this always a trap?

The four followers of James walk discreetly backwards from the fracas, returning to the sanctuary of the central courts.

Paul yells that he has committed no crime, that Timothy is a circumcised Jew.

But a crowd has formed; a ring of ruffians has organically appeared. Men who were seemingly dispersed in every direction, seeped into the corners, strolling, admiring the frescos, taking the shade of colonnades or half-heartedly haggling with stallholders, are suddenly gathered here. In cases where the likelihood of detection is so slight, the sanction must be heavy, or else where is the deterrent? For the warning signs to work, it must be known that the throng will enforce the toll. Judaea is a vendetta land under vendetta law. An eye should be gouged out for an eye lost. And this dreg riff-raff – suspiciously swift to emerge – seem extremely keen on gouging. Were they in wait for Paul, or do they always hope for the chance to commit murder countenanced by God?

Someone in the crowd shouts, 'Kill him!' And assailants tear into Paul. He is pummelled by fists. Knocked to the paving. The sky above him is dimmed by snarling shapes. Sandals stamp on his head. But Silas claws men from his master, swinging like a granite hammer. And Timothy jumps onto the back of one of the attackers and rends at his eyes. Mnason flees, but the two score of Paul's other supporters charge into the mass of aggressors and what was a brutal assault on one man becomes a swirling skirmish on the forecourt of the Temple. Though outnumbered, Paul's followers have advantage in knowing each other instantly, while the chaotic mass of their attackers faces confusion as well as pugilism. The violence is stilted and gusting – men grapple and are wrenched apart again. The battle is a vortex; centripetal Paul sucks in defence and aggression, many men fathoming who to fight in the brawling whirlpool only by how other combatants behave when close to the apostle.

Then Secundus, wrestling away an adversary who tries to strike his master, is knifed from behind in the small of his back and shrieks out at the pain as a sickle-shaped dagger is withdrawn. He drops to his knees, seeming puzzled, as if he feels an overwhelming urge to sit down and think about something, but he will not need to dwell on it for long. The assassin who struck the blow looks calm and satisfied. If he is angry, it is fury born of some slow-boiling hatred; he is not carried away in the heat of events.

But for a moment it is as if the fight has paused, while those nearby take in this escalation. And all who have seen, and are able, then draw their own blades and the pace of combat slows as the ripple of drawn daggers spreads and consequences climb. And the two sides disentangle and separate, backing away from knife slashes. Some of the fallen are dragged from the ground into their own lines.

Paul and his disciples are encircled by a force of greater and growing numbers. The apostle's followers gather around their master and the injured Secundus; silent Secundus, robe rooster-comb red, face translucent as a stilled bird-chick. And though the crowd hesitates to rush at the opposing knives, they begin to lob objects and feint lunges, as the bravery of superior numbers is bolstered. There is no way for the apostle's men to escape; it is stark clear how this will finish. The only remaining doubt is how long it will be before they are overborne and butchered. They will bleed out on the forecourt, like so many beasts. Because sacrilege demands sacrifice. There is no atonement without the shedding of blood.

But then, as a division of *deus ex machina*, a formation of Roman spearmen comes running, Mnason at their head, leading the cohort to the battleground. Mnason had a message to deliver in case of trouble and he has conveyed it, compelling as an angel. Legionary boots troop across the Temple court and the crowd must burn with the urge to pelt them or charge them, but to do so would mean death. The mob's blood is up, but they still hold on to the greasy edge of reason sufficiently not to challenge the trained killers of Rome. Not just yet.

The soldiers come to a practised stop with javelin points like a stockade buttress between the two factions. And the tribune of the cohort draws Paul from the mass of his followers and demands of him: 'Is it true what this man Mnason says, that you are a Roman citizen?'

And Paul, whose face is raw-bruised, who bleeds from his nose and his lip and one ear, laughing with fear-rush and relief, replies, 'I am. And, praise God, it was worth every drachma.'

Forty-nine Years after
the Crucifixion

Drusilla can feel a headache coming on. At least, let it be only that ... For sickness is no respecter of wealth or station: the *mal aria* – the bad-air fever that comes with the muggy summer humidity – robs from palace and shack alike, and even here at the seaside one is not completely immune. Life is a near-death experience. If you get ill, one of two things happens: you get better or you die. Physicians can do little more than predict which of those it will be and charge for whatever quackery they prescribe, if they think you might survive. Only dreamers really believe that healers cure disease. In this world a tiny incision can cost a limb or a life in gangrenous creep. Or lock your jaw, spasms spreading, muscles seizing and arching in orgasmic parody until ceased by suffocation. Or that small cut can become a funnel to ease into the body a plethora of amorphous pestilences – small wonder that men so shy from circumcision – but there are any number of ways to die. Ways beyond counting. Life is hard and death is easy. That is to say, for most people life is hard. For Drusilla, that has rarely strictly been the case.

Drusilla claps her hands to summon the slaves, growing tired of the expectant emptiness on the table in front of her. The naked girl who brings in the wine is newly bought, and Drusilla is rather pleased with her. She speaks perfect Greek, but is very pale-skinned, as if she came originally from some northern province, even from Germania perhaps; the girl herself doesn't know. Her breasts are pearls tipped with pink and her hair a white like gold in moonlight. She really was an awfully good purchase.

The girl fills Drusilla's gilt-silver goblet, with timid attentiveness. Drusilla seems to recall it came from Lesbos, this batch of wine, as much of the best does, from the isle of Sappho. To look at this slave, Drusilla wouldn't blame that girl-loving poetess for her preference. Drusilla could have half a mind to order this little one to her chamber tonight, in compensation for an absent husband, though she probably wouldn't even feel like it by the time the dreariness of the dinner party is over.

The thought draws Drusilla back to the moment and she smiles at the two ladies beside her on the couch. One is the wife of the *duoviri quinquennales*, the most important politician of this little Italian coastal town. The other is from the Rufus family, among the oldest and wealthiest lines in the area. The three women arranged on the opposite couch are similarly consequential. Life has taught Drusilla that such alliances are important and often they must be paid for, not only with the expense of fine tipples and delicacies but also with boredom.

The gorgeous slave-girl returns with a platter of durum sweets, fried with oil and absolutely drenched in honey. Drusilla takes a syrupy handful and passes some words of chatter with her guests, but cannot help her eyes being stolen once more by the slave-girl's effervescent rump and the heart-shaped gap where light shows between her upper thighs; she really is divine. She can't be any older than Drusilla was when she first married.

Drusilla shudders at the memory of those days. One might suppose she would have been glad to marry a king. But when you're born a princess, that is only what is to be expected, and Azizus was not a terribly kingly king.

He was a dreadful little man actually, all belly between his genitals and his beard. He barely passed ten words a day with her outside the bedchamber, and in it he huffed and puffed away, squashing her down like he was sealing a letter, yet was still quite convinced he was a lover to humble Apollo. As doubtless every courtesan and concubine had always told him it was so.

The slaves bring in bowls of warm water, muslin towels and oil of orris so that the diners may wash their sticky fingers. Though drawn from many races, Drusilla's slaves are uniformly comely; she does like to look upon beautiful things. But not one of them, save perhaps the new girl, could have matched Drusilla in her youth. She was once a beauty who made even her own ravishing sister envious.

Ageing is tedious for one who has been radiant when young. But even now, at forty-two, Drusilla still draws admiring gazes when she goes into town. She is helped in that by fame, of course, but largely it is her looks; this Italian resort is full of the second homes of senators and patricians; people are accustomed to celebrity here.

Most of the town's denizens are probably only dimly aware of who Drusilla is. Doubtless they have heard that she is some kind of Judaean princess, but it has been a tangled tale, this dynasty of the Herodians, even for those involved.

Drusilla's great-grandfather was Herod the Great; he had ten wives, until he executed one, and even though he had three of his own children murdered too, he still left such a superfluity of descendants alive as to cause succession crises and confusion for generations to come. After Herod's death, Rome divided his kingdom between three of his sons, but shortly reneged and deposed two. And Roman prefects ruled Judaea after that. Except, that is, for a brief spell when Drusilla's father was tried out as a client king; this was around the time that Drusilla was born, so she didn't know much about it until after the decision was revoked again. Later her brother, King Herod Agrippa, was given token rule over Galilee and Golan. But that, too, was annulled when revolt occurred, even though Agrippa naturally sided with the Romans in the war. The Herodians were Jewish up to a point, but certainly not to the point of suffering for it.

As if to underline Drusilla's own practical approach to her religion, the next course the slaves bring is of oysters, scallops and sea urchins, cuttlefish and clams, all cooked in a mint and cumin sauce, a dish absolutely prohibited, of course, to those who adhere strictly to the Torah, but rather fine to eat for all that. And there are also stuffed sow's wombs and barley cakes and honeyed mushrooms and lobster, with a little vinegared cabbage and dressed cucumber. All the lounging diners comment on what a marvellous spread it is and how they must repay Drusilla the compliment when they can.

And it is well to be entrenched with influential people because the Romans give and the Romans take away. Even as a princess married to a king, Drusilla was perceptive enough to realize where the real power lay. Her husband, Azizus, was king for precisely as long as Rome allowed it. Ruler of a small Syrian city state, client king of an anthill and a patch of sand.

Next the naked slaves bring in capon, filled with lamb brain and ginger, sprinkled with crushed pepper and pine kernels. A capon is a castrated cockerel; Drusilla has never really worked out how one would go about castrating something that doesn't appear to have anything to cut off. Just another of those tiny mysteries of life, which would be simple enough to solve if one could be bothered to ask a slave.

Drusilla's second husband had once been a slave himself. Strange thing, to exchange a king for a freedman. But when she had first seen Felix, he was no slave: he was prefect of Judaea. He came with a retinue of legionaries into her husband's court, and by the way that fat Syrian flustered and abased himself in trying to ingratiate, it was apparent which man was the nobler.

Felix was handsome, in a rough-cast soldierly way, and he had the look of one who would be just as hard and commanding when he fucked; which Drusilla had thought might be rather nice. And she was so thoroughly bored with her little tin-pot king in that regard.

Drusilla herself barely spoke at that initial encounter, but she had made sure that Felix took in her best side. She had looked down, as if demurely, but really to lure his eyes to the shadow-slit between her breasts. And she crouched up on the cushions as she readjusted, curving up her back like a little cat. And she could see that Felix was glued as an ant in honey.

And why shouldn't she have trapped him thus? That being all the power she had. Felix was a brute, the kind of man so domineering that he thinks he can plunder whatever he wants from the world. So Drusilla let him take what he wanted, without him ever realizing that the choice wasn't truly his. *Felix* means 'lucky', but in spite of this, the prefect believed he carved his own path through life. He believed he made his own luck, as lucky people invariably do.

Drusilla snared Felix so utterly that in his entrapment he supposed himself to be the hunter. He sent a magician to the court to woo Drusilla secretly on his behalf, and she allowed them both to dream that her seduction was accomplished by their cunning. How is it that men can believe they rule the world when they would risk and lose it all for the chance to screw a beautiful girl? They don't even rule their own selves. So Drusilla said farewell to her chubby, stumpy king and plucked herself a freedman Roman prefect. She eloped, like she was Helen of Troy, careless as to whether she would leave war in her wake.

And those first years together, Drusilla and Felix were almost like Adam and Eve, so often were they naked and alone. Maybe the fruit of that forbidden Eden tree was a metaphor for language itself, Drusilla thinks, because all words must have been sex noises in the beginning. When there were only those two first people, grunts and moans were all the communication required. But afterwards we had to learn to promise because we had invented lies. We needed words; we needed consonants and vowels and verbs in order to conceal our true selves and obfuscate real intentions. But in sex, we return to Eden.

The first murmurings of that headache coming on seem to have gone, to Drusilla's relief. A few cups of wine invariably work better than anything a physician might prescribe. Opposite her, on the other couch, the wife of Lucius Caecilius Jucundus holds a ball of amber, rubbing it occasionally and smelling its delicate fragrance. It's a bit of an affectation, to Drusilla's mind. Noble ladies do that in Rome in order to mask foul stenches, but there is no need for it in a fine villa in a delightful little seaside town like this one and among such aromas of food. It is borderline insulting, in fact; Drusilla wonders whether she ought to strip the woman from her future invitations altogether. Her husband is only a banker, after all, a dreadfully vulgar occupation. A banker is no better than a goatherd, save for proximity to money.

Goat is the diners' next delight, when the slaves bring it in. Or not goat, but a plump kid, as tender-fleshed and juicy as a peach, so young it must have had more milk in its veins than blood when it was slaughtered.

It has always seemed to Drusilla that the Torah rule, *Do not cook a kid in its mother's milk*, was probably supposed to be a reference to the age of the animal, rather than some vague prohibition about combining meat and dairy. For a people teetering near survival's edge, to kill a beast still suckling makes no sense; much better to let it fatten up first and eat it once weaned. However it was, Drusilla is no subsistence desert-dweller and she has long since left off worrying about those Laws.

Her first husband, good King Azizus, had been obliged by her brother to convert to Judaism before marrying her. But Herod Agrippa made no such terms for Felix. How could he? No one but the emperor tells a Roman prefect what to do. The Jerusalem high priest Jonathan had rebuked Felix on how he was governing and Felix simply had him murdered. One did not even give unsolicited advice to Felix.

Though Felix had seemed to enjoy talking with that curious man, Paul. He was about the only Jew Felix much listened to; the one who said the Law of Moses was ended. It was almost as if Felix was looking for confirmation that he was right to ignore the Torah. Though, so far as Drusilla knows, no one was ever brave or foolish enough to suggest to his face that he ought to convert anyway.

That thing with Paul was a funny old business start to finish. They were at the Herodian palace at Caesarea, which had become the prefect's residence; Drusilla had been asleep, curled around the hard-body form of Felix, when the messenger came. The slave who had been fanning them throughout the night must have stirred Felix to alert him to the news, because Drusilla herself woke to the noise of Felix saying, 'Go on then, read it out.'

And a centurion cleared his throat as he broke a scroll's seal and told how the man Paul had been seized in the Jerusalem Temple and was about to be killed, when the tribune of the cohort had saved him, having learned that he was a Roman citizen. The tribune wrote that although Paul was charged with questions about the Torah, there was no charge against him under Roman law. But reliable sources had informed the tribune that more than forty men had taken a Nazirite Vow, which would not end until they had killed Paul. Whether these men were of the sect of the Nazarenes or not, the tribune didn't know, but the assassins were supposedly unafraid to ambush Paul even while he was in Roman custody. And the tribune must have taken this threat to be very real, because the prisoner Paul was immediately dispatched to Caesarea guarded by two hundred legionaries and a cavalry detachment of seventy, with a further two hundred light skirmishers to protect the flanks.

So Felix had ordered the centurion to hold Paul guarded in the palace, though under open arrest, to let him have some freedom and not to keep any of his friends from visiting or caring for his needs. And the funny thing was, over time, Felix had seemed to grow rather fond of Paul. He did have this way about him, hard to define; it wasn't that he was terribly congenial, yet people were pulled towards him, like the tides to a shore. He was a man hard to ignore; his presence demanded one decide whether to love or hate him. He was quite a small man – in fact the name Paul even means 'small' – yet he seemed to occupy a great deal of space.

Deputations of Israelites from Jerusalem came asking for Paul to be delivered over to be dealt with by the Sanhedrin, but Felix would have none of it. And, anyway, the man had the right of appeal to Caesar's court: Paul was a Roman citizen – he had the proof of it in twin inscribed bronze tablets, folded together and wax-sealed – and even if that citizenship was newly purchased, it was no less of a fact. And Felix himself being a freedman, he had a certain disdain for old lineages; he believed a new citizen to be every grain as much a Roman as a man who could trace his family line for five centuries; a point on which the law agreed.

So for two years Paul had stayed with them at the palace in Caesarea. Felix wouldn't hand the prisoner to the Jerusalem council, but neither would he release him. It wasn't only that Felix grew affectionate, of course: he also had hopes of a bribe from Paul. Felix's informants had learned that Paul had access to a great deal of money. And it must have been a very large sum indeed to have maintained the attention of a man like Felix. A proconsul might earn four hundred thousand sesterces per year – a sum sufficient to keep eight hundred average families – in wage alone, never mind what he could wring from the province he ruled. Felix must have had strong evidence that Paul had substantial gold stashed away. But, so far as Drusilla knows, no bribe was ever paid. There might have been remuneration here and there for upkeep, but the big pay-off seems never to have arrived.

So Paul was still there, at the palace in Caesarea, when Felix was recalled to Rome. And Drusilla went with her husband, leaving the land of her ancestors and leaving their customs too.

The slaves bring in a large silver platter; it takes four of them to carry it, their buttocks jiggling as they take little shuffle steps so as not to shift the whole roast porker on the salver. It is lying there, on a back crinkled with salted crackling, sprawled as if asking for its tummy to be tickled, but that belly is slit open and inside it are baked thrushes, mussels, figs and sweetbreads, spilling over as if trying to escape.

'Such ecstatic creations,' says Alypia, one of the couched women. 'You really are spoiling us, Drusilla.'

Alypia's husband is in *garum*, the ubiquitous

fish sauce that Italians seem unable to cook or eat anything without using. Alypia is a little excitable and young, but she at least seems fun, and her husband is obscenely rich. He staged a gladiator show in the town's stadium with thirty pairs of fighters earlier in the summer, without even seeking election, just for the spectacle of it.

Hopefully Felix will shortly come down from Rome to join Drusilla in their seaside villa. She yearns for him; she aches when they are apart. Over the years, she has come to truly love him. And more than that, when you are with a man like Felix, a man who fears nothing and believes he can do anything, you feel so invulnerable; maybe Felix perceived that same quality in Paul. But Drusilla cannot bear Rome, even to see her husband; she goes there as seldom as possible. The summer stink is intolerable and disease is rife and everything is just so much more pleasant when you can look out across the sea.

After this last dish, she might command that pastel Nordic slave to perform an erotic dance, perhaps with one of the other slaves. That might be rather nice. See if it shocks the stuffy, amber-rubbing banker's wife.

It is a little tedious to have to entertain, but not so bad, and one must try to ingratiate oneself with the influential locals. Drusilla is contented in this prettiest of Italy's resort towns, cooled by gentle zephyrs of breeze, surrounded by farmlands and the plump grapes growing on the fertile slopes of Mount Vesuvius. A mountain that has started smoking of late, like the gentle breathing of a contented god; like the billows that once flowed up from the Temple at Jerusalem. The local wines aren't nearly as good as those from

Lesbos, of course, but still, it is a fine hideaway
in which to settle and enjoy a blessed life:
Pompeii.

Twenty-nine Years after the Crucifixion

For two years Paul was detained in the palace at Caesarea – less than guest and more than prisoner – with the governor Felix and his wife Drusilla. But after Felix is recalled, Porcius Festus is made prefect.

Porcius arrives in an increasingly unstable land, nationalist banditry rife in the countryside and Sicarii, crowd-mingling, sickle-daggered assassins, murdering collaborators and the impious in the cities with rising regularity. Compared to Porcius's other problems, the issue of what to do with Paul is just a minor irritation. But it is an irritation nonetheless.

Felix used to enjoy talking with Paul, but upon hearing the apostle preach for the first time, Porcius Festus declares, 'You are raving mad, Paul. Learning has sent you insane.'

Aware of this altered stance in governance, the Jerusalem authorities renew their petition that Paul stand trial for blasphemy before them. But Paul once again claims Roman exemption.

If Porcius Festus dismisses the charges outright he may face uproar, but if he condemns a citizen, simply to placate the ire of provincials, his political prospects could be lastingly marred. So Porcius comes to a prudent and plain solution: Paul has appealed to Roman justice so let him face justice at Rome.

* * *

For the journey, Paul is transferred to the custody of a centurion called Julius of the *Frumentarii*, a group of detached legionaries who secure supply lines, courier messages and perhaps spy. Julius has a ruddy, broad farmer's face, which belies a mind dark and supple as a mole viper. For the assigned task, Julius commands a unit of auxiliaries from the Augustan cohort and they all board ship on the fifteenth day of the Augustan month.

The soldiers are necessary because Paul is not the only prisoner under transport. A group of manacled *damnati* – thieves, tax absconders and the merely unlucky – are also on their way to Rome, so that their blood can fertilize the arena's barren soil.

But Paul is not herded with those others. He is no convict, but a person awaiting Caesar's court, who should be extended some courtesy. Paul is a man of substance and a citizen. During his time at the prefect's palace, the apostle has even taken to wearing the toga, a hot, woollen encumbrance. A cloth sixteen feet long and ten across, which drapes upon the body, held in place under its own weight. But which carries weight also in what it signifies: that one is a person of wealth and standing. To add to the picture, Aristarchus and Timothy pose as Paul's slaves and because of this are allowed to accompany and attend to him.

Centurion Julius accords Paul so much respect that when the ship ports at Sidon in Syria, on the first leg of the journey, Paul is allowed into the town to visit supporters there and to stay with them while the vessel's captain awaits favourable winds. The other prisoners remain on board, manacled and caged, sickening from the swells and close-confinement.

As soon as the weather allows, the ship travels onwards, skirting the coast, far to the sheltered east of Cyprus. A voyage of ponderous progress, making creeping use of the changeable local land breezes and the steady westward currents, frequently anchoring as advance is thwarted. When the days are clear, the ship passes within sight of many places that have shaped Paul's life: Antioch, which once was his great base, until he was driven from it by those Judaizers; the Taurus Mountains, behind Tarsus, his boyhood home; Perga, where John-Mark deserted; and numberless sites of triumphs across the shores of Pamphylia and Cyprus, where communities of the sanctified were founded.

More than two weeks it takes, of nautical dawdle, to make port in Myra. The ship is ultimately bound for Troas, where it will harbour for some months. Sailing becomes ever more dangerous as autumn progresses and not even the unhinged take to the seas in the turbulence of winter.

The centurion Julius had planned to travel overland for much of the route from Troas. But by chance, while at Myra, a grain-ship docks, having come from Egypt. More than half of the Nile delta's crop props up the Roman corn-dole. A premium is paid to those captains brave enough to deliver late in the sailing season and this ship, large enough to cross open seas, still intends to make direct route to Rome.

Julius's rank secures passage for his soldiers and prisoners and the ship is then a skillet of grain and blood, all that buttresses the Emperor Nero from the urban beast he rides.

Including crew, Paul counts seventy-six souls on the ship that might be saved, but few are of a mind to listen to him. The west wind continues to run against them; progress is hard and slow. A distance past Cnidus, which could have been done in a single day with a following draught, instead steals the best of a week.

When the wind shifts even worse, to north-west, exactly opposing the direction they should be travelling, the captain is forced to sail past Crete and seek refuge in the natural harbour called Fair Havens, on the southern side of that island. And there they are stranded, at anchor for so many days that the Israelite Day of Atonement passes while they are there. Not that any on board fast, but it is a measure of how perilously late into the sailing season they are running. It begins to seem likely they will be forced to spend all winter in the bay.

As it is, the ship is marooned deep into the month of Octobris, but then a slight southerly breeze starts to blow, and a council is taken on how to proceed. A person of rank and an experienced traveller, Paul is allowed to attend and give his view, which is that they ought to remain precisely where they are. But the captain thinks it better to use the beneficial zephyr at least to sail further around the Cretan coast to the port of Phoenix, which is better shielded for the ship to winter in and will allow them freer access to supplies and is in any event in the direction they must ultimately travel so might promise a faster spring departure. The grain-ship being under the command of Rome, the centurion Julius has the final decision and naturally he favours the advice of the mariner; they hoist anchor and resume sailing along the shore of Crete.

But the ship hasn't covered half the distance to Phoenix when there tears down from the Cretan mountains the wind they call Euraquilo: a violent north-easter, typhonic in ferocity. The squall strikes with sudden force, near to tearing the single square sail from the mast, or the mast from the ship. The hull groans with the leverage of the great beam, and old hands cry that the clinkers will burst and send them all to choking death.

Such oars as the ship has are only for manoeuvring close to port, useless in a gale. The crew has no choice but to let the ship be ripped away from the Cretan shore and further out to sea, running with the wind to avoid being sunk by the strain of resisting it. Rain comes thick as ropes, so dense the passengers fear they will drown each time they breathe. Waves lift the ship high as city walls. The decks shudder and the sea grows black.

By helmsmanship, or luck, or both, they are able to steer the craft into the lee of a small island called Cauda, lying off Crete. The storm is still violent and it is impossible to anchor; billows, white-crested as if toothed, continue to crash against the craft, but in the part-shelter of the isle they are at least able to perform urgencies that had been impossible in the full squall. The crew lower the sail that had threatened to undo them; it might even have blown them to the wrecking sandbars off Libya, had they not got it down. Then they undergird the ship: running a double length of rope from stern to bow and torquing it tight, to stop the hull bending with the force of the pounding. While the sailors are at these tasks, the soldiers and passengers are ordered to haul in the ship's boat, which, after the practice of the time, had been drifting on a line behind them, threatening to capsize. It takes all their strength to get it on board, with the ship wrenching and the wind blasting. Their eyes sting from the salt spray and driving downpour, and it is hard even to grasp the rope, their hands are so slick with water.

The *damnati* shriek that they should be freed from their chains, or they will certainly die if the ship goes down. But the centurion tells them every man on board will drown if the ship sinks, and those in chains will be blessed to perish fastest. They should be grateful to be fastened and caged, when the wash that sweeps across the decks threatens to tear better men overboard.

Timothy vomits in the constant rolling churn. He retches until his stomach is empty; then he dry-retches the lining, then he vomits again with all the water swallowed in the retching.

Paul tries to lift his spirits with a psalm:

> *'Some went out on the sea in ships;*
> *they were merchants on the mighty waters.*
> *They saw the works of the Lord,*
> *His wonderful deeds in the deep.*
> *For He spoke and stirred up a tempest*
> *that lifted high the waves.*
> *They mounted up to the heavens and went*
> *   down to the depths;*
> *in their peril their courage melted away.*
> *They reeled and staggered like drunkards;*
> *they were at their wits' end.*
> *Then they cried out to the Lord in their*
> *   trouble,*

and He brought them out of their distress.
He stilled the storm to a whisper;
the waves of the sea were hushed.
They were glad when it grew calm,
and He guided them to their desired haven.'

But the storm is not stilled with a whisper and the waves are not hushed and it does not grow calm, and the only guidance to be found is the wind Euraquilo.

The crew swing the ship so that its prow points into the gale. Then they rig a small foresail, only big enough to hold the bow position, in hope not to be sunk by wave-crashes from the side. And they throw out sea-anchors to steady and slow. But they can do nothing more than this and the ship courses with the storm, dragged ever further from safety.

The breakers are blasted skyward and the rain comes drenching as a sea and the heavens are half as often at the side as above, so that no one even knows which way is up or where water ends and air begins. One wave hasn't passed before the next hits and they join and tear apart again. The deck is treacherous and terrifying, lit only when lightning flashes, but to go below is to sit in rocking, slopping liquid in darkness and misery and to know that water lies on every side and even overhead.

On the next day the tempest has not diminished and the ship is tossed so fearfully that it's decided they must jettison the cargo, to lessen the force of the waves on the broadside. Valuable sacks of Nile grain are heaved from the hold in human chain over slippery, pitching boards and fed to Poseidon's white horses. But if that salt god is pleased by the gift, he doesn't show it and the storm continues to rage.

The third day, to further lighten, for fear the planks will be torn apart, they hurl into the billows all the ship's goods and tackle, everything any less than vital. And the wounds caused by falls and splintered wood are first washed clean and then washed raw. And the passengers follow the crew in lashing themselves to those parts of the ship they deem least likely to be swept away.

The gale still doesn't abate. And after many more nights' drifting before it, fear itself is just a distant memory, replaced in most with the certainty of despair. For more than a week the sailors see neither sun nor stars nor any land, so that they cannot do better than guess where they are. Some fear they will be crushed on reefs or rocks and others that they will disintegrate in the open water. And old salts, who had thought they had known and conquered every hazard of the sea, cry tears masked by the rain and the sprays and sob supplications hidden in the howls of the gale.

They can't make cooking fires on deck to bake the remnants of grain, and all the hardened biscuits and salted fish are long gone, so they eat raw, mortared corn, damp with blustered sea water. Most hunger and all are cold. The soldiers and seamen have woollen cloaks waterproofed with oil and Paul and his pseudo-slaves have thick travelling clothes, but all of these are drenched and heavy. The *damnati* shiver in their shackles, clustered tight together like a colony of seabirds. Not a nail or pot or inch of skin on board has known dryness in a week. Chains and ropes have snapped; the taut foresail barely holds. And the ship sometimes leans so hard that a man at the side could stretch a hand into the deep, but all are strapped at the centre away from waters that yawn like jaws.

More days they suffer in hopelessness, still blasted towards they know not what fate by the storm; perhaps even until they drop off the edge of the world. Each time they think they feel the tempest lighten, it proves to be a dream.

Paul reminds them of how they should have followed his advice: never to have left the anchorage at Fair Havens. But they resist the urge to send him over, like a Jonah, for long enough to hear him also say that an angel came to him in the night and promised they would all be saved. Some of the mariners pluck small comfort from this because – though no man saw this angel – it is clear from Paul's countenance that he earnestly believes what he says, and there is no other comfort to be found.

They will not even know a grave or pyre when the ship goes down, only the ocean and the stripping fishes. Some have travelled half the world to be here and some who are slaves had no choice in that. And men who have never prayed in their lives pray now. To Poseidon, Thalassa and Oceanus; to Triton and Palaemon; to Castor and Pollux; to the sea nymph Thetis and the white goddess Leukothea; and some even wager a prayer to that resurrected God of Paul's to see if He might bring them back from this oblivion.

It is near midnight on the fourteenth day adrift in the tempest when the first sailor senses that land is near. And others, too, believe it to be so, either smelling soil, as some old tars can, or picking out the resound of breakers upon a shore even amid the still-blowing storm.

Though water washes across the deck, so deep it is sometimes hard to be sure they are not sunk, the mariners take a depth-sounding over the side and find it twenty fathoms and then a little later fifteen fathoms. But because it is double dark from cloud and night they can't risk drifting in to smash upon cliffs or rocks so they throw out four anchors from the stern, which by miracle catch in clay, to hold the ship fast. The vessel slews about, like a bull at the end of a charge, and with the groans of planks in the last of integrity, the prow faces a shore the voyagers cannot see.

Some deckhands lower the ship's boat, saying that they are going to lay more anchors in advance of the bow – each two-armed of jujube wood and iron – so that the ship can be eased slowly into land when daylight comes. Probably their intentions are honest – it would seemingly be suicide to make for an unknown and stormy shore in a small craft in the dark – but Paul is convinced the men are trying to escape to save only themselves and he persuades the centurion of it. So Julius slices the lifeboat's rope and it is set adrift, an empty vessel on a shadow sea.

Daylight reveals a coast that no one on board recognizes but which has at one point a sandy bay. Because the ship is anchored from the rear, it is proposed that they raise the foresail, cut the lines and attempt to beach the ship.

So they slot the steering oars, and at the captain's signal, as the cloth fills, soldiers hack all four anchor ropes at once and the ship, under full sail for the first time in two weeks, ploughs at speed towards the land. Their course runs true at the bay and even the *damnati* cheer and laugh. But then, still some distance from shore, the ship strikes a sandbar and every man is thrown from his feet.

The fore of the ship is held fast by the bank, but

waves continue to pound into the stern, and the much battered boards begin to fragment. Many weep then, to have come so close to salvation, only to face the water, after all. Those of the sailors who can swim, seeing that the ship is breaking up and knowing the first will have it best with the sharks, leap into the sea and make for the beach. The prisoners plead to be freed from their chains, so that they, too, might try for land. Some of the soldiers would sooner put them to death, to prevent escape. But Paul repeats to Julius the angel's promise that all would be saved and the centurion orders that the *damnati* be released. And the soldiers leave their weapons, to better their chances with the billows.

The ship wails, while the waves tear it apart, as if it came alive only in death. And those men still on board aid in their vessel's destruction, rending from it such pieces as they hope will float. Some jump and some tremulously descend upon ropes. But all take themselves into the swells, grasping at planks and debris.

Paul, Timothy and Aristarchus cling together on a section of cross-shaped flotsam, which once had formed part of the aft, and supported by it the three of them kick their way towards the land. And not only they, but every single man of the ship – bone-cold, bloodied, drenched and starving – staggers up the sand alive.

* * *

Through the darkness of the tempest they drifted from Crete more than five hundred miles to Malta. And they will stay wintered on that island, until another vessel carries them onward to Italy.

Over the quarter-century of Paul's missionary

journeys, he travelled perhaps as many as ten thousand miles. But upon arrival he will never leave Rome again.

Thirty-four Years after
the Crucifixion

There are white flakes down the crease of Paul's mouth, where drool in his sleep must have dried. One side of his age-wrinkled cheek is squashed flat from the unyielding pillow of the prison's stone floor. These days, Paul's eyes take a long time to focus when he first awakes. He doesn't recall that this used to be the case. Paul has spent a long lifetime resisting sleep. Always he has been the last to bed and the first to rise. Sleep is sister-son of death, an oblivion once to be feared, before God's promise. Yet, if denied its release for sufficient time, even strong men break. We might give up almost anything for sleep in the end.

In the near darkness of the cave-gaol, some pray and some cry. They rock and sob. And rats scuttle and couples rut. And you can't blame them for it and the Christ forgives. Man is born into trouble, as surely as sparks fly upward, and the Christ forgives. The rich take it hardest in here. Those who have always known the quiet violence of poverty adjust to new horrors more easily.

Yesterday, if day it was, Paul told the story of Job, a righteous and prosperous man, who the accuser Satan said was pious only because he was so blessed with wealth and family. So God granted permission for His servant Job to be tested, to prove that his love of God was true. And Job's oxen and asses were stolen from him. And his sheep were burned and his slaves were murdered. And all his children were struck dead. And Job himself was afflicted with hideous, hurtful boils that covered him from the soles of his feet to the crown of his head. And Job cursed the day he was conceived and wished he had died in the womb, but he did not curse God. Thus God won his wager with Satan.

Paul had meant the story to give them heart, but one of the hearers had softly said, 'Then this new God you have brought us to is no different from the gods of Rome: they destroy men for diversion.'

* * *

The torturers who took Silas's speech and sight might just as well have killed him. Though Paul does all he can, Silas cannot or will not eat, and he grows weaker every day. His breath stinks even above the putrid prison because of the infected wound where once his tongue was attached and because his body is consuming itself. He seems resolved to death; though emotions are hard to ascertain from a voiceless, eyeless man in a domain of permanent dusk.

Paul thinks back to the assembly of Thessalonica. The despondency that struck them when the first of his converts there died. They had been told they were baptized into eternal life so had not expected death. Perhaps Paul had not wholly expected it himself, though in retrospect it made sense: the dead in Christ will be the first to rise when He returns but, of course, this doesn't mean that no more will die until that time. Some things are best clarified through looking back on them.

Other things should be forgotten. Past pains cease even to be scars, if allowed to fade from view entirely. Yesterday is what we say it was, as long as it doesn't return. But all too often it does return. All too often it comes back in the same stony shape.

* * *

Many of the Christianoi are praying when the hole in the ceiling is opened. The voices of the women chime and mingle. So often have they said these words that they have fallen into a rhythmic cadence, like song. The men unconsciously harmonize, high and low become one. A hum is produced at the edge of the words, a vibration that murmurs back and throughout the cavern.

The rope is lowered and another prisoner is let down. It is a marvel that the hemp doesn't snap with the strain because the figure who descends is almost the same size and shape as one of the great rock obelisks Roman road-builders use to sign a parting of the ways.

Even prison is no protection, Paul thinks, but he raises a hand in some sort of greeting and smiles, though the smile is thin and sore as rope burn.

When his bare feet touch the damp rock floor, Cephas warily acknowledges the wave and comes to Paul, with an old man's slow lumber. Cephas eases himself down and blankets the hand of silent Silas in one of his own, squeezing gently.

'So do you still say that Caesar is a noble God-appointed ruler now, Paul? Will you say it even as they cut off your head?' But there is perhaps more tenderness in Cephas's rheumy old eyes than anything else.

'Our differences don't matter now, Peter. The veil is about to be lifted. The truth will be shown soon enough. The axe is at the root of the tree. This is the moment that was always coming.'

'Yes, the axe is at the root of the tree, where it's been these thirty-odd years. But if you've changed the head with a new blade and changed the haft with a different handle, is it still the same axe? Perhaps it is no longer even an axe. Maybe you now hold a mattock or a hoe.'

'Well, presently we'll know. And if this is not yet the end of days, be content that your vision of The Way will be the victor, Peter. My stoutest supporters will try to continue, I don't doubt it, but without me they can't stand against the authority of James, the Lord's brother.'

'You don't know, then?' Cephas says, his voice in pebble waver. 'I thought the whole world would have heard by now. James the Just is dead, Paul. James is dead.'

Thirty-two Years after the Crucifixion

Last night James stayed in Bethany. At the home of an enduring friend, the same house where his brother was once anointed with costly oil, as all kings must be. Thus James now descends the Mount of Olives as he walks to the Temple. It distils one's mind, to pass through that place where so much happened. And so much did not happen. Where they prayed in the darkness for all that Zechariah had prophesized and promised. But the earthquakes didn't come and the Romans did.

There is a leafy smell of plenty in the olive groves. A scent much missed in recent years. And everything cries of the Galilee Sea, strangely, because those Galilee days are far away in distance and time, but the wind rolls in James's ears, the trees sway like the waves and it's cool and fresh as the breeze on a boat.

Some of the trees are old as Methuselah, with trunks thicker than the backs of a plough-pulling brace of oxen. How would these ancient olive trees be with wild shoots grafted on to their roots? Would they thrive as they do now or would the struggle to combine kill both parts and whole? James knows the alluring maniac Paul has written that his Gentile communities are just so grafted on to the nourishing sap from the root of Israel, from which he says the Jews themselves are now snapped off. Who knows if Paul really believes such things? Paul's lips drip honey and his speech is smoother than oil, but James is sure God loves His people. That is life's one certainty. God covenanted this land to prove it. And presently Yeshua will return to free it.

James treads stiffly down the path towards the Kidron valley, winding between the coin-round rolling stones of the ossuary caves hollowed into the hillside. That was another certain truth: James was witness to the empty tomb; he and Cephas saw with their own eyes that Yeshua's body was gone. There are Sadducees who say it wasn't so, but they are flatly wrong.

From here, the Temple is barely as big as one of James's dark thumbnails, but only as everything is decreased from a distance: nothing can negate the Temple's importance; like a guardian, the Temple watches over Jerusalem. And the Roman Antonia Fortress watches over the Temple. Jerusalem's walls of quarry-cut limestone, higher than the tallest trees, look impregnable, yet they have been pregnated: enemy seed lies within, multiplying. But shortly Yeshua will return to defeat all oppression and usher in the true Kingdom of God.

There have been other would-be messiahs, of course, during the period while James and those of The Way have patiently waited for Yeshua's reappearance. Just a few years back there was the one they called the Egyptian, who was convinced that he could bring Judaea liberty and a new dawn. The Egyptian had gathered a multitude of common people right here on the Mount of Olives – from where the new age must indeed begin – saying he would collapse the fortifications of Jerusalem – perhaps he hoped for earthquakes. Then he and his believers would march through the tumbled defences and defeat the Romans and their collaborators. The prefect of the time, Felix, had unleashed a force that killed four hundred of the Egyptian's followers and captured another two hundred alive, later all crucified.

Before the Egyptian, there was the man called Theudas. Roman horsemen had decapitated him and slaughtered many of his acolytes, without waiting to see if Theudas could indeed perform the miracles he claimed. Which, of course, he would not have done: Yeshua is the true anointed one, of the line of David, and any day now he will come back to prove it.

* * *

James prays in the Temple so frequently and for so long that his knees have grown swollen and calloused, like those of a camel. It pains them now to walk great distances; not that this is such a long way – the Kidron valley is not even wider than a dog's bark, for dogs on one side can cause retaliation from the other – but the steep uphill from its bottom still takes its toll. James is past sixty years, a venerable enough age for any man to reach in these times, but he won't be going anywhere until Yeshua returns. That much is sure.

James rests when he reaches the vast steps of the Temple, which lead to its double and triple gates. There's a vagabond at the foot of them, with a grey-faced monkey in a little tunic. And when the man plays his reed pipes the monkey dances for him. A watching toddler flaps his arms and shrieks with joy that such a thing should be. Too young yet to know that in Jerusalem all things are.

When the Greek-Seleucid Empire outlawed and tried to extinguish the religion of the Israelites, women were thrown from this corner of the Temple Mount, for having their babies circumcised. And people who hid to observe the Sabbath were burned alive. Many were tortured and slaughtered for refusing to eat swine meat. These things that Saul of Tarsus would surrender are not convention or etiquette. They are the very essence of a nation. They are the people's portion of the contract agreed with God.

As he approaches the leftmost gate, James hands a coin to a ragged and ancient crone who sits there, not seemingly begging but without other obvious pursuit. And she says she'll give it to the poor ones, though the idea that there could be anyone poorer than her seems improbable. And then she says, 'I met him, you know. I knew him, if only for a moment of a day. That day in the Temple. He was like the sky wrapped in a skin.'

And she looks as though she might be mad – she puts a hand over her mouth, as if to stop her speech, or else to hide it – but she speaks the truth, because who could she mean but Yeshua? And if that's who she means, then it's as good a description as any.

James passes through the gate and into the glorious colonnaded courtyard of the Temple, a space so huge that it occupies perhaps a tenth of the entire city. A feat of engineering near mystical. Mostly the pale stone is smooth as kidskin but here and there are blocks left irregular, just as they came. Parts a builder could have left aside, but which have become corner stones.

Everything is about stone in this land. Yeshua named a fisherman Cephas – Peter, in Greek – Rocky. Then he with James and Jochanan became the Three Pillars. And now James, already surnamed the Just, is also known as Oblias – Rampart of the People – not only a pillar, but a bulwark wall that protects them. James has risen in populist prominence to become almost a rival high priest. He wears the white linen robes and turban of a priest this very day. There are even rumours that James has entered the Holy of Holies, the innermost sanctum, where only the high priest is allowed. If James has really done so, it is blasphemy. But if he has done so and lived, it is a sign of confidence and power and of God's favour.

Many among the Jerusalemites have long doubted the legitimacy of high priests chosen by Rome. James now speaks openly against the present incumbent: Annas the Younger; Annas son of Annas; offspring of the man who had a hand in Yeshua's death.

James has publicly called Annas ben Annas a sack-swollen tick, bloated from feeding, the blood of others swirling within translucent stretched skin. A ruler who oppresses the poor is like a dustbowl wind that obliterates crops. James says that Annas and all the rich should weep for the miseries that are going to come upon them once Yeshua returns. But some in Jerusalem already tire of waiting for Yeshua's return and call for his brother to be anointed in his stead.

A hooded crow, black but for its tunic of grey chainmail, lands clumsily in James's path and stares at him, one-eyed, with a twisted head.

It is not because of the bird, but James senses that something is wrong. Is this premonition, or does he subconsciously spot subtleties too small to define, imperceptible differences on the courtyard that lead to his stomach so rapidly sickening with a feeling of ill?

James crouches a moment, as if struck by a sudden need to pray, but he does it rather to take pause on his route and have a guarded look about. He sees nothing amiss, but whispers scripture anyway:

'For man knows not when his hour will come;
As fish are caught in a cruel net,
And birds are snared with a noose,
So are the sons of man trapped in an evil time,
When it falls suddenly upon them.'

James takes a further vigilant sweep. The bright white marble and burnished-gold Temple – wider at the front than at the back, like a prone lion – glows with glory. Low murmurs of prayers drift about. And the incomprehensible chatter from clusters of foreigners, words that sound like whoops and hoots and yelps. The tang of rich incense on the air. Stallholders shout and beasts bleat. People gaze in wonder, looking serious and worshipful. Others gossip as if by a village well. A nose-tied bull raises a suddenly rigid tail, a right-angle removal, to defecate with audible exhalation. And two small brothers laugh to witness it, as James and Yeshua might once have done. Pilgrims meander with pale palms held out before them, as if they carry invisible loads. Men nod gravely as they encounter those notices that warn of the death deserved by Gentile trespassers past that point; they physically acknowledge as if outwardly to declare that they understand and agree and that the penalty does not apply to them. An Ethiope limps by, one foot held out sideways, slowed by some ailment. And in the shades of the outer colonnades, merchants spit on their hands to seal deals. Wealthy men, most of them, who will howl when Yeshua returns. For the sun rises with scorching heat and withers the plant; its blossom falls and its beauty is destroyed. In the same way, the rich will fade away even while they go about their business. But for the moment they are engrossed and pay no attention to the kneeling apostle. Neither can James see anything else to account for why he should feel so suddenly fearful. There is not even a single Temple Guard in sight.

And, as James thinks this, the realization sinks, because there should be. He becomes conscious that the thing he senses is in fact an absence: there are no Temple Guards to be seen. When there should be. There always are. And if they cannot be seen, then it means that they are unseen.

James pushes himself up and starts to make for the eastern gate. Maybe he shouldn't have come alone, but Jochanan and Cephas are both abroad, converting the colonies of that exiled enemy, Paul, brushing away his lies, which are as fragile as spiders' webs. And James should have nothing to fear, here in the Temple, in public. He is the Just One, a Pillar, the Rampart of the People. The Pharisees would clamour for retribution if the high priest dared to touch him.

But it seems that Annas son of Annas has decided that risk is worth it, to silence a rival and a critic, because his Temple Guards now pour forth. In two columns they troop across the courtyard. Crowds clearing before them. James flees as fast as he can, but his knees are crick and gristled from his life of prayer. The guards close and there is no doubting their purpose. James flings out with his staff to ward them back. But they grapple him; six or seven of them have him by the arms and the legs. One pulls his turban off and throws it away. James thrashes, but vainly against such numbers.

Some in the crowds cry out against the guards. But the guards just push aside such people as hinder them. They are at least three squads strong: thirty men, armed with swords and fullers' clubs. One has a bandage, filthy as his soul, wrapped about his head. They haul James to the parapet of the eastern wall of the Temple Mount. And, as if he was but a dockside sack of grain, they heave him over.

James shrieks, like a gull in flight, as he falls. But ceases with a grunt when he hits the steep side of the Kidron. He still lives, though, as he rolls down the ravine. A herd of goats first watches, then flees the person hurtling towards it. A bundle of white linen and blood, tumbling, unable to stop itself. Eventually the body reaches the base of the valley. Even now James twitches. He cannot rise, but he tries to. It is clear he isn't yet dead.

The Temple Guards trudge down the path towards him. And then they gather stones. Many of them haven't been in Judaea for long but already they know: everything is about stone in this land.

Thirty-four Years after
the Crucifixion

While it was still dark, people poured into the Circus Flaminius. It has nothing like the capacity of that incinerated Circus Maximus, so best to arrive early to secure a decent seat. Many of the spectators have also lately taken in the Gardens of Sallust or the Gardens of Maecenas, not to admire those imperial parks but to witness the ranks of Christianoi nailed to trees therein. Or to watch those sentenced to the flames and burned, who serve as nightly illuminations.

The plebeians who made the effort to get a good view in the theatre will be well rewarded: the day's programme promises to be rich and varied. The first chariot racing since the fire will be held today. Almost everyone in the city, from the Emperor Nero himself to the youngest child, is a passionate supporter of one of the four great charioteering stables: the reds, whites, blues and greens. But whichever of those teams will be today's victor, that the contest takes place at all will buoy the spirits of Rome. There are also to be some legendary tableaux acted out: the death of Actaeon, hunted by his own hounds; Laureolus killed by a bear; Prometheus devoured alive; the ravishing of Pasiphaë by a bull. And you can guarantee the acting will be first rate, because the beasts will play themselves and the screams will be real.

It's just a couple of *andabatae* on the programme now. No one got up early in the hope of seeing them, but the *editor* has a whole day to fill, and it's all good family entertainment.

The *andabatae* have been goaded within earshot of one another by iron-masked Charon and his assistants. This bout's conceit is that two elderly men have been chosen from among the ranks of the *damnati*: a brace of stiff-limbed old patriarchs instead of gladiators; their beards of bone-grey concealed beneath helms with no eye-holes. But, though wrinkled, withered and diminished from who they once were, they both look of a type who might have wielded a weapon when in their florescence. One is bow-legged, as if he walked half the world in his younger days; the other, a monster to make daemons afraid of the dark. They were paired to fight because the prison guards caught them in a rancorous argument, but this will be no mere battle of wits or arthritic fists: each is now armed with an evil *gladius*.

'Better you die swift by the sword,' one shouts, the enveloping visor muffling a voice deep and with the guttural quality of a Galilean. 'Come to me and I'll cut you cleanly. Who knows what horror awaits the victor?'

'Your offer is generous,' the other replies, 'but I am not the sort to lie down quietly. Or to strike empty air. I would offer you that same favour: the kindness of a quick death.'

Were they real gladiators, they would have enjoyed the *cena libera* last night: the unrestricted feast where warriors can eat and drink what they please. But these two, in the stink of a gaol-cave, dined only on a corn *puls*, watery as fish piss. One of them sincerely believes that it transformed into the body of his saviour-God; for the other, such ideas are blasphemy and lunacy.

But there will be time yet for other people to ponder those impenetrables. Things are currently in flux; rituals are sprung and growing, but remain pliable shoots. Some will fall on stony ground, some will be wrenched out entirely and some will become deep-rooted as oaks, tenacious as weeds.

And these two men here, clothed only in loincloths and helms scarred from former blows, share more in common than divides them. Both of them believe that the end of the world is nigh and in this, in a way, they are correct: they will most certainly die this day.

As iron whets iron, each has been sharpened through the years of interaction with the other. And now they stand, opposed and motionless, on the hot sands, listening for the slicing of air. Blindfolded before the view of thousands. Sightless in plain daylight.

Forty-three Years after
the Crucifixion

The sounds of the earthworks cease only at night: the pounding of dirt being packed; the clatter of poured stones and thud of boulders; the hammering of timber; the shouts of slave-masters. Noises that fill him with the same shiver that the night screech of the bittern did as a child, only now numbed to a constant dull dread.

A dust devil swirls on the fortress square, a little whirl of life. Credulous men believe they are djinn, but the Highlander knows them to be sand and wind. The Highlander has seen all the wonders under the sun and most turned out to be nothing but ephemeral trickeries, pursuits fruitless as grasping at olive oil, or chasing after the wind.

The Highlander came from the Golan Heights of Galilee, though he has spent most of his life outside that plateau. Of course: since one does not gain a name like 'The Highlander' except by leaving a place where it could be applied to anyone. It was Jerusalemites who gave Yosef the appellation Haramati, a word that might sound like 'Arimathea' to those who don't speak Hebrew. But there is no such inhabitation as Arimathea; one might just as well seek the end of the wind as Arimathea.

This is a fitting enough place for a highlander to end his days: the highest inhabited point in a boundless realm of red rock. Distant cliffs stratified, as if they have layers within them, almost as if it was not all God-moulded in just a single day. There is desert on every side from up here and that wet-desert of the Dead Sea in the distance. A sea in which no creatures can live. Such strange waters there are in this covenanted land. What a queer gift God gave. They say that Galilee's great lake also became a sea of the dead: turned red with blood by the fighting that took place there. Six thousand bodies finished within it, putrefying under the sun, the stench corrupting the air.

Galilee's waters and highlands are some way from here. But this is still a fitting enough place for a highlander to finish. Even if Yosef can't help wishing that end could be delayed.

One would think that an old man should be less afraid of death. But somehow death's proximity makes what little life you have left all the more precious. Dying is a young man's game. That toll of Roman tools – which began three months ago, imperceptibly distant then, impossibly far off – cuts into the Highlander's bowels and marrow. The end will not be long now.

Nature knows nothing of the ills of man. Soft-squeaking orange-winged starlings still call to each other, gentle as the noise of leather sandals on tiled floor. A tender eek-eek, familiar somehow to human ears. It is the song that we would sing if we were birds. We wouldn't whistle, like larks and jays, or hoot, like plovers. We would peep as starlings, saying: *Come to me my brother, sister, please. I get lonely on this breeze. I'll share my*

*catch with you. I have enough for two. I just don't
want to be alone any more.*

But soon enough those orange-winged starlings
will be gone and this cliff-top castle will belong to
the carrion crows.

Many people said that all the things which
subsequently befell Judaea were to avenge
James the Just. But the Highlander is of a view
that causes are invariably more intricate and
complicated than that; unless, perhaps, they are
even simpler: maybe war came only because war
was always going to come, sooner or later.
Whatever the real cause, many named it redress
for the death of James.

The Highlander never knew James but was a
great admirer of his brother, though not, of course,
a disciple. Jochanan was the last of the Twelve,
and they say he died back at the destruction of the
Jerusalem Temple.

The constant drums are the worst. The Romans
beat drums to keep their slaves in rhythm as they
haul dirt and rock on the ramp. And Roman
signallers sound trumpets to relay orders, blasts
that echo one another up and down, always
reminding that they are coming.

At first defenders of the fortress fired down
upon the builders of the slope. But Roman
engineers constructed a great tower, plated with
iron against flame and crammed with bowmen
and slingers and engines for flinging stone and
ballistae with bolts long as loom arms. And after
that, even to lift eyes above the battlements would
immediately bring a volley so dense that the sky
would turn black.

It was futility and fear that ceased the activity of
the defending archers, not the knowledge that the

scarp-builders they killed were fellow Judaeans, enslaved.

But, then, if this hideous war has taught the Highlander anything, it is that the Romans do not have a monopoly on cruelty. At the very beginning of the Jewish rebellion, the legionaries stationed in Jerusalem were induced to surrender, with a promise they would be spared, then were murdered once they gave up their swords. And those Sadducees who might have sued for peace had their throats cut in cold blood. The high priest, Annas son of Annas, was found hiding in an aqueduct and killed without trial. And ambassadors under truce were executed, against every code of war. And the Zealots fought the Sicarii for domination of the insurgence. And the poor killed the rich and burned the archives of debt and ownership. And Jerusalem at the finish was divided between three battling factions within, even as the Romans besieged it.

Such atrocities have forced Yosef to confront the sickening possibility that, if it were Judaea that ruled the earth, maybe Roman peasants would be broken by tax and tribute and brave sons of Italy would hang from trees.

But that, of course, is not how the world is: Rome is the great power and through that the great evil. No nation can stand for ever against Roman discipline and fearful efficiency. Though Judaeans fought hard and had many victories, at the end of four years of war, four legions closed on Jerusalem, a city already torn by bitter internal fighting. Much as they have now done to little Masada, the Romans surrounded Jerusalem and built fortified banks and siege towers and stationed their great trebuchets, out of range of Judaean arrows, but able to hurl back boulders.

Starvation found those trapped inside and the Romans found those who fled. In the depths of the half-year Jerusalem siege, five hundred or more of those who tried to escape were crucified every single day. It became so mundane to the legionaries doing the nailing that they tried to outdo each other in the imaginative poses chosen for those they put to slow death. They crucified so many that they ran out of space for the crosses and ran out of crosses for the prisoners. The land was stripped of trees for ninety furlongs around. And even in the evidence of the agony of those captured – nailed as far as the eye could see – multitudes still deserted the city, so desperate was the famine inside. Families suspected of having cached food were tortured to reveal its whereabouts. People ate girdles and sandals and even plundered old animal dung for the wisps of hay within it.

The Highlander fled before the worst, but he has witnessed sufficient hunger in his time to imagine how it was. He has seen how children begin to look like imps through starvation: their eyes grow big in their heads; their faces are drawn down to show their cheekbones. Children gain an ethereal beauty in dying, which only increases the horror.

The Highlander is sore with sorrow for the woes of his adopted city, echoes of the words of Lamentations: the tongues of nurslings stuck with thirst to the roofs of their mouths; children begging for food which no one gave. The rich who dined on dainties, rotting in the street; those who once lay on scarlet rugs huddled on ash-heaps. Bodies ruddier than rubies, corpses veined like sapphires, their skin drawn tight over bone, dry as kindling. Better to die by the sword than by starving, skin like a furnace, glowing from the delirium of hunger. They say that the hands of women cooked their own children, making that their food, amid wreckage more darksome than the night. And many said it was all for the sin against Jerusalem's prophet, for the crime of those priests who shed in her the blood of James the Just.

Up here in the fortress of Masada there is plenteous food: there are store rooms filled with dates; durum wheat; barley; nabali olives; fig cakes; lentils; salted fish. The defenders of this fortress could have held out for many years. Maybe even indefinitely: there are dovecots and parcels of fertile, tillable soil. There are rain-catchers and storage cisterns replenished from springs. Only two ways lead up to this walled cliff-top keep and both are single-file and serpentine, chasms beneath them, perpetual precipitous winding paths, either of which a child with a slingshot could defend against a cohort, while the stronghold has a copiously stocked armoury within the safety of its towers and casement walls.

Herod the Great, unloved by his people, fortified this citadel in case it should be needed as protection against them. Great men, perhaps, are always a little tainted with madness. Who but a madman would dream of a palace redoubt upon a mountain in the middle of a desert? Perhaps it was the ambition of insanity, but it was certainly ambition.

And who but the Romans would seek to capture such a place? They could have let these last few survivors be, with maybe a million dead at Jerusalem and the entire city in ruin, the Temple dismantled, stone from stone. Masada threatens no supply lines, little but wilderness. The Israelites are long since crushed. Victory has already been declared. Rome minted coins to celebrate the conquest so long ago that some have even drifted up here: *Judaea Capta* they read and show a weeping Jewess beneath a Roman standard. What would it matter, a handful of rebels holed up in a place from which they could not come down?

But that is not Rome's way. Her Empire can only be held if rebellion is publicly crushed, ruthlessly, brutally and utterly. The expense is irrelevant: Judaea and the world must know that every thimble of resistance was rinsed. No one can be seen to escape the maws of the wolf. So the nine hundred and some at Masada, larger part women and children, are encircled by Roman siege camps and the full-strength Tenth Legion. There will be no escape: you might just as well try to outrun the wind.

A black kite wheels in the sky, yellow claws only half sheathed. Ready to dive on such rodents as dare to live on the mount: golden spiny mice; soft furred jerboa; bushy-tailed jird. All beautiful in their way, but quick and fearful of the open. Even the desert rats know that a burrow must have an escape route, or all is lost.

The finish will be soon: the Romans draw near. Their ramp is visibly closer every day. They have already trundled into view a chain-slung battering ram for the breaching of Masada's wall.

The defenders have built a second wall, of loose earth around logs, that a ram will not easily smash, but only pack. But no one really believes it will stop the legionaries for long. It was not built in the hope of victory, but only of preserving some spirit of fight.

The real plan is of a darker weave and few are privy to it for now. The night before the Romans look ready for their final push, everything of any value will be burned. And then each man in Masada will end the life of his wife and children. Better it be done with a loving hand, if that is all the love that is left. Better that than the alternative. All know well what comes to pass when Rome takes female prisoners. There are but a few hundred women and girls and ten thousand Roman aggressors. Any loved ones who survived such plunder might be murdered anyway and would certainly be enslaved. Not as house servants, or even field slaves, but as military chattel, or sent to the quarries and the mines; condemned to death though still alive. Far better it be done by the loving hand of a husband and a father, if that is all the love that remains. And then ten men drawn by lot will kill all the other men. And one man drawn from them will finish the final nine. And this last will kill himself. The enemy will take possession of a worthless empty vessel. Three months and ten thousand troops and they will not find a beggar's treasure or capture a single slave.

Was it ever worth it, for a piece of land, the Highlander wonders – not just Masada, but all of it – such unending bloodshed for this parcel of goats, boats and Jehovah?

You cannot blame those Jews who rose up because if you believe it to be true that God killed the first-born of every single family in Egypt, why would He suffer the Romans? To rebel might seem insane, but not if you trust scriptures that say Yahweh once killed a hundred and eighty-five thousand Assyrians in their sleep for the sake of His people. Not if you believe that God sent giant hailstones down on the Amorites, and stopped the sun in the sky to give Joshua sufficient daylight to butcher the survivors. Not if you believe that God bewildered Sisera's army, so that they slew one another, without the Israelites having to draw a sword. If you believe that this is God's country and these are God's children, then how could you believe that He could let them fall? If you believe that Gideon with just three hundred men slaughtered a hundred and twenty thousand Midianites, why would an entire nation fear a few legions? If you believe that Samson killed a thousand men, with just the jawbone of an ass. If you believe that God smote fifty thousand and seventy Bethshemites. If you believe that David massacred every male in Edom and all the people of Ammon and sixty-nine thousand Syrians. If you believe that Ahab killed a hundred thousand foes, because they mocked the God of Israel. If you believe that the Lord slew twenty-seven thousand men in Aphek by crushing them under the walls, and uncountable by the same act in Jericho, why would you think He would let Caesarea stand? If you believe that God struck dead a million Ethiopians in a single day, for daring to attack Judah, it hardly seems possible that He would not assist at all in fighting Rome.

Which is why Yosef has come to discover that he no longer does believe: he no longer credits that the scriptures can be true.

He is seemingly alone in this: most of the others here in Masada cling to their faith, like the last flotsam remnant of a smashed ship.

There is a group of twenty-four or so, who are followers of The Way. They keep themselves a little apart, but not so much. After all, they don't differ greatly from the religion of the rest: they believe in a Messiah of the line of David – as most Jews do – only they believe he has already come and will soon return, having already risen from the tomb.

The Highlander could perhaps tell them something about that, if he had a mind to, because he was the one who pleaded with and bribed the prefect Pilate to be given Yeshua bar Abba's body. It was Yosef Haramati who undertook to accord the corpse the rites that should have been its due. And one might say that if a fellow has made it his business to see that a man he esteemed is buried properly with respect and expense, as soon as the Sabbath is over, then that is just what that fellow would do. One might say that the Sabbath ends at nightfall. And while women may fear to leave the safety of Jerusalem's walls in the dark, the servants of a wealthy highlander would have no such compunction. One might say that, of course, the tomb was empty by the sunrise of the next day: why wouldn't it be empty? It wasn't Yosef's tomb after all: it was a tomb that he had temporarily availed himself of. One might say that if a fellow had put it upon his honour that the proper duties would be accorded at the earliest opportunity, just as they should be, then for a fellow not to have fulfilled what he had undertaken would have been a queer gift. A fellow might say that was the simple truth of it.

But what is truth? Maybe something can be true even while it is not true. Or, rather, perhaps it can be real, as a lived experience, without being objectively true. Because are they not happier, those followers of The Way? Doesn't their faith give them something that others lack? Doesn't it fill a breach otherwise evident in the world and in the person? Is it really better to be wise and empty than to be foolish and filled with love?

But what does that all matter now anyway? Yeshua is dead, and those who awaited his return in Jerusalem must virtually all be dead too. Baptizer John is dead. James the Just is dead. The Judaean nation is in shattered fragments and the Temple utterly destroyed. The Way is certainly finished. What further truth could matter now?

Sixty-two Years after
the Crucifixion

... if Christ has not been raised, then our preaching is futile and your faith is empty. More than that, we would then be lying about God, because we have testified that God raised Christ from the dead, whom He did not raise, if it is true that the dead are not raised. For if the dead are not raised, then not even Christ has been raised. And if Christ has not been raised, your faith is worthless ...

The *episkopoi* reads aloud those glorious words, such gravity within them, from one of the letters Paul wrote to the Corinthian believers. The *episkopoi* – the bishop – has made it his solemn responsibility to gather as many of Paul's epistles as he can. An unknown number has been lost. There were years when those didactic distortionists sent from Jerusalem were gaining such ground that the words of Paul came close to heresy. Who knows what magnificent missives were discarded as worthless or burned as dangerous? It seems scarcely conceivable these days, but at one time Paul was no longer even welcome among the congregations of great Ephesus; he left the city *so utterly unbearably crushed* that he *despaired of life itself.* But now one of Paul's most loyal followers is Ephesus's bishop.

For time has proved it evident that Paul was right all along: the age of the Torah has indeed been ended. How can one conduct sacrifices at a Temple that is no longer in existence? God has lit the true path with fire and fury. The whip hand has changed. Judaea has paid for the death of the Christ; and those Judaizers who once so plagued the righteous Paul have likewise received due recompense.

Lately, a copy of another work has come into the bishop's possession – the original was written at Rome, so they say. It is an attempt to tell the tale of the Christ's life, or at least the last year of it. It makes apparent that Jesus in fact prophesied the Temple's destruction. And it shows how the Messiah's family rejected him and how his weak and vacillating followers constantly misunderstood his nature and purpose and finally betrayed him. It reveals that a Roman centurion was the first to recognize that Jesus was the Son of God. And it tells how the noble prefect, Pontius Pilate, tried hard as he might to release the Messiah, but those obdurate Jews wouldn't have it.

Such revelations come as small surprise to the bishop, who knows well how his own master Paul was plagued by Jesus's family and misjudged by the disciples and betrayed by the Jews. In fact, the Jesus in the story is almost a reflection of Paul, though filtered, as if seen in a glass, darkly.

Paul never mentioned the details of the Christ's betrayal; seemingly the apostle was unaware of them. In fact, he spoke of an appearance to *the Twelve* at a time when there would only have been eleven, had one of them turned traitor. But, then, the bishop has noticed, in all his letters, Paul never once cited a single teaching of the earthly Jesus.

Paul was much more concerned with the exciting urgency of what was to come than with mere history.

Perhaps it had not seemed important for anyone to record the Christ's earthly deeds, when he was expected to return to rule at any moment. But now it begins to seem as if the Day of the Lord has been delayed indefinitely. Those who knew Jesus as a man are long gone, and most of the generation that came after sleep too.

This new chronicle, though, the bishop was pleased to discover, finally provides a little literary completeness. For just as Judah – from whom all the Jews are descended – sold his brother Joseph, so the disciple Judas sold Jesus. Was this villain Jesus's brother, as Joseph's betrayer was? It is left in mist. Jesus did have a brother called Judas, but all his brothers are faint and hard to find in the story; James the Just has virtually disappeared. What is plain is that – though it must in some sense be admitted that the Christ's disciples were all Jews – this Judas is even more 'Jewy' than the rest: his name means 'Jew' and sounds like 'Jew'. And he is dubbed *the Iscariot* from Sicarii: an assassin; a nationalist; a warmonger. So, even if Paul didn't know the story of this traitor, it certainly has a ring of truth about it.

The separation of The Way from such dastardly Hebrews is complete now, of their own volition: the scribes have recently inserted a curse on the sect of the Nazarenes into those daily prayers said in all the synagogues of the diaspora. It is no longer really possible to be Jewish and Christianoi; one must choose. Though there are rumours of remnant straggler groups in ruined Judaea, named Ebionites – the poor ones – who still claim the

Messiah Yeshua was a mortal man and fulfil the Torah, as best they can, and spit diatribes against Paul.

It came too late for Paul, but the persecutions against the Christianoi in Rome ended once crazed Nero was deposed and Vespasian, hero-general of the war against Judaea, became emperor. But Paul would not have wished for sorrow to be spent on him anyway. Didn't he once tell the bishop, with his own dear lips, that he feared not to die? He was even half eager for it, grown impatient of the Christ's return.

In his dotage, by assembling and preserving Paul's texts, Episkopoi Onesimus cannot help thinking that he might finally live up to his name. He has ended the volume of his collection with a letter written about him by Paul, well aware that this act holds an intimation of vanity, for the letter is almost without theological value. But so many of Paul's mighty words have been lost that all those that remain should be cherished, and that littlest, simplest epistle – asking for a slave's crimes to be pardoned – may bring comfort to many, not only to the bishop referred to in it. For are we not each of us in some sense a slave begging for our sins to be forgiven? Are we not all of us trying to be useful?

Useful's offence was not really so great – though, of course, sufficient for execution – just a little figure added and subtracted here and there from accounts and bills, money that would one day have been returned to Philemon anyway: Useful had hoped only to use it eventually to buy his freedom. A debt that was in the end settled by Paul's powerful words.

It is an irony not lost on Useful that the crime from which he fled all those years past was that of fraud, for as well as collecting Paul's letters, Useful has himself created a few. Though those fabricated epistles are, he thinks, the kind of things Paul might have said, were he still around. Paul would doubtless have wanted to update his beliefs, in the light of events – or, rather, the lack of events, for the Christ has still not returned – so it is hardly forgery as such to write in Paul's name. More like a flattering emulation. And if a little can be done in the process to scatter a bit of bracken over old disputes that no longer seem to matter, then all to the good.

Useful has begun to wonder, in fact, if it might not be sensible to write down the events of Paul's life as well. For now, he can still remember much of what Paul once dictated. Grievously, the scrolls themselves remained with Paul during Nero's persecution and must be long since lost. But Useful could likely produce a good enough replication from memory, of the acts of that apostle. And it would be well to begin the endeavour soon, for the past is a city harder to reach even than Rome.

Bishop Useful has already noticed that Paul is less vivid than once he was. And when described to other believers, the apostle must be abridged, when he was not an easily encapsulated man. It is simple to explain unwavering faith and unrelenting drive, but they were only part of Paul. In his letters you can still see glimpses of his contradictory complexity: quick in anger and filled with love; boastful and humble; convincing and irrational; tender and condemning. Without the reminder of those letters, Useful sometimes thinks that Paul's humanity would disappear entirely. He might, like Jesus, become half-God.

During his youthful travels with Philemon, Useful passed through many an abandoned town.

To look at them, you would think that the world was composed only of stone. When of course it isn't: lives are largely formed of straw, plank, cloth, wicker, bone, baked clay and dried dung, but when all that has gone, when the rest has decomposed, what is left is stone. Stone tells lies, because it survives, and the frailer stories didn't.

THE END OF THE AGE OF APOSTLES

The first men of the Tenth Legion march up the ramp to the fortress of Masada at dawn. They arrive as a slot-eyed tortoise, a shield barricade against arrows. They come braced to battle desperation. A metalled centipede clambers through the breached wall, and enters a realm of terrible solitude.

Some surfaces are glazed with blood as butchers' blocks; some rooms are filled with people; but nobody is home.

Rome has been chasing the wind.

* * *

And a scar-throated rock badger of a codger crawls from the tumbled wreckage of a portico at the Jerusalem Temple. The forecourt is in flame and ruin; soldiers in havoc hack and violate and loot.

And a Son of Thunder ought to do something. He ought to do what he should have done when they took Yeshua: he ought to charge the enemy and care not for the certainty of death. He should have done it when he was young and strong, when he still had his brother by his side and a king to fight for. But his king told him not to – nobody is perfect – so this will have to do. And he pulls a new knife from an old scabbard.

Bodies are piled in the *mikveh* baths. And human blood, Judaean blood, runs down the gutters of the altar. Roman boots soil the Holy of Holies. Legionaries tear the golden grapes from the gates, as they have ripped all the fruits from this land; and they smash the tiles of the cloisters, as if so many skulls; and they rend apart the tapestries like maidens' skirts. And everywhere there is fire, so bright it stains the sky. And shrieks fill Jochanan's ears. And smoke is in his teeth and his eyes.

And if this is not the apocalypse, it will suffice until one arrives.

* * *

And the Temple is whole again and James the Just is lying at the foot of the Kidron, amid thickets of bramble, dense as lamb's wool. And though they are little more than lackeys of the aristocracy, it is still Jews who are gathering the stones – good Jerusalem stones, lime and pale. They are Temple Guards, they should be defenders of the faith, but they pelt him with rocks. And even then he lives on. So they finish him with fullers' clubs. They swing down as if threshing corn. They have killed the Just One. And many will say that all the things which befell Judaea were revenge for this.

* * *

349

And in the centre of the sands of the Circus Flaminius, two men come at one another, sightless before the eyes of Rome. Each is armed with a honed *gladius*, and as they close the final steps to striking distance, each takes a swing of his weapon, feels the heft of it. Iron cuts the muggy air and the crowd begins to chant and cheer.

And then both men toss their swords away.

They hold one another, momentarily sharing strength. Two wrinkled old veterans, in helms with no eye-holes, embracing before the multitude. And doubtless cruel Charon will not tolerate it for long. And the mob must have its blood. But what use the tongues of men or angels if they don't, in the end, speak of love?

* * *

And in Corinth people remember. People pray and people sing.

* * *

And in Galatia, someone reads aloud a letter.

* * *

And in Antioch, those pierced and painted and branded, with hair and hat and apparel of every folk and fashion of the Empire, share a single table, long as a grain-ship, in a building that was once a ruined warehouse, but which now has a new cedar roof and a big oak door, always open.

* * *

And in a market square in Hispania, Timothy wipes away with his palm the tear that threatens to form, and begins to speak.

* * *

And in Colossae, old Philemon clasps to him, and won't let go of, the lumpen, useless bulk of that prodigal son, who isn't.

* * *

And on a hot road towards Alexandria, John-Mark looks behind him at the two children who follow. They are not his offspring: he found them on the trail, somewhere between the desolation of Jerusalem and here. He would make better time and be safer without them and he isn't over-fond of little children; but a man he loved once said he should suffer them, so he is. Their faces are tight-skinned with thirst. They have already walked far further than any child ever should. The smaller doesn't look like she will last another mile. So John-Mark drops his refugee's bundle and picks her up instead. To discover she's less a burden than he feared. She brushes the dust from his grey dandelion hair, and John-Mark laughs.

* * *

And in Philippi, Lydia frees her slaves. Because, because, why should she not: so the axe is at the root of the tree, why can't they meet it free? Surely, if today is the end time, then tomorrow something begins.

IN THE BEGINNING

This Galilee basin is dry, but fertile; the chalky soil is flush with thickets of thistle and wild flowers. The donkey – draped with battered rags of saddle blanket – would doubtless like to stop and graze, but the man leading it doesn't allow that. The man is not so old, but is already a little toil-crooked. Though covered with road dust, he is agreeably proportioned, in a creased kind of way.

His son walks beside him. The boy's skin is smooth as settled butter, but dark as one who spends his days in the sun. He wears an oversized *simlah* that he is the third to own. Inherited from his grandfather and passed through a now deceased brother.

A breeze blows, only as strong as the breath the boy's open mouth expels when he sleeps, but sufficient to lift the heat a little.

As the pair and their animal come to the edge of a village they would pass through, they find themselves at the tail of a strange procession: an angry-looking group of men are going somewhere; somewhere it looks like the lone woman in their midst – beautiful and pitiful – would rather not go. Several of the men are shepherds, dressed in the amateurishly tanned skins of fat-tailed sheep that died in ravine falls or from wolves or disease. They carry slings at their belts to drive off predators and hooked staffs in their hands. But most of the group look like peasant farmers; those with a parcel of land to their name can still just about keep a family from penury in this fruitful corner of the country.

'What's happening, Father?' the boy asks.

'I don't know,' the man says, though he suspects that he may.

'She's been taken in adultery,' one of the shepherds says, looking back at the pair.

What's adultery? Maybe she rode half the village, with the relish the boy used to ride the donkey. Maybe she sought a little solace when her husband was away for months on end. Maybe she sought a little solace because she has no husband, in a place and a time that defines her only by who owns her. It doesn't matter right now: she's an adulteress. Or, at the least, she has been taken as one.

She is already bloodied from beating and grabbing. The father would like to divert his path, but he supposes that the boy must eventually learn that things like this happen, that life and people can be sickening and brutish. So they follow the morbid procession, only in that it heads in the direction they would take in any case. They accompany, only in that they do not deliberately alter their course.

There is spittle in the corner of the woman's mouth. Some kind of fear foam that she can't wipe off because her hands are bound. Tied up, as if there was a way in which a lone, terrified woman could threaten a big group of righteously outraged men.

The men drag her to what must pass as the village square: an open area around the well. A Hasid is there – a holy man – with a few of his followers. Cheap incense smokes, to keep the flies away, next to a basket of puncture-ripened sycamore figs. The Hasid is scratching symbols into the dust; he does not look up, as the mob presents their prisoner.

Many among the throng hold rocks that they have picked up on their route, which suggests that they don't consider the ending of this story to be in doubt, yet they still wish for the blessing of the Hasid.

The boy's eyes glisten, like broken eggs, but he wants to stay and watch what happens. His father is torn, unsure if that would be good for his lad or not. But the boy must be a man one day. A day not as distant as the far shore of that lake they call the sea. So maybe this is a good enough time to learn a little of the evil of men. Not a stoning, no, they won't stay for that. But for this thing here now. For whatever this thing is.

It isn't a trial, because the Torah lays down strictly what happens at trials. Nor is it quite a lynching, for these men pretend to follow some kind of process. It is an attempt to kill without responsibility for the death; but the man doesn't know the word for that thing, or if there is one.

'Who is the Hasid?' the father asks the shepherd who answered him before.

'Yeshua bar Abba.'

The father nods: he has heard the name, of course. People round these parts now talk of little else. They say that he is not only a rabban, a magician, a healer and an exorcist, but claims to be a king.

There are three others with him: a massive ox-man, who could look threatening but doesn't because his smile is soft and sweet as a slice of sabra fruit; and a fellow so similar to the Hasid that he can only be a brother, if not a twin, lean and full of life; and another, who shouldn't be alive at all, to judge by the wound, scarlet and recent, across his windpipe. But they all three of them seem over-brimming with hope and happiness, like they believe that anything is possible and everything will be well.

The Hasid lifts his head from the riddles he has scribed in the dirt and stares at the crowd, as if noticing it for the first time.

The father and son are too far away to hear exactly what the Hasid says. But the woman, who was hunched and shrunken, gradually straightens. And the man who had a guard's grasp of her arm steps uncertainly back a pace. That shepherd who answered their questions lets the stone in his hand drop, to dent the earth. And other rocks drop too. They fall to the ground. They do not maim. They do not flay. They slip to the dust.

There are a lot of stonings in this land. Who knows if they will ever stop? But there won't be one just here. Not today. And that is a better lesson for the boy than the man could have hoped for. He signals with his head that they should continue their journey, and gives the donkey's hemp bridle a little tug.

'Is he the king, as they say, Father?' the boy asks, scampering the three steps he had fallen behind.

'Well, if you mean is he the rightful descendant of David, the one who should be king, I just don't see how anyone could know that any more: our people have been to Babylon and back as slaves since then, have been conquered by Assyria, Persia, Alexander's Greeks, the Ptolemies of Egypt, the Seleucids of Syria, the Herodians and Rome. It must be ten centuries since David. I'm not sure anyone knows that now, not really. But someone has to be the one in line, so why not? Maybe it's him.'

'No, I mean *the* King. Do you think he is the anointed one who will free us, Father?'

'What I think is that you're getting a bit old for all that stuff, lad. There's not going to be any saviour coming. But the Romans will go eventually, like every other empire has. Probably not battled away by the Zealots, or prayed away by the Essenes, but ultimately they will return to their own lands. Likely not in my days, perhaps not even in your children's, but in due time they will leave, and our people will survive somehow, as they always do.'

'So he is not the Messiah?'

'Sometimes, lad, we want our heroes to be greater than they really are, because that excuses us for being less. It's easy to glorify, but that shrugs off our own failings. If Elijah and Daniel were people like us, then only our own weakness, our own petty evils, our own leather hearts prevent us becoming people like them. If this Yeshua is just a man, it means that if you stay brave and kind and true to yourself, maybe you could grow up to be a man a little bit like him. But even if you don't, you're still my child. That's enough for me. The Pharisees can keep their resurrection. You're the only afterlife I need.' He loops an arm over the boy's thin shoulders. 'He's just a man, son, not so very different from those who would have stoned her.'

The father looks back, as he starts to walk on, at the barefoot teacher, still scribbling enigmas in the dust.

'But he's a prince.'

Acknowledgements

Deborah Bernard
Amanda Preston
Sarah Castleton
James Gurbutt
Sam Greenwood
Professor Yan Wong
Simon Pearlman
Clive Hebard
Hazel Orme
Emily Burns
Anna Davis
Elliot Soll
Meriam Mohammad
André Ivangine
Mum and Dad

The kindness and generosity of the peoples of the Bible lands, Turkey and Italy. With special thanks to La Maison d'Abraham in Jerusalem; Eva Gerbi and The Home in Rome; and the Rumshines camp in Jordan.

Manchester University, my alma mater, for the use of their research resources and for Professor Gerald Hammond, who perhaps planted the seed of this story, almost twenty years ago.